BURIED BONES

PALMETTO
PUBLISHING
Charleston, SC
www.PalmettoPublishing.com

The cover artwork was prepared by Inanna Mitchell, graphic designer, inannaamw_hat@gmail.com.

Paperback ISBN: 9798822955905

BURIED BONES

Bonnie Moore
A Maggie Anderson Mystery

CONTENTS

MAIN CHARACTERS IN BURIED BONES

THE INVESTIGATION TEAM:

MAGGIE ANDERSON, Former Prosecutor, Lead Investigator

Maggie, an attractive, tall, and athletic woman of seventy-five years, formerly head of the sex crimes unit in the DA's office in Washington, DC, retires to Salt Lake City and surreptitiously meets Ben Stillman, the suspect in Buried Bones, in a country diner near the small Utah town of Medford in Madison County.

Her hard-won career had been the focus of her life. She gladly took on challenges and approached crimes with a strong intuition and compassion for her victims. However, in therapy after the traumatic vigilante death of an innocent suspect, she questioned her skills, and her therapist uncovered a lifetime of over-achieving in order to please her difficult parents.

She hesitates to become involved as the lead investigator in Ben's case because she no longer trusts her abilities and must recapture her confidence.

She was in three unsuccessful marriages and has many doubts about her ability to be in a successful romantic relationship until she meets Robert Parsons.

ROBERT PARSONS, Retired Architect, Maggie's Sidekick on the Investigation

Robert, tall and handsome, with twinkling eyes and a gentle demeanor, is the boy whose mentor, Carl Stevenson, saved him from going bad. He is from Medford and becomes a successful big city architect with the support of the Stevenson family.

His life changed forever when his wife died of cancer and he became the single parent of four teenagers. With his children grown and scattered, his friends have become his family and he longs for a new love.

He is mesmerized by the worldly Maggie and seeks a way into her heart. He becomes the shoulder she leans on, the sage giver of good advice, and the one who opens doors to those who can solve the murder case she has taken on.

His hometown connection and his emotional loyalty to Carl Stevenson becomes so strong, he is forced to choose between his past and his future.

GWEN SIMONS, Former Trauma Nurse, now a Private Duty Nurse, Maggie's friend who joins the Investigative Team

Gwen is the prototype of the Energizer Bunny. She is short, roundish, and keeps going, and going, and going...with a perceptive smile.

In her career, she was a trauma nurse in Chicago and handily dealt with gang shootouts. She lives with her sister in Salt Lake City, Utah, and has a clientele of older women that she cares for as a private nurse. She never married or had children, so she gently 'mothers' her clients and her friends when she isn't advocating for a social cause.

She becomes an embedded 'spy' nurse in the Stevenson family and listens unobtrusively. Her forte is quietly sorting out the truth for the investigation team.

PETER MATTHIEU, Former Medical Research Doctor, Maggie's other friend who joins the Investigative Team

Peter is the tall, thin, quiet man of wisdom, a former medical research doctor who asks questions and digs for answers until he is fully satisfied with the results. He now considers the greatest pleasure in his life to be a solitary ski run down a tall mountainside, spraying thin lines of powdered snow in his wake.

He becomes the collector of clues and the interpreter of facts for the investigation. He provides the knowledge and skill to interpret the evidence that breaks open the case.

THE MAIN TOWNSPEOPLE:

AUDREY STILLMAN, the Victim. Her body was secretly buried for four years

Audrey's life was marked by traditions. She was born in Medford, went to the local schools, and married her high school sweetheart, Ben Stillman, in 2001. As an only child, she wanted a big family, and they agreed on three children. They lived in a log cabin in the woods, and she developed a business growing herbs and packaging them into teas and herbal remedies. After fifteen years of marriage and countless medical tests, she never became pregnant.

When Ben asks for a divorce, Audrey's life crumbles. She pours her troubles into a secret diary and her heart goes to a new boyfriend. She senses trouble and hides the diary shortly before she is murdered.

BEN STILLMAN, the Suspect, accused of his wife's murder

Ben wanted to be part of the fabric of Medford when he grew up. He wanted to have children and raise them with Audrey, but eventually a nagging voice convinced him he was gay and Medford was not ready to accept his choice. He does the only thing he knows he should do...he divorces Audrey and moves to the city.

Four years later, the sheriff calls and asks him to identify a body found in a shallow grave behind the cabin where they had lived. Dental records prove the body to be Audrey. Because he is openly gay, the town assumes he wanted out of the marriage and wants him to stand trial for her murder. No one in town believes him when he says he is innocent.

LOGAN HARRIS, longtime DA for Madison County, a country lawyer and part of the local political machine

Logan is the aging misogynist gatekeeper on the charges against Ben Stillman. He badly wants to win the case against Ben Stillman as his last big success before retiring. Going into it, he thought he had a slam-dunk case until Maggie shows up.

He still practices western frontier law where you do your best to follow the rules, but when the man with the biggest gun wants to enforce his own rules, he slowly backs down and hopes that the problem goes away.

He meets his match in the big city female prosecutor, who isn't afraid of anything.

RANDY STEVENSON, Grandson to Grammy Stevenson, friend to Audrey Stillman

Randy was raised to be the son and heir of a rich man and he won't let you forget it. Charismatic? Well, sorta. Assertive? In a bullying kind of way. Thinks he can do no wrong? Absolutely. In need of a comedown? Just ask Maggie Anderson.

Randy was friendly with Audrey after her divorce from Ben and had a schoolboy crush on her, even though she was ten years older.

In the end, he knew too much, and keeping his secrets was too much for him.

"GRAMMY" STEVENSON, Matriarch of the Stevenson dynasty family, and widow of Carl Stevenson, the town's patriarch

Grammy was raised in a remote polygamist community in southern Utah where the men made the decisions and the women did what they were told. She was disowned when she left for a different life in the city and became the wife of a man from Madison County.

She was active in her community as Carl's wife; she was obedient and never asserted herself; and she raised six children. Her years of public respectability concealed secrets and lies. One lie, in particular, ate at her heart for more than forty years. When it surfaced, she could not bear the shame.

CHAPTER 1

Maggie

Friday, September 4, 2020

A tall, thin man in his early forties opened the rickety, wood-framed screen door of an old Utah diner nestled in the foothills of the Wasatch Mountains. The spring was loose, causing the door to bang behind him.

In the first half-second, it sounded like a gunshot. Maggie Anderson was still accustomed to life in a big city and she automatically flinched before turning, with a frown, to see what had happened. *That's so distracting. They should fix that door.* He looked exactly like her long-ago favorite TV character, but with darker hair. As a college student in the 1960s, she had swooned over the handsome Dr. Kildare.

His gaze darted nervously around the room. No one greeted him. The sounds of conversation and laughter died. The clang of silverware stopped. Johnny Cash's throbbing words in "I Walk the Line" became a lonely echo from the sound system.

Maggie glanced at the other patrons. All appeared to be farmers and ranchers. Some stared at the man. Others glared. Parents reached for their children and pulled them close.

Maggie and her three friends—Robert Parsons, Gwen Simons, and Peter Matthieu—had driven to the mountains above Salt Lake City for Labor Day weekend and planned to stay at Robert's ancestral log cabin near the village of Maxwell on Old Highway 84, now a service road, east of Ogden. Before settling in, they were grabbing dinner at the only place to eat in Maxwell. In their North Face outdoor gear, they contrasted with the locals and their weather-beaten overalls.

She was about to speak to Gwen, but the man piqued her curiosity. She paused as her prosecutor's mind churned. *Who is he? What's wrong with this scene?* He stood out from the locals in his light-blue polo shirt, crisp chinos, and lack of a cowboy hat. He adjusted his collar, reminding her of another role played by the same ageless actor, Father Ralph in *The Thorn Birds*.

The locals turned back to their meals and spoke hesitantly in quieter tones.

The man chose a booth and plucked a stained menu from its ancient holder.

Next to Maggie's table, four unshaven men, all in their 30s and 40s, in sweaty T-shirts and cowboy hats, gawked at him and muttered churlishly. One of them, wearing a white hat, listened but remained silent. When he straightened in his chair, tipped his hat back, and loudly cleared his throat, the others fell silent.

"What's that all about?" Maggie eyed Robert, gesturing toward the stranger. "Last time we were here, everyone was friendly."

Robert laid his fork on his plate and fiddled with the cuff of his dark plaid shirt. Now in his late sixties, he had retired as a big city architect, and his family roots often brought him back to these bucolic neighborhoods, farms, and ranches, where he was still part of the community. He seemed to shrink from his imposing six feet and stared at his plate. "That's Ben Stillman." His dark-brown eyes hesitantly met Maggie's. "His ex-wife's body was dug up near my place about a week ago." He surveyed the energy of the room as if he didn't want to add any negative thoughts, and reluctantly nodded toward Ben. "He's the suspect."

Gwen, an inquisitive take-charge nurse, instinctively brushed back her short salt and pepper hair, pulled her glasses off her face and set them on the table, and stared, listening intently.

Maggie pulled up the zipper of her red fleece vest. *So much for a pleasant weekend.* She stared at Robert. "What do you know about it?"

"Not a lot. I've heard rumors. They were a nice couple, no problems." His eyebrows drew together and he lowered his voice. "About four years ago, he moved away. Turned out, it wasn't a good situation. She disappeared. We presumed she had moved on." He leaned in. "No one saw her again until last week."

"How did they find her?" Gwen copied Robert's intensity while lifting a forkful of salad to her mouth.

Robert slowly dipped a fry in ketchup. "New owners bought the place a few months back. The old cabin was in bad shape, so they decided to build a new one. The body was found when their contractor started digging the foundation. She hasn't been officially identified yet, but they think it's Audrey." He put his fry down and pushed his plate away. "Everyone liked her. If he killed her, they're gonna want to do something about it."

"If he's been gone for four years, why is he a suspect?" Peter, the wiry, balding, former medical researcher, cautiously leaned over the bowl of vegetarian soup he had insisted be made just for him. He spoke with the crispness of a stoic upper midwestern accent.

"The body was decomposed. He could've done it four years ago."

Maggie narrowed her eyes. "I suppose the good people of this town want him hanged?"

"Of course. Around here, people judge first and ask questions later. That's the way it is." Robert slowly shook his head.

"Has he been charged?" Gwen asked.

"Doesn't look like it." Robert gestured toward him. "He's not in jail."

Maggie frowned knowingly. Her eyes gravitated toward Ben. "He's making a mistake showing up here. His lawyer should've cautioned him to keep a low profile."

The cowboy in the white hat rose from his chair with a sense of purpose. He ambled menacingly toward Ben with a pronounced limp. The room became quiet except for the sound of his boots scraping against the uneven floorboards.

He slid into the seat across from Ben, leaned forward, and crossed his arms. "You don't belong here. I'm askin' you to leave." His raspy voice filled the room.

The other cowboys stood and quietly formed a semicircle at Ben's booth, their thumbs hooked into thick leather belts. A subtle smirk crossed Ben's face. He took a drink of water.

"Are they going to grab him and force him out?" Maggie whispered to her friends.

Robert spoke quietly. "The one in the white hat is Kevin, one of the Stevenson cousins. His relatives practically own the town. He and his buddies have been troublemakers since high school. He's already had his knee taken out in a fight, but he didn't learn anything. He's as bad as they get."

The waitress bustled out with a cheeseburger platter and stopped short. She put the food on a counter and yelled through the door, "Hey, Cookie! We got trouble."

A tall, heavyset man in his fifties, wearing a cook's apron over a stained T-shirt, came through the door. He picked up the platter and walked to Ben's booth.

"Excuse me, boys." He spoke as if he'd seen this before. He set the food down, draped his arm around one cowboy's shoulders, and eased all of them back to their table. "Let's take it down a notch, okay? How about another round of beer, on the house?"

Cookie motioned to the waitress.

Retreating, Kevin turned and pointed toward Ben. "You." He jerked his thumb toward the door. "Out. Now."

His buddies sneered.

Gwen inched closer to Robert. "Will they attack him in the parking lot?"

Robert's voice pierced the air. "Everyone knows those cowboys. They believe they have a God-given right to do as they damn well please. I wouldn't put it past 'em."

The stiffness in his shoulders suggested he was preparing to confront them.

"What can Ben do to safely get away?" Peter said.

"I know him. Not well, but enough. He knows them. He'll understand what to do."

Robert's rising tension worried Maggie. She stared at him, unable to put her mind at ease. "Ben's set himself up for trouble. He's outnumbered. There's no one to defend him, and he'll end up dead." She tried a quick sip of water to keep her heart from beating faster, but the blood drained from her face.

Robert noticed and cocked his head to the side. "What's wrong?"

"This seems like a prosecutor's nightmare." She stared at nothing, but couldn't stop her hand from shaking. The distant memory of a charred body had ensnared her.

He touched her hand and raised an eyebrow. "How so?"

She blinked. "I've seen this before. My office always feared having an innocent suspect up against an angry crowd before we could sort through the evidence." She took another sip and swallowed hard to regain her composure. "Sometimes we detained people temporarily for their own safety, and we definitely advised them to stay out of sight when they were released."

Leaning back, she breathed deeply. Her muscles tensed. Memories took her back to her old job in DC. "Sorry. I'm still haunted by two innocent people I lost that way. They were both killed by vigilantes." She twisted her paper napkin into a knot.

Peter turned to her, puzzled. "What are you saying?"

"Ben Stillman could be innocent. If they found the body last week, it's too soon to know what happened. Those cowboys are going to punish him without knowing all the facts."

"You mean he's innocent until proven guilty?" Robert was friendly but sarcastic, as if he understood her underlying angst.

"Yes. Strange things happen when a case is investigated with a team of experts. Usually, the truth comes out, and it's not what the angry crowd believes. A vigilante mob usually murders someone who is innocent, but it's hard to convict any of them."

"Point well taken." Robert studied her face. "Are you okay?"

"I felt responsible. I retired after my second inno-cent suspect died." She tried one more bite of her chicken breast, but it had lost its appeal. Raising her face slightly, she again felt the pain of her failure. She met Robert's eyes and felt his concern.

"I'm sure you did your best, but it sounds like your situ-ation got out of control. Anyway, your retirement to Utah was DC's loss and our gain, right?" Robert's eyes twinkled before perusing the table. "Looks like we're finished. Ready everyone?"

They stood. Robert towered over Gwen, but he was only a couple of inches taller than Maggie and Peter.

Still feeling tense, Maggie hesitated before pulling Rob-ert aside. "I can't walk away and leave that man to those wolves. This could go bad in a heartbeat. I'd like to check in with him, see if I can convince him to leave."

"Are you sure? You just had a bad memory triggered. It sounded like that experience in DC almost destroyed you."

"I can't think about me right now. We're far away from any law enforcement. If we do nothing and he's injured or killed by those cowboys, I'll feel responsible because I knew what could happen, and I didn't do anything. I need to say something, even if he decides to stay." She nervously brushed hair from her forehead.

"You think something bad is about to happen?"

"I don't know. It doesn't feel right to just walk away."

His frown softened. He laid an arm around her shoul-ders. "You've got a lot of courage. Be careful."

"I'll only be a minute."

Peter and Gwen stared in confusion.

Robert shrugged. "She's our favorite bloodhound, and bloodhounds are stubborn. When she's locked onto some-thing, you need to let her go for it." He grabbed his Stetson and leather jacket from a peg and turned to Maggie. "We'll be outside."

CHAPTER 2

Maggie

Maggie wrote her cell number on a business card. She felt nervous because she was about to talk to a suspect, something she vowed she would never do again after she retired.

Before leaving her job, she had always moved like a big-city prosecutor on the warpath. Her hiking boots hit the floor hard, but she willed herself to relax enough that she wouldn't frighten the locals. Silence fell in the diner. The anxious stares of the patrons followed her.

Reaching Ben's table, they locked eyes. Instead of Dr. Kildare, she saw someone putting on a brave front.

She waited and stifled a deep breath. "My name is Maggie Anderson. I heard you're caught up in a legal situation. I'm a lawyer and might be able to help. Mind if I sit for a minute?" For a surprising moment, she was in the game again.

He hesitated before waving for her to sit where Kevin had been moments before. A thin frown line between his eyes deepened. Distrust lurked on his face. His tone was wary. "Nice to meet you. I'm Ben Stillman."

"I don't know if you have an attorney. Sometimes in situations like this, people need to chat with a legal professional. If you still need someone, I might be able to help you find the right person."

"I don't need an attorney."

She slid her business card across the table and spoke gently. "If things change, and you want to talk to someone, feel free to call me."

"You from around here?" His tone was wary. He slowly pulled out his wallet and put the card in it.

"No, I retired to Salt Lake three years ago. I'm up here for a weekend with friends."

"Where you from?"

"I lived in DC for twenty years and San Francisco for thirty years before that. I went to college and law school in San Francisco."

"Must have been a big change, moving to Utah." His shoulders seemed to relax.

She felt the stares of the cowboys burning into her. "I like the slower lifestyle."

He hesitated. He seemed to wrap himself up in feelings and memories. "After Audrey and I divorced, I moved away. I didn't even know she was missing until the sheriff's office called yesterday. They wanted to know where I lived and whether I would go to the coroner's office to ID her." His grief came suddenly and unfettered. He leaned back, his shoulders against the seat's cushion, and closed his eyes. Tears trickled down, undisturbed.

"Didn't she have relatives who could do it?"

"Just her mom. Her dad died several years ago." His voice hitched. "The sheriff said her mom didn't want to see the body. I live in Salt Lake, so it was easy for me to go this morning."

"Did you make the ID?" She sounded like her old professional self.

Eyes glistening, he swallowed hard and shook his head. "It's too decomposed. Mostly, it's a skeleton. We knew it was a woman because there was a long white dress. They thought I would recognize the dress, but I didn't. The medical examiner is looking for dental records now."

He clenched his fists on the table. "They think it's Audrey. I'm feeling a lot of grief. My parents live over in Medford. I came up here to tell them. They really liked her." He shrugged as if throwing off the pain. "I decided to get something to eat before heading home."

"If it's her, I'm very sorry. I don't mean to be intrusive." As a distraction, and not wanting to seem like an ambulance chaser, she found a paper napkin and absentmindedly twisted it. "You should speak to a lawyer to help you navigate this."

As if hearing her for the first time, he stiffened and crossed his arms on the table. His eyes questioned; his confidence disappeared. "What for? We divorced four years ago. I just learned about her death yesterday."

"Almost all ex-husbands are suspects. If you're innocent, you may still need help getting through it. It's unfortunate, but that's the way it is." She switched to a gentler tone as a way of creating trust. "I'm retired, but I have connections and could help you find the right lawyer."

"Thank you, but I didn't kill her. I'll keep that in mind, though."

He doesn't believe me. She scooted to the outer edge of the red Naugahyde seat. "I'll let you finish your dinner." She hesitated. "Please be careful. This isn't a good place for you to be right now. It could be dangerous."

She stood. He had been very direct. Her instinct was to believe him, but she had not succeeded with her mission. "Feel free to call me."

He nodded, as if appreciating her effort.

She joined her friends in the parking lot.

"Everything okay?" Gwen asked.

"He viewed the body this morning but couldn't ID it. Obviously, it was traumatic. He says he's innocent. I told him he still needs a lawyer, and I could help him find someone if he wants." She faced Robert. "I hope I didn't embarrass you in your old hometown."

"Oh, hell no. You're just being scrappy. Can't stay away from a good murder mystery, can you?" He tried to hold back a playful grin.

Gwen eyed Robert, overcome with concern. "Can we do anything?"

"Can't drag him out against his will."

"I'm not getting involved." Maggie shook her head, already starting to feel empathetic. "He deserves an impartial jury, and that's hard in a small town. I just wanted to change the atmosphere in there, maybe suggest it wasn't a safe place for him." Robert opened the front passenger door of his electric-orange Jeep Wrangler.

"It felt like vigilante justice was about to happen." She said as she climbed in. "For all we know, it still could."

CHAPTER 3

Maggie

Eerie solitude filled the Jeep as they drove along the old highway in the deepening dusk.

Maggie dwelled on her effort to warn Ben, even though he did not take her advice. It was a small step for her after reliving the tragedy that had ended her career. She tried to shift back to her carefree vacation mood, but her prosecutorial mind had been aroused and she kept wondering if Ben was innocent. Her professional success had come from intuitively sensing guilt or innocence and then proving it, but her instincts had become rusty, and she wasn't sure.

She had joined a social group for seniors when she moved to Salt Lake and met Robert at one of the events. He helped her move to a new condo a year ago, and she thanked him with dinner at an upscale restaurant. Not long afterward, he invited her to his mountain cabin along with two others. While soaking in the fresh air, they fished along the river's shores and baked the fresh rainbow trout they caught.

Robert spent many weekends at his cabin and often invited friends to join him. He was instinctively liked and trusted. Everyone who knew him wanted an invitation, and he liked to oblige. Several flirty women had found his small-town charm irresistible, to no avail. He stubbornly remained the group's most sought-after bachelor. He charmed Maggie as much as he did other women in their group, but she shied away from flirting.

Five minutes from the diner, Robert turned onto a narrow dirt road that led to an enclave of old log cabins along the northern bank of the Weber River. The sun had almost vanished behind the nearby mountain peak. Weeds and scruffy brush lined the road. Scattered trees were full of leaves, flaunting their proximity to an endless water supply. These trees became ungainly patches of dark as the sunlight disappeared.

Robert flashed Maggie a grin. "As many times as I've been down this road, I still love leaving the world behind. It feels like coming home."

He pulled aside for an oncoming pickup and returned a wave as the driver passed. The locals still considered him one of their own.

Maggie noticed the dark majesty of the rugged mountains nearby and the sound of distant water. "Mother Nature at her finest. I'm imagining coming home as a pioneer. Enticing, isn't it?"

"Those old pioneers were seldom enticed. The Native Americans weren't happy, and times were tough." Robert chuckled. "But I have to say, my ancestors overcame everything."

Maggie glanced at him, amusingly. *Yes, you've got the ruggedly handsome genes of John Wayne, Jimmy Stewart, and Will Rogers all rolled into one.* He had a full head of dark wavy hair, twinkling eyes over full lips, and a whisper of a mustache, but she had a habit of keeping her admiration to herself. "They picked a pleasant spot to settle down."

Peter leaned forward. "Robert, is it safe here? Someone killed that woman in one of these cabins." Tall and thin, he had an oval face and the searching, inquisitive eyes befitting the leader of a medical research team. He had retired to the mountain resort town of Park City and often talked about how much he enjoyed a long, solitary glide on his skis at one of their famous Olympic ski runs. "What would you do if there was a problem? We're far from the local police."

Robert looked at him in his rearview mirror. "Buddy, you're definitely a city slicker. We've got it handled. The sheriff lives a few doors down from my place. In all my years here, this is the first hint of trouble." He winked at Maggie. "Besides, I keep guns at my place. You're safe with me."

Peter's high-pitched laugh sounded nervous. He didn't seem reassured.

Maggie turned toward the back seat. Gwen had retired, lived with her sister in Salt Lake, and worked part time caring for private nursing patients. During the previous state legislative session, Maggie and Gwen had lobbied at the state capitol on behalf of a national gun safety group.

Gwen shook her head. "Someone killed that woman in this neighborhood. Would your guns have stopped that?"

Robert smiled diplomatically.

Before they could dissect gun laws, the moon appeared. A clearing known as Stevenson's Row emerged after they passed the first row of trees. The moon quickly disappeared behind a cloud, and only the outlines of the rustic cabins were visible. The second cabin was Robert's. Far enough from the others to offer privacy, it was close enough to be part of the small community along the river.

Robert pulled into his parking space. "We're here, folks."

He killed the engine but left the headlights on and lit a kerosene lamp he kept in the Jeep. The men lugged heavy items and brought in wood as the stirred-up road dust started to settle.

Maggie quietly listened to the myriad cricket sounds and took in a deep breath of mountain air. The temperature had dropped since leaving the diner. The cozy country feeling from her first trip to the cabin returned as she and Gwen carried kitchen supplies in.

Robert started a fire in the fireplace before giving a quick tour to Peter and Gwen. His great-great-grandparents had built the original structure in the 1880s. Much later, a log addition expanded the cabin into the four-bedroom home where he lived as a child and where he brought his family for outings. His wife had died twenty years before, and he often said that part of the cabin's continuing lure was her memory. His grown children now lived in other states, so his friends had become his family.

Gwen remarked on the patchwork quilts as Robert assigned rooms. Peter asked questions about the log construction. Robert was pleased to show him the details while Gwen returned to the living room and an old rocking chair with a thick foam cushion. She and Maggie listened to the crackle as the fire came to a blaze in the iconic cabin that suggested many generations had lived well and prospered under its eaves.

After a few minutes, Gwen suggested that she and Maggie put the food away.

As they worked, Gwen whispered, "Did you notice that Peter and I got the upstairs bedrooms and you and Robert got the downstairs bedrooms? I wonder if Robert thinks we'll have midnight maneuvers."

Maggie chuckled. "Oh, that's funny. I've already made the point to Robert that I'm no longer interested in romantic encounters."

Gwen stopped for a moment, a container of milk in her hand. "Oh, that's a shame! Why is that? Can't you see how our handsome Robert has been favoring you?"

"I'm too old for that. And besides, I don't have a great track record with men and romance."

"Well then, open your eyes. Your past is behind you. That man is a catch, and he has zoned in on you. You don't want to miss out on this one!"

Maggie chuckled and slowly shook her head at the thought. What she had wanted most in life had failed to appear, and she had become content living her second-best dreams.

Gwen paused and her voice became soothing. "Life is all about continuing to love. Even if you've been disappointed or hurt, don't stop loving and letting people love you. It's what keeps us going."

Maggie considered Gwen's comment and smiled. "You're a sweetheart. Thank you." When they finished, she went to her room to unpack.

After settling in, they grabbed warm coats and breathed in the cool night air from the small porch. Gwen and Maggie claimed the white plastic chairs near the door. Robert took the top step, and Peter watched the darkness from a metal chair in the corner. Light from their lantern reflected in their wineglasses.

A wind rushed out of the canyon, kissed their cheeks, and reminded them to button up. Trees became dancing silhouettes against the moon, and plumes of smoke filled the air with the smell of wood burning in nearby fireplaces. Rustling leaves suggested an eavesdropping animal. The river gurgled, and crickets chirped their soothing tune.

Gwen sipped her wine and turned to Maggie. "At dinner, you mentioned losing a couple of innocent suspects. It sounded like when I lost patients. No matter who they are, it's hard, isn't it?" She had been a supervisory nurse in the crime-ridden South Side of Chicago and handled the fallout of many gang shootings. "The cops always expected me to know who the bad guys were and to save their lives so they could be taken to court."

Maggie stared into the darkness as if peering into her thoughts. She felt relieved she had finally been able to trust her close friends enough to share one of her worst memories. "Probably similar. Prosecutors have to develop thick skins just like nurses." She silently perused her minefield of thoughts and set her glass on a small round outdoor table between the chairs. "Like you, I've seen and heard stuff I don't want to remember but can't forget. It's like a scar on your soul."

"Didn't it give you a lot of satisfaction when you convicted someone?" Peter asked. "I've always thought our criminal justice system was good at catching the right person." He moved his chair a little closer.

"Oh yes. There's satisfaction when you're right. The media makes it look like we're right all the time, but we had to be aware that someone could be framed, or an eyewitness could be mistaken. DNA testing helps, but it isn't always available."

"Are you glad to be away from it?" Robert hesitated. "I had four children. You're reminding me of feeling guilty for punishing the wrong child. You always remember it."

Maggie looked at each of them and shifted in her chair. "You're my best friends. I think I owe you the full story of that awful memory I had at dinner." She swallowed hard. "You all know I was the head of the sex crimes unit. It wasn't easy being chief." She shook her head. "I've been gone long enough I'm beginning to feel normal, but some cases were so gruesome they made my skin crawl. I couldn't punish the perpetrator enough. But sometimes I wasn't sure." She sipped wine to distract her emotions. "We always had a team of investigators who confirmed the evidence. What bothered me at the diner was a couple of situations when our investigators had suspects and we cleared them, but then everything went south on us."

"That's a positive thing, isn't it, clearing people?" Gwen frowned, putting her wine down. She pushed her glasses to the top of her head, as if expecting the conversation to become more intimate.

Maggie hoped the darkness would hide her rising anguish. "Toward the end of my career, I had two innocent suspects who were released and then killed by angry vigilantes in situations similar to what we saw at the diner." She cringed as she remembered walking out of the courthouse soon after the second suspect was release, and one of her colleagues caught her with news of what had just been reported.

"The last one was especially tough on me. His name was Trevor. A couple of angry old white men believed he raped and murdered a seven-year-old white girl, so they killed him without knowing he had been cleared. He was a nineteen-year-old college student, a Black kid."

She blotted away a tear. "He was the pride of his family, and by the time of his funeral we had identified the actual killer. I can't imagine the pain of losing one of my children like that." She coughed. "There was no justice in what happened to him. I went to his funeral and apologized to his mother. Afterward, it was too much for me. My job had consumed me, but it still wasn't enough to protect an innocent person."

Gwen took her hand. "But, you know, it wasn't your fault."

"He was accused of a brutal crime, so I held him in lock-up longer than I should have. I put a lot of pressure on his lawyer, and on him, to confess and take a plea deal. He kept claiming he had big plans for his life and wouldn't admit to a crime he didn't commit."

"Why did you pressure him so much? Didn't you have evidence?"

"We had an eyewitness who picked him out of a lineup. We thought we had our suspect," Maggie said. "Stereotypes influenced our witness and me, I'm sorry to say. If the skin color of the witness is different, two people can look alike. It's something law enforcement is having a hard time with. Our witness was wrong."

Peter moved closer. "Is an eyewitness enough to convict?"

"Not in that circumstance. We didn't have enough hard evidence to hold him even after he was ID'd. My department should've worked harder to keep his name from the press, but it leaked. Old-fashioned thinking still exists in DC, even though they don't think so." She shuddered. "When we let him go, I suggested he lie low and go to his mother's house down in central Virginia. That was the mistake. Virginia is worse than DC on racial issues. I should've known better."

She hugged herself as she spoke slowly and painfully. "Those vigilantes followed Trevor down there. He stopped at a 7-Eleven. Some people inside saw the men throw gas on him when he got back to his car. They touched a burning match to the gas, and fled. No one was close enough to identify the men."

Maggie closed her eyes and slumped in her chair. "I went to the crime scene. By the time I arrived, it was dark. Police lights blazed garishly on the remains of Trevor's old blue

Ford. An officer who was waiting for the morgue vehicle showed me around." She choked. "I saw the remains of his body in the front seat. His head and torso had burned, and his jeans and lower limbs remained grossly out of place."

She turned away. "We traced the girl's murder to someone else using DNA. Prosecutors make mistakes sometimes. It was a hate crime and Trevor was innocent." She drained her wineglass. It felt good to share the details she had kept to herself for so long. "After that happened, I retired." She buried her face in her hands.

"I'm so sorry." Gwen put her hand on Maggie's knee. "I've also seen a lot of tragic situations. Let me know if you want to talk more. I have plenty of time."

"Thank you." Maggie looked up. "That's why I reacted. Ben Stillman might be guilty, but the DA needs convincing evidence, the bullies need to get out of the way, and Ben deserves his day in court."

Robert finished his drink, stood, and reached for the door. "Thank you for reminding us."

Peter touched Maggie's shoulders as he moved inside. "You did the right thing today. I hope Ben takes your advice."

Maggie continued staring into the night. Under her watch, she had cost an innocent person his life. It was the worst moment of her career. Coping with crime had darkened her judgment. She became angry because Trevor deserved better. Her supervisor sent her to therapy. Her therapist had suggested she was obsessed with her sense of responsibility.

Gwen gave her a hug before going inside.

Alone, Maggie stood and leaned across the porch railing. Feelings swept over her. Trevor's face was still there. Ben's innocent-looking face flickered in her mind. She couldn't let it happen again, not to anyone. Justice was necessary.

Robert stepped back outside. "Are you okay?" He brought reality back.

"Yeah, I'm all right," she said over her shoulder. *Was I too open with my feelings?*

The lantern cast his shadow across the road as he stood next to her. "I'm glad to hear that." He smiled wryly, his eyes revealing what he actually suspected.

"Everyone thought I was good at it, but I failed at doing my job."

"You want to tell me more?"

"I wasn't supposed to let the job get to me. But the work I did was horrible. I talked to mothers every day about their children. Every week, I had to interview a child who had been sexually abused. These were innocent children!" She wiped away a tear. "Every week I went to the hospital to interview rape victims. Some of them had been beaten. I would go home and cry where no one could see me. The following day at work, I would badger any suspect I had."

Her tone hardened. "Every time I convicted someone, two more cases landed on my desk. No one knows how many times I felt like I was about to snap, but I didn't. We weren't supposed to let it cloud our judgment." She faced him. "How could it not?"

He reached for her hand and held it gently. "Take a deep breath."

"What?"

"Breathe. Slowly. You're still human. Your heart is hurting. Let it slow down for a minute."

She let go a little and focused on relaxing and inhaling the cool night air until she could feel its gentle effect.

"Need a hug?" The gentleness of his tone calmed her tension.

"Yes, I do."

She had spontaneously opened up and talked about one of her greatest mistakes. He had understood. As his arms closed around her, she felt his spirit like a warm sun.

"What was in your heart?" he whispered near her ear.

"What do you mean?" She pulled away just enough to make eye contact.

"What was your intention when you talked to Trevor?"

"I was releasing him. I believed him and wanted him to go to his mother and be safe. My son got into trouble at that age, and the cops understood. I had the same goal."

"You did the right thing."

"He died."

"You couldn't have foreseen that. It wasn't your fault."

His arms surrounded her again. She snuggled against his heavy sheepskin-lined jacket, letting the earthy smell distract her. It was the safe hug of a friend without romantic overtones. To release the pain, she held him tightly.

His warmth brought her back. Her mind felt calm. She began to wonder if she would hear from Ben and how she would handle a conversation with him.

CHAPTER 4

Maggie

Saturday, September 5, 2020

Maggie's phone rang the following morning as they finished their eggs, sausage, and toast. It was Ben Stillman.

"I'm sorry to bother you on a Saturday morning. I hope this isn't too early."

"No, you're fine. We've just finished breakfast." The moment of silence that followed felt awkward.

"I've thought about what you said yesterday. I appreciate you took the time to talk to me. Do you have a few minutes?"

"Certainly. I'm glad you called. We were just talking about how you were threatened. Were there any issues?"

"No. I suspected those cowboys were up to no good. I went out with another group so I would have witnesses in case there was an ambush. The cowboys waited for me, but they did nothing."

"Glad to hear that." *He sounds better.* Using a thumbs-up, she let her friends know there was no problem after they left. Still dressed in her maroon pajamas and a plaid flannel robe, her short auburn hair uncombed, she moved to the living room and sat in the rocking chair.

"I'm sorry if I was rude last night," Ben said. "It was a rough day. Audrey was my best friend for so many years. I'm still shocked to know she could be gone." He cleared his throat. "You said you could help me find a lawyer?"

"Yes." After revisiting her feelings the night before, she had hoped he wouldn't call. She was now bound by her commitment to help him.

"Again, tell me why I need a lawyer? I didn't do anything. I knew nothing about this."

"Ben, I'm a retired prosecutor, so I'm going to see this from a jury's point of view. I'll probably be more blunt than you would like. I don't know the details, but the circumstantial evidence against you seems to be strong enough to involve getting an attorney on your side."

"Can they convict me on circumstantial evidence?"

Maggie stopped rocking and sat on the edge of the chair. She needed to listen carefully to his questions and hear his underlying concerns. "Sometimes. Depends on what the jury thinks. If they like you, they'll acquit. In a case like this where exculpatory evidence will be hard to find, it could be a guilty verdict if they don't like you."

He didn't respond.

Maggie waited. *Something concerns him. He doesn't know me well enough to talk about it.* She rose and paced. "Ben, do you have any more questions?"

"What's the circumstantial evidence against me?"

"I don't know much about your case, but burying a body at a remote cabin isn't typical for a random murder. Audrey was most likely killed by someone who either lived with her or in the neighborhood. It's the cabin where you lived until four years ago." She hesitated, needing to let him know the worst evidence. "Something went wrong with your marriage, so you had a motive."

"I haven't been there since I moved out. The last time I saw her was when we signed the divorce papers."

"The coroner will estimate her date of death with about six months on either side. You told me the body was almost a skeleton, so she's been dead for a while. If she died three and a half to four years ago, you'll be a suspect regardless of where you live now."

"How can they be that exact?"

"Forensic science works wonders with decomposing bodies."

"Why would they accuse me?"

"You had marital issues that ended in a divorce. That circumstance provides a motive."

"Our divorce was amicable. This is all so new to me. What happens? How do I defend myself? The sheriff wants me to come in and give a statement. What do I say?" He paused. "Will they arrest me if I go in?"

Maggie winced. *Is he afraid the sheriff has hard evidence? Am I reading him wrong?* "First, they need probable cause to arrest you, and the circumstantial evidence isn't good enough yet, but the sheriff may have more evidence than you know about. I suggest you talk to a criminal defense attorney before giving a statement. I don't have a law license in Utah, so I can't say much more."

He sighed as if finally accepting her suggestion. "How do I find an attorney?"

"There are several ways. Some people look up local defense lawyers on Google. I can also recommend someone, but I'll need more information."

"What do you want to know?"

"It's too complicated for right now. Let's meet in Salt Lake and talk about it again."

They planned a call for Monday evening. Maggie returned to the kitchen table.

Gwen's eyes were full of questions. She sipped her coffee slowly.

Peter had made notes on a paper napkin. He put his pen down and looked up.

"He knew how to handle the cowboys. No issues," Maggie said.

"Good to hear that," Peter said.

"Well, Counselor?" Robert sat back with his arms crossed.

She hesitated. "The first conversation isn't enough to make a judgment call." Her mind whirled from Ben's questions. "My instincts are still rusty."

Gwen smiled. "My favorite supersleuth, Jessica Fletcher, would say that as well. But she never let it stop her. I don't recall you ever backing away from a challenge. What does your gut feeling say?"

"How strong is the fact that it was a remote cabin?" Peter asked.

Maggie stared at him, pausing for emphasis. "Devastating."

Maggie shook her head. "Defense attorneys don't make immediate judgment calls about whether a person is guilty. They get the basic facts, and hopefully the truth, and then put forward their best defense case. I don't have a gut feeling yet, so I'll refer him to an attorney who will dig into it. He's either innocent and needs someone to stand up for him, or he's worried about something that might be incriminating and has a right to a vigorous defense."

"But you're going to meet with him and ask more questions?" Gwen said.

"Yes. I need to know if he's being honest. I won't refer a bad case to my colleagues." Maggie poured a cup of coffee and stirred in milk and Stevia.

She glanced up. "Robert, I would like for you to show me where they found the body."

CHAPTER 5

Maggie

She and Robert made plans to walk to Audrey's old cabin and then catch up with Peter and Gwen on the river trail. While Robert checked the fireplace, Maggie stepped outside and zipped her silver parka against the chill. She turned toward the sun, taking deep, cleansing breaths. A morning fog meandered through shadows in the forest. Birds skimmed among the trees and called to one another. All seemed right with the world.

The nearby water in the river gushed over large, jagged boulders from ancient rockslides. After leaving the rocks, the water slid into the crevices of Weber Canyon. Thurston Peak was on one side and divided Madison County from the more populous Davis and Weber counties. Salt Lake City lay at the southern end of the mountain, south of Davis County.

On her first trip to the cabin, Robert had told her about the enclave's pioneer history. Established in 1870, the nearby village had become Maxwell, with the county seat of Medford about five miles east. Pioneers had cut a dirt trail to the river and built log cabins under the juniper, fir, pine, and box elder trees. Fish became trapped in a natural water inlet and provided food.

Over time, the pioneers constructed ten one-room cabins. Four of them had been enlarged to two stories, while six had become two-bedroom bungalows.

When Robert stepped outside in his heavy jacket, his ruggedly handsome appearance impressed her again. Still warmed by his hug, she wished she had met a man like him before giving up on finding a romance that suited her. In the past, she had been lured by charm, only to later feel manipulated. She now reasons that her independent lifestyle no longer allowed room for a very personal 'someone' in her life.

"How far is the cabin?"

"Not far." Coming down the steps, he looked concerned. "This murder is going to shake things up around here. It's always been a tight community."

"How?"

"Like you said to Ben, if it wasn't him, a neighbor could've murdered Audrey. That's going to create suspicion of the rest of us." His eyes questioned her as if he wanted reassurance.

A yellow Labrador lay nearby, lazily wagging its tail as it watched them.

Robert waved toward the first cabin. "That one belongs to summer folks. Their car is gone, but the dog is here, so they must be up for the weekend. I can't imagine them being involved in a murder—or any of the other folks here."

They started walking. Maggie was accustomed to a fast pace and had to consciously slow down. The change felt calming.

Robert motioned toward the large cabin just beyond his, which belonged to one of the county's founding families, the Stevensons. "They still own a cattle ranch, a house, some buildings in town, and two of the cabins. The old man, Carl, was a major player in the county before he died a year ago."

"When he was alive, I presume he was one of the local good ole boys who controlled everything. Am I right?" Maggie laughed, hoping to lighten his concerns.

"You might say that, but he was one of the good ones." Robert softened. "He was a mentor to me after my dad abandoned us when I was ten, and I've tried to be like him. His widow still lives in their cabin. Their oldest son, Hank, runs their businesses now. None of them would've been involved in a murder."

"Why do you say that?"

"Status. Reputation. They're the most important family in town. Most are married and settled down. And besides, I know them pretty well. I grew up with Hank."

They reached the next cabin, a single-story building. "Hank's son, Randy, lives there. He returned from the army about five years ago."

"Did he serve in a combat zone?"

He stopped. "Why do you ask?"

"He could've been in Afghanistan. Post-traumatic stress. It could've triggered a reaction that resulted in Audrey's death."

"Not Randy. I'm pretty sure he didn't see combat."

Maggie frowned. *Robert is too close to the Stevensons to be objective.* "You know, it's probably best if we don't speculate about the neighbors right now. I don't want any outside influences when I meet with Ben. I need a clear head when I assess his veracity."

They walked a short distance in silence. Robert had always been respectful, and she trusted him. "Tell me about Carl and his mentoring."

Robert approached a tree along the side of the road. "One time, I was getting ready to carve my initials in the trunk of this tree. Carl stopped me. He told me that trees are also living creatures and how carving on them wasn't good. If the tree is damaged enough, it could kill it." He fell silent, as if reliving a special memory.

"And?"

"Well, I was just thinking about what else he said that day. He said I was like a young tree and I shouldn't let stuff get under my skin and eat away at me. I think he saw I was a teenager heading for trouble."

They started walking again. The dirt road through tall trees seemed to invite an intimate conversation.

"He always watched out for me. Carl stayed my mentor for the rest of his life. I miss him. I've always tried to be calm like he was."

"It's hard to lose someone close. I bet he was always proud of you."

The dirt road stretched a few hundred yards ahead. Robert seemed lost in his memories.

Walking in silence, Maggie pondered her lack of roots. She had grown up in a military family and never had a forever home or neighbors who watched her grow up.

"Carl was right," she said.

"What do you mean?"

"Oh, nothing. Life maybe. You were lucky to have Carl. It sounds like he helped you find a direction in life."

She silently mused on her own life. Through their friendship, she had already told Robert about her challenging history and how she had overcome it. Her parents had been locked in an unhappy marriage. They were old school and believed criticism was the best way to be a parent. Each of them had tried to control her in conflicting ways, and she had barely kept her adolescent anger in check.

With no guidance or help from her parents, she had struck out alone and found the world to be a painful place. Wanting a different life, she had become a hippie in the 1960s. Later, she became a rebellious feminist in the early Gloria Steinem mold, intent on creating her own identity and career.

Maggie had wanted to experience everything. She wanted a family and a big house in the country with a white picket fence. She tried marriage three times and always walked away feeling burned. Her therapist said she didn't pay enough attention when selecting the men she married.

"Have you thought about mentoring kids?" she asked.

"Oh, I tried with my kids, but it's hard being a father, a mother, and a mentor."

Robert's wife had died of cancer, and he finished raising their four teenagers. He claimed his marriage had been so good he feared trying it again and had become wary of commitment. Two years before, his youngest had found a partner, and Robert hesitantly talked about moving on. A new relationship had become a big challenge for him.

"Just curious. Why did you become a prosecutor?" Robert asked.

She walked a few steps in silence. Often, she didn't trust people enough to tell her stories, but Robert had become a trustworthy friend. "It's actually a broader question. Why did I go to law school? Why did I jump up and down and take to the streets for women's rights? I lived in San Francisco. It was the late sixties and early seventies. That's what we did." She grinned, thinking about her old Haight-Ashbury days. "All my life, I've had a certain idea of who I was, and I found it in San Francisco. Back then, my generation cared about each other and our well-being. We were social activists. After my first divorce, I became a volunteer on a rape crisis hotline. My cause was violence against women, and I wanted to make the law stronger for women." She paused. "Not much has changed. It gets more attention, but there are as many rapists now as there were then."

Privately, she remembered all the victims she had represented over the years, especially the ones who died. She often carried a small item belonging to the victim as a good luck talisman. It allowed her to connect with the spirit of the victim and feel her energy, and sometimes, in private, she would hold the object and chat with its owner as though the woman was still alive.

Robert grinned. "You're a crusader, aren't you?"

"Yeah, I guess that's my style. I've never been well-behaved."

"I'm impressed by your commitment to social issues."

They reached the curve in the road that turned to the right along the river. *I can't tell him what it's like to feel the spirit of someone whose been violently abused. Robert would never understand those conversations and how often I uncovered clues by simply talking to the victim.*

Robert waved to the fifth cabin on the left at the bend. "That one belongs to the sheriff." He indicated four more cabins along the road, two on the left and two on the right. "Those places belong to families who come in the summer, and sometimes they're rented out."

He pointed straight ahead. "That last pile of rubble at the end of the road is where Ben and Audrey lived. They found her body buried behind it."

In the morning sun, the old cabin stood desolate. One corner of its roof had collapsed where the timbers had rotted. It sloped down between the walls of the living room, splitting halfway up so rain and snow got inside. Vines grew haphazardly along the jagged edges.

"Sad." Maggie stared at the cabin's remains, which were inside a barrier of yellow police tape. "What do you know about Audrey? How did they get along?"

"I knew her, but not well. Before I retired, I didn't come up often, and that's when she and Ben lived here. Nice-looking woman. *Charming* might be an easy way to describe her. She sold herbs from her garden. They were both good people and seemed to get along fine. It's hard to believe Ben killed her."

"At the diner, it sounded like you had already made up your mind about him." She mused before gesturing toward the cabin. "How close can we get?"

"Let's find out. Ben doesn't seem like the type, but we're so remote it's hard to imagine it being anyone else. I'm glad I'm not the prosecutor on this one. It would be like a blind man in a dark room trying to find a black cat."

He picked up his pace, easily went under the yellow police tape, and beckoned to Maggie.

For a moment, she contemplated trespassing on a crime scene. The authorities had already examined the location. The area was very isolated. She was curious. With only a moment's hesitation, she went under the yellow tape and followed him.

Coming close to a backhoe sitting idle on the rise next to the river, Robert pointed toward the cabin and the logs haphazardly piled around it. "Not much left of her garden, but over here on the bluff, see where they've started digging a foundation for the new cabin?" He pointed to the partially dug trench. Whiffs of the fresh soil greeted them as they got closer.

He motioned toward the river. "See how the ground under those trees has washed away? That's a high-water mark from an old flood. That land above the trees is safe."

Robert turned back, descended the slight hill, and jumped across the small rainwater ditch along the road's edge. He scrambled close to the cabin's ruins, raising dust on his boots.

"This place is incredibly remote." Maggie removed her sunglasses and absorbed the view along the river before following him, stumbling over a loose snakeskin the wind had been tossing about.

Robert found his way to the remains of a log fence next to the cabin. "This was her garden." He moved inside the area, knelt, and examined a couple of scrawny plants. Picking a leaf, he rubbed it between his fingers and sniffed. "This one's a mint."

Maggie joined him. Despite the overgrowth, she could make out the gravel pathways and raised beds. Dried-out stalks on small trellises looked desolate. She gently touched a struggling dill plant before moving to the back of the garden and gazing across a small, sunny field covered with blooming plants.

"Look, Robert. The lavender survived, but it needs pruning. Thankfully, the rain and snow were enough to keep it alive."

She worked her way through dead leaves to the front of the garden, climbed two steps, and approached the doorway of the cabin. Small, bright wildflowers grew chaotically in the crevices of the fallen logs. She picked a yellow one.

"Be careful. That building's not stable."

"I won't go in."

Scanning the rooms in front of her, she saw a fireplace standing solidly in the rubble of the collapsed roof. Weather-damaged sofa cushions sat on a log frame against a wall. The remains of a kitchen were evident. Cabinets hung loose. A few old utensils were scattered on the floor. A wooden table holding a rusty kerosene lantern was against the window. The careless wind caused a ragged curtain to dance.

This was once Ben and Audrey's home.

The cabin felt eerie and seemed colder than its surroundings. Maggie shivered. She breathed in and out, feeling like something strange was happening. Her eyes glazed over and shut. When she opened them again, the cabin was charming and cozy. The roof was once again solid, a fire burned in the fireplace, and the couch was clean. In the kitchen, a young woman with long dark hair, wearing a white apron, peeled potatoes in the sink. A calico cat rubbed against her leg as if asking for his empty bowl to be filled. The woman turned and smiled shyly. *That must be Audrey. I've never seen a victim's ghost before.*

Maggie blinked, squeezed her eyes closed, and shook her head. When she opened them again, sad vibrations filled the air. The woman lay on the couch, her hand dragging on the floor. The cat was curled up on a rug. The fire had died, and the room seemed cold. *Was Audrey killed in this room?*

She turned to Robert. "Did anyone live here after Audrey disappeared?" *He won't believe me if I tell him what I saw.*

"Well, it's been several years. It's possible. The Stevenson family sold it a year ago when the roof collapsed."

She moved carefully toward the far end of the porch. Cautiously peering into a dusty bedroom window, she noticed an old iron bed with a bare mattress. It had become home to forest vermin.

Two wooden steps off the side of the porch beckoned her to explore. Walking along the outside wall, she scanned the trees, the rocky landscape, and the vastness of the forest.

A man's shout rang out. She quickly returned to the front porch. An older, paunchy man was running down the road toward them.

"Uh, Robert," she called. "Someone's coming."

Robert came to the front of the garden.

"Hey, Bobby Parsons." The man shouted and waved a brown hat. With an air of authority, he slowed to a fast walk before he spoke. "I can't let you go on that property right now." In his sixties, he wore a dark-blue western shirt, Levi's, and cowboy boots.

Maggie started toward the man, turning to Robert. "They still call you Bobby up here?"

"Yep. I'm still little Bobby Parsons. When I was growing up, another kid my same age was also called Bobby, so everyone gave us two names to tell us apart. I changed to Robert when I moved to Salt Lake. It's more professional." He smiled as he went toward the man. "Up here, I'm still the kid in the neighborhood."

"Hey, Sheriff. Good to see you. I'm not touching anything. Just wanted to get a better look."

"Can't do it. Sorry. Come on over this side of the tape." He motioned with his hat. "View's good enough here."

Robert ducked under the yellow tape and walked toward him. Maggie followed.

Robert was taller by a couple of inches and slung his arm around the sheriff's shoulders. "Hey, buddy, you got quite the crime scene here. Maybe you should put up a barrier to keep the tourists out. What do you think?"

"If I can't keep the locals out, how am I gonna keep the tourists out?"

Robert led the sheriff down the road a few steps and lowered his voice. "Speaking of being a local, think you can tell me what's going on?"

The sheriff pointed back toward Maggie and raised an eyebrow.

"Don't worry about her. She's cool."

"New girlfriend?"

"Nah, she's a good friend. A bunch of us came up for the weekend." Robert motioned for her to join them and introduced his childhood friend, Sheriff Jeffery O'Brian.

"Howdy, ma'am." The sheriff touched his hat, moved to include her, and addressed Robert. "You may be my oldest friend, but I can't tell you much right now."

"You think it's Audrey Stillman, don't you?"

"I'm going to let you think whatever you want."

"Didn't Carl's family sell the place after he passed?"

"Yep. After ole Stevenson died, it was so run-down they wanted out from under it, so the estate sold to a family who's been after it for years. Name's Miller from Salt Lake. They wanted to build a fancy new place, but they wanted it over there." He waved toward the bluff.

"They got their plans drawn up, got all the permits, and brought the backhoe in to dig the foundation. You can see over there where it's staked out and where they started digging."

All three turned to view the piles of dark soil alongside the small trench.

"Ole buddy, I guess I can tell you some. I just can't talk about who it is. The story will be in the local paper this week anyway." The sheriff cleared his throat. "That day, I hadn't gone into the office yet. I was getting ready to leave, and some guy came running over to my place, yelling at the top of his lungs. If I hadn't opened the door, he would've knocked it down and sure as hell would've woken up the dead."

The sheriff's eyes darted around. "Guess I shouldn't have said that. Well, anyway, he dragged me up to the job site. He was blubbering and stammering so much I couldn't get straight what he was saying. The guy running the backhoe was on the ground, looking at something by the bucket."

He grimaced. "When I got there, I got on my knees where they were digging and saw something that looked like cloth, dirty cloth. The bucket tore it, and when I got down and pulled, there was more there. Just on the other side was a bunch of hair—long, dark human hair. I felt along the other side of the cloth and knew I had a skeleton.

"I didn't have my phone, so I sent the first guy back to fetch it and have my wife call for backup." He pointed. "If you look where they were digging, you can see the hole where they took her out of the ground."

"It's Audrey, isn't it?" Robert asked again.

"I have my suspicions but can't say anything until the body's identified. Like I said, I won't address the rumors. The press is pushing me for a statement, but I can't oblige them either." His tone became wary. "Whoever buried her thought she'd never be found."

"Who dug her out?" Maggie asked.

"I called a couple of deputies to come clear the space, and I took pictures. I can do simple investigations, but for this, CSI at the state coroner's office had to be called. Their crime scene people did the actual digging."

"May I see what she looked like?" Robert said.

"Buddy, that's against the rules. My photos are evidence. I can't be showing them around to curiosity seekers."

"Has anyone ID'd her?"

"Well, to tell you the truth—and you have to keep this to yourself—you're probably right about the ID, but we're not sure yet. Her mom's the only relative, and she refused to look at the pictures or go to the morgue. We tracked down Audrey's ex-husband and asked him to go in, but I think they'll have to go for dental records."

"I knew her. Not well, but I might recognize her."

"I don't think anyone will recognize her." The sheriff shook his head and grinned as if friendship trumped the rules. "But I guess I could show you the picture, just in case." He pulled his phone out of his pocket and scrolled. "Let's see what I have." Finding the one he wanted, he handed his phone to Robert.

Robert stared at the picture. "She's all bones. Pretty gruesome. You're right. It's impossible to identify her." His voice was sober.

"May I see the picture?" Maggie asked.

Robert gave her the phone. The sheriff frowned but didn't object as she turned away to create shade. CSI had pulled aside the folds of a large, dark-green tarp that enveloped the woman's skeletal remains. She lay in her grave, exposed as if floating in a pool of dark water. What remained of her white dress touched the bones that had been her feet. The tarp had protected her long dark hair. Her deep black eye sockets were haunting.

Her arms were crossed across her chest. Hands emerged from the remnants of her sleeves. Traces of dried flesh were visible on her hands where her skin had been protected from the dirt. A small wooden cross, two sticks tied by an old string, lay on her chest with her fingers entwined around it, giving the impression that a brief ceremony was held.

Consumed by pity and horror, Maggie drew back. The eye sockets stared back at her. She couldn't help remembering the victims she had buried. In retirement, she had gotten away from the underbelly of society, but these haunting eyes brought back memories.

Maggie's stomach churned more than when she had seen other corpses, as if she was absorbing the pain of this person. She heard a faint wailing, like a call for help. She raised her gaze to see if the men heard it. They seemed oblivious. She looked away as she handed back the phone.

"We bagged that wooden cross after taking pictures," the sheriff said. "That's the only clue we have, other than her location."

Maggie moved a few steps away and stared toward the empty trench. Instead of clearing her thoughts, they became more vivid. Some people called her intuitive skills her sixth sense. In her vision, she tried to see who was handling the body, but only saw a shadow folding the tarp over the body and guiding it into the ground. *Was a prayer said as someone put the cross in Audrey's hands? Was there any remorse?*

"Maggie?" Robert touched her arm. "I was just telling the sheriff that we met Ben last night and you're going to have coffee with him when we get back to Salt Lake."

The sheriff turned to her like a kindly grandfather. "I'm sure your intentions are honorable, but it's not a good idea for you to get involved. You should let law enforcement handle this."

"I was law enforcement at one time," she said, trying not to bristle. "When I met Ben, I suggested he needed a good defense attorney. I plan to encourage him to hire someone."

"It'll be a waste of money, if you ask me. But I guess even a guilty person needs a lawyer." The sheriff tipped his hat, warned both of them about going on the property, backed away, and hurried home.

Maggie closed her eyes again. She was still connected to the corpse. She could not walk away from it. "I'm sorry, Robert, but viewing that corpse was hard. I'm not up to finishing our walk to the river."

"Anything wrong? You're looking pale." He gently embraced her shoulders.

"Did you hear anything when we saw the picture? Like the skeleton was crying out?"

"No, can't say that I did."

She pulled away. "This woman has gone from being a sentence spoken in a diner to being someone who was alive. I've seen bodies before, many times, and I've never been spooked, but this one affected me. I saw a vision of Audrey. Something strange is going on in my head." She shuddered. "Even with my parka on, I had chills."

A corpse speaking from the grave was more than she had ever encountered. Chills ran down her spine. *The thin mountain air made me dizzy. It must have been the breeze and the gurgling of the nearby water. Dead people don't cry out from the grave. Do they?*

CHAPTER 6

Robert

Maggie stopped briefly as they walked back. Her eyes looked haunted. "Robert, I still hear crying. It's like I'm hearing Audrey's voice and the voices of my old victims, especially the cases I couldn't solve. I moved out here and worked hard to put all of that behind me, but it's back."

Robert draped his arm around her shoulder. Since first meeting her, he had found Maggie to be both intriguing and intimidating. Smart and tough was the way he described her. She was more ambitious and adaptable than any woman he had known. Her urbane style exuded confidence. She spoke with the clipped accent of an Easterner and sometimes interrupted like the New Yorkers he had seen on TV. She talked about worlds and people that intrigued him but he had never experienced, like high-stakes players in DC who checkmated their political opponents with decisions that affected the entire country. She casually spoke about traveling the world, another of his pipe dreams. Yes, she was intimidating at times, but that was part of the challenge. To see her spooked by a corpse in the woods of Utah made her human and unsettled him.

He hoped he could calm her with a hometown distraction. "I've known that ole buzzard since we were kids. I called him 'sheriff' when he was still a deputy. Almost forgot his real name."

She offered a weak smile at his joke.

A new feeling that was difficult to put into words crept into his heart. He had done well in life, had many friends, felt happy, loved his privacy, and was glad he no longer had any responsibility for someone else. The more he got to know Maggie, the more he wanted to be her best friend and make memories with her. When he hugged her on the porch, he felt her vulnerability and wanted to take care of her. It was like a schoolboy crush, but it felt important.

His arm tingled. He wanted to pull her close again, but she seemed tense, as if she wasn't ready for it. Maybe he wasn't either. He knew the stories of her unsuccessful marriages and wondered if he could be different from the other men in her life.

He needed to be careful about Ben's case because it was close to home. There was nothing more to see or discuss until Maggie met with Ben. He searched for a distraction for today.

Walking a few more yards, he stopped. "I should stop and say hello to Carl's widow. She treated me like one of her own, and I haven't seen her all summer. Would you like to meet her?"

"Sure."

She was still spooked, and he wasn't sure a visit would help, but it was the best he could do at the moment. Approaching the Stevenson cabin, he noticed a red pickup parked in front and a couple of teenagers throwing sticks for the yellow Lab to catch.

"Hey, Spanky!" Robert yelled. "Go tell your mom and grandma that I'm out here and want to say hello."

The boy ran into the house.

Moments later, a middle-aged woman came out and waved. "Hey there, Bobby Parsons. Mom's still having breakfast. I'm running late for a Boy Scout meeting. Why don't you come around in fifteen minutes and have coffee with Grammy?" She waved toward Maggie. "And bring your friend."

He waved back before turning to Maggie. "That's Carol, Hank's wife."

Gwen and Peter had already left for their hike. They waited in his cabin until the red pickup pulled away.

As they sauntered over, he said, "Grammy was friendly with Audrey, so it's probably best not to mention Ben. It might upset her."

He tapped on Grammy's cabin door, which was ajar.

"Come in. Come in."

Robert entered the front hallway, tossed his hat on a mounted deer antler, playfully scooped up the tiny wisp of a woman in the kitchen, and gently twirled her. "Good to see you, Grammy. Here's that hug you've been missing!"

Stray white hairs fluttered from Grammy's pinned-up bun, and her cane swung in the air. After gently slowing down, he led her to a recliner facing the living room, seated her among the pillows and her knitting bag, and placed her cane nearby.

He noticed she had aged, and an air of sadness clung to her. Her skin, sporting a hint of makeup, resembled a withering leaf. Sunken, dusty-blue eyes peered through wire-framed glasses perched atop her prominent nose. She wore light-blue knit pants and a zip-up jacket. Socks and sheepskin slippers kept her feet warm.

While Robert tended to Grammy, Maggie moved into the living room at the rear of the cabin and looked down from the large picture window facing the river. The ground noticeably sloped behind the cabin, and light filtered through the trees, making it feel like a tree house.

"Grammy kept me out of trouble when I was a teenager." Robert said, putting Grammy's TV tray in front of her. "Don't know what I would've done without her." He kissed her lightly on the forehead.

"Bobby Parsons, you've been avoiding me all summer. Glad you stopped by, and tell me who your friend is."

"I brought three friends with me this weekend. This is Maggie Anderson from Salt Lake."

Maggie turned from the window and leaned forward with a gentle smile. "Very nice to meet you, Mrs. Stevenson."

"No, no, I'm Grammy to everyone in the neighborhood, including their friends." She pulled a gray shawl over her shoulders. "Take a seat, please."

Maggie moved an old wooden kitchen chair close to Grammy and sat.

"Carol set up the coffee for you and put the cups out. Help yourself. There's water boiling for my tea."

Robert went to the kitchen. "Still like your tea with lots of sugar?"

"Of course. I always have sugar, and there are some chocolate chip cookies somewhere on the table."

He adjusted her tea and laid two cookies on the saucer. He asked Maggie how she took her coffee and set two cookies on the saucer for her.

Robert followed Maggie's gaze as she looked around the living room. A TV and fireplace occupied the far end. A large framed sepia photo of pioneers in nineteenth-century wedding garments hung over the fireplace. On the other side of Grammy's recliner, a small bookcase held baby pictures and family photos. Prominent among them was a photo of Grammy and Carl. Maggie lingered on the photo as Carl's warm smile captivated her. She smiled at a small toy box in the corner with a couple of Raggedy Ann dolls on top. He was glad she no longer had a haunted look.

Robert sat on the couch nearest Grammy. "How're you doing? How's your health?"

Her hand trembled as she raised her cup and gazed out the window. "I've been better." She became quiet. Her face softened, and she looked away. "Carl's been gone fifteen months. Our fifty-ninth anniversary would've been last month. I'm alive, but you don't want to hear about me. It's just my turn to be old and have regrets. Tell me about your family."

He obliged, quickly bringing her up to date on his children and grandchildren, who were scattered around the country, before asking about her six kids.

"We still live a simple life up here, not like you city folks. Hank has taken over doing everything Carl used to do. Jimmy runs the ranch with Eddy. My girls have families over there in Wyoming. They're all married except for Eddy, and they all have kids except him. I don't think he'll ever become a family man." Her voice became tense. "He's never amounted to anything and had to stay with us a while back because he couldn't get along with his brother."

Robert hadn't seen Eddy in several years and remembered him as the youngest brother, whose three older sisters adored and spoiled him. *What had Eddy done to cause her such concern?*

She sighed deeply. "I sure miss all those grandkids. Guess I'm not relevant anymore. I only see Randy every once in a while, and he's no help. Anyhow, none of them come to see me except for Carol, who's a godsend. If it wasn't for her, I don't know what I'd do. Sometimes I don't even get out of bed unless she's coming."

"Aren't there people in town you could visit?" he asked.

Grammy hesitated, as if there was a misunderstanding, then shook her head. "They don't let me go anywhere, and I don't drive anymore. I gave Carl's pickup to Carol, and Hank sold my car. I don't care about visiting people anyhow."

She shivered. Maggie reached over and pulled her shawl closer to ward off the chill.

Grammy nervously touched a small necklace at her throat before bending forward with a studied expression. She bit her lip. "Bobby Parsons, what do you know about that body they found down the road? No one will tell me a thing."

He eyed Maggie and hesitated before turning back to Grammy. "Not much. I heard about it. Some people think it's Audrey Stillman. Didn't I hear you were good friends with her? What do you think?"

"Of course it's her. Who else would be buried over there?" Grammy's facial muscles hardened, and her body became rigid.

Maggie leaned in, paying closer attention.

"Has anyone been arrested?" Grammy spoke carefully while moving her knitting bag to the floor.

"No, it's too soon. They need to do an investigation," Robert said.

"They're saying that ex-husband of hers did it."

"I've heard those rumors. An arrest takes time. The authorities need to investigate."

"They also need compelling evidence." Maggie picked up a cookie.

"It's Ben's fault. He's connected somehow," Grammy said. "After he moved out, Audrey told me about his evil ways. All they need to know is the Bible is strictly against sodomy, and he's a sodomite. A man who's evil in one way will be evil in other ways." Grammy wrung her hands. Her piercing stare shifted from Ben to Maggie. "Why else would he secretly bury her like that? The quicker he's arrested, the better we'll all be."

Robert had ignored innuendoes from the people in town, but did not realize how much the rumor had spread. Maggie's brow scrunched into a frown. She seemed as shocked as he was at Grammy's attitude. *Did she pick up on what Grammy implied?*

Grammy leaned toward Maggie. "Did you know Audrey?"

"I've only been up here once." Maggie's tone was measured, as if she had heard something important but didn't want to address it yet. Needing a distraction, she walked over to the fireplace and examined the large photograph on the wall.

Grammy watched Maggie. Her voice rose. "Ben didn't know right from wrong. He had no morals."

Robert had never heard Grammy speak this way. "Why do you dislike Ben so intensely?"

Grammy scowled. "He walked out. Abandoned Audrey. Left her with nothing and no man to take care of her. All for his own evil purpose. He had an obligation to her."

He inched forward. "Grammy, sometimes things go wrong in a marriage. It's not our place to judge. Because they got divorced doesn't mean Ben killed her."

"He killed her. I know it. The scriptures tell us how evil he is, and I know it in my heart."

She was determined to judge Ben. Robert needed to change the conversation.

He rose, cranked open one of the side windows, and breathed in the fresh air. "I love that river. Listen to it,

Grammy. Life is so gentle here. Remember all the times Hank and I canoed on it? He was younger than me and wasn't strong enough to go the distance most of the time."

"Well, he's plenty big and strong now. He looks a lot like his father. He's not at all like that wimp, Benjamin."

Grammy's attacks on Ben made Robert uncomfortable, and he tuned her out. As a distraction, he scanned the room. Carl's heavy winter coat still hung on a coat hook in the front hallway.

He deflected two more biting criticisms of Ben before deciding it was time to say a polite goodbye and leave. He gave Grammy a perfunctory promise he would come back soon, headed toward the front door, and grabbed his hat from the antler rack.

Maggie followed and closed the door. "I'm sorry your visit didn't turn out well."

Robert shook his head. "I don't know what's gotten into her. I've never seen her like that. Maybe she's still mourning Carl and is lashing out at everyone."

Maggie glanced at the hat in his hands. "Is that your hat? It looks a little different."

He looked closely at the hat. It was a darker shade of tan and older than his. "You're right. It's Carl's old hat." He stepped back inside and found his own hat.

He came down the steps. "She's still living in the past. She hasn't gotten rid of Carl's things. I was like that for a while when my wife died."

CHAPTER 7

Maggie

"Those cowboys back at the diner could be the beginning of a lynch mob, couldn't they?" Maggie asked as they walked back to Robert's cabin. "My guess is that no one up here will calm them down."

"You're probably right. Robert kicked a small rock. "Ben needs to stay away for his own health."

"I hope he understands that. Is the whole town reacting the same way?" She started up the porch stairs wondering what other information she would need before referring the case.

"Not as strong, but they have it in for Ben Stillman." Robert opened the door. "I'd sure like to know what evidence the DA has besides the fact that Ben and Audrey divorced. Do you think he wanted out badly enough to kill her? Rumor is that Audrey was saying bad things about him after he left, and he wanted to stop her. That's what people are saying." He shook his head. "I don't like to spread rumors, so I didn't say anything last night."

"I appreciate that you didn't. Why does Grammy believe the rumors?"

He shrugged. "Why does anyone believe rumors?"

She followed him into the living room. "Tell me more about Randy, the grandson who was in the army. What's he like?"

"Oh, him? A bit spoiled, but harmless." Robert sat on a three-legged stool and pulled off his boots before placing a new log in the fireplace. "The family worried because Carl was gone so much on business. When Randy came home, they set him up next door to keep an eye on Grammy."

"Does he do a good job of it?"

"Not that I can see. He's about thirty years old. How many boys that age take good care of their grandmothers?"

She frowned. "Is Grammy in a fundamentalist religious group?"

"I wouldn't describe the locals as fundamentalists. When we were kids, she was more pragmatic." He leaned against a doorframe and laughed. "The women around here make sure the men and kids go to church, but religion isn't everything. She never quoted Bible verses."

Memories of her mother's religious obsession intruded on Maggie's thoughts. She turned to the kitchen faucet for a glass of water as a distraction. "Did she grow up in a strict religious community?"

"I don't know how she was raised. Carol would know more about her background."

"Is the whole town reacting the same way?" She followed Robert into the living room. "Ben seems completely different from his reputation. Besides him, who else would have a motive to kill Audrey? So far, none of this is making sense. What am I missing?"

"Don't know. That's the problem—it isn't clicking. You may be the perfect person to solve whatever happened."

"It's sad that Grammy's family doesn't visit much. It must be hard being out here alone. She seems very lonely."

"She can't be that lonely. Carl was on the county council. Everyone in town knows her. I guess being out here in the woods makes it hard for someone to stop and visit." He shook his head. "You and I both know it's hard for kids to stay in touch when they have their own families. Sometimes we expect too much. I don't see my kids all that often."

"I know. I had to move to Utah to see my grandkids more than once a year. You and I are both still active, but we'll need our kids eventually."

He became thoughtful. "Grammy has become very agitated. I remember her as much happier, and I've never known her to be stubbornly religious. She's also acting like she's just waiting to die, which is hard to take."

Maggie felt conflicted about Ben's case. What more did she need to know? She chose the rocker and nervously rocked for a few minutes. It sounded like Ben was being accused of murder simply because he was gay. She got up and thumbed through a box of old rock and roll CDs, examining three of them.

"How old do you think she is?" She placed a CD in the slot of the player.

"Well, Hank's her oldest, and he's about eight years younger than me, so he must be around fifty-seven, maybe fifty-eight. She said it would've been their fifty-ninth anniversary, so I would put Grammy at seventy-nine, maybe up to eighty-five, something like that."

Maggie had assumed Grammy was at least mid-eighties. The contrast was striking, considering she was seventy-five and still enjoyed working, did yoga, and had no hesitation about adventure traveling alone. She grimaced. "She's close to my age...maybe a few years older. She had a good husband, a house full of children, prestige in the community, and financial stability, yet she seems so bitter."

She pushed the button for the music. She felt a gut instinct sink in and spun around. "I think there's something else going on with Grammy. Consider this—I think she knows something about Audrey's murder that she doesn't want to talk about."

"Why do you say that?"

"It's what she doesn't say. It's the behavior we just saw. She's trying too hard to blame Ben. She's evasive. She's hiding something that's on her mind. She knows more than she's willing to say."

"That's the prosecutor in you. Interesting theory. I wish I could tell you how to get it out of her or why she's gotten so crabby."

"It's more than a theory. An instinct is telling me something is not quite right. I've always trusted my instincts."

As the music started, Robert's demeanor became playful. "That's 'Pretty Woman,' by Roy Orbison. Love it!" He grabbed her hand and twirled her, singing along. "'No one could look as good as you, mercy!' Remember how to dance to this?" He kept hold of her hand, gently embraced her, and did a few jitterbug steps.

Crabby wasn't how Maggie would describe Grammy. *Lonely* and *conflicted* would have been better.

Her growing friendship with Robert had become a pleasant distraction. She looked forward to seeing him and enjoyed his attention, but she would have pushed him away if he became romantic.

"It's strange how things turn out." Robert put the CD away. "I suspected Ben was gay, but I wasn't sure because he was married."

Maggie grinned. "I wondered why I immediately liked him." She also wondered if that was the source of Ben's hesitation on the phone and whether he would get a fair trial in a conservative small town. His only chance would be to find evidence that cleared him without question, and it needed to be found before the town's fragile self-control snapped.

"Oh, you like gay men but not straight men?" Robert joked, but she heard a serious question.

"No, it's not that. Gay men aren't on the prowl. Makes it easier to be friends."

"I've gotten to know a few gay men in architecture. They're pretty creative. I don't understand the attraction but, hey, to each his own."

Robert turned a kitchen chair around and sat on it backward, watching her fill two glasses of water. "I'm having a hard time with Audrey's murder. Wish I could give you a different answer, but who else would've done it?"

Maggie rested her back against the kitchen counter and closed her eyes. *The first question is always, why was she murdered?* She couldn't help wondering how she would approach the case as either the prosecutor or the defense counsel.

"Counselor, your wheels are spinning, aren't they?"

She opened her eyes. "I know. Bad habit. Interesting drama in the woods, isn't it? I'm even more curious about Ben's story now."

"Theoretically speaking, how would you get involved?"

"I'll help him find a good defense attorney, and I know someone who might be interested. I can't represent him because I didn't transfer my law license to Utah, and I certainly don't need to get back into the fray." She grinned. "After all, I'm enjoying retirement."

Robert looked disappointed. "That's all you would do?"

"I'll talk to him. If he has a believable story, I'll refer him. My friend would do a good job."

"What if you think he's guilty?"

"Even if he's guilty, he deserves a good defense. The DA needs to prove his case. A four-year-old murder won't be an easy conviction."

His brow wrinkled.

"The DA has a tough job with this one," she said. "He'll need to have solid evidence, and that will be hard. Sometimes I had to take a case to trial that still needed investigating. We were fairly certain about the guilty person but didn't have the budget or the manpower to keep looking for evidence, so we took it to a jury and let them decide. Sometimes the jury let someone go that I believed was guilty. Sometimes they convicted someone who turned out to be innocent, which was heartbreaking and hard to undo."

She sighed. "I'm now free of those concerns. If the evidence points to Ben, so be it, but if the DA is prosecuting him simply because people want to blame someone and Ben is someone they don't like, I have a problem with that."

The front door opened. Gwen bounced in, clearly exhausted, but still full of energy. Peter panted behind her, ready to rest.

"Sorry we didn't catch up with you," Maggie said. "I needed to recuperate."

"That bad?" Peter said.

"That old cabin was a little creepy."

"What a great place for a hike. The mountains are stunning." Gwen put her red sunhat on the table. "We followed the river trail for two or three miles. There are other old cabins upriver, and we talked to some people on the trail."

Robert and Peter moved aside to talk about the old cabins.

Gwen sat at the table. "How was your visit to the gravesite?"

Maggie chuckled. "The sheriff lives right down the road from it. He caught us trespassing at a crime scene."

Robert turned to them. "Then he showed us a picture of the corpse when they pulled her out of the ground. It was pretty gruesome. She's a skeleton."

"We also visited the lady next door. She's called Grammy. Her husband's ancestors helped settle this area. He died a year ago, and she's pretty lonely now."

"How old is she?" As a visiting nurse, Gwen cared for older people who lived alone.

"Robert estimates she's between seventy-nine and eighty-five. She's a little younger than your clients. She's pretty negative. I wonder if she's depressed."

"Does anyone take care of her?"

"Her daughter-in-law comes once a week. Grammy said that sometimes she doesn't even get out of bed unless Carol is coming."

"That sounds like depression. It happens a lot." Gwen opened the door and stepped out into the sun.

Maggie followed.

"It would be difficult when you're isolated like this." Gwen looked around. "Many people don't realize how hard ordinary life is when you're older and alone."

"I guess we rarely think about aging until it arrives." Maggie crossed her arms. Gwen might be just the person to discover what lay under Grammy's caustic demeanor. "Do you have a business card with you? She's very difficult, but if I get involved in Ben's case, I may suggest getting some extra help through your Visiting Nurses' agency."

"Sure. I'll find one in my purse and give it to you. Are you thinking of jumping in?"

"I'm planning to talk to Ben, and I'll help him find a lawyer." Her insides clenched. Gwen was too easy to talk to, and she had revealed her private thoughts too quickly.

After a few minutes of sunshine, Maggie excused her-self to take a nap.

Opening her bedroom window, she reflected on the sit-uation. Had Ben already been judged as guilty? Something beyond the scant details of Audrey's death niggled at her. *It's my old crusading spirit. I suspect Ben is facing prejudice and can't defend himself. No matter how hard I try to dis-tance myself, I know I won't be able to pry myself away until justice is served.*

CHAPTER 8

Maggie

Evening fast approached, and the weather was warm. Robert suggested they take their dinner down to the group patio and sit near the river. He was sure others would come to the regular Saturday dinner and his guests could meet the neighbors. It promised to be a quiet and cool evening under the trees.

Years before, the residents had cleared a space, built a large wooden platform, installed a permanent grill, and set up picnic tables and seating. This patio became their favorite meeting site. Away from TVs, computers, and household routines, friendships were formed, children grew up under watchful eyes, summer renters were welcomed, and local news was shared.

Robert led the way along the path. He pushed aside stray branches with one hand and carried a small cooler containing two six-packs of beer. Maggie followed with a potato salad wrapped in a tablecloth. Gwen had a chocolate cake in a carrier. Peter brought up the rear with a cardboard box packed with steaks, hamburgers, and other fixings.

Gwen and Maggie spread their supplies on a table. A small cabinet next to the grill contained charcoal, starter fuel, small pieces of wood, and grilling tools. Robert and Peter started a fire and began cooking the meat.

Once everything was ready, Maggie wandered over to the riverbank. She inhaled slowly and absorbed the sound of rushing water, then followed a few dirt steps down to the narrow gravel shore. At this stretch of the river, the water was smooth and flowed in silent splendor. A giant seagull swooped low and snatched a fish from the water.

Maggie needed to come to grips with the hatred and anger she heard from Grammy. She wished she could whoosh down and pluck it out of existence. She had grown up influenced by religious and social prejudices. She had changed her way of thinking and wondered how Grammy had held on for so long.

Silently, she compared Grammy to her father, who had grown up in the Deep South and was forced to accept racial integration as a military officer. She remembered his uncontrollable anger when Central High School in Little Rock was integrated in 1957. Before dying in the 1980s, he had abandoned his rigidity, joined a group of retired officers, and was friendly with several African American men. Would he have accepted gay people in the same manner? Why couldn't Grammy learn to be more accepting, like he had been?

Maggie put her concerns aside and rejoined the group. She looked up and saw Grammy watching them from her window, and wondered if she would come down to the picnic.

A couple arrived. They added their steaks, fruit salad, and bottled water to the offerings. The man joined Robert and Peter at the grill. The woman was in her late twenties and had long blond hair. She looked like a rodeo queen with her matching western-style orange shirt, Levi's, and a white cowboy hat.

Maggie approached her. "Hello, I'm Maggie, Robert's guest for the weekend."

"I'm Karen, Randy's new wife. We were married about three weeks ago." She blushed and gestured toward her husband while placing their items on the table. "We got back from our honeymoon last week."

The tall, muscular young man wore an embroidered orange western shirt matching his wife's and had a full head of curly dark auburn hair. Since he would have known Audrey, Maggie hoped they would find time to talk about her.

He lifted his hat slightly. "Nice to meet you, ma'am," he said with a hint of military discipline.

Moments later, Randy approached the table with a full plate. "Ladies, these hamburgers are ready to roll. Is everything ready?"

Karen scrambled to make room on the table while the others found places to sit.

"Steaks are coming off," Robert said. "I've got one medium rare ready to go."

"I'll take that." Randy quickly held his plate under the steak. "Karen will want the next medium rare coming off." He handed Karen's plate to Robert.

The rest of the steaks were claimed within minutes.

Randy turned to Gwen. "I don't believe we've met. I'm Randy. My dad is Hank Stevenson."

"That's nice. I don't believe I know who Hank Stevenson is," she said.

Maggie grinned. Gwen had told many stories about patients who had tried to curry favors because of their social status. It seemed Randy had already made a poor impression on her.

"You're not from around here, are you?" Randy asked.

"No, I'm also Robert's guest this weekend."

"The Stevensons are one of the major historical families here. My grandpa helped build this town. Grandma still lives in one of these cabins, but she's too old to come to the picnics."

Maggie glanced up and saw Grammy still standing at the window. She wondered if he had thought to escort her. It might have been as simple as Grammy needing an arm to steady herself.

"My dad runs half the businesses in town, and I'm being trained to take over when he retires."

Gwen gave him a bored look, then addressed Karen. "I heard you say you're newly married. Congratulations."

Randy grabbed a bottle of water and placed his hat on the table. "We just got back from our honeymoon in Hawaii."

Maggie rolled her eyes. He exuded privilege and arrogance despite his efforts to be friendly. She toyed with bringing him down a notch.

Gwen focused on Karen. "How was Hawaii?"

"Beautiful. Stunning. We were on Maui most of the time."

Randy squeezed Karen's hand. "Tell her about the helicopter ride."

"We flew over the volcano. It was amazing!"

Randy nodded to Peter. "Are you also staying at Bobby Parsons's place?"

"Yes. First time I've been in Madison County." Peter unpacked a six-pack of beer.

"Are you up here from Salt Lake?"

"Well, I retired and moved to Park City about a year ago. I like the skiing in Utah."

"Where are you from?"

"I was a research doctor at the Mayo Clinic in Minnesota."

"Welcome. We enjoy our small town. The air is fresh. The mountains keep the Salt Lake smog from coming over. We're family-oriented here. It's nice when you know everyone."

Robert grabbed two beers and handed one to Maggie as he sat next to her.

Randy smiled at Robert. "It's good of you to bring your city friends up here and show them our country living."

Maggie could see by their strained expressions that Randy was wearing thin on her friends. She sipped her beer. "Gwen, what are your plans for tomorrow?"

"I thought I would take the river trail heading toward the canyon."

"Good idea. May I join you?"

"Absolutely!"

With that cue, their group set up activities for the next day, and Karen and Randy fell into a separate conversation.

Later, over dessert and with a sarcastic tone, Randy stood and asked the gathering, "So what does everyone think of the latest buried bones news?"

Peter glanced around. "It's rather sad and morose."

"You may end up with a ghost haunting that new cabin," Gwen said.

Maggie winced. She broke off a forkful of chocolate cake and raised it halfway. "Randy, if it's Audrey, you must've known her. What was she like?"

"You would have known her better than I did, Randy," Robert said. "You probably also knew Ben fairly well. What's your opinion?"

Randy placed his hat on his head. "Oh, I liked Audrey. She was sweet. They used to come down here to the patio dinners. She was the one who socialized. My grandpa loved talking to her, but he talked to everyone. Ben was weird and didn't talk much."

"Were you friends with Audrey?" Maggie lifted another bite of cake.

He glanced toward his wife, blushing. "I would say I was friendly with her, not friends. In the army, they stationed me in England, and she wanted to know what I'd seen. She was into Shakespeare and old stuff like that."

Amused by his embarrassment, Maggie wondered if he'd ever had a romantic interest in Audrey. She expected him to brag and decided to tease it out of him. "What do you mean?"

"Oh, she liked to dress old-fashioned with long skirts, almost like a Shakespearean costume, and she tended that garden like it was something from the past. You know, everything had to be old-fashioned, like composting." He chuckled. "No modern chemicals for her!"

"Did you ever help with her garden?"

"And she enjoyed being dramatic. She couldn't just wear a coat or a jacket. She walked around in one of those big, long cloaks that women used to wear in the old days."

"Was she a homebody, or did she have lots of friends who visited?"

"No, she didn't have many visitors. She was in her garden most of the time."

"Did you ever help with her garden?" Maggie repeated.

He shot an apologetic look at his wife. "Well, I helped her clean it out once. Cut the plants back and took out the dead branches."

Karen's face perked up. She seemed to listen more carefully.

"Was that before or after her husband left?" Maggie said.

"After." His face flushed bright red. "In November, when the plants died. My grandpa asked me to help her."

When he blushed again, Maggie shook her head with a slight smile. *There's more to it.* "Did she act in local Shakespeare plays? Was she an amateur actress? I once knew some people from the Renaissance Faire who dressed like that. They did a lot of local acting."

"I don't know. I don't go to local plays." Randy sounded annoyed. "All I know is she dressed the part. She walked around with her long skirts, bonnets, and old-fashioned baskets. When it was cold, she wore that heavy cloak with the old Gaelic cloak pin." He turned to Gwen. "When she had the hood up, she looked like a ghost or something."

"What's a Gaelic cloak pin?" Gwen asked.

"The Gaelic cloak pin?" Caution entered his gaze. "It used to belong to my grandma. It surprised me when Audrey had it, but they were good friends. Grammy got it from her Scottish ancestors. In the olden days, it was used to fasten their cloaks. Grandpa said Grammy gave it to Audrey to use with her cloak."

"I've seen it," said Karen.

Randy shot a questioning glance at her.

Robert finished his chocolate cake. "What do you think of Ben?"

"Ben?" Randy's eyes narrowed. "He was quiet, never said much. I guess we know why."

"What do you mean?" Maggie asked.

"He's a queer." Randy smirked. He acted as if he was providing important news. "Around these parts, we know what's normal, and we stick to it. He was in a marriage he didn't want. Maybe he had a boyfriend, and for a couple of years, he planned to kill her."

"Don't you think you're jumping to conclusions? Just because someone is gay doesn't mean they're a murderer." Maggie's blood heated up. She clenched her fist under the table. *Randy's more than just offensive. He's a jerk.*

"I'm not just talking for myself." Randy waved his bottle of water around. "Ask anyone in town. We all knew him. He went to high school here. We're angry." His voice went up an octave, his gaze darting around. "We should've known because he didn't play sports or do what the other guys did. We're asking around to see if he ever made a pass at anyone. He should've never married Audrey. That was wrong of him, trying to be straight."

"Randy," Maggie said, taking a deep breath. *Now is not the time for a rebuttal, but a response is needed.* She reached for her almost empty beer can. "I lived in San Francisco when the gay culture emerged, mostly in the seventies and eighties." She deliberately drank the last drop. "I had several good friends who were gay. Most of them didn't realize it when they were in high school. From what I heard, they just tried to be normal teenagers."

"Are you one of those gay sympathizers?" Randy's voice quivered. "How can you be friends with them?"

Gwen and Peter frowned at each other. They got up, tossed their trash, and moved to lounge chairs for a separate conversation. Robert sat forward, listening closely.

Maggie spoke carefully, both hands circling her beer. "I'm not trying to pick a fight with you."

"It's not natural. Those people are dangerous, and they're the ones who go after kids."

"No, they aren't." She squeezed the beer can until it bent and leaned toward Randy. "Before I retired, I was in charge of the sex crimes unit at the DA's office in Washington, DC. I prosecuted child molesters. Eighty percent of them were straight male relatives or the mother's boyfriend. In my entire career, I never prosecuted a gay man for molesting children."

Randy walked to the platform's edge and stared at the river. When he faced the others and spoke, he sounded almost petulant. "I knew Audrey. My family knew her. She was from around here. She didn't deserve to be killed. Ben told her he was gay, and he moved out. She was angry and told people. That's what got her killed."

He scowled. "Grandpa said she wrote him a note saying she was moving and disappeared. Grandpa didn't know it was Ben. He thought she left town." His voice rose. "What really happened is Ben went after her for telling on him. She didn't move. She was killed and buried. It's anybody's guess who wrote that note."

Maggie swallowed hard. "You're right. She didn't deserve to die. I hope they find enough evidence to figure out what happened. I met Ben yesterday over at the diner. He was also sad and hurt. He didn't seem like a killer." She paused. "What happens if there's evidence it wasn't Ben?"

Randy came back to the table and drank from his water bottle. He shook his head. "I heard about what happened at the diner. He's guilty. I ain't got time for this equality bullshit. We just finished dealing with a lot of racial stuff at the schools." The veins on his temples pulsed. "They demanded the whole damn school district teach Black history! Why couldn't they just study American history? What makes them so special? We don't need those gays doing the same thing. We don't need his kind in this town, period."

He sneered. "And we don't need people coming in for the weekend telling us how to run our town." He tossed his water bottle in the trash, picked up their salad bowl, and jerked his head for Karen to follow him.

Karen glanced back at Maggie, a hint of fear in her eyes.

When they were out of earshot, Maggie drew in a deep breath and smashed the beer can with her foot. She leaned forward with her forearms on her knees and looked up at Robert, shaking her head. "Excuse me for saying this, but that kid is an asshole."

She was loud enough that Peter and Gwen heard her and moved closer. The four of them silently followed Randy and Karen as they return to their cabin.

"Maybe you could do more than just refer Ben to an attorney," Robert said. "Randy's no longer wet behind the ears. I wouldn't put it past him to be more connected to this than we know. Maybe you could get involved. We've got your back if you need it."

"Absolutely," Peter said.

"I'd like to help if I can," Gwen said.

Peter and Robert nodded.

Maggie glared up at Randy's cabin. "Sounds to me like the straight white men of this county feel threatened, and Ben Stillman will be convicted because he's gay. That's an issue."

"I agree," Robert said. "And there isn't a lawyer in this whole town who will help him."

"How many lawyers do you have here?" Maggie asked.

"Oh, I imagine there're a couple who handle divorces and maybe a couple who do business-type work. The rest of them live here but work in Ogden or Salt Lake. Any time there's a criminal case, it usually goes to the public defender's office."

"So, if Ben Stillman doesn't qualify for the public defender, you think he's out of luck?"

"He'll have to go to Ogden or Salt Lake to find legal help. No attorney in town will want his reputation affected. I'm just telling you how it is, not that I like it this way. Medford is pretty backward."

"It's like going back about twenty or thirty years, isn't it?

"I'd call it about fifty years. You're just the outside person he needs." He gave her a knowing look. "Maybe duty calls?"

She looked at each of her friends apprehensively. "I can't practice law in Utah."

She had no one to talk to about her hesitation to practice law again or her concern about being responsible for the life of someone caught up in a criminal case. She wished she had the courage to go up against Randy and his ilk.

CHAPTER 9

Maggie

Tuesday, September 8, 2020

Maggie's ride home from her weekend in the mountains was uneasy. She had her gut instinct and couldn't turn it off, but she wasn't convinced of Ben's innocence. She had met him and the accusation was hard to believe, yet there was no other reasonable explanation.

Ben called late on Monday and they arranged a meeting at a Starbucks for the next evening. Being able to look him in the eye, question him, and pick up on body language were all vital to her.

The air was hot and dry. She wore a navy T-shirt and jeans to their meeting. She saw Ben at the counter as they each ordered coffee and a dessert. In a pale-green shirt, he loosened his tie as they settled in. Smiling slightly at his movie star-quality appearance, she collected her thoughts and pulled out a small spiral notebook.

"Ben, I have a lot of concern for your situation. What happened at the diner was bad enough, but I talked to some of the local people this past weekend, and you don't have many friends in Madison County." She raised her cup, watching for his reaction. It felt like she was confronting a suspect. "The town thinks you murdered Audrey. Until the matter is resolved, you should stay away."

He shook his head slowly. "I understand. I'm not a social person, so few people really get to know me. All I can tell you is that Audrey was alive the last time I saw her, and I had nothing to do with her death." He picked up his cup. "You had questions. What would you like to know?"

"I'm going to ask about a lot of details. Things your attorney will want to know." She leaned back. "For the moment, please tell me a little more about yourself."

"Sure." He became reflective, glancing out the window as he spoke. "I was born and raised in Madison County. My family goes way back. My mother wrote a book about the county's history. My parents aren't taking this well." His tone spoke of pride and concern.

"In 2001, two years after high school, I married Audrey. She was the only girl I ever dated. Her dad was the county assessor, so half the town came to the wedding reception."

"When did you move into the cabin?"

"About the time we got married, Carl Stevenson was looking for a tenant. He wanted someone local, not a weekender or a seasonal family. Audrey wanted an herb garden, and we thought it would be a great location. We enjoyed living there."

"How did you get along with the neighbors?"

"Good." He sipped his coffee. "I miss being around old friends and the people I grew up with. I miss the cabins. You know the place by the river called the patio, don't you? It's a special place, and you get to know everyone. I was always on the quiet side, but Audrey was friendly and loved going there."

"Did you get to know Carl and Grammy?"

"Carl was friendly at the patio dinners, but Grammy usually stayed home. Carl often said she wasn't feeling well. I think she had a medical condition or something, and she didn't socialize much." He stopped to take a bite of his brownie. "I heard Carl was out on his ranch and died about a year ago. It must be hard on her now."

"Tell me about your marriage and the divorce." Maggie made notes. "How long were you and Audrey married?"

"Fifteen years."

"Why did your marriage break up?" She sliced her blueberry tart.

He hesitated.

"I've been married three times." She bit into her tart and took a sip of coffee. "There are always many reasons. I'm not asking for details, just a general idea."

Ben spoke as if he had nothing to hide. "I realized I was gay."

She had hoped he wouldn't hide it and relaxed at his response. "Okay, tell me more. Your lawyer will need to know the story. How did it all go down?"

Ben leaned back, which showed his confidence in her and his openness to talking about it. "In the beginning, we tried for children. Everyone expected a pregnancy, but it just didn't happen. After about five years, we started drifting apart. I worked as a salesman at the Ford dealership, and Audrey was selling herbs and crafts. I was taking computer classes and hanging with friends from class, and she was building her business and had separate friends."

He sighed. "One day, maybe ten years after we got married, this guy came into the dealership to talk about a truck. He didn't buy, but a few days later, he called and asked me to meet him at a bar. I'm not a bar person and didn't know the place. It's east of town, very remote. I went out to meet him. We talked about trucks for a few minutes. He asked me if I knew what kind of bar it was. I looked around and saw it was all men, which wasn't a big deal, but then I saw some guys in a corner getting too friendly and realized where I was.

"I'm not going into detail, but you get the picture. At first, I was uncomfortable, but I started hanging with the truck guy because we got along well. I thought I was being politically correct by being his friend." He shrugged and grinned.

"Then I went through a phase of fierce denial as it sank in. It took me a while to come to grips with the idea. Medford's a very macho town, and I never knew anyone who was openly gay. It's hard to come out when you wonder if all eyes are staring at you. It was even longer before I started an affair. By that time, Audrey and I had been married about fourteen years, and we were more like friends."

"After fourteen years of marriage, you told her?"

"Well, by the time I told her, it was fifteen years."

"So for a year, you were having sex with both a male lover and your wife?"

He picked up his last bite of brownie. "Yes."

"Didn't you consider it risky for health reasons?"

"I'm sorry to say I paid very little attention to that."

"When you finally told your wife, how did she take it?"

"Not well. She was shocked and angry and took it personally. There were some pretty nasty fights before I moved out. I still loved her, but it was more like loving a friend. At first, I wasn't sure what to do, but I had to do something."

"Do you understand why she was angry?" Maggie had to stop before she defended Audrey. She put her pen down.

How would any woman feel if her husband left her because he was gay? "I'm sorry. It's an awkward position. Thank God it's becoming more acceptable, especially for younger people." Silently, she reflected on her best friend in San Francisco who had died of AIDS. She swallowed hard to keep her emotions in check. "Tell me about the fights. Was there anything physical?"

"No. I never touched her in anger. All I could do was be truthful and let it play out. There was one time she pounded on my chest. I grabbed her hands to stop her, but that was it."

"Do you remember when that was?"

"The last time we were intimate was in July 2016. I couldn't stand the deception anymore and told her then. The chest-pounding happened about a week later." He shook his head. "It probably wasn't the best way to handle it. I started looking for a job in Salt Lake and moved out in August 2016. I stayed in a hotel for two weeks before I could find an apartment and get some furniture."

"Was Audrey religious?"

"No. She was raised Mormon, but we never went to church and didn't participate in any church activities."

"What was Audrey like? How would you describe her?"

He bowed his head remembering her. "She was the sweetest, kindest woman I've ever known." He looked up. "She made me feel good about myself."

"Did she have the means to support herself after you left?" She thought about the financial fallouts from her own divorces, and anger welled up inside her.

His forehead wrinkled. "Not really. When we were sorting things out, I suggested she move in with her mom to save money on rent, but she didn't like me telling her what to do."

Both of them finished their coffee.

"I need some details about the divorce. Did you take any of the money or any possessions?" Maggie said.

Ben sounded more businesslike. "We had two joint checking accounts. One was for her business, and I had nothing to do with it. When I left, she had enough money in our regular account to pay the rent and expenses for two months. I took half of the savings account and a few papers out of the safe deposit box. She had enough for six months with none of her business income. I took my laptop and a few other things. The furniture was a rustic style made from bleached logs. It was perfect for the cabin. I wanted something different in Salt Lake."

"Did Audrey have a car?"

"Yes, it was an old clunker. It wasn't worth anything, but she liked it because she could carry her plants without worrying about the car."

"Were there any life insurance policies on Audrey that you would benefit from?"

"No. We did okay financially, but we didn't have any life insurance on her. I had insurance through my job but lost it when I moved to Salt Lake."

"What happened to the cat?" *I wonder if my vision of the cat was real.*

"The cat? She kept it when I moved. I don't know what happened to it after she disappeared."

"When was the last time you saw her?"

"In October, I hired a lawyer in Salt Lake. We worked things out and signed the papers in November. There wasn't much to it. No kids, no house, nothing much to divide after I left."

"November 2016?"

"Yes. It was November 17."

"Did you see her after that or talk to her?"

"No. When I saw her then, she was still bitter. She told me she had a new boyfriend, and he had so much money she didn't need anything from me."

"Did your attorney hear her?" Anticipating a witness, Maggie felt a surge of excitement. "Did she give you any clues who the new boyfriend was?"

"No, that's all she said. No one else heard. I was a little surprised because she never cared about having lots of money."

"That could've been defensiveness on her part. Do you think the corpse is Audrey?"

"I hope not, but it seems likely. I'm still feeling a lot of grief. She was a good person. This must devastate her mom. I hope they find the person who did it. I can't imagine what would've caused someone to kill her."

His empathy for her mother is good, but does he really understand how emotionally devastated Audrey would have been? "Did Audrey have any enemies? Anyone who would want to see her dead?"

"Not that I'm aware of. Everyone liked her. She was always kind. She visited Grammy, who was hard to get to know, and they became good friends. Grammy even came down to our place a few times. Audrey used to say she felt like a granddaughter to her."

"You told me the sheriff's office contacted you. Have you heard from them again?"

"No."

"You know, if they prove the body is Audrey, you'll be the prime suspect."

"I didn't kill her, and I didn't bury her. I knew nothing about it until last week. I guess that's why I need a lawyer."

"The problem is you have to convince a jury." Maggie turned away. *I wonder if he knows about the items at the gravesite.* For effect, she relaxed. "Robert and I talked to the sheriff a couple of days ago. They found several things that could be linked to you. Do you remember owning a large dark-green tarp? Maybe you covered the firewood, or Audrey used it in her gardening?"

Ben frowned. "No, doesn't ring a bell. We kept our firewood under the eaves, so we didn't need to cover it. I wasn't the outdoor type, so I wouldn't have much use for something like that, and I don't think Audrey had one. I could be wrong, but I don't remember it."

"One other thing. Even if she wasn't religious, did she keep any religious symbols? Anything like a Bible or religious pictures? Maybe a cross or even a hand-carved wooden cross?"

"No. Like I said, she wasn't religious."

"I heard she liked old-fashioned costumes. Could she have had a cross as part of a costume?"

"Not when I was there."

"It's good you don't remember any of that stuff. The sheriff might try to connect those items to you." *And if those items were yours or Audrey's and you're not telling me, my friend, you're in trouble.* Maggie couldn't help that she still thought like a prosecutor; she had been fooled before. "What are you doing for work now?"

"I work in Bountiful for an independent stockbroker and live in North Salt Lake. Mostly, I do computer work. I'm studying to become a broker myself. When I get my license, I plan to move to San Francisco."

"It's an interesting town, but it's changed a lot since I was there."

"So I've heard. I'd like to know more about it when we get through this difficulty."

"Sure." She didn't want to get distracted. "Let's go back and fill in some details. Can you remember the people who were living in the cabins when you were there?"

She took notes as he recalled the residents of each cabin. He had sold vehicles to some of them. "Do you remember if any of these neighbors disliked Audrey?"

"No one disliked Audrey."

As Maggie asked questions, she quietly assessed Ben's honesty. He had talked about his feelings, his money, and his career. He showed none of the telltale signs of lying, answered her questions without hesitation, didn't fidget, and maintained eye contact. She surmised he had become accustomed to telling the truth about himself, and always being truthful came with that. He came across as innocent, but the circumstances and public sentiment were overwhelmingly against him.

It felt good to be back in the game, even for a moment. Ben was depending on her help. She suspected it was a quarrel gone bad or an accidental death, and he was trying to hide it. Much of what he said contradicted her theory, but he could be covering it up.

She made her decision. *Even if he's guilty, he deserves a good defense lawyer and a fair trial. He might even get a plea deal or probation.* "I know a criminal defense lawyer, Charles Cameron. I'll introduce you to him. He's low key, but handles things well."

"Thank you."

"You should start looking for documents that will verify your story. Find the hotel records from when you moved and those divorce papers with her signature. That will prove she was alive in November 2016. Also, since you were a signatory on both bank accounts, see if you can get copies of bank statements for both accounts for 2016 and 2017. You'll want to be transparent with the DA. It'll help if he doesn't have to dig them out. Be aware, of course, they'll be looking for any suspicious transactions. Keep thinking about anything else that might be relevant and let your attorney know about it."

The next step was to take his story to Charles. She wondered if she had become too emotionally involved to objectively assess Ben's chances in court. She also pondered why she was drawn to Ben's case and how she would diplomatically step away after turning it over to a Charles, her friend who was a defense attorney.

CHAPTER 10

Audrey

Monday, July 4, 2016

It was deserted where Audrey sat near the river. Almost everyone had gone to the July 4 picnic in town and would stay for the fireworks. *Everyone* really meant the ten or fifteen people who were at the cabin enclave for the holiday weekend. Audrey had not gone because Ben said he had plans and disappeared.

Instead, she grabbed her gardening bonnet, walked down the dirt road, and turned at the pathway leading to the patio. She carried a jug of iced tea and a package of Oreo cookies, sat at a table shaded by trees, and listened to the water. She needed to talk about her scariest thoughts. It felt urgent, but her best friend, Stacey, was happily married, busy with her kids, and wouldn't understand.

Dear diary, Audrey wrote in the large dark-blue spiral notebook she had recently purchased. Her soft, feminine script gently sloped forward, flaring into loops. *I've been lonely lately, and my mom suggested I start a diary, so here I am. I have thoughts I can't tell anyone, so at least I'll have you to talk to.* She wrote the date in the top right-hand corner. *I only wish you could talk back and give me advice.*

I don't know what happened or even how it started. It was so perfect in high school. Ben was the kindest and most gentle boy I knew, and he always spent time with me, just talking. My friends kept complaining about their boyfriends who always wanted to kiss and touch them, and do even more, but Ben wasn't like that, and I was so glad. But when he did kiss me, it was special. She gazed toward the river but only saw memories. He had been the best dancer in school and her steady back then. It was important to have someone who was good-looking and easy to get along with, and who spent a lot of time with her.

She wrote about how she had recently pulled out her yearbooks and looked at the pictures of them together. They sat next to each other in the bleachers at graduation. He leaned over and quietly asked her to marry him. She had made no plans for after high school, except perhaps she'd take a few secretarial courses like her father wanted. She found a job at a fast-food place and saved money for a wedding. Ben wasn't sure about his future, either. He thought maybe he would go to college in Ogden, but he didn't know what he would study. He found a job where he started out doing deliveries at the local Ford dealership. They were going to figure out how to grow up together.

There were so many feelings she had kept hidden inside, and so she wrote page after page, reaching into far corners for the forgotten promises they had made to each other.

Because she had been an only child, she wanted children more than anything, lots of them. He wanted to make her happy. The hormones were there, and it was hard, but they had waited until after the wedding to have sex. They decided on three children and talked about names and how they would need to move from the cabin when the second one was on its way.

They were disappointed for more than five years. For a while, her mother's friends would ask discreetly, but that had stopped. At the patio dinners, the eyes of her neighbors were full of expectations, but they also stopped looking and asking.

She and Ben talked about the possibility of medical issues and went to a fertility clinic in Salt Lake. No one could find anything wrong. With nothing to tell people, all she could talk about were the herbs she was planting and the customers she was finding.

She never doubted Ben's devotion to her, but after a while, it felt like they were drifting apart. He was taking classes that would help him find a better job. She couldn't complain about that, but she missed him. When she asked questions, she didn't understand what the classes were about, so she stopped asking and just knew it would be good for them. When she wanted to spend time together, he had homework to do. They never talked about splitting up; they were just two people clinging to separate dreams, and they slowly lost those dreams.

She wanted to do everything a wife was supposed to do to make her husband happy and busied herself by making the cabin into a charming home and building her garden. She loved living in the woods and feeling like a modern-day pioneer who burned wood in a fireplace for heat. She sewed her own curtains, canned vegetables from her garden, crafted a patchwork quilt, learned to cook, and always had a good meal on the table when he came home. For her own enjoyment, she took long walks in the forest and made a log fence for her garden.

But their relationship changed, and she wasn't sure when it happened or why.

She would make dinner for two and would eat alone because he was late. Sometimes on Saturday evenings, he would remain in town long after work, and she would go to the patio for dinner so she could share her casseroles with others. Their cat became her companion.

He came home later and later. Sometimes he smelled of beer and stale smoke, but she said nothing. She didn't want him to feel like she was trying to control him. He continued to treat her well, and they never fought, but after fifteen years of marriage and their disappointment about children, little affectionate things stopped, and sex was almost nonexistent.

She thought maybe this was normal, but still worried. *What's he doing on Saturday nights? I want to follow him, but I know that won't work. My old car is so beat up everyone would recognize it. What would I do if I caught him with someone else? How embarrassing would it be? I'm just sitting around here, waiting for something to change, throwing rocks in the river, and reading books from the library. I'm so thankful for the library. I've taken up an interest in old England, and I'm reading books about a monk in an old monastery who solves murders.*

It felt good to write it all down. She reached for her tea and cookies. She twisted apart an Oreo and licked the frosting, just as she had done long ago, and watched the fish jump in the river while wondering what had gone wrong. The gentle sound of the water calmed her troubled mind. All she could wish for was that she and Ben would be the same as before.

Diary, I still love him. I want my husband back. I want our marriage to work. What did I do wrong? What do I do now?

CHAPTER 11

Audrey

Monday, July 18, 2016

Oh, diary, oh, diary, please help me! Two weeks ago, I told you I was worried. Now the very worst has happened. I'm so embarrassed; I can't tell anyone. Please help me understand all of this. I need you. A soft rain had fallen during the morning, and, despite her tears, she had been careful walking on the muddy path down to the patio. She watched the raindrops fall from the trees like the insidious drops of her agony.

Ben has asked for a divorce. There, I said it. I can't believe it. I need to say it again. Ben has asked for a divorce. And I thought we might mend things. I'm overwhelmed. I'm hurting like I've never hurt before. What went wrong?

The sun came out from under the clouds, and she tried to collect herself. *This past weekend, he was very nice to me. On Friday evening, he took me to a nice place in town for dinner. We talked about old times, some of our favorite memories. He asked about my business. My garden has been* a sanctuary for me, so I haven't said much. He stayed home on Saturday and fixed some things around the house.

The second night, we made love, and it seemed like old times. He was interested. He was gentle. I slept in his arms just like I used to. I thought he had come back to our marriage.

Tears formed in her eyes again. She came to the hard part. *The next morning, it happened. As I poured coffee, he asked me to sit down. He wanted to talk about something. He lit the old kerosene lamp on the table. I closed my eyes and smelled the burning oil. It's still vivid.*

As he moved across the room, there was a look in his eyes that scared me. I put an extra spoon of sugar in my coffee.

"I need to tell you something," he said. "This isn't going to be easy for me or for you." He silently looked at me for a long moment. "You're the only woman I've ever been with, and we've been good for each other. I've never regretted marrying you, and I'm sorry we weren't able to have children. I know how much you want a baby."

The dread took hold. I felt it in my muscles and ran my fingers through my hair.

"Something has happened," he said slowly. He didn't look at me. Instead, he spoke to the stove on the opposite wall. "It started about five years ago, but I wasn't sure. I wasn't comfortable—until a few months ago."

"Have you been having an affair?" I had the courage to ask. My voice quivered. He said I was the only woman, but was he lying?

"Well." He bent his head and scratched the back of his head where his hair was thinning. "It's not quite like that."

"What is it?" I was tired of waiting and held my coffee until my knuckles became white.

He turned to me, his eyes pleading for me to understand. "I'm gay."

"We had sex last night," I finally said. "You didn't have any trouble with that."

"We've been doing it for fifteen years, and I've always enjoyed it, but it's not the same. I know that's hard to understand. I still love you, Audrey, but I can't live with you anymore." He turned back to the stove, and his words seemed almost involuntary. "I've dreaded this moment."

I'm clutching my pen right now, just thinking about it again. "How did you expect me to feel?" Under my frozen exterior, I wanted to scream at him, to pound his chest and make it painful. I felt humiliated.

"I expected you to be hurt. You've depended on me so much, and I'm letting you down. I'll try to make it as easy for you as possible."

We continued to talk, slowly and carefully. We were both hurting, but the words came out. He told me how he discovered it. He asked me what he could do to make it less painful. I looked around the cabin, wondering if anything would help. He went over our finances and his income and proposed how we should split the money. He said he would give me some money, but I don't earn enough to support myself after that. What will I do when his money is gone?

I realized he had been planning this for a while.

When it was over, he got dressed and went to work, and I cried. I got dressed and came down here. Tears are still coming, and I'm messing up this paper right now.

Biting my lip is the only way I can stop my feelings.

CHAPTER 12

Maggie

Wednesday, September 9, 2020

Charles Cameron was glad to hear from Maggie. He arranged a meeting for the next afternoon at his office in Farmington, just off the interstate a few miles north of Salt Lake and Bountiful. The three of them settled into the brown leather chairs in his conference room with assorted drinks. Charles asked her to summarize the facts.

"The crux of the story is that about two weeks ago, a corpse was dug up at a remote cabin in Madison County, where Ben lived when he was married. He and his wife separated in August 2016, and he last saw her in November 2016. The corpse hasn't been officially identified, and there's no estimated date of death yet, but several people think it's Ben's ex-wife, Audrey, who disappeared a few months after the divorce. Ben's the prime suspect." Maggie faced Ben. "Is that the big picture?"

He nodded.

Charles, a thin, lanky man of about forty-five with wire-framed glasses, disheveled hair, and wearing shirtsleeves, finished his notes before looking up at Ben. He had the look of a man who had heard and seen everything. "And what's your side of the story?"

"I moved to Salt Lake when we split up, and the last time I saw her was when we signed the divorce papers in November 2016. Several months after that, my parents heard a rumor that she had moved out of town."

With gentle prodding from Charles, Ben repeated his story about growing apart, realizing he was gay, and separating. He talked about how Audrey was devastated and angry. Ben showed Charles the hotel records and the signed divorce papers. He also talked about Audrey's comment regarding a new boyfriend.

Maggie picked up the divorce document. Sipping coffee, she carefully read it. Her prosecutor's mind whirled in the background as she searched for weaknesses in Ben's story.

Charles focused on the investigation. He wanted to know exactly how the body was found. Maggie repeated the sheriff's story and described the photo she had seen.

"Within a few days, the coroner should have the body identified, and he'll estimate the date of death within a range," Charles said. "Right now, they have insufficient evidence for an arrest."

He spoke to Ben firmly but softly. "But if it's Audrey and if the date of death is anywhere near the time of your divorce, you'll be their prime suspect."

"I already am. That's why I need a lawyer. I didn't kill her, and I didn't bury her." His voice didn't waver.

"All they have now is circumstantial evidence, and it's flimsy at best, but if they come up with better evidence and the jury doesn't like you, you stand a chance of being convicted. You can expect the DA to pore over every detail of your life. You need to be prepared for it."

Charles reviewed his notes. "Were your fights ever public? Did anyone ever see anything physical? Did either of you ever go to an emergency room?"

"No, it was never physical," Ben said. "I don't recall any emergency room visits. Probably the only one she talked to about us, if anyone at all, was her mother."

"Did her mother like you?"

"I think so, especially in the beginning. Her mom wanted a grandchild. But she's also religious, so I don't know what she thinks now."

Charles evaluated his notes. "We need to find out who that boyfriend was. We need to build a case of reasonable doubt. Maybe the boyfriend did it."

"How do we do that?"

"I don't know yet. Think hard about it. Was there anyone in the neighborhood, in town, or connected with her business she might have gone to for comfort after the divorce? Someone she might have taken up with?"

"No one I can point to. We grew apart. Those last couple of years, I wouldn't have been aware if she was seeing someone."

"And she was reaching the end of her childbearing years, which might have given her motivation. You had someone on the side. Maybe she did too, and it went sour." Charles looked at Ben quizzically, as if trying to pry loose a memory.

"What about revenge? Is there anyone who held a grudge against you? Someone who blamed you for something that went wrong?"

He didn't wait for an answer. "Those are things I want you to think about. Maggie says the town has turned against you. If you're arrested, I'll ask for a change in venue. We don't want this case tried in Madison County, but we'll cross that bridge when we come to it. Since there's no evidence against you right now, I'll postpone the interview the Sheriff has requested."

He contemplated. "In the meantime, I've known Maggie for a while, and I know she's talented. I'd like to hire her and let her dig up more facts, maybe see if we can identify the boyfriend." He turned to her. "Maggie? You would work under my law license as my investigator."

Not expecting an invitation to join the defense team, she hesitated. Her first reaction was to say she couldn't take it on. Ben's face showed his confidence in her. Looking away, she thought of the hundreds of people she had prosecuted and wondered if she could defend someone accused of killing an innocent woman. She cringed at the thought of Randy and his ilk influencing the investigation. Concern about her past mistakes haunted her. "Could we talk in your private office for a minute?"

She looked at Ben. "Would you excuse us for a moment? There are some professional issues we need to discuss."

"Certainly. I didn't mean to startle you." Charles led Maggie to his nearby inner office. He closed the door. "What's up?"

Maggie sat in one of his orange upholstered guest chairs. "Charles, I'm a prosecutor. I've never defended anyone, especially someone accused of murder. I'm not sure I can do this."

A pause filled the air before Charles spoke. "In law school, did you ever have a mock trial class where you had to take one side of a case and then turn around and take the other side?"

She hesitated. "Yes."

"Pretend you're still in that class. Look at both sides equally. What are the strengths and weaknesses of Ben's case?"

"His weakness is he was the husband. They got divorced around the time of her death. Sounds like a marital quarrel got out of hand and he covered it up." She hesitated. "The other side is she signed divorce papers several months after he left so she was alive after they split up."

"Did he kill her after the divorce was final?"

"Could have, but most people get over their anger enough to move on."

"Ben is innocent until proven guilty." He spoke with authority before pacing the floor. "You like him well enough, but you're the best person to cut holes in his story and find the truth before the DA does. This case needs expert and meticulous investigation. If he didn't do it, we need to find the actual killer. If either you or the DA come up with inculpatory evidence against Ben, I can always negotiate a plea deal."

She leaned back. Charles was a good defense attorney. Getting involved felt crucial to her sense of justice. *Am I genuinely drawn to Ben's innocence? Can I believe his story?* "Charles, I'm retired."

"I know you well enough to suggest you can't just sit on your hands. I suspect it bores you to tears to be without a major project." He smiled. "I'm handing you the perfect solution for your retirement boredom."

She grinned, but had to tell him the truth. "Charles, just before I retired, I was responsible for one of our innocent suspects being murdered by a vigilante group. He was a very promising college kid. We never got justice for him. I left the department. I can't go back to practicing law. I'm not good enough."

He sat in the other guest chair and took her hand. "I've known you long enough to know you belong with us on this case. The best thing you can do for yourself is to jump back in."

She wondered what her friends would say. Sweat appeared on her brow. A lifetime of making career decisions flashed before her.

The words came out before she could come up with another excuse. "Okay. I'm willing."

She held her head in her hands, still feeling her conflict. *What if I mess this up? What if...?* She had to believe in herself again. It would be hard.

Swallowing hard, she stood. Her hands fell to her sides. Charles gave her a quick hug.

They walked back to the conference room.

"Ben, before anything goes to court, both sides need a lot more evidence. Maggie has agreed to be the investigator, if you're comfortable with it," Charles said.

"Sounds good to me."

"I would like for her to meet with the DA and go over what we know so far and see where he expects to go with the case," Charles said. "Maggie can check in with me every few days. I won't have to be involved unless something incriminating surfaces. Ben, is it okay for us to disclose the information you've given us today?"

"Sure. I have nothing to hide."

"I know the DA in Madison County, Logan Harris." Charles picked up his phone. "It's a little late so he won't be answering his phone, but I'll leave a message and confirm with you tomorrow."

He made the call. "Logan, Charles Cameron from Davis County here. I'm representing Ben Stillman on the unidentified corpse case you have. We both know it's too soon for an arrest, and we both need more information. I also know you're always shorthanded with investigators, so I'm offering to help. I've hired a very good gumshoe and would like to send her over to touch base. She's a retired prosecutor, so you should get alone well. It's early in the case, and we all need to understand it better. Let me know if you're willing to meet with her."

"Charles," Maggie said as he hung up, "is it all right if I enlist a couple of retired friends as volunteers? They were with me when I met Ben, and I think they would be helpful."

"Who are they?"

"All three are friends. Robert Parsons is from Madison County and knows the people up there. He's a retired architect. Gwen Simons is a private-duty nurse, and Peter Matthieu is a retired research doctor from the Mayo Clinic. They would be helpful in getting the legwork done."

"They sound fine to me. Just keep me informed of what you're doing. Ben?"

"Are you talking about Bobby Parsons and the others who were with you at the diner?"

"Yes."

"I don't have a problem with them."

When Maggie got home, she plopped on her couch. *What did I just agree to? I'm supposed to be selfishly enjoying myself in retirement. Why am I the compulsive crusader for justice?* She called Robert.

He chuckled. "I thought you would end up on the case." He congratulated her, asked what he could do, and offered the use of his cabin. "I get the feeling you become obsessed with your cases. Am I right?"

"I plead the Fifth." She grinned sarcastically. "But honestly, I may get Ben killed."

A moment of silence followed before Robert said, "Didn't you tell me a few days ago that you spent your whole life fighting for underdogs?"

"Yes, but...it's a whole new ballgame. I'm not sure I can stand up to all those Randy Stevensons who live in Medford."

"Maggie...Maggie, my dear friend. Of course you can. You'll have us standing behind you, if needed."

"You're sure you can handle me and all the problems I create?"

"I'm sure."

With his assurances, she called Gwen and Peter and asked if they still wanted to be involved. They both readily agreed to be part of the team.

Robert called her back after thirty minutes. "Are you going to be okay with this? It brought up some personal stuff for you when we were at the cabin."

It surprised Maggie that someone asked about how she felt. She had gone through life with no one really caring about her feelings except her therapist. She had become enmeshed in the law profession, where there was a distinct barrier between the rule of law and personal feelings. In her career, when the everyday horrors of her job hardened her, she had always tucked away those emotions and plowed ahead.

"Of course. I'll be all right. I always am." Her voice wavered.

"You'll talk to me about it, won't you?"

"Yes."

"We'll do this together. Don't forget that. When it gets rough or when those people in Medford get to be too much, call me."

"You're a sweetheart. Thank you." She intended to be cavalier, but his concern and the softness of his voice pleased her.

The next day, she set up a Zoom call to organize the team and plan for a weekly meeting.

"First off, I'm very glad to have this group of fellow sleuths," Maggie said. "Thank you for volunteering. They pulled me in because of my background, but I think you're here for the adventure. Am I right?"

"I love the idea of investigating an actual case," Robert said. "However, we need a name for our new team."

"Okay, that will be homework." Maggie made a note. "Actually, to get started, I'd like to assign responsibilities." She looked at her planning notes. "One thing before we start, we all need to eat. I propose we start our meetings with a potluck."

They loved the idea. Gwen offered to coordinate the menu.

"Robert, you know the people in Madison County, and everyone likes you," Maggie said. "I suspect there's a lot of gossip. I'd like to see you tap into it. Someone knows something, and they'll talk about it to the right person."

"That's easy."

"Gwen, I have a gut feeling that Grammy knows a lot more about Audrey's death than she's willing to tell. I'm going to try to meet her son Hank, pass along your business card, and suggest you as a backup caregiver for Grammy. I don't know if he'll agree, but I know you're good with your ladies. If you can gain her trust, Grammy might open up a little to you. Would you contact your agency and let them know you want that assignment if he calls?"

"Absolutely. She'll be an interesting challenge."

"Peter, I think you would be perfect at keeping track of our details and doing the research. I can send you everything I have so far. You'll be good at finding what we miss."

His eyes twinkled. "I'm on it."

"I'll handle the initial contacts and send out updates. Charles Cameron arranged for me to meet with the DA in Madison County on Monday. If I need to, I'll bring you into later meetings, but it's better if no one knows the three of you are part of this team." She smiled and felt professional again. *I'm feeling my stride.*

"We're going to nail this."

CHAPTER 13

Maggie

Monday, September 14, 2020

While driving up to Medford, Maggie contemplated how to convince DA Harris he didn't have a case against Ben.

Her GPS easily led her to the freeway exit for the small country town, fifteen minutes east of Robert's cabin. It was the type of place that stayed the same, never grew, never died, but kept on bragging about its place in pioneer history. An eclectic mixture of small buildings and homes greeted her. Their one concession to modernity was the county office complex, which still looked new and was a bold effort to be part of the twenty-first century. It took up an entire block.

"Mr. Harris, nice to meet you," Maggie shook hands with a husky man in a western-cut brown tweed sports jacket, a string tie, and scuffed cowboy boots. He met her eye to eye at five foot ten, and was close to sixty. A bit doughy and dumpy, he had a weathered, ruddy face and deep bags under his eyes. Exhausted, he appeared to be the perfect small-town lawyer who simply tried to keep the peace and punish the bad guys.

"Call me Logan." He led her down a hallway from the reception area.

"And I'm Maggie."

Even though she had dressed casually in a black sweater and pants, she still looked like an outsider next to his small staff, who were wearing torn jeans and T-shirts. For a split second, she compared his team to the vast open room of investigators at the DA's office in DC, the sixth largest in the country. She made a mental note to shake off her East Coast experiences and blend in, even if it meant wearing torn jeans.

Logan's office contained a wooden desk with a computer, a side table full of case folders, two guest chairs, and a coat rack with a brown Stetson. Important certificates and his law school diploma hung on the wall.

"Maggie, what can I do for you?" He said as if it really didn't matter, and sat behind his desk.

"Charles would like for me to go over the case with you." She intentionally softened her normal professional attitude. She had found it beneficial to start out gently when working with older men. "We've interviewed Ben Stillman and want to pass along what we know."

"He's the most likely suspect, isn't he?" Logan spoke as if he was the decision-maker and the case was already decided. "The sheriff wants to arrest Ben, but I can't give him the go-ahead yet because the body hasn't been identified." He stared at her. "I hear you're from DC?"

"Yes. I was in the DA's office. Retired three years ago."

"This isn't DC. We do things differently. Can we be clear about that?"

"Not an issue." She eyed him carefully and braced for what would come next.

"You know, Maggie Anderson, Medford's a small town in a big rural county. We've less than twelve thousand people in the whole dang county, and we like to know who our neighbors are. We pride ourselves on having a safe culture where children run free, people don't lock their doors, and no one suspects anything of their neighbor. We try to keep it that way and don't like some of the changes going on in the outside world. Having a murder here is a big concern for everyone."

"I totally understand." She already knew the egos of small-town cops and DAs were inversely proportional to the size of their department. Privately, she knew Medford's legal landscape did not differ from any other place, apart from its size.

She decided to cut to the chase. "Do you have enough evidence for probable cause against Ben Stillman?"

"If it's Audrey and if she died when Ben was living here, we do. Not many people have a reason to be down that dirt road, and they had marital problems. Circumstantial evidence suggests he solved his problems by killing her and moving out."

"And if he wasn't living in Medford when she died?"

"He's still in our crosshairs. He's the only one who had any issues with Audrey. For whatever reason, he came back and did it." His voice had a strict and serious undertone. "We don't have much of a staff, so if you know anything that would help solve this, I'd appreciate your saving us the trouble of an investigation." He picked up a pencil and intentionally drubbed it on his desk.

"Charles Cameron and I believe he's innocent. We're more than happy to cooperate on this, at least to get the basic evidence. We both need the same documents and the same information. At some point, I will need to work independently, but right now, I think we both want justice for Audrey Stillman."

"Since there's no arrest yet, I think we can discuss this openly and collect the background documents, if that's what you're talking about. You're going to be an outsider here, especially since you're from outside the state, so don't be coy and hide evidence from me if it goes against your client. I've got the county council breathing down my neck and the local newspaper itchin' for a headline." He shook his head. "I won't even tell you what the Salt Lake TV stations want."

She kept her chin high. "You can be assured that I'll be totally transparent with you." She had come of age when women had to claw their way to the top by acting like men and had learned that the better way to influence someone was to be polite while controlling the details. If she did most of the work, she would steer the case in the right direction the way she had done her entire career. "What's the latest on identifying the body?"

"I don't have a report from the coroner yet." He fell back in his chair. "I'll call them."

He punched in a number. When he got through to the attending coroner, Aaron Jenkins, he switched to speakerphone and identified that Maggie was in the room.

"Any news yet on the woman we sent over?"

"We don't have a positive yet. We're still waiting for dental records to see if it's the Stillman girl. We've got a couple of dentists searching old records."

"What about an estimate on the date of death?"

"She's been dead three and a half to four years. Right now, we're calling it between October 2016 and April 2017, based on a chemical analysis of the bones and the soil acidity. It could go a month or two on either side of that.

"It's mostly skeletal remains. There was some flesh on her hands where they were not close to the dirt. We sent a sample of the skin and hair to toxicology to see if anything pops up. Other than that, there are no deformities and no marks on the bones that would indicate a knife wound or a bullet. No broken bones or anything that would show an assault and no broken neck bones that would suggest strangulation. We think she was between thirty-five and forty. It could've been a poisoning or a natural death, even though she was young."

"Anything else?"

"We looked at the pictures you sent, the wooden cross, and the tarp she was wrapped in. The cross was hand-carved out of mesquite, a common wood around here and even more prevalent in Utah's drier south and central land-scapes, but it was old. Judging from an analysis of the carving, it was made fifty or sixty years ago. From the way it was placed in her hands, our profiling expert suggests that either your corpse was religious or the person who buried her was. It was most likely done by someone who cared about her, if that helps. A random murderer wouldn't have bothered."

"What about the tarp? Any telltale clues on it?"

"The tarp was old even before it was used to wrap her up. There's a spot or two of oil or grease that has been there quite a while. We're trying to identify it. We think it's motor oil but don't have a final on it yet. If it's oil, the tarp would have been used to crawl under a vehicle at some point."

"Is that it?"

"No, there's one more finding. You're probably going to be interested in this."

"What is it? Don't keep me waiting."

"She was pregnant. A fetus's cartilage and bones are identifiable at around ten weeks of pregnancy. The spine usually starts coming together around eight weeks, and the arms form by about fourteen weeks. From the size and development of the baby bones, we think she was twelve to fourteen weeks pregnant."

"Holy shit!" Logan's eyes widened. "Aaron, can you do a DNA test on those baby bones?"

"Sure."

Maggie furiously wrote notes.

"Get me a DNA on the mother and the baby." He inhaled deeply. "See if you can do a profile on the father. We have a whole new case here."

"Should take about a week. I'll also have the official toxicology and lab reports by then."

"Call me when you have it." He ended the call and stared at Maggie as if he had already evaluated the new information. "Stillman's gay. You know that?"

"Yes."

"So, here's the new story, and it's a slam dunk. We have a motive. He wants to leave her. Join the gay lifestyle. They have sex one last time. She gets pregnant. It spoils his plans. He won't let that stop him. He kills her. Buries her. Thinks no one will ever find her. The deal is done and he's free."

"Some of our evidence is going to make that a hard case to prosecute." Maggie's confidence rose. She pondered whether she should mention the new boyfriend. "Can we put some details up on a whiteboard?"

"Sure." Logan's self-assuredness was evident as he canceled a meeting and opened a door off his office. "I have a small evidence room here."

The room had a table, four chairs, industrial-style shelves with evidence boxes, and an extra-large whiteboard. He cleaned the whiteboard.

"Here." He handed her a couple of markers and sat. "It's your show. Convince me. I've got a pregnant female skeleton in the morgue, and we think it's Stillman's ex-wife. The most logical answer is that he did it. From what I hear, she was angry about the divorce. Maybe she was angry because he left her when she was pregnant. Then she's found buried in the backyard. It's pretty solid to me, and I think a jury would agree."

Maggie remained calm and deliberate. Instead of convincing a jury of Ben's guilt, she needed to convince a DA of his innocence. "Let's go over what we know, and I'll add what we got from interviewing Stillman." Her boyfriend theory was ready to be revealed...slowly.

First, she needed a timeline. She drew a series of vertical lines on the whiteboard, creating columns six inches apart, and labeled the top of each column, starting with *July 2016* and ending at *April 2017*.

"The coroner says she probably died between October and April." Near the bottom, she drew a horizontal line across the whiteboard from the column labeled *October 2016* to the one labeled *April 2017* and made arrowheads on each end. "This is the range."

She turned to Logan. "In July 2016, Ben told Audrey he was gay and wanted to end the marriage. In August, he moved out. He went to Salt Lake. He can prove it with hotel charges on his credit card. Audrey was angry and hurt. She talked to people. Who did she talk to? We don't know yet." In the column labeled *August 2016*, she wrote *Ben leaves* and *Who knew?*

"Ben took half of the money from their savings account and left the rest for her. There was enough money left in their checking account to pay the bills for two months, and with her share of the savings, she could pay all the bills for six months. He can prove this with bank records." She put dollar signs in the *September 2016* and *October 2016* columns.

"The coroner says she was three to four months pregnant. Could it be Ben's kid? Maybe. Ben says the last time they had sex was in July. When would she know?" She counted with her fingers. "August, September, October?" She drew a line from the July 2016 column to the October 2016 column. "Yes, it could've been his baby, but she would've known, and it would've been in the divorce papers." She waited for her comment to sink in.

Logan frowned. He shifted uncomfortably in his chair and didn't say a word as his eyes went back and forth, reviewing everything she had written.

"In October, Ben found a divorce lawyer in Salt Lake. I've seen the divorce papers. It was simple. No kids or pregnancy mentioned, no house, no investments, no retirement money, and they split the minimal debts fairly. She got half of the savings account. They met in November at the lawyer's office to sign the papers. The lawyer was a witness." She wrote *divorce* and the date *11/17/2016*.

With a scowl, he leaned back in his chair, arms crossed. "Not buying it. Maybe she didn't know yet. It has happened, you know. If she's pregnant, he's not doing much for her, just trying to get out of the marriage. He didn't even offer to pay child support."

She sighed. Apparently, she needed to educate him, and was willing to make him look a little foolish. "If she got pregnant in July, she would have suspected by November. Every good divorce lawyer asks that question and addresses it in the divorce papers."

Near the bottom of the *November 2016* column, she drew a black vertical line across the coroner's estimated date of death. "She was still alive at this point, and Ben had moved out. He didn't talk to her on the phone after November or even wish her a merry Christmas. Nada. Nothing. You'll see that when you subpoena his phone records."

"There's nothing that would stop him from coming back and killing her. He didn't bother with Christmas because he knew she was dead."

"You'll need to find evidence of that. Our client says he had a busy life in Salt Lake and stayed away from Madison County."

Logan's face was full of bluster. "Maybe she wasn't pregnant when the divorce papers were drawn up." He sounded less confident. "They could've had one last roll in the hay to celebrate the divorce, and she got pregnant. It happens. He didn't want to tell you. Then he made sure it wouldn't destroy his plans. Still within the coroner's time frame."

"A last roll in the hay would've been damn foolish, but it happens. I will grant you that." Ben had a different lifestyle. She doubted he would go back to a woman. "Her phone records will show if she called Ben. You might also discover if she was calling someone else."

She allowed Logan to have his new theory with one twist. She drew a line from *November 2016* to *February 2017*.

"There's one more piece of information that will be in Ben's testimony. In November, when they signed the papers, Audrey mocked Ben and said she had a new boyfriend who had much more money than he would ever have. No one else heard her. Was she spiting him, or was it for her own ego? We don't know. Is Ben lying about this to throw the scent off? We don't know." In the *November 2016* column, she wrote *New Boyfriend* in red.

"If she had a new boyfriend, she would've started dating in September at the earliest. Give it a couple of months before she's pregnant or knows about it. Maybe she celebrated the divorce with the new guy, and they forgot to use a condom."

She tapped the board with her marker. "So now let's assume she got pregnant in November with the boyfriend. Count it out with me—November, December, January, February." She drew a red line from *November 2016* to *February 2017*. "By January or February, she knows she's pregnant. She tells the boyfriend. Maybe he's married. Maybe the last thing he wants is a kid or a marriage.

"Audrey had to consider her options. Abortion? There could be some pushback in Utah. Force a miscarriage? Can she make it happen? Risky. Should she go public and humiliate the guy? What does that get her? She could've been desperate and committed suicide, but who found her? Who buried her? Who wanted to keep it a secret?"

She straightened. "Who secretly dug a hole in the ground and laid her to rest?" She spoke slowly. "Why didn't that person go to the cops if he was innocent? Where did the tarp come from? Who loved her enough to put that little wooden cross in her hands? Was the ground soft enough to dig with a shovel, or was it frozen? Maybe this happened in March when the ground was softer."

Before sitting down, she drew one more line from *February 2017* to *March 2017* and labeled it *Burial*.

"You're talking about a boyfriend only Ben Stillman knows about, right?" Logan snickered. "No one is going to admit to dating her. He'd be afraid of being charged with murder."

"True, but that's the challenge. It's your case, but I think we're looking for that mysterious boyfriend. Ultimately, DNA from the baby bones will tell us who we're looking for."

From the angst in his eyes, Maggie could see Logan was having a hard time admitting that his case against Ben was probably falling apart.

He frowned and shook his head. "If DNA shows Ben isn't the father, you've established reasonable doubt. Can't take that to a jury." He looked toward the wall as if deep in thought. "I have to answer to the honchos around here, and I have reporters breathing down my neck. This case needs to be solved." He returned his gaze to Maggie. "Right now, there aren't any other suspects. What do you suggest?"

She understood he was asking for her cooperation, which was exactly what she wanted. Even though most district attorneys were tight-lipped, she needed his cooperation and local contacts.

"First, we aren't sure of the ID, but we can assume it's Audrey," Maggie said. "Charles Cameron would be happy to bring Ben in for a statement, but you may want to wait until you get the basic records first and maybe some questionable evidence."

Logan wasn't happy, but he had to start somewhere. "Once we get the ID confirmed, we can open a case. Ben can furnish his hotel and divorce records. It would be faster if I subpoenaed the phone records instead of you. I could also contact the DMV about her tags and see what happened to her car. If someone killed her and sold her car, we could find him."

The game was suddenly afoot, and Maggie grinned. "I've asked Ben to get the joint bank records so we know what happened to her money. We should also determine the last time she paid rent. That would narrow down the date of death."

"Carl Stevenson was the landlord when she was there. He died a year ago. Hank runs things now. He'll be cooperative." Logan's response confirmed that he knew it was no longer a slam dunk case. "I can get the subpoenas out easily enough."

"I suggest we keep it quiet about the pregnancy. I need to tell Charles and ask Ben if he knew about it. That's the kind of evidence you keep out of the papers until you establish paternity. It must be on a need-to-know basis. If the boyfriend hears about it, he may skip out."

"Agreed."

"Is it okay if I talk to Hank about the rent records?" *He's also the one to talk to about getting better care for Grammy.*

"Sure. You've got the right to talk to witnesses as much as I have."

"Thanks. Charles and I are confident Ben didn't kill Audrey. I know it's not normal for the defense to be actively involved, but we'd like to help find the actual killer." *If we back off too soon, Audrey's death will become a cold case, and Ben will never be cleared.*

Logan checked his cell phone and provided Hank's number. He sent Hank a text to let him know she would be calling.

Maggie snapped a photo of the chart on the whiteboard.

Logan locked the door to the evidence room behind them. "Let's get Ben in for a DNA test. We don't want him to come here. We've got some angry folks, and it might be dangerous. He can go directly to the coroner's office in Salt Lake."

Maggie called Charles with the new information about the pregnancy and told him Logan was requesting a DNA test. Maggie then called Ben. She didn't tell him about the pregnancy because she wanted to see the results first. Arrangements were made for him to go directly to the crime lab for the test. She also asked for Audrey's cell phone number and passed it to Logan.

Maggie reached out for a handshake. "Logan, let's agree on a premise. This case isn't about Ben's sexuality or his divorce. It's about a murder that happened after he left town. Let me suggest that someone is trying to frame him because this town doesn't approve of his gay lifestyle. I know we're on opposites sides, but I think the focus is to find out what really happened to Audrey." She hesitated momentarily and decided to influence his attitude. "I appreciate your willingness to take a broader view. I'm looking forward to working with you."

He was uncomfortable but said nothing and shook her hand as if they had an agreement.

As the door closed behind her, she sensed Ben would have been railroaded without a lawyer, but he was on equal footing now, and she was, de facto, in control of the investigation.

CHAPTER 14

Maggie

"Hank, this is Maggie Anderson." She called him after she got to her white Ford Escape. "I'm an investigator for the defense on the case of the body found out there in Stevenson's Row."

"I heard someone was poking around. Logan told me to expect a call. Didn't I hear you're a friend of Bobby Parsons? He and I grew up together. What can I do for you?" Hank's voice was firm and self-assured. He sounded like someone who always got his way.

"Yes, we're friends. We don't have an ID on the body yet, but we're assuming it's Audrey Stillman. Logan and I are trying to narrow down the date of death. We're wondering if you would provide her rental records."

"Of course. I'm happy to oblige. Are you in town?"

"Yes, I've just met with Logan."

"There's a little café a few blocks from you and across from my building. Let's meet for a cup of joe in an hour, at three o'clock. You can tell me exactly what you're looking for."

She got the address, pulled her sunglasses from on top of her head, and drove the short distance over. The café was on one of the few remaining historical streets.

Weather-beaten wooden and brick buildings lined both sides for several blocks. Old doors had transom windows, and treasured goods were displayed for window shopping. Maggie parked a block away. She watched a clerk putting Halloween costumes in one window and walked past an old-fashioned hardware store, a bakery, and a title abstract company. After checking the time, she stopped at a small gift shop next to the café.

The shop was the perfect place to spend her extra minutes among the teas, trinkets, and handmade crafts on the shelves. An older woman with short graying hair, in a printed dark-green floor-length cotton dress, said hello and asked if she needed any help.

"No, I'm just looking, but thank you." Maggie moved among the display racks of herbal teas and noticed beaded necklaces on an antler tree. "Your shop is so pleasant! I love the smell of the teas." From the discount table, she picked up a scented sachet in a loosely woven cloth bag stenciled with "Audrey's Finest Herbs" and wrapped in lavender cellophane.

"The artist who made that is no longer in business. That's the last item I have from her."

"Was it Audrey Stillman?" Maggie sniffed the scent.

"Yes, did you know her?"

"I know of her."

Holding the sachet, her hand tingled. She could almost see hands stitching the lavender flower on the front and stuffing the fragrant dried lavender leaves inside. She wanted to find something Audrey had touched, and this was perfect. She would feel as if she was connecting with the victim's life. She bought it.

"Was Audrey one of your regular vendors?" Maggie asked.

"Oh yes, she was one of my favorites. My customers loved her crafts. This sachet was one of our biggest sellers." She carefully placed it in a small brown bag. "She had the eye of an artist and grew very fragrant plants."

"She was a local girl, wasn't she?"

"Yes, grew up here. It's a shame she's gone. Do you know anything about what happened to her? The whole town is asking questions."

"I'm from Salt Lake. Actually, I just started working with the DA, Logan Harris, on her case. We don't know much right now." Maggie checked the time. She wished she could ditch Hank and interview this woman. "I was up at Audrey's old cabin about a week ago. Her field of lavender is still growing well."

"Oh, I hope you're able to sort it out. She was such a sweet person. We all loved her. Maybe we could get someone to dig up what's left of those plants."

"I'll do my best on the investigation." Smiling at the prospect of getting more information, Maggie turned as she headed toward the door. "It would really be great if someone rescued those plants."

CHAPTER 15

Maggie

At three o'clock, Maggie entered the coffee shop. Old Co-ca-Cola signs still hung on the walls, and red-checkered vinyl tablecloths covered the tables. Photos and memen-toes from bygone patrons were everywhere, and a jukebox played Sonny and Cher's "I've Got You, Babe."

"Maggie Anderson?" A tall, husky, middle-aged man approached her with a friendly smile. He had the same dark-auburn hair as Randy, but streaked with gray, and he wore a brown leather jacket and jeans. It was as if Grammy's picture of Carl had come alive.

"Yes, and you must be Hank? Nice to meet you." She shook his hand. "I met Randy on Labor Day weekend. He's a younger version of you." Silently, she hoped Hank was a nicer version.

After ordering coffee, she gave him a business card, which he put in his shirt pocket.

"So, Maggie, how did you get involved in our little mur-der mystery up here?"

"I was Robert's guest at his cabin. I'm a retired prosecutor. It's in my blood. I've been hired by Ben Stillman's lawyer as an investigator."

"You switched sides? Sure that was the best thing to do? Ben Stillman's guilty, isn't he?"

"You're getting ahead of the game. The best approach is to find the evidence and then decide guilt." Her interrogator instinct instantly rose, but she was determined to be sociable with the most important man in town. "Robert told me your dad died about a year ago. My condolences. It's always hard to lose someone in the family. That made you the landlord out at Stevenson's Row, didn't it?"

"Kind of you. Well, I took over managing most of the properties in 1999 when my dad retired, except he wanted to manage the cabins. My brothers run the ranch. Dad continued to go on buying trips for cattle, but Mom didn't want to go anymore, so he stopped traveling." He momentarily lost himself in a memory. "Actually, he stopped doing a lot that last year. When he died, I became the executor of his estate."

"How did he die, if you don't mind my asking?" Maggie fixed her coffee and took a sip. She knew she was being more assertive than most women in Utah and hoped it wasn't too much.

Hank shook his head. "He was counting cattle out on the ranch and had a heart attack when no one was around. We thought he was in great health. He was only eighty-two. Goes to show, you never can tell."

"How's your mom handling it?"

"She's tough as nails. She raised six kids and stayed married to my dad for all those years. Dad retired so he could take care of her when she had breast cancer. I'm sure she misses him." He relaxed with his coffee cup in both hands. "We thought Mom would go before Dad. The clean air out there in the woods must be good for her."

"How often do you see her?" Maggie tried to sound small town friendly and concerned even though she had an ulterior motive.

Hank chuckled. "Well, my wife, Carol, is an angel and takes care of her every week. Gets her to the doctor when she needs it, buys her groceries, stuff like that. I get out there occasionally when a repair is needed. Always stop by to say hello."

"You've got children, don't you?"

"Yes. Randy's our oldest, and we have three others."

"Sounds like Carol's pretty busy." Maggie knew it was none of her business, but decided to ask anyway. "Would it be useful for her to have a backup caretaker when Carol can't get out there?"

"What are you getting at?" He laughed. "Mom won't leave that cabin. We'd never attempt to move her."

"Oh, I wasn't thinking about that. We visited Grammy when I was up here with Robert, and I could see how settled she was. I was thinking about a sudden medical need, some medical monitoring, maybe helping with housework or something like that. That's all. You know, it's possible to get a visiting nurse to come up once in a while. Someone who could be on call when Carol needs a break." She sounded like a busybody, but she was still bothered by Grammy's lonely stare from the back window.

Hank narrowed his eyes and scratched the back of his neck. "I've never heard of that. Don't think it'll happen. Have to say, though, Carol could use some help sometimes, but there's no way you can get someone to come out here to the boondocks."

"You'd be surprised. I have a friend who's a visiting nurse. She goes all over. That's why I mentioned it. She has a group of ladies she takes cares of and visits once a week."

Maggie sipped her coffee. *Seems like he always needs to have the upper hand. I'm outside his norm for women, and I need to be a little more careful.* "Anyway, I didn't mean to get distracted." She laid her sunglasses on the table and pulled Gwen's business card from her purse. "Here's the number of the agency my friend works for if you want more information."

He took the card and put it in his shirt pocket.

"So, what's this about the rental records?" His voice seemed a little uncertain.

"As I mentioned on the phone, Logan and I are trying to establish a timeline for when Audrey died. We thought it would be useful to get the rent records. Would you be willing to provide those?"

"Oh, sure. Anything for law enforcement." He cleared his throat. "I've got the best bookkeeper in town, Mrs. Madison. She's been with us for over fifteen years. She's very organized. What do you want to know?"

"I understand Audrey moved. When was the last time she paid rent?"

"Can't tell you offhand, but I can find out."

"We'd also like to know if you have a forwarding address for her and whether anyone else moved in after she left." She softened her voice. "I also heard Audrey left a note for Carl when she gave notice. Do you think Mrs. Madison would have that note?"

"All of that was before my time. I'll check and get back to you within a day or so. That place was so run down, I don't think anyone lived there after Audrey disappeared."

"Off the record, what do you know about Audrey's disappearance?"

"Nothing really. She was my dad's tenant, and I heard she left town after her divorce. No one paid much attention until her body was found."

Maggie's forehead wrinkled. "Wasn't Audrey's dad the county assessor? You must have known him. Wasn't there some concern about his daughter?"

"She was a grown woman. I assumed she decided to leave town and acted on it." He raised his eyebrows and crossed his arms. "You're barking up the wrong tree if you think no one cared. No one is going to tell you that."

"So, by dying, she finally disturbed the peace of this happy little town?" *That was meant to be mild sarcasm, but came out as snarky. Why did I say that?*

He shook his head and put his left arm on the table. Leaning in, his face flushed. "We thought she left of her own accord. We finally know she didn't go anywhere."

The change in his demeanor puzzled Maggie. He was sensitive to anything that sounded a little like criticism.

He glared at her, his face was turning red. "Mark my words, that corpse is Audrey, and her murderer is that fag who almost got away with it. If he steps foot in this town, we're going to disturb the peace even more and take care of him. Permanently."

Maggie stared. She had expected a more nuanced attitude. Hank was a bully. Her intention in meeting with him was to gain an ally. She rattled him too easily, and he revealed himself too quickly. "I believe you just threatened my client. Did you mean it that way?"

"You know what I meant." He sat back and scowled. His face was turning red. "We don't want his kind corrupting our children. You need to keep him away for his own good."

"Hank." She was as polite as possible, considering she was having a hard time with self-control. *It's time to leave before I get in more trouble with him.* She stood and picked up her sunglasses. "Perhaps I was a little flippant. It's difficult to talk with someone who threatens to kill over a mildly sarcastic comment. Please remember that Ben is my client. That's a threat to his life. At the very least, it's an attempt to intimidate a suspect."

Her grip tightened on her sunglasses. "I'm going to ignore your comment and assume you said it in haste, but I suggest you be more careful about your threats. If it happens again, I'll file a complaint with the court." She swallowed hard. "I look forward to hearing from you about the rent records."

She left the café and cautiously looked around. *Now what? My temper just exploded. I should have known better. I've blown my chances and made a huge mistake.*

CHAPTER 16

Maggie

Maggie reckoned with what had just happened. She had been too eager and too confident. She called Robert for reassurance and left a message. "Robert, I just blew the case. I met with Hank and got flippant and walked out on him. I think I've made a mess of this."

It was a paradox. She was proud, despite her brashness. She would never admit it, but there were times when she had used the same slur Hank had used. Growing up, she learned prejudices against anyone who did not conform to her parents' ways of thinking. Her attitude had been wrong. She had changed and had little tolerance for others who remained prejudiced.

Walking to her car, Maggie calmed down. She had come through for someone who didn't fit the mold, someone she barely knew. She had learned to stand up for others because she had struggled to find respect and still appreciated those who had stood up for her when it was tough. She understood people like Hank, but she would not accept his behavior. She would deal with the fallout.

People stared at her. She debated whether to stay in town overnight. Robert had given her a key to his cabin, and she had brought an overnight bag, just in case. By the time she unlocked her car door, she had decided to stay. She would be far enough from town to feel safe, but close enough for her presence to be felt.

Ben had talked about Grammy's close relationship with Audrey, so Grammy's attitude toward Ben was puzzling. Staying overnight would allow another visit and perhaps she would learn more. She assumed Grammy's attitude was the result of a rigid religious upbringing, so she didn't expect her to open up easily, but it was worth a try.

She needed to call Robert again. He had asked her to let him know if she decided to use the cabin. His extended family had keys, but he kept the calendar. Anyone wanting to use it had to check with him first. She also needed to talk about her mistake with Hank. Her message went to voicemail again.

Her first stop was a supermarket. As she approached the checkout, she noticed a display of cut flowers. On an impulse, she selected yellow chrysanthemums in a crinkly orange wrap as a gift for Grammy. As part of unwinding from her difficult career, she intentionally made small efforts of kindness even if it was just holding a door or helping someone carry groceries. Flowers for Grammy would be today's effort and might have a softening effect.

At the cabin, Maggie unpacked her purchases, setting aside a small package of shrimp to take to Grammy's, and removed the cellophane from her new sachet. Sitting at the kitchen table, she gently squeezed the small cloth bag to release the energy of the woman who had made it. Closing her eyes, she sank into a meditation and imagined Audrey was present at the cabin.

"Audrey," she whispered in the same way she had talked to her old victims. "I've seen your garden. It was lovely at one time. I've also seen you. I care about what happened to you. Please talk to me."

Maggie didn't hear a voice, but when she opened her eyes, the shadow of a woman in a long, hooded cloak appeared a few feet away. The woman stooped to examine a tall plant with drooping flowers. As she pointed to the plant, her image faded away.

Puzzled, Maggie put the sachet in her pocket. *Am I seeing things again? Did the woman really appear, or am I so anxious about Ben's case that I imagined it? Was there a message? What was it?*

* * *

A few minutes later, Maggie walked over and knocked on the cabin next door.

Grammy opened her door a crack. Her hair was a mess and she wore a blue bathrobe. "Yes, what can I do for you? Oh, I know you, don't I?"

"Grammy, it's Maggie. I'm Rob—I mean, Bobby Parson's friend."

"Yes, I remember you. Weren't you here a couple of weeks ago?"

Maggie waved to the other cabin. "I'm borrowing Robert's cabin for the night. I thought I would stop and say hello." She reached out with the flowers. "These are for you."

She floundered. "Me? Why me? No one has ever given me such beautiful flowers."

"Go ahead. Take them."

Grammy's thin hands cautiously reached out. Maggie placed the bundle in her arms. She was after information for the case, but Grammy intrigued her on a more personal level, and she simply felt the pleasure of giving.

Grammy turned to go inside, hesitated, and looked back. "You want to come in?"

"I'd love to. I hope I didn't disturb you." She followed Grammy to the kitchen.

"I...I don't know what to do with these." Grammy laid the flowers on her kitchen table. "I don't think I have any vases big enough."

"What about a pitcher?" Maggie pointed at a large plastic pitcher on the counter. "May I use this?"

Grammy nodded, and Maggie filled it with water as she wondered how to approach Grammy to get the information she wanted.

Maggie took the wrapping off the flowers, set aside the small packet of chemicals, and asked for scissors. "This stuff helps keep them fresh longer." She poured the chemicals in, arranged the flowers, and placed the makeshift vase in the center of the table. "There. You can enjoy them now."

"Why did you bring me flowers?" Grammy's sunken eyes were distrustful.

"I keep hearing what a wonderful person you are!" Maggie hoped she wasn't being too obvious.

Grammy shuffled toward her recliner, sat on the arm, and leaned against her cane. "No, no. I'm not. I'm unworthy. My life was my family. Now I'm a burden on everyone." She moved to the window and stared out. "I've seen so much out this window." She turned back to Audrey. "So much has changed since he died. I eat alone if I eat anything at all. I have no one to talk to since my dog died. I'm here by myself most of the time." Her fearful gaze shifted to

Maggie. "What if I were to fall? There's no one who would even know. I'm invisible." Eyeing the TV program, Grammy pressed the off button on the remote before sitting in her chair. "There isn't much use in living any longer."

Maggie realized her concerns were valid. She regretted that her brashness with Hank had probably ended any prospect of a visiting nurse. "You certainly gave it your all, and your kids turned out well. You had a long marriage and a good life. Do you have friends you could chat with?"

"My friends have all died. All I have left are my children and grandkids."

"What about Randy?"

"He's a young man. Boys don't learn how to care for old folks." She sighed. "We're boring to them."

Maggie returned to the kitchen, opened her package of shrimp, and found a couple of small plates. "I brought an appetizer. Do you like shrimp?"

"I don't get shrimp very often. Yes, I like them." She dipped one in sauce and set it on her plate.

Maggie wondered if she would be able to connect with the woman who had been like a grandmother to Audrey. She began asking gently prodding questions and soon realized Grammy's toughness had masked someone whose day was spent hidden in a cloud of depression.

"I understand you're from southern Utah. How did you end up in Madison County?"

"Oh, it's a long story. It was many years ago." Grammy fidgeted.

"I'd like to hear it if you want to tell me."

Grammy bit her lip. "I wanted to be a nurse. They let me go to nursing school in Salt Lake. I was supposed to go home when I finished, but another war was starting, and they needed me at the veteran's hospital. I was there for five years."

"Let me guess...Carl was wounded in the military. You nursed him back to health."

"He had joined the navy. It was just before the Vietnam War. He was injured on the ship, and they sent him home."

Maggie bit into a shrimp. "These are delicious." She glanced around the room and stopped at the picture of the pioneer couple above the fireplace. "Are those your ancestors?"

"Yes, those were my great-grandparents. That picture is from 1883, when they got married. I had a small one, and my husband had it enlarged and framed for me."

"Were they Utah pioneers?"

"They were children when they came with the early Mormons. It was a group from Scotland, and they traveled across the plains in covered wagons."

"I moved to Utah three years ago. I've been reading about the pioneers. They were very determined people. Where did your ancestors settle?"

Grammy's spirit improved. "They had to be. They dealt with a lot. My great-grandmother's family settled in Mapleton, south of Provo. They were the first to plow the ground and dig the ditches. My great-grandfather's family was in American Fork. They met at the old Brigham Young Academy in Provo and were married a few years later."

"Where did they live after they got married?"

Grammy's tone became defensive. "My great-grandmother was a second wife. They moved to central Utah, where he had his other family." She raised her chin defiantly. "There were three wives and fifteen children." She nibbled a shrimp. "Those two had five children. Two of them lived to be adults."

"Were you born in that community?"

"Yes."

"Did you have many brothers and sisters?"

"My grandmother was one of those who lived. She had twelve children. My mother was one of them. She had nine children. I had five brothers and three sisters. Five of us lived to be adults. I was next to the youngest."

"Are any of them besides you still alive?"

A pained expression came over Grammy's face. "I don't know." She looked away.

Maggie regretted asking the question. She had recently learned that many fundamentalist families disown children who leave the communities. Perhaps Grammy had been one. She had more questions, but needed to be careful. "I'm curious. What was it like being in a family with several mothers?"

Grammy glanced around her living room. She ate another piece of shrimp. Her mouth flattened into a grim line. "There were good times. There were bad times. The men made the decisions and did as they pleased. The women and children did what they were told to do. The boys grew up to be in charge, and it started all over again."

Maggie wasn't sure how to respond. Even in the confines of a small community, Grammy understood the issue that bothered so many women. She thought about her upbringing in a 1950s military family. "You and I grew up in similar circumstances."

Maggie had another shrimp. It was time to ask the important questions. "I heard you and Audrey became good friends. Do you miss her?"

Grammy's sharp tone pierced the silence. "Who told you that?"

"Several people."

"Yes, she lived here a long time and became my friend." Grammy sounded wistful. "She made wonderful teas and enjoyed showing me her plants. She gave me her ointments and told me about her ancient recipes. We often had tea together."

"Sounds like she was fond of you."

Grammy hesitated. "Well, she was fond of many people."

"Did she stay in touch with you after her marriage ended?"

"For a while."

"By any chance, did she tell you she was dating someone new?"

Grammy froze. "No."

Maggie's shoulders tensed. She had stumbled onto something. "Do you miss her?"

Grammy's face hardened. "No." She faced the window. "Life moves on."

Why did Grammy suddenly turn cold to Audrey's memory?

Maggie continued her effort to learn more about Audrey until the shrimp was gone, but Grammy became vague. When she was no longer getting meaningful answers, Maggie carried the dishes to the kitchen.

"Grammy, I would love to visit again. Would that be alright? You've led such an interesting life. I'd like to get to know you." *There's more, but I don't know how to get past her resistance. I don't know what that is all about.*

"I always enjoy company, even if I'm not in the best of moods. You're welcome to come, but my life is nothing to talk about." She walked Maggie to the door.

A little later, while she baked a chicken breast for her dinner, Maggie pondered Grammy's unwillingness to talk about Audrey. She picked up the sachet and cushioned it gently. "Something is bothering Grammy about you. What is it?"

She waited, but the shadow did not appear.

CHAPTER 17

Maggie

Tuesday, September 15, 2022

Maggie's phone rang as she finished her breakfast of a toasted bagel and coffee.

"Maggie, it's Hank Stevenson. First, let me apologize for my comment yesterday. I meant it as an expression of frustration, not literally. I'm not someone who would kill anyone. We're a small town, and attitudes change slowly. I was out of line." His tone sounded as if he was making a necessary political gesture, not a sincere apology.

"Thank you." She could thank him for the apology, but she wasn't going to trust him again.

"I have some rental information for you."

"Great." She grabbed her spiral notebook. She was glad he had kept his promise in spite of her brashness.

"The last time Audrey paid rent was September 2016, but we don't have any forwarding information, and we don't have any note from Audrey. The next time we rented the cabin was on May 1, 2017, to someone named Christine Donahue. She stayed for six months. I have records on her."

She took down the contact information for Ms. Donahue. She was in nearby Ogden.

"Thank you, Hank, although it adds a new wrinkle. We need to find out where Audrey went when she moved." She cringed. *I need his cooperation, but he's a jerk, and I don't want any further interaction with him.*

"Mrs. Madison will be happy to oblige if there's anything else you need."

"I'm still in town. Is there a chance I could go by this morning, get copies of her records, and chat with her?"

"Not a problem. I'll call the office and tell her to cooperate and give you whatever you need for the case."

Maggie said she would be there within an hour and got Mrs. Madison's phone number. She poured another coffee and tried to clear her mind of Hank Stevenson's earlier rudeness.

She was still tired. Noise had awakened her during the night. She had double-checked the doors and windows and finally decided it was just animals. Being alone, she wished she knew where Robert's guns were. She knew Grammy was home, and Randy still had a light on. Down the road, the sheriff was probably home, but she wondered if she should have gone out to verify that it was just the wildlife.

She returned to her notes. Randy had said that Audrey had moved suddenly and left a note for Carl. Apparently, she moved in October. Randy had also speculated that Audrey didn't really move, and that someone had killed her. These facts didn't fit with Audrey signing the divorce papers in November. Something was wrong with the timing. The puzzle pieces didn't fit.

She called Ben. "Did Audrey ever talk about moving from the cabin?"

"No. Not while we were still communicating. At the end, we talked about her moving to her mother's place, but she wanted to be on her own."

"I've just learned that Audrey's last rent payment was in September 2016, so she moved before your divorce papers were signed. If Audrey didn't live in the cabin anymore, where did she live when you saw her in November?"

"What are you suggesting?"

"If she moved in October, it no longer makes sense. Hank Stevenson said her place was vacant from October through April and someone moved into the cabin in May. Audrey was living somewhere else when she died. Why would someone bring the body back to the cabin to bury it? Maybe it isn't Audrey."

"Her mother should know where she was living. Could someone ask her?"

"Sure. Good thought. I'll ask Logan to contact her."

After cleaning up, her last task before going to Hank's office was to pour the remaining coffee into her travel mug. When she opened the door, a sheet of paper was taped to it. In large, sloppy letters written with a thick black marker, it read: "LEAVE TOWN BITCH."

Maggie backed into the cabin feeling exposed and defenseless and locked the door. She had forgotten what it was like to be alert all the time and should have suspected something when she heard noises in the night. Her knees became weak.

She called Logan, hoping he would send someone to escort her, but got his voicemail. Fighting to stay calm, she left a message. "It's Maggie Anderson. I stayed over at Robert Parsons's cabin last night. This morning, I found a threatening note taped to the front door. There may be fingerprints. I'm leaving shortly to meet with Hank's bookkeeper. I'll phone when I'm finished."

She called Robert. She needed to hear a warm, friendly voice. Still forcing herself to be calm, she described what happened. "I won't stay here again."

"You're scared to death. I hear it in your voice. You need a hug. I'm sorry I couldn't call back last night. I wish I was there now. Have you called anyone for help? Do you have the sheriff's number?"

"I also wish you were here. I called Logan but got his voicemail. I don't have the sheriff's number. I'll leave in a few minutes. I'll be okay."

"I'll try to reach the sheriff to get you an escort." He called back a few minutes later.

"The sheriff's already at work, and his deputies are out. Is Randy's car there?"

She looked out the window. "It was there last night, but it's not there now."

"Where are you right now?"

"I'm sitting at the counter in the kitchen."

"Do something for me, please. Walk into the living room." His voice was gentle.

She hesitated. "Okay."

"See that rocking chair in the corner? Go sit in it."

Puzzled, she did so. "Now what?"

She heard the smile in his voice. "Rock. It's good for the soul."

She closed her eyes as she moved with the chair and became comfortable. Her heartbeat slowed. Her tension eased.

"How does it feel?"

She rocked for another few seconds and breathed deeply. "I'm remembering when I rocked my babies back to sleep. I like rocking chairs."

"Good, you're more relaxed. Now we can talk. I know you aren't going to drop the case, but it's not a good idea for you to be out there by yourself. There are people who insist on having their own way, and they want Ben convicted."

"What should I do?"

"Next time you need to go up there, just call my name and I'll be there. I'll have your back. Even though you're playing footsies with the DA, those people think you're on the wrong side."

"So, the investigator needs a bodyguard, is that it?" As much as she wanted to be aloof and independent, she longed to feel his arms holding her again.

"Something like that."

She stopped rocking and leaned forward. "Robert, you know what that note tells me?"

"No, what?"

"Someone in this town knows what happened, and they're afraid I'll find out. You don't send goons out to scare someone unless you're afraid of being caught. This isn't about me. It's about the person who's afraid of me."

"Any idea who that person is?"

"No. I'm going to need your help on that one. You know this town. If we figure out who the goons are and who they work for, we'll find that answer. In the meantime, I promise I'll play it safe and be nice to people. I need to go over to Hank Stevenson's office, but I'll go home afterward."

"Hank's a good man. I've known him all my life. He's not going to be behind anything, but a lot of those cowboys work for him, and some of them are messed up. Don't say too much and don't let anyone know your schedule."

"I'll call when I get home." She paused. Robert was taking care of her. It felt good, and she didn't want to worry him. "Thank you for calming me down."

Cautiously, she opened the door and looked around. No vehicles were parked in suspicious places. She glanced toward Randy's cabin. *Could it have been him?*

She left.

Concentrating on her rearview mirror, she watched for any vehicles making the same turns she made.

CHAPTER 18

Maggie

Maggie parked in front of Hank's building, a modern two-story white stucco on the edge of the old business district. The receptionist notified Mrs. Madison. Looking around, Maggie wondered if a phone call about her presence would be made to the goons who threatened her.

Mrs. Madison greeted her. She was short, mid-fifties, wore a purple flowered dress, and spoke with precision. They went to her impeccably organized office, and Maggie settled into a guest chair.

Can I trust Hank's bookkeeper? "Hank gave me some rental information on Audrey this morning. Would you give me a few more details?"

Mrs. Madison seemed happy to help. "We store the paper records in the back, but I can get them. I can also show you what we have in our computer system."

"Let's look at the computer first."

Mrs. Madison pulled up the account for Ben and Audrey Stillman. She moved the screen so Maggie could see a steady stream of payments that ended in September 2016. Maggie asked her to print it.

"I heard Audrey left a note for Carl that she was leaving. Do you have that note?"

"No. If she left one, he didn't give it to me. I checked when Hank asked me this morning."

"What about forwarding information?"

"I put that in the tenant's profile. I don't have anything for Audrey or Ben."

Maggie leaned back and intentionally changed her tone. *People like Mrs. Madison will be bothered by someone else's frustration and will try to solve the problem.* "This is such a small town. I'm sure you heard that Audrey had moved out of the cabin. Was it soon after she and Ben separated, or was it a little later?"

Mrs. Madison glanced at the floor before raising her eyes. "Oh, I don't want to gossip about anything. Carl brought me the rent checks or told me someone was leaving. I remember hearing that Audrey moved suddenly, but I can't tell you when it was. All I can go on is what the records say, which is that she stopped paying rent in October 2016."

"Would you show me when the cabin was rented again?"

Mrs. Madison nodded. She created a report showing the cabin's monthly income and expenses for 2016 and printed it. She changed the dates to 2017, printed it again, and showed where the rental income stopped in September 2016 and resumed in May 2017.

Maggie examined the reports. "The rent went up after Audrey moved out."

"Ben and Audrey had very few rent increases. We rented it as a short-term vacation cabin in May 2017 for six months. Then, we found someone for the ski season and another couple for the summer in 2019. The cabin was put up for sale after that."

Maggie frowned. "Why was it vacant from October 2016 to May 2017? That seems like a long vacancy. Wouldn't that be a ski season opportunity?"

Mrs. Madison blinked. "I don't know. Carl handled the leases. I just pay the bills and keep the records. Perhaps he was doing some repairs. I don't remember."

Maggie scrutinized the reports again. "I can see where the utilities were paid when it was vacant..." She moved her finger down a few lines. "But I don't see any repair costs."

Mrs. Madison performed additional inquiries. "That's correct. We paid the power bill from October to April, and it looks like there were almost no repairs. That's a little unusual, but Carl was a generous man. Perhaps there was someone from the church, maybe a small family who needed a place to stay, and he gave them free rent for the winter. He was known to do that."

"Do you know who the person or family was?"

"No. He wouldn't have mentioned it. He may have known some people in need and helped them out. He was that way, bless him." She sounded defensive.

"Okay, that makes sense." Maggie bit the inside of her cheek. *I want to stay on Mrs. Madison's good side, so I won't push it.* "Would you see if Audrey gave any notice?"

"Certainly. It'll take a few minutes to find their folder. Can you wait?"

"Absolutely."

Mrs. Madison disappeared, returned with a file folder, and sifted through the papers. "There's no written notice or any forwarding address. I copy all the rent checks, but they would be in other files. Do you want me to get those?"

Maggie reviewed the lease and saw nothing unusual. "No. You've already been a big help. I need two copies of the reports and the lease, one for the DA and one for Ben's lawyer."

After the copies were made, Maggie thanked her and assured Mrs. Madison she would call if anything else was needed.

Sitting in her SUV, Maggie called Logan.

"Good to hear from you, Maggie. Are you okay?"

"I'm fine. A little thing like a nasty note doesn't shake me up for long. Did you send someone out?"

"Yep, the sheriff sent someone over."

"Good. I got rental information. It's our first puzzle piece. Audrey stopped paying rent after September 2016. Randy said she left a note saying she was moving, but Hank's bookkeeper didn't have it, which is a little odd. Ben saw her in November when they signed the divorce papers. He wasn't aware she had moved. Can I drop off your copies of the rental records?"

"Sure. I heard about that note when it happened, but the timing seems off. Where're you headed after that?"

"Home."

"Good. Let's keep you out of the way. Call me when you're in front of the building, and I'll send someone out."

"Logan, it's strange that Audrey would move in October without saying anything to Ben or the landlord. It's also strange that she didn't leave any forwarding information for her business mail. We know she was alive in November, so she died after that. Why would someone kill her and take her body back to the cabin to be buried?"

"I'll check with the post office and see if they had forwarding information. It's a little odd, but Ben knew the place was isolated. He would've done that because he didn't want the body found."

"Ben didn't know she had moved. The bookkeeper thinks Carl may have let someone stay rent free for six months. Ben wouldn't have known about that. The last thing the killer needed was for someone to see him digging a grave." She took a deep breath. "We need to know where Audrey moved to. Her mother would be the best person to ask, but since I represent Ben, it would be too sensitive if I tried to talk to her."

"Gotcha. I can do that. I know Mrs. Williams. She's a talker when she wants to be. I'll also expand the subpoenas and ask for utility bills in Audrey's name. We may find her new address that way." He paused for a minute. "This is getting stranger by the minute."

Next, she called the new tenant, Christine Donahue, explained the reason for her call, and verified that Christine moved into the cabin on May 1, 2017, and moved out six months later. Maggie made an appointment to meet with her in Ogden the following Monday.

When Maggie reached her home, she called Robert and asked if he knew anything about Audrey moving in October 2016.

"No," he said. "I'll have to think about that. Seems to me she came to the Christmas party the sheriff has every year for our little community up there."

CHAPTER 19

Maggie

Wednesday, September 16, 2020

Robert, Gwen, and Peter arrived promptly at Maggie's condo on Wednesday evening for their first team meeting. Robert and Peter walked in as if they were serious detectives. Robert had on a brown plaid Sherlock Holmes deerstalker hat and carried a traditional curved pipe. Peter sported a false mustache identical to Hercule Poirot's, a black bowler hat, an impeccable black suit, and a bowtie. He made a point of dusting off imaginary specks of lint.

"Gwen?" Maggie perused her seemingly normal outfit.

Gwen laughed. "Unfortunately, Jessica Fletcher didn't have a costume. However, I intend to solve as many mysteries as she did!"

"We're going to be real detectives," Robert chuckled.

Maggie rolled her eyes as she closed the door. "It's not that glamorous."

Maggie supplied a Costco pizza, Robert brought a green salad from a deli, Peter provided wine and beer, and Gwen furnished a homemade apple cobbler. Everything was spread out on the dining room table, and they carried plates to the living room.

"This is the first time I've been in your new place." Gwen glanced around at Maggie's eclectic combination of antiques, art, and personal treasures. She peered closely at a safari memento on the wall with other travel mementoes. "Someday soon, I want to hear all about your adventures." She found her spot on the couch.

"I helped her move all this stuff." Robert sat on the loveseat. He waved toward her bookcases. "I hauled every one of those books and helped put them away. Maggie has her own unique Dewey decimal system."

Maggie giggled. "And it works well!" She pulled a chair over to the coffee table.

Peter joined Gwen on the couch and opened his laptop. Robert's deerstalker and Peter's bowler graced the coffee table.

"What have you come up with for our team's name?" Maggie asked.

"It will be elementary, my dear Watson." Robert had a new accent, his pipe resting comfortably on his lower lip. "These compatriots of mine share my love of all that is bizarre, and they will, indeed, be ideal helpmates."

"*Mais oui, mon ami*," said Peter. "We must have a French word in our name." He tapped his head. "A word that shows it's the little gray cells on which one must rely."

Maggie stared at him. She smiled but held her tongue, contemplating whether the joke had gone too far.

"You have the grand gift of silence, Watson," Robert said.

Maggie looked at Gwen and gestured toward Robert and Peter. "This is serious business. Our client's life is at stake."

"Proceed, Watson. Proceed," Gwen said without a moment's hesitation.

Maggie tossed a wary look at Robert before turning to her yellow legal pad.

"First, we need to treat this case with more concern. A woman has been murdered, and our client has been accused. If he's arrested, I suspect he'll be facing the death penalty. We believe he's innocent, but that's not enough. We must prove that someone else did it."

She looked around, making sure she had everyone's attention. "Here's your first lesson in being a detective. The basics are three words: *why*, *how*, and *who*. If you can discover the motive, which is *why*, then you ask *how*, and that leads you to *who*."

She drummed her fingers on her thigh. "We have our first clue, which might answer the *why* question. I met with the DA, Logan Harris, on Monday. I educated him on the fact that he doesn't have a slam-dunk case. In fact, all he has is weak circumstantial evidence, but that could change, and we have to be ready for anything."

She cleared her throat. "Logan called the coroner's office while I was there. The body hasn't been officially ID'd yet, but we're assuming it's Audrey Stillman. We'll probably know by Monday. The coroner believes she died between October 2016 and April 2017. There's no evidence of any wounds or strangulation. He suggested it could've been from natural causes or poisoning. Natural causes don't fit with the fact that someone secretly buried her, so the assumption is, for now, that she was poisoned. This next piece of info was a big surprise and is confidential, so let's treat it with care—Audrey was three to four months pregnant when she died."

Gwen gasped. Her hand rose to her chin. Peter typed.

"You're kidding. Ben's?" Robert said.

"We've gotten DNA from him, but I'm fairly certain it isn't. Logan is also getting a DNA test on the baby bones. I'll be very disappointed with Ben if the results show it's his child, and he kept that from me. If it's him, he had a motive, and his entire case goes out the window."

"If it's not Ben's, who's the father?" Gwen asked.

"She was single and pregnant. Audrey made a comment to Ben in November 2016 that she had a boyfriend. Maybe that boyfriend wasn't happy with the situation. Maybe he wanted her to get an abortion, and she refused. Finding that boyfriend should either give us the killer or lead us to him. By the way, I didn't tell Ben why we needed the DNA. This is top secret right now."

"Who knows about it?" Robert asked.

"Logan Harris, Charles Cameron, me, and now you guys." She looked at Robert. "We need to find out who dated Audrey after Ben left. It could be someone she had to keep secret, but I bet the gossip circuit knows."

"A whole lot of men would've jumped her bones, but it sure doesn't sound like the Audrey I knew. She seemed like a loner." He shook his head and took a long draw on his beer.

"It's your assignment, Robert. Don't say anything about Audrey being pregnant. Use your magical way with people, and see if you can flush him out."

With a smile, Robert leaned forward and saluted her with his beer. "Your wish is my command."

She passed out copies of her chart. "This is the result of my meeting with Logan Harris." She went through the explanation. "I think she got pregnant after Ben moved out. We'll know more when we narrow down the date of death with phone and bank records, which we should have next week.

"I'm not sure how this is connected, but I think Audrey moved from the cabin. Randy said she gave notice, and I got rental information from the landlord. It looks like this happened in October 2016, but we don't know where she went. Randy mentioned a note she wrote to the landlord, but the note isn't in the records. If she moved, it may be connected to the mysterious boyfriend."

Finally, she told them about the threatening note at the cabin and her theory that someone was trying to scare her away.

"And madame does not scare easily. *N'est pas*?" Peter asked with a twinkle in his eye.

"You're right." Maggie grinned. "Our first puzzle piece right now is to figure out why Audrey moved and where she went. I'll work on that while Robert is looking for the boyfriend. Peter, I'll keep sending info as I get it, and, Gwen, I need to get you connected to Grammy. You'd be great at getting her to talk. I think I blew it when I talked to Hank, but we can look for another way."

As he prepared to leave, Robert turned to Maggie. "You're doing the right thing on this case, but don't let the slow start get to you. Every great detective starts with a situation where everything goes against him or her."

Maggie gently pushed him out the door. "Sherlock, we'll definitely need to reason backward on this one."

Gwen lingered and was the last to leave. "It looks like Robert is someone you can trust, doesn't it? He certainly wants to take care of you."

Maggie laughed. "Oh, stop being a matchmaker! I don't need a boyfriend."

CHAPTER 20

Robert

Thursday, September 17, 2020

The next afternoon, Robert drove up to his cabin. He looked around to see what needed to be repaired, made a shopping list, and drove to a small hardware store in Medford.

"Greetings, Bobby Parsons! We haven't seen you around for a while," Shorty, the owner, said as he helped another customer. He was an older man, five foot four, overweight, and clad in brown bib coveralls. "What ya looking for?"

This was Robert's first stop on the gossip circuit, and he wanted to sense the lay of the land. Shorty had a reputation for chasing after women, young and old, and talking about it.

"Gotta do some work on my cabin. Gettin' it ready for winter." He took a shopping cart into the aisles.

Shorty followed him. "Anything I can help you find?"

"Well, I know your place pretty well, and I've got a list. I'll let you know if I can't find something."

Shorty came closer and spoke quietly. "You know more'n most of us about that body they dug up. What can you tell me?"

"Don't know much. No ID yet. It'll be a shame if it turns out to be that Stillman girl. She was just too damn pretty to be dead." Robert gave Shorty that look between men where they both knew what they were really talking about. "After Ben left, the guys kept telling me I should try to hook up with her. Sorry I missed my chance." He felt sleazy, but knew it would work.

Shorty shook his head. "You're not the only one."

"She seemed to keep it pretty close to home. I never saw anyone with her. Was it all talk, or did some lucky guy score?"

"Well, there were always rumors. Don't know if it was just bragging."

Robert plucked a can of spackling paste from the shelf. "That so?" He moved his cart down the aisle for a can of weatherproofing for the porch. "You'll have to let me know if you hear anything solid."

Shorty returned to the counter to ring up a customer. Robert continued shopping and moved to the front counter after the customer left.

He handed Shorty his credit card. "If I learn anything important about the case, I'll come in and tell you." He picked up his purchases. "Maybe you'll be able to tell me more about Audrey." He handed him an old business card. "Call me on my cell if you hear anything important."

"Deal. I'll stay in touch."

Robert visited three other stores and left cards with the owners he knew would likely spread the word, but none of them seemed to be the right connection.

His final stop was a run-down honky-tonk at the edge of town called the Lazy Q Tavern. It was still early afternoon.

Only three cars were in the parking lot of the old one-story building with rusted beer placards tacked around the entrance. Neon signs glowed in several windows. The inside lights were low, it smelled of stale beer, and two patrons sat in a far corner booth.

Feeling like Columbo, Robert walked in. All he needed was a rumpled raincoat.

The bartender whirled around. "Well, look who the dogs drug in. How ya doing, cowboy? Haven't seen you in a long time." He dried his hands and reached across the bar for a handshake. "Need a beer?"

"Yep. Michelob." Robert sat on a red-seated chrome stool at the end of the long bar and looked around. Hundreds of carved initials scarred the old wooden bar's surface.

"Place hasn't changed much, Harvey. You hanging in there?"

"It's been pretty rough." Tall and skinny, he was at least sixty years old with a gray mustache. His stained apron covered a worn green T-shirt.

"How are things in town?"

"A lot of places are just plain shutting down. Businesses don't like it, but folks are stayin' home." Harvey leaned against the mirrored cabinet where the hard liquor was kept. "What ya doing up in these parts?"

"Gotta get my cabin weatherproofed for the winter. Came for supplies." He took a long drink of his beer. "Got some chips or something to go with this?"

Harvey pulled a bowl of popcorn from under the counter. "Try this." He wiped down the counter before venturing a question. "You know that old broad who stuck her nose into the investigation, don't you?"

"Yeah. I know her." Robert shot him a glare. "She's a friend of mine."

"Didn't mean no harm. She have a name?"

"Maggie."

"How'd Maggie get mixed up in this?"

"We ran into Ben at the diner in Maxwell. She's a retired lawyer. She's helping him out." He shook his head. "You know how lawyers just can't stay away from it."

"Damn that son of a bitch. He had no business killing Audrey. Hope they hang him. You're mixed up with it. What d'you think is going on?"

Robert cringed and shifted sideways on his stool. "I don't know much about what they're thinking, but there's something suspicious. That's all I can gather right now."

He took another drink and crossed his arms on the bar. "You know anyone that Audrey could've been dating?"

"What d'you mean?" Harvey seemed to stall.

"I'll tell you what I think. I'm betting that Ben caught her cheating on him and he knocked her upside a few times. Probably got out of hand, and he went too far. When she died, he had to hide it." It was hard for Robert to put a voice to these lies.

"He was a fag. He wouldn't care." Harvey's face was skeptical.

Robert nibbled on the popcorn. "She was still his wife. He wouldn't let her embarrass him like that. Hurts a man's pride if his woman is cheating." He grimaced, but he had to sound like one of the cowboys. "Even a fag."

"I see what you mean. Makes sense."

"They don't have anything right now. If they could find the guy she was seeing, they might get enough evidence against Ben." Robert picked up his empty beer bottle. "Hit me up with another. Make it as cold as you've got."

"Interesting." Harvey reached into a fridge under the counter and brought another Michelob to Robert.

"Do you know if she was hanging out with anyone? She ever come in here?"

Harvey thought for a minute. "Don't recall anyone braggin' about her. It's been a while." He glanced at the ceiling, as if reviewing his past patrons. "Don't think she was ever here."

Robert reached into his wallet and placed a hundred-dollar bill on the counter.

"Forget it. It's on the house. Just good to see ya."

Robert leaned across the bar. "That's for you. You know everyone, and you hear everything. You can help me find the guy Audrey was seeing."

Harvey stopped and stared back. He eyed the money suspiciously. "You serious?"

"Yeah. I can make sure you're taken care of if you come up with something that sticks. I think Audrey was cheating on Ben, and you're the one who can find out."

"Well, a lot of cowboys come through here." He moved away and dried some glasses before turning back. "Those Stevenson boys up at the ranch come into town every couple of weeks. They might know somethin'."

"Don't tell anyone I'm asking. Just see what they'll tell you." Robert smiled. "Sure would appreciate it if you could be of assistance." He took a business card from his wallet. "The cell number on here is still good. Call me if you hear anything useful."

He placed the card on top of the money, asked Harvey for his personal cell number, and programmed it into his phone.

CHAPTER 21

Maggie

Monday, September 21, 2020

Midmorning on Monday, Maggie knocked on the door of an attractive Tudor-style home on the east side of Ogden. Christine Donahue answered. She was in her early fifties with graying temples and wore dark-rimmed glasses, gray sweats, and a green environmentally branded T-shirt. She invited Maggie in and offered tea.

Maggie pulled out her notebook. "As I mentioned on the phone, I'm working on a case involving a corpse that was dug up at the cabin in Madison County. I'd like to ask a few questions."

"Sure. I saw a mention of that on the news recently."

"First, why did you rent that cabin if you live so close?"

"I teach creative writing at the local university. I was working on a book that summer and needed a quiet place to write. My children were home from college, and there were too many distractions for me to concentrate. The family agreed I could get away if I came back on Sundays, so that's what I did. The log cabin was perfect."

"Did you finish the book?"

"Yes. In fact, it's been published."

Maggie learned that Christine had found the cabin through an online search and had talked to Carl, who was quite personable. He had come out once a week, worked on the landscaping, and maintained the garden.

"Did you have to furnish the place, or did it come furnished?"

"The furniture was there. It was a rustic style crafted with bleached logs. I brought my own linens and most of my kitchen items."

"Did Carl ever mention the people who lived there before you?"

"Not really. He told me the previous tenant had planted the garden and I could help myself. A couple of neighbors came over and asked about her. I think it was a woman living by herself, but I never knew anything about her."

"The husband moved out in 2016, and she stayed. She may have moved suddenly, but we haven't located where she moved to. Some people think she's the corpse, but the body hasn't been identified yet. Right now, we're tracking down anyone who rented the place to make sure the corpse isn't one of the other tenants."

She laughed. "Well, I'm alive and well."

"One more thing. Was there a stray cat that hung out around the cabin?"

"It would have been nice, but no."

Maggie's phone rang. It was Logan Harris. "Excuse me. I need to take this."

Christine nodded politely.

"Hello, Logan," Maggie said and then listened. "Okay, I'm in Ogden right now. I'll come over directly. Give me about thirty minutes."

Maggie turned to Christine. "The body has been identified. I need to go over to Medford and meet with the DA. Thank you for your time. You've been helpful."

"Not a problem. Good luck on the case." She waved as Maggie pulled out of the driveway.

The trip to Ogden had been worth it. Maggie learned Carl had kept Audrey's furniture. She wondered why he volunteered to do all the yard work. Did he want to prevent someone from seeing a fresh grave? Maybe it was innocent, and he furnished yard services simply because it was a short-term lease.

Maggie called Robert and told him she was on her way to the DA's office. He said he would head up to the cabin, would text her when he got there, and asked her to stay out of the public eye.

Maggie drove down Harrison Boulevard, past the university campus on the left and the McKay-Dee Hospital complex on the right, and connected with the interstate that headed up Weber Canyon. She pulled up to the county office complex precisely twenty-nine minutes after Logan had called.

CHAPTER 22

Maggie

Maggie met Logan in the hall and followed him to his office.

"Have a seat." He stepped behind his desk and handed her the coroner's report showing that dental records confirmed the corpse to be Audrey Stillman. "This came about two hours ago. Also, we didn't get any fingerprints on that note stuck to the cabin door. Probably had gloves on. No one seems to know anything, which doesn't surprise me."

"Robert Parsons is going to escort me for a little while. He's on his way up from Salt Lake. I'll be fine."

"Good. I'll hold a press briefing tomorrow. I'm going over to see Audrey's mother this afternoon. At least she'll have closure."

"Do you want us to tell Ben?"

"If you would..." He frowned. "I could try to have Ben arrested, but I don't think I have probable cause anymore. I need to talk to the mayor." Clearly, it was a hard admission for him to make. "I've got a lot more to go over with you." He headed for the evidence room. "C'mon."

Maggie's earlier sketch was still on the whiteboard.

Logan handed her a marker. "You're good at this. I'll tell you what I have. You figure out the impact."

Maggie erased the July column. In its place, she made a new title, *Facts*. "Has the estimated date of death changed?"

"No, but we're closer to the actual date. We'll get to that in a minute."

She made her first entry in the *Facts* column:

VICTIM: Audrey Stillman
DOD estimate: 10/1/2016 to 4/30/2017
Alive on November 17
3 to 4 months pregnant at death

"Do we have the toxicology report yet?"

"Yes." He took it from a folder and passed it to her.

With a grimace, she read it. "Poisoned? How did they get that?"

"Some flesh on her hands had not decomposed. It was tested three times to make sure. Read the type of poison."

She read the report silently:

The poison is consistent with tropane alkaloids from the perennial bushy herb Atropa belladonna, commonly called deadly nightshade or belladonna. This greenish-purple ornamental plant is native to the Mediterranean, Western Europe, and Hima-layan Mountain areas and has been introduced in North America. The plant has a long history of me-dicinal use in smaller and microscopic quantities and is deadly in higher doses. The purple-black sweet berries have a higher concentration of poisonous alkaloids. Though widely regarded as unsafe, small amounts of belladonna are taken by mouth as a remedy for certain conditions, and it has been used in ointments for joint pain and other nerve conditions.

She wrote *Poisoned* on the board and stared at Logan. "How did a poisonous plant native to Europe get to a cabin in the woods of Madison County, Utah? Is there a possibility Audrey would've had that in her garden?"

"Hell if I know, but that's what we're dealing with—a poisonous plant called belladonna. She grew herbs that were used in teas. Why she would have that one is beyond me."

She shook her head and wrote *Baby* on the whiteboard, underlining it. "Do we have DNA on the baby yet?"

"Yep." He picked up another paper. "They did a DNA test on Audrey and the baby and have a profile of the father. Caucasian. Western European and English ancestry. Nothing unusual. It fits 85 percent of the guys in Madison County. Not much help."

She added *Father???* to the board. "Do we have Ben's DNA?"

"Yep." Logan handed her another paper. "It's not him." He sounded disappointed, his voice hitching. "That's why I can't arrest him. We know she died months after he moved out, and he's not the father."

She read Ben's report carefully. There were no significant matching markers to link him with the unborn child. She put *Not Ben* on the whiteboard. "How was Audrey poisoned? Did she accidentally poison herself?"

"That plant is used in making ointments. That may be something she was doing. The poison could've come from a tea using the leaves. She was pregnant and was no longer married. She probably wasn't sure about the boyfriend. She could've drunk it on purpose."

"Someone either fed her the poison or found her body. Either way, someone secretly buried her." Maggie sank into a chair and covered her face with her hands, feeling momentarily stymied. She looked up. "Time for a break."

Logan and Maggie grabbed drinks from the break room and again surveyed the whiteboard. She stopped to read a text saying Robert was at the cabin. She texted back that she would contact him after her meeting.

Stepping up to the column labeled *October 2016*, Maggie wrote with a red marker, *10/1—Rent stops*. She added a new word, *Moved???* "Did you talk to Audrey's mother about whether she moved?"

"Yep. She says Audrey didn't move in October. She doesn't know why the rent wasn't paid. They had talked about Audrey moving to her mother's place, and she was waiting until spring to move the plants. Audrey was at the cabin until she vanished in March 2017. Mrs. Williams filed a missing person report the last part of March."

"Hank's bookkeeper said Carl was known for helping people," Maggie said. "Audrey's husband had just left her. She didn't earn a lot. Maybe Carl felt sorry for her and just let her stay rent-free starting in October."

"Carl had that reputation, but six months of rent is a lot." Logan flipped through his notes. "Mrs. Williams seldom went to Audrey's cabin. Audrey usually went to her mother's place when they visited."

"Carl could've been motivated for a reason beyond just being Mr. Nice Guy. Got any ideas on that?" Maggie asked.

"He was always a womanizer, but I never heard anything about him chasing after Audrey. After Ben left, I never heard that she was dating someone."

"Carl was a womanizer? And Grammy put up with it?"

Logan nodded.

Maggie stopped writing. "Grammy told me she grew up in a polygamist community."

"Yep, that's probably why she tolerated it."

Maggie shook her head. She had put up with a womanizing husband once and understood. "Do you think any of her kids would talk about it?"

"Well, her three boys live here. I'll have to think about how to approach them. They aren't going to want to say anything bad about their parents. Leave that one to me."

"Could Audrey have been spending time with a boyfriend and kept it a secret?"

"Yep. She must have."

"Do you think it could be Carl?"

"I knew Carl well enough. She was a bit young for him. He liked women, but he seemed to like them older."

Maggie erased the word *Moved*. "For now, let's assume Carl did nothing more than give Audrey free rent. If anything comes up, we can look at him again." She reviewed the board. "She's living in the cabin. The comment about her moving could've referred to March. When was the last time Mrs. Williams talked to Audrey?"

"Early March 2017. Audrey went over to celebrate her mother's birthday."

"What day is her birthday?"

He looked at his notes. "March 8."

She wrote *Mom's birthday 3/8* near the top of the *March 2017* column. "She's alive on March 8. What do you have for Audrey's phone records?"

Logan briefly reviewed them. "She's making calls through mid-March, and then it goes quiet. Nothing. Her bill was never paid, and her phone was disconnected. We traced the numbers. Nothing to Ben after early November, so that checks out. She's calling her business contacts, her mom, and a girlfriend named Stacey Lighthouse. We also have calls to Randy Stevenson in late November and calls to the landlord all the way through February, suggesting she was still living there. We didn't identify anyone who could be the mysterious boyfriend."

"I can see having a girlfriend, but why would she be calling Randy?" Maggie went back to the board, wrote *Contacts*, and listed Stacey Lighthouse and Randy Stevenson. "We need to talk to both of them."

"Interesting question. Yeah, I'll arrange interviews."

"Are any of her business contacts suspicious?"

"No. The local ones are all women."

Maggie handed him the bank records. "There's nothing unusual about her checking accounts except she stopped using them."

Logan leafed through the pages. "These accounts are still open with no activity since March 2017."

Maggie carefully examined Audrey's phone records. "There are no calls to Randy in December, January, or February. I would expect her to stay in touch with the boyfriend once she knew she was pregnant."

She placed the phone and bank records side by side. "Her last bank transaction was on March 15, and her last phone call was on March 16." She turned to Logan. "I think we probably have a DOD of March 17 or 18."

"I was thinking the same thing. Let's go with March 18."

Establishing the date of death gave the case a sense of momentum.

Maggie pulled out her phone, found her calendar, and scrolled backward. "March 16 was a Thursday, so March 18 works for now."

She put a red *X* in the *March 2017* column. "Help me count backward...February, January, December. If Audrey died in mid-March, she got pregnant sometime between

November 15 and December 15." She made an *X* in the *No-vember 2016* column and drew a line connecting *November* and *March.*

"She talked to Randy Stevenson during that period," Logan said hesitantly. "What do you think of that?"

"I'm guessing he's ten years younger than Audrey. I have a hard time believing she would be involved with Randy, but we need to talk to him. He was single back then, had recently returned from the army, and was probably looking for a girlfriend. He told me he helped with the gardening once. She bragged about a boyfriend in November, but I think she stopped talking to Randy too soon. If he was the father, she would've called him when she realized she was pregnant." She thought about what Audrey had said to Ben. "Does Randy have money?"

"Not right now, I don't think. He may have some trust money from his grandpa. But he'll inherit from Hank, and it'll be sizeable. He's going to college and getting trained to run the businesses. Don't forget, Audrey could've walked down to Randy's place to talk to him face to face, so don't dismiss him too soon."

"Okay, Randy's a maybe. Do you have any other evidence?"

"We checked with the DMV. Audrey's car was an older Chevy station wagon. The tags haven't been renewed since February 2017. We don't know where the car is. If someone killed her, that car is somewhere up a lonely ravine out there, or it's been junked. We can follow up on that." He shuffled through his file. "The post office didn't have a forwarding address. We checked the utility bills and came up with nothing."

"When did Mrs. Williams report Audrey's disappearance?"

"The end of March 2017. The sheriff investigated. Carl Stevenson said she had impulsively moved. There were no clues. She didn't answer her phone. We couldn't find any trace of her car. The investigation was closed."

"Do you have a file on that? Sounds like it was soon after she disappeared."

"Yep. I'm sure the sheriff has it."

"Shouldn't we review it?" Maggie wondered if it was an investigation based on the word of one person.

"I'll see what I can do."

His hesitancy didn't sound good. She had doubts about Logan but didn't want to make a snap judgment about how Audrey's disappearance was handled. She would listen, evaluate, and weigh it carefully.

Maggie stared at the whiteboard. "Here's how I read the motive." She retrieved her notebook and flipped the pages as she talked. "Ben and Audrey split up in August. She's angry, maybe a little frantic about money. She tells the landlord she just lost her primary source of income, and he gives her free rent for a while because he's a nice guy. She finds a boyfriend, possibly in October, maybe early November, and maybe he moves in with her, or she moved in with him. Maybe he's married, so she can't call him. That's why we don't have phone calls. In November, she brags about the new boyfriend to Ben."

Maggie reached for her coffee. "In November or December, she gets pregnant. She figures it out and tells the boyfriend, probably around February. There are no suspicious phone calls, so it must've been face to face."

She paced. "Audrey had resources to get herbs, but I wonder why she would buy a poisonous plant. Maybe someone else knew about it and used it to kill her. Maybe that someone else was the boyfriend. Maybe she was despondent because of the pregnancy. Either she intentionally drank the poison or someone gave it to her. She died, and someone buried her. I go with the boyfriend because it was kept a secret. Boyfriend got scared, but he cared enough about her to put that little wooden cross in her hands."

"Who's the damn boyfriend?" Logan asked. "Could she have taken the herb, hoping it would cause a miscarriage? Maybe the boyfriend told her that would work."

"Don't know. Before we speculate too much, we need to ID him. You may need to do a lot of DNA tests to find him." Maggie sat across from Logan. "We know it's not Ben. I'll need to go over all of this with Charles Cameron. There's nothing to tie Ben to Audrey's death, so he may want me to pull out."

Logan's eyes widened. His voice was anxious. "Don't leave me with this mess. I've got a killer out there. This happened on Hank's property, and there's a lot of politics at play. Everyone from the county council to the dog-catcher wants me to arrest Ben. I don't have any evidence against him, and I don't have the budget to put anyone on this case full time."

"Ben's paying for my time. Your DNA test clears his name."

Logan frowned. "We're looking for other evidence to pin it on him."

"What evidence?"

"I don't know yet. We have a date of death. He knew where she lived and that she had herbs and probably that she had a poisonous herb. He also knew she was saying horrible things about him. Maybe he wanted to put a stop to that and didn't even know she was pregnant. Maybe the boyfriend had nothing to do with it. Ben could've driven up to her place with no one knowing. She would've opened the door to him. He could've brewed a cup of poisonous tea, sat with her until she drank it, and then buried her. Mark my words—someone will remember seeing him at her cabin during that week in March. His every movement is going to be suspect."

He sighed. "If he was in town and bought gas with a credit card, he's a suspect. If someone remembers him stopping for a beer, we've got him close to her place. We want his credit card charges for March 2017. You know as well as I do, we're going to have every theory in the books on this one. We might as well be ready for it."

"That's how innocent people get charges." She narrowed her eyes. "You're confusing the town's prejudice with the obvious truth. In March 2017, Ben had moved on and had no motive. He wouldn't have benefited from her death. He wasn't the father of her baby. Whatever Audrey was saying or doing didn't affect him."

She glanced at Ben's phone records and laid them on the table next to Audrey's phone records. "I don't see any contact between them."

"I'll go over the phone records again. Maybe he called from work. She would've let him in. He planned this and didn't want to establish any personal telephone records. This has to be airtight. My job depends on it."

Maggie glared at him. Logan was making a feeble excuse. He didn't want to face the mayor. She hoped it wasn't his job security that motivated him the most.

"There's another question for Mrs. Williams you should follow up on when you see her this afternoon. Carl cleaned out Audrey's cabin when she disappeared, but he kept all of her furniture. That bothers me. He should've given it to her family. He might have offered Mrs. Williams the furniture, and she told him to keep it. That would be believable, but we need to establish that's what happened. Would you ask her about it? You might also get some clues from her mom about Audrey's relationship with Carl. How well did they get along?"

"Yeah. I'll follow up." He seemed afraid of losing her help in the investigation.

"I'll get you Ben's credit card information. You're going to want Audrey's credit card info as well. I'll see if Ben can get me her account number."

Logan crossed his arms. "I still think your guy did it." He was determined to remain in control.

"You're certainly free to pursue that angle, and we'll cooperate if you need more evidence from Ben. I think the mysterious boyfriend knows what really happened. If we stay in the case, I'm going to try to find him."

She asked for copies of Logan's new evidence.

Logan paced. "I've got a lot of political pressure. They're going to roast me alive if there's anything against Ben that isn't checked out. I've got to look for more."

"We'll cooperate fully. We both need to speak with Randy and Stacey before going in our separate directions. Would you set up interviews? Those witnesses will be much more cooperative if you contact them and not me."

Maggie texted Robert to say she needed to make one stop before she would be on her way to the cabin.

CHAPTER 23

Maggie

It wasn't in her nature to worry about her own safety first, so Maggie forgot about the need for security and walked over to the gift shop. She needed a gift and wondered if the shop had anything appropriate. In addition, she was curious to know if the shopkeeper had any useful information.

"Good afternoon," the shopkeeper said.

Maggie was the only customer there. "Nice to see you again." She selected a jasmine tea and approached the counter. "I need a gift for a friend. This will be perfect."

"Glad to hear that."

"Do you remember we talked about Audrey Stillman?"

"Yes, of course. You're the one who's looking into that. Such a tragedy."

"My name is Maggie Anderson, by the way. Didn't you tell me Audrey was one of your regular vendors?"

"Yes. Mostly, I carried her teas and herbal remedies. Her handmade crafts were adorable. My name is Claire, Claire Pascal."

"Claire, I'm wondering if you could help me. We're trying to establish Audrey's date of death. Do you recall the last time you purchased inventory from her?"

"I can look that up. I have my old financial records in the back. If you would keep an eye on the store, I'll find out." She disappeared into the back room and emerged a few minutes later, carrying two pieces of paper. "Here are the last invoices from Audrey."

They examined the documents together.

"My last order was placed on February 26, 2017. I was stocking up for the spring crowd," Claire said.

"I presume you simply called her with an order. How quickly did she deliver? Did she keep a supply of dried herbs?"

"It depended on the time of year. When I ordered in January and February, I got the teas that were packaged in the fall. She used some herbs to make salves, which were available all year. Over the winter, she made the crafts."

"Do you know if she bought plants from a catalog?"

"Oh, yes. I buy some of my teas from the same catalog." She pulled out a three-ring binder from under the counter. "It comes out quarterly. Here are the last four."

Maggie flipped through several pages of hand-drawn pictures of herbs and natural remedies that included descriptions of their uses.

"Sometimes Audrey and I would split a minimum order," Claire said. "I would sell the raw product, and Audrey would make an herbal remedy and sell it through this catalog and at other shops."

Maggie quickly looked for belladonna in the catalog, but found none. A notation of the website went into her notebook. After scanning a few more pages of the catalog, she asked as casually as she could muster, "Just curious. Did you and Audrey ever talk about her divorce?"

Claire's face hardened. "Not really. Ben was quite a rascal. He never deserved her anyway."

"Did Audrey ever tell you she had a new boyfriend?"

"No. I knew she was angry and frustrated in the beginning, but she seemed to get over it. The last time we spoke, she sounded so much better, so I asked how she was doing. She said things were looking up, but she couldn't talk about it yet."

Was she talking about her secret pregnancy? Audrey probably wouldn't have told her friends about it yet.

Maggie picked up the last invoice from Audrey. "When would these items have been delivered?"

"About a week later."

"How quickly did you pay for them?"

"I always gave Carl a check when he delivered. I didn't like to keep Audrey waiting."

"Carl?"

"Carl made her deliveries. He started bringing them about three or four months before Audrey disappeared. He said he understood very little about herbs or gardening and was just dropping things off for Audrey when he came into town. He joked he was bringing me her extra vegetables."

"Why was Carl involved?"

"Saving her a trip, he used to say. He was like that, always helping people out. That's the way people from small towns are."

"Was Carl the one who told you Audrey had moved?"

She fell silent for a minute. "Yes, I believe so. I needed to place a new order, but Audrey didn't answer her phone, which was odd. I finally called Carl, and that's what he told me. He said she left a note telling him she wanted to start a new life. Her car was gone, and she left some of her things behind." She shook her head. "It seemed strange to me that she never said goodbye."

"I've started over a couple of times. Sometimes a clean break with the past is important."

"Oh, I know that story! Now that I think about it, Carl gave me the inventory Audrey left behind. Told me he was cleaning out her place and found some things I could sell."

"The landlord always gets stuck with the things people leave behind." Maggie chuckled and turned to leave so she wouldn't show what she was feeling. *Carl seemed to know about Audrey's disappearance before anyone else. He gave away her stuff. What else did he do?* "It's good seeing you. Perhaps when I'm in town again, I can stop by."

"Please do, and please feel free to tell me how the case is going." She took a business card from a holder and gave it to Maggie. "The whole town is up in arms about this, and we're hoping for a quick end to it."

Maggie slipped the card into her purse and said goodbye. She sat on a nearby public bench and made notes. Claire was a great resource. She would go back.

CHAPTER 24

Maggie

Maggie was still thinking about Claire's information as she walked toward her SUV, which was in the parking lot of the county office complex. Just before reaching the street corner, she heard someone take a step behind her on the old wooden sidewalk.

The footstep was hard. The person was too close. She paused briefly.

"Yes, you. Turn around."

She did so, slowly. A man moved farther out from a doorway. Tall and slender, with the beginnings of a beard, he wore a white cowboy hat, black shirt, and black Levi's. His hands were on his hips as if he was about to reach for a six-shooter. She remembered him from the diner as Kevin Stevenson.

"We don't need no lesbo lawyers messing things up. When you're told to leave town, you need to pay attention and follow instructions. Leave now, and don't come back, just like that fag client of yours needs to keep his sorry ass gone."

She sensed someone else and turned around.

A tall cowboy reached out and blocked her way forward. "We know how to take care of people like you."

Without a word, she quickly stepped sideways on the sidewalk. She wasn't going to respond. Nervous but determined, she started to go around the second cowboy, but was too slow. He blocked her again. He put his hands on her shoulders, forced her to turn around, and pushed her into Kevin's face.

"Bitch, we don't want to see your ugly face in this town again. You understand?" Kevin's breath reeked of beer.

The man behind her snickered and casually lowered his arms.

She remembered a self-defense tactic she had read about. She quickly changed her expression and became animated. "Excuse me. Do you know what time it is?"

Kevin's face twitched with confusion, but he automatically looked down at his watch.

In this moment of distraction, she jumped off the sidewalk and dashed several steps into the middle of the deserted street. The cowboys jumping down to the road. Kevin tried to keep up with his gimpy leg. His friend stayed near him. She ran and turned a corner. They were a few yards away. With the way their bodies meandered while they walked, she surmised the cowboys were drunk. *You're not going to touch me again.* With her heart in her throat and sweat pouring down her temples, she walked fast with a firm step until she reached the parking lot.

She jumped into her vehicle, locked the doors, called Logan, and left a message. "Just want to let you know two drunken cowboys accosted and threatened me on a downtown sidewalk. I'm in your parking lot right now. They followed me and are blocking my car so I can't get out. I've seen one of them before. His name is Kevin, and he's one of the Stevenson cousins. Looks to be around forty, wears a white hat. Logan, someone wants me out of town, and I'm wondering why. Hope you have some ideas."

Her vehicle bounced as the cowboys leaned against the back of it, preventing her from backing out.

She called Robert and explained why she couldn't leave. He told her to hang tight; he would be there. Fifteen minutes later, his Jeep pulled around a corner. He grabbed a nearby parking spot and called her. She apologized for not staying safe, identified where the cowboys were, and told him they were drunk. He slowly walked over, being careful to stay out of their line of sight.

After briefly checking with her, Robert walked along her driver's side until he got to the rear. Putting one hand on the roof, he confronted them. "Who are you working for, and why are you trying to intimidate this lady?"

The cowboys smirked.

Kevin stood and tried to get in his face. "We've got orders, and we don't have to tell you." He stumbled forward and took a swing at Robert while the second cowboy laughed.

Robert caught Kevin's forearm and twisted it behind his back, causing him to lose his balance. "Sorry, pal, you're picking on the wrong person." He pushed him to the ground. "Go tell your boss that you had too much beer and couldn't do your job."

As Kevin got up, Robert grabbed both of them by their shirts. "I'm going to give you five seconds to get so far away that I can't beat the shit out of you." He pushed them away.

The men turned and comically ran as fast as they could.

"I don't want to see your sorry asses around her again, ya hear? If I do, I'll bust your skulls open!" Robert yelled.

He walked around to the passenger side of Maggie's car, opened the door, and spoke gently. "You're right. Someone is after you."

Maggie stared at him with admiration. "Where did you get your John Wayne training?"

"There were many summers I worked on a ranch. It's tough work. Gets you in shape."

She leaned on the steering wheel with an overwhelming sigh of relief. "Thank you."

A big grin covered his face. He shook his head. "I'm in charge of rescuing damsels in distress this week. What else you got for me?"

CHAPTER 25

Robert

"Want some lunch?" Robert was proud to be her knight in shining armor and welcomed her brief thank-you hug.

"That would be great. Let's not do any place in town. Maybe somewhere that caters to travelers."

"There's a really nice place called Jensen's Grill up the road a piece in the other direction. Best restaurant in the county. It's big enough, so you'll be okay. Let's move your car over next to the police department. We'll pick it up later."

After moving her car, he gallantly opened the Jeep's door. "Cinderella gets to ride in the pumpkin today."

Maggie smiled as she climbed in and her jitters seemed to ease. "Why are those cowboys so angry that I'm investigating this? Don't they have cows to take care of?"

"Obviously there's more going on than we think, especially with Kevin Stevenson involved." He didn't want to tell her, but that was a bad omen.

It was almost two o'clock. Jensen's was a clean, modern, one-story building with an extensive menu.

Just inside the door, Robert took off his hat and waved toward the tables in one smooth gesture. "It's your choice."

Maggie chose a circular booth in the bar area, far away from other diners. The room was dimly lit, and soft music played in the background.

Maggie ordered a salad, roast chicken breast, and white wine. He selected a thick steak, a baked potato, and a tall beer.

He looked at her plate, smiling. "You know, this is beef country. You're lucky they have some East Coast food here."

She chuckled. "Someday I'll have to teach you there are other things that are edible besides beef."

He cut into his steak. "After you asked the other day, I've been thinking about the last time I saw Audrey. It was definitely the Christmas party at the sheriff's house. I don't come up much in the winter, but I always come for that. She was there. Pretty as she could be, too." He wanted to tell Maggie that she was prettier, but he held his tongue. "She was alone all night. Word was out that Ben had moved, and people were talking about him being gay. Almost no one talked to her. We didn't know what to say."

"Logan and I think she got pregnant sometime between mid-November and mid-December. Do you remember if she left the party with anyone?"

"Not that I saw. Some of the guys pushed me to take an interest in her, but she was too young. She wanted babies—we all knew that—and I didn't. I wasn't going to take any chances. Besides, I left a little early because it was snowing. Had to heat my place up."

Robert sipped his beer. "Are you okay? You had a bad experience out there."

"I'm okay." She breathed deeply. "See, you taught me something."

"Did they threaten you?"

"Yes."

If they hadn't been in a public place, he would have pulled her close and hugged her. All he could do was meet her intense blue eyes. After her ordeal, she needed to hear his praise. "Can I tell you something without you getting embarrassed?"

Her face turned wary.

"You're a beautiful woman. On the outside, certainly, but I also admire your courage and your spirit. You're someone special." He scratched his chin to hide that he was outside his comfort zone and was blushing.

He had never seen her embarrassed. Something about her eyes changed. She looked toward the empty tables to her left. Her face softened into the gentle face of a child. Her eyes glistened with tears. After a moment, she brought herself back from whatever memory had been triggered. "Thank you. No one has ever paid me such a nice compliment."

He reached across and took her hand. She held his gaze. Her eyes were no longer wary.

Maggie looked around and slowly eased away from him. She nodded toward a tall man coming toward them who wore dark clothes and a black cowboy hat. "Isn't that Randy?"

"Yes. Keep your cool, okay?" Robert shifted in his seat.

"Order me another wine, please."

"Bobby Parsons, good to see you." Randy tipped his hat to Maggie. "You too, ma'am." He frowned when they didn't invite him to join them. Finally, he pulled a chair from a nearby table and sat on it backward. "You know anything about the case yet?"

"Naw, not much," Robert said nonchalantly. "What d'you hear?"

"Nothing official yet, but I heard rumors it's Audrey. They got dental records. We only have two dentists, so that was easy."

"What else do you know?"

"Was wondering how soon ole Ben will be arrested." Randy nodded toward Maggie smugly. "You might know that, ma'am."

Maggie glared at him but didn't say anything. Robert kicked her gently under the table. She couldn't afford to antagonize him again.

"That's going to be between Logan Harris and the sheriff. It's really not for me to speculate."

"Do they know how she died?" Randy asked.

"Another question for Logan Harris."

"Can they pinpoint when it happened?"

"Robert was just telling me he saw Audrey at the Christmas party in 2016, so we know it was after that. Did you see her there?"

Randy eyed Robert. "Well, yes. Everyone in the neighborhood went to the party. I talked to her briefly."

"Were you there with Karen?"

"No, we didn't meet until last year." His gaze shifted to Robert. "That particular party was almost four years ago, wasn't it?"

"Were you there with a girlfriend?" Maggie sounded like she was cross-examining him.

"No. I came home from the army in 2015. I didn't have a girlfriend then."

"Did you see Audrey leave with anyone?" She watched him carefully.

Randy leaned in and sneered. "You're sounding like ole what's-her-name, Jessica something or other. You know, the old lady who played detective. Can't really remember."

She ignored his insult. "Did you leave alone?"

He sneered. "My uncle Eddy was there. He was staying with Grandpa. We walked back in the snow."

"Wasn't that the year you helped Audrey clean out her garden?"

"Look, lady, you ain't gonna get me on anything, so stop trying. Besides, that was already done. We finished before Thanksgiving, as I recall. The Christmas party is always two weekends after Thanksgiving."

"Did you meet up with Audrey after the party?"

"No." He glowered at her, visibly uncomfortable. His mission to get information had backfired. "I'm meeting someone for lunch." He got up and left just as the new round of drinks arrived.

Robert toasted Maggie. "Good work, Counselor."

"Please notice it was easy for him to answer all of those questions except for one."

"You got me. Which question?"

"He wouldn't tell me if Audrey left with someone."

"Do you think she hooked up with Randy?"

She was quiet for a moment. "I don't know. I don't trust Randy. He's the type who will lie and hide evidence. In your gossip circle inquiries, see if you can find a romantic connection between Audrey and Randy. He would've bragged about it. Maybe you can get some guys together with a couple of pitchers of beer and flush some answers out."

"Good idea. Beer usually works."

CHAPTER 26

Robert

They picked up Maggie's car and drove to the cabin. Robert worked on his weatherproofing project while Maggie relaxed until it was time to drive home in their separate vehicles. Her day had started peacefully and had turned into something exhausting. A quick nap was perfect.

As he drove back to Salt Lake, Robert felt the warm connection with Maggie that had started at Jensen's Grill and decided to move his agenda along. He called her and suggested they stop for a hamburger at Wendy's that was about halfway. He asked what she wanted and said he would go through the drive-through and she could join him in the parking lot.

After they shared their impromptu meal, he turned to her, his left arm resting on the steering wheel. "You don't flirt, do you?"

Maggie blinked and stopped gathering the trash. "No. I'm past that. Men don't date women my age. I'm free to be whoever I want to be. Don't have to think about impressing anyone."

"What would you think if someone was interested in you?"

"I'd think he was a little bit crazy. I'm rough around the edges, you know, school of hard knocks and all that. Not good girlfriend material."

He grinned. "You're not the first person to call me crazy."

She stared at him. "Robert, are you trying to tell me something?"

"When I appointed myself as your bodyguard, there was a little more to it. I like the person I'm guarding. You're Cinderella and Nancy Drew, all rolled into one."

"Robert Parsons, every woman in Salt Lake knows you're off-limits. You and I both know how many women have flirted with you and gotten nowhere."

He leaned toward her as if he was disclosing a secret. "We're not in Salt Lake anymore. Maybe I'm approachable when I'm someplace else." He felt like a teenager ready to make his first romantic move. "She just needs to be the woman sitting next to me."

Maggie laughed nervously. He sensed that every bad romantic event in her life was flashing before her eyes and telling her not to do it.

Shyly inching toward her, he broke into a wide grin and batted his eyelashes. "What I'm trying to say is...I would like to kiss you."

"Okay," she blurted out, to his surprise.

Before she could take it back, he carefully pulled her toward him. His lips barely touched hers. The kiss became firmer. Her resistance melted. He felt the warm current of being connected and hoped she did, too. She didn't pull away.

"You kiss like a genuine princess," he finally whispered. He gently kissed her forehead. "It's been a very long time since I kissed a woman. Thank you."

She laid her head on his shoulder.

He savored the moment while the sun disappeared behind the mountains to the west and sent its last rays of warmth into the Jeep. The silence was like a toasty blanket.

Maggie finally pulled away. "Really hate to break this up, but I need to get home." With a peck on his cheek, she said a gentle goodbye and went to her vehicle.

Just before taking his exit from the freeway, he called to say good night. Hearing her voice made him feel warm all over again.

CHAPTER 27

Maggie

Tuesday, September 22, 2020

The next morning, Maggie woke up thinking about how her relationship with Robert had changed in one day. He had responded to her with compassion, never once finding fault or blaming her for what happened with the cowboys. He had a quiet force, a way of being that acknowledged who she was, flaws and all. She wasn't sure if she deserved him, but she felt good about herself, and powerful.

She set up a meeting with Ben in Charles's office for later in the day and asked him to bring a picture of Audrey. She planned to use the photo in interviews to watch the witnesses' reactions, anticipating that someone who was hiding information about Audrey would avoid looking at the picture.

"She was about twenty-five in this photo," he said, setting it on the conference room table. It showed a beautiful woman with long, dark hair, sparkling eyes, and an impish grin.

"I've already given both of you bits and pieces of the evidence, but I'm going to lay out the big picture for you." Maggie said, cradling the sachet in her pocket. "Ben, I'm sorry to be the one to tell you this, but the body has been positively identified as Audrey through dental records. The DA will release that information today." She waited while Ben absorbed the news. "I'm sorry."

"I've been expecting that. At least we know." His eyes glistened with tears.

"The relevant time frame for our investigation is from December 2016, when the Christmas party was held, to March 2017. Her last phone call was made on March 16. We believe the death and burial took place a few days after that. Did you have any contact with Audrey between December and March? Think hard. Any phone calls? Any emails? Any social media contact? Did you visit her? Did you accidentally see her at a grocery store?"

"No. I visited my parents a couple of times over the holidays, but I don't recall going back to Medford for any other reason. She had a new boyfriend. I was glad. I left her alone."

"What about your romantic interest? Did you continue to see him?"

"He came to Salt Lake twice, but that didn't last. I needed a clean break."

"Could he have done something to Audrey in retaliation?"

"I don't think so. It wasn't a difficult breakup, but I can follow up on that."

"The DA will want to know his name, and he'll need to come forward at some point," Charles said.

"I understand, but it'll be awkward. I won't give you the name yet, but if it's really needed, you'll get it."

"Fair enough. The DA wants to see your credit card records from November 2016 through March 2017."

"Maggie asked me to bring those." He handed copies to both of them.

She perused the new charges for March 2017. None of them originated in Madison County. However, he had charged gas in nearby Ogden on March 18, 2017. "Ben, how often do you go to Ogden?"

"Rarely."

"Do you recall why you purchased gas in Ogden in March 2017?"

He took the statement from her and stared at it. "I'm going to have to think about that and go through my calendar. Right now, I can't remember why I was up there at that time."

"The DA wants to make a case that you drove up from Salt Lake, murdered Audrey, and drove home again. He'll hone in on this charge, and it could be enough for a jury to convict. We're going to need an explanation."

"I'll do some research. I'll get back to you in a day or so."

"Next major fact," Maggie said. "When she died in mid-March, Audrey was three to four months pregnant. Counting backward, we estimate she got pregnant sometime in November or December."

"I wondered why you needed a DNA test. I couldn't imagine why any of my DNA would still be around." Ben looked away and spoke softly. "She always wanted a baby, but we just couldn't make it happen." He turned back. "It's a shame she died and never had the chance to be a mother."

Charles straightened. "Your DNA test clears you. The father was someone else. Her getting pregnant certainly strengthens your assertion that she had a boyfriend."

"Have you identified who he was?"

"Not a clue. By the way, this pregnancy is confidential," Maggie said. "Only the necessary people know. Keep it quiet."

Maggie pushed the coroner's report in front of Ben. "There was enough flesh on her hands that the coroner was able to prove she was poisoned, which brings up the possibility that it was self-inflicted, especially if she was pregnant and her boyfriend was unhappy about that. How does that strike you?"

Ben glanced at the report and looked at her photo. "The Audrey I knew was always optimistic. She desperately wanted a baby. She would've raised the child alone with her mother's help."

"The town won't believe she intentionally drank the poison," Charles said. "Someone buried her."

"How much did you know about her herb business and her garden?" Maggie asked.

"I didn't follow her business closely. I knew she advertised in catalogs and bought supplies from them. She had old-fashioned recipes that were handed down for generations and used the spare bedroom to store inventory and make her creams."

"Do you know which plants she had in her garden? Did she ever talk about being careful because of a poisonous plant?"

"No. I didn't know what was there. She talked about her plants sometimes, but I don't remember what she said. I didn't do any of the gardening."

"That reminds me." Maggie rummaged through the documents in her case file. She held up a photo of the small wooden cross in Audrey's hands. "You mentioned she wouldn't have typically worn a cross, even with a costume, but she was buried with this cross. Have you ever seen it?"

He looked at the picture quietly. "I don't recall ever seeing it."

"Could it have been some type of decoration in your home?"

"No. Not while I was there, anyway."

"The cross could've belonged to the person who buried her. Someone dug a shallow grave and held a brief ceremony where Audrey's hands were positioned around the cross," Charles said. "Then someone wrapped the body in a tarp and put her in the grave. He must have brought the cross with him. This could make it premeditated unless he can prove the poisoning was accidental."

"The bottom line is that someone buried her. That's all we have. The boyfriend is the prime suspect, but we don't know who he is." Maggie cleared her throat. "Any questions?"

"At one point, you thought she had moved. Did you find anything on that?" Ben asked.

"She stopped paying rent in October 2016, which seemed odd to us. Hank's bookkeeper said Carl was a generous person, so we speculate he felt sorry for her and let her live there rent-free. Her mother said she was living at the cabin when she disappeared in March."

"Where does this leave me?"

Maggie raised an eyebrow at Charles. "What do you think?"

Charles eyed Ben. "You're not the father of Audrey's baby, which is important. The key times are November to March. Someone got her pregnant, and someone either found her dead or killed her and then buried her. Right now, nothing links you to either, but the town is going to demand that every rock be looked under in order to implicate you. The boyfriend needs to be identified. Once we know who that is, we either have the killer, or we have someone who probably knows enough to identify who the killer is."

He rubbed his eyes. "Your DNA test clears you, but that gas purchase is evidence that puts you in Ogden in March 2017, and your explanation will be critical. Once word gets out that you were in Ogden, someone may try to manufacture seeing you in Maxwell on the same date, but we have to wait and see. We could back away from this now and see if they come up with anything that ties you to Audrey's death. They may never find anything strong enough to arrest you."

"What do they need to tie me to her death?"

"The DA will find witnesses who'll say that Audrey was bad-mouthing you around town and you were angry," Maggie said. "He thinks you drove up to the cabin in mid-March, made tea from a poisonous plant in her garden, and made sure she drank it. Then you dug a hole, wrapped her in a tarp, put that cross in her hands, buried her, and left with no one seeing you."

She watched for his reaction. He did not act like someone whose actions had been uncovered. "They will need proof that you were near the cabin around the time she died. You could've been in town and not made any phone calls, but your cell phone would have pinged on one of the local cell towers. We might be able to get ping records before the DA does, but we would be required to give a copy to the DA. Under the circumstances, if your phone pinged anywhere in the county, that would probably be enough to convince a local jury."

Ben studied his credit card statement. "I'm fairly certain I wasn't anywhere near Madison County in March 2017, so my phone wasn't there. I'm sure there's an explanation for a trip to Ogden, but no one is going to believe me." He looked up. "I could live with this hanging over my head for a long time. True?"

"That's about it. From what Maggie has told me, the town is determined to pin it on you," Charles said. "Even without an arrest, you'll be considered the murderer who got away."

"Which means the actual facts will never be known unless we find them?"

"That's what it looks like."

"What are the alternatives?"

Charles tapped his chin. "We could end our investigation now and let the DA take it on by himself. If that happens, they will focus on you until they exhaust every possibility. If they can't find anything, it'll become a cold case. If they find strong evidence linking the murder to someone else, it'll clear you. However, that's not likely to happen, and the public sentiment won't change unless there's a conviction. In the town of Medford, you'll always be known as Audrey's killer."

Charles shifted in his chair. "Or we could keep Maggie on the case a little longer and see if she can piece together who really killed Audrey. She could also neutralize any new theories that don't hold water."

Ben faced Maggie. "What do you think?"

"Right now, there's no DNA evidence that implicates anyone. Logan Harris needs to get DNA from the men who had contact with Audrey. It'll be a process of elimination until we find a match. That doesn't mean that when we find the father, we also find the killer, but it's the only clue we have."

She paused. "We've got one puzzling situation. Someone is trying to drive me out of town. They left a threatening note for me when I stayed at Robert's cabin, and last week, someone sent two goons to confront me on the street. My opinion—and I could be wrong—is that the person behind these scare tactics knows something and doesn't want to be found out. It could be the man who was the father, or it could be someone directly connected to the murder. We don't know yet."

She sighed. "It's just my opinion, and maybe I'm jaded by big-city politics, but I think there are strong political influences up there. Anyone in the Stevenson family—and there seem to be a lot of them—will have political protection, and no one with the name Stevenson will be charged. Even if we find the smoking gun, the reality is the DA isn't going to take the hit by arresting anyone named Stevenson. If the evidence gets too close to one of them, the DA will shut the case down and make it a cold case."

Charles frowned. "I don't think it's quite that bad. We've cleared you, Ben, but it's highly unlikely that we'll be able to solve this case. I have concerns for Maggie's safety, but she's willing to keep digging to find out why someone is trying to chase her out of town."

Ben held the photo. "Let's give it a couple more weeks and see what happens. Audrey was my wife. I loved her. Even if there's no arrest, I would like to know what really happened. Maggie, are you sure you're going to be safe if you keep working on this?"

"I'm not going to stay overnight anymore, and Robert Parsons is escorting me around town as a bodyguard. I'll be all right."

"If we proceed, where do you want to go with this?" Charles asked.

"The big question for us is who Audrey had contact with. Who got her pregnant? Who secretly buried her?" She closed her hand around the sachet again, as if she was also asking these questions of Audrey.

"What's next?" Ben asked Maggie.

"The DA is still focused on Ben. It's time for us to do an independent investigation. We need to track down the boyfriend. If we think someone is suspicious, we'll try to get his DNA. That will answer the first question, but it won't tell us who the killer is."

She pointed to the credit card report. "Ben, we can anticipate they'll jump on that gas charge on your credit card because the date appears to coincide with Audrey's death. Let me know as soon as you have anything that would explain your trip to Ogden."

She tucked her hair behind her ears and glanced at Charles. "It's been three and a half years, so I don't think either you or the DA will get cell tower records on Ben's phone. Usually, the requests need to be submitted before they delete the records. We always had to get our retention orders in within two years."

"You're probably right on that," Charles said. "I'll check it out."

Maggie put the picture of Audrey in her case file. "I'll take good care of this. And I'll check in with Charles every time I go up there, so people know I'm okay."

CHAPTER 28

Maggie

Wednesday, September 23, 2020

"Can I have one quick hug before the others come?" Maggie whispered to Robert, closing the door. She was glad he had arrived early for the next team meeting.

He beamed as he quickly put a bottle of Italian wine on the table. "I'm glad you like hugs." He enveloped her in his arms and kissed her on the cheek.

"I'd like to keep this just between us for now." Heat coursed through her. She was still fighting her instinct not to trust men and against her impulse to shut down and protect herself. A door to her heart had opened, and she was peeking around the corner, checking it out. She didn't want her fears to win out.

"I promise to behave myself tonight, but it won't be easy." Robert pulled back and gave her a quick kiss. "I'll practice my best detective manners."

The doorbell rang again. It was Gwen with homemade spaghetti and meatballs, which went on the table next to Maggie's salad. Peter soon arrived with gelato and Italian cookies.

"I'm now an embedded spy!" Gwen said. "Hank called my agency and hired me to look in on Grammy one day a week. Apparently, his wife insisted. I already told Maggie, but I'm telling everyone now! I've already been to see her twice, and we spent an afternoon getting to know each other."

Maggie breathed a sigh of relief and squeezed her secret sachet as thanks. She started the meeting by putting Audrey's picture on the coffee table and bringing the team up to date on her meeting with Logan. Having Audrey with them gave the room the somber feeling it needed.

"We're still working on a motive, but we know she died by poisoning," Maggie said. "It's beginning to fit together—the boyfriend got her pregnant, and he wanted her to end the pregnancy. She refused, so he took matters into his own hands. I also stopped by the gift shop and got info about an herb catalog Audrey used. I asked Peter to research the website for a belladonna plant."

"Is that a plant she would've had in her garden?" asked Gwen.

Maggie looked at Peter. "You may have an answer."

"I do. The website features a wide variety of herbs, books on growing a pharmacy garden, and equipment for making tinctures and medicinal plants." He read the research on his laptop and added his own comments. "A belladonna plant and its seeds are labeled as poisonous in high-ingested amounts but are still available for purchase, which seems dangerous. The dried leaves can be made into a tincture to treat muscle and nerve pain and motion sickness. There's a history of the belladonna plant, which I won't go into, but it's been the poison of choice for centuries. What all of this means is that the amount of the dose is what makes it poisonous."

His eyes gleamed. "I also found a website about the recent reconstruction of a Civil War pharmacy farm in Maryland. Civil War doctors used a tincture made from the plant's leaves for treatments. Parts of the plant were used for whooping cough and hay fever remedies. These methods have survived in homeopathic medicine, and the farm in Maryland is producing various medicinal plants again, including belladonna." He glanced at Maggie. "Did Audrey make tinctures and salves?"

"Grammy said something about creams that Audrey made. I'll follow up with Claire. She may be able to confirm whether Maggie purchased the plant."

Maggie picked up Audrey's records. "I sent each of you the phone and bank records to review. If anything strikes you as odd, let me know." She touched Audrey's picture. "Logan and I are using March 18 as her approximate date of death. From that, we calculated back and decided that she got pregnant sometime in November or December. We're looking for someone she was seeing then."

She hesitated. "Carl claimed he had a note from Audrey, which no one has seen. We aren't sure how this note fits in with her death. Audrey's mom, Mrs. Williams, said Audrey was planning to move in with her, so what Randy said about the note doesn't make sense. We also know Carl kept her furniture. He should've given it to Mrs. Williams. I've asked Logan to follow up with her. Logan also said that she filed a missing person report, and I've asked to review the file. I'm waiting for him to produce it."

She frowned. "We know Carl was a womanizer, but with him gone, it's going to be hard to find out if he pursued Audrey, but I think he should be a suspect. I don't know how much we can get from Grammy about Carl's behavior. Gwen, you're our best hope for that."

"I'll see how snoopy I can get," Gwen said, winking at Maggie. She sat back and started watching Robert and Maggie carefully, as if she sensed something different.

Peter consulted his notes. "I need to check with you on something. Didn't Claire tell you that Carl said he knew nothing about plants and gardening?"

"Yes, Claire told me that. He simply acted as a delivery person for Audrey. He joked that the herbs were Audrey's vegetables."

"Didn't you say he worked in the yard every week for the new tenant?"

"Yes, Christine told me that. Carl took care of the garden and the surrounding area."

Peter smiled. "He was lying when he told Claire he knew nothing about plants. The poisonous plant was in the garden, and Carl knew about it. Otherwise, he wouldn't have bothered making excuses. If he told the new tenant she could help herself to the plants from the garden, it means he removed the belladonna before she moved in and made sure it didn't grow back. Also, I suspect he didn't want anyone to see the fresh grave. I also think he's a suspect."

"Could someone else have known about the plant?"

"Yes, that's possible, but we don't have evidence that someone else took care of the garden and probably hid the grave after Audrey died. That's where he made his mistake."

Maggie contemplated. "That's an interesting idea. Before we can go with it, I need to verify that Audrey had the plant." She sighed. "If Carl is a possible suspect, we don't have any way of getting his DNA."

Robert's expression was stoic. "I've put feelers in place that should lead to the boyfriend. I'll add Carl to the list of possibilities. I have my methods, so I must be careful about disclosing anything right now. I expect to get some feedback by next week."

Gwen giggled. "Robert, you're something else! I also have something that's important."

Everyone turned to her.

"Hank came by on my second day there. He said he needed a private moment with his mother. I was folding clothes on the couch, so I took the clean laundry upstairs. What he didn't know was that I could stand at the bend in the stairs and hear everything." She edged forward. "As soon as I left the room, Hank asked if anyone had been asking questions about Audrey. Grammy said no, but she has been worried about Audrey's diary—"

"A diary?" Maggie said. "Did Grammy know what was in it?"

"I don't think so, but she sounded concerned. She said Audrey talked about the diary being her best friend. Grammy asked Hank whether it had been destroyed."

"What did he say?"

"He didn't know about the diary."

"I thought Grammy knew more than what she was saying," Maggie said. "Carl must've done something with Audrey's stuff when he cleaned out her place. The furniture remained, but we need to know what happened to her personal stuff. Gwen, good work! Keep listening."

Wrapping up the meeting, Maggie identified three issues: they need to find out if Audrey bought a belladonna plant, they need to find DNA for Carl if possible, and they need to find out what happened to Audrey's diary.

"I have an idea that may work on the DNA issue." Robert turned to Gwen. "When will you be at Grammy's place again?"

"Tomorrow afternoon."

"I'm coming for a visit. It needs to be a surprise. Just expect me."

"I'll go back to the gift shop and ask about the plant," Maggie said. "I'll also find out about Audrey's personal belongings. That diary could be revealing."

CHAPTER 29

Robert

Thursday, September 24, 2020

Robert went to his cabin again. He worked on the weatherproofing until he saw Gwen's car pull up. He gave her an hour before he tucked a small white plastic trash bag in the pocket of his Levi's, put on his Stetson, and knocked on Grammy's door.

Grammy stared when she answered. "Bobby Parsons, what are you doing here today? Come in."

"I'm up here doing some work on my place, and I saw Gwen's car. Thought I'd come over and say hello."

"Oh, that's right. She's your friend. I knew that. Come in. She's upstairs. Have a seat." She shuffled over and called Gwen.

He tossed his hat on the deer antlers and walked over to the window.

Gwen bounced down the stairs. "Robert, I saw your Jeep when I came in. What brings you up this way in the middle of the week?"

"Gotta get my place ready for the winter. I've ignored it for a couple of years, so there's a lot to do. Thought I'd take a break and see if you had any coffee brewing."

She winked at him and headed for the kitchen. "We can take care of that."

"Grammy," he said as she moved over to her chair, "you're looking chipper today."

"Oh my, yes. Gwen's making sure I take my vitamins. She put them in seven little paper cups in the kitchen." She pointed to the coffee table. "See that photo album? I showed her some of my pictures last week, so this week she brought an album from when she lived in Chicago. She was about to show it to me."

Gwen came in. "Robert, I don't know what you take in your coffee."

He fixed his coffee, then sat on the couch. "Don't let me stop you. I'm interested in the pictures as well." He was pleased to see Grammy's improved mood.

Gwen pulled a chair over close to Grammy, placed the album half on her lap and half on Grammy's lap, and commented occasionally as she leafed through it. Robert stood and looked over Gwen's shoulders.

He allowed about thirty minutes before he thanked the ladies for their company. Gwen walked with him to the front hallway.

"How are things going with our favorite bloodhound?" Gwen tried to sound casual.

Robert looked puzzled for a minute before grinning. "Gwen, my friend, I've known you quite a while. Can't get anything past you, can I?"

"She's a good catch. Keep trying."

Robert took his hat, and held it casually as he opened the door. Except it wasn't his hat.

After closing the door, he cautiously placed Carl's hat inside the plastic bag and knotted the opening.

When he was safely in his own place, he called Maggie and told her what he had done. "Carl had a robust head of hair. I imagine we can find some of it inside his hat."

"Excellent!" she said. "I need to get authorization for us to take it to the lab for analysis." She fell silent for a moment. "However, we may have a chain of custody issue with it."

"What do you mean?"

"There's a strict procedure for law enforcement to identify and track evidence. We don't have that here. If any significant evidence is found on the hat and if it's used in a trial, someone must testify that the hat belonged to Carl and it has been on that hat rack since his death."

"Grammy is the only one who could say that."

"That's my point. She would never testify. If someone else has put that hat on and mixed his own hair with Carl's, the lab test will be useless."

"You mean the way I almost did a couple of weeks ago?"

"Yes. We may be able to get Logan to test it, even though the results wouldn't be admissible in court," she said. "How are you going to get your hat back?"

"Oh, I have another one I can wear for a while. When I get Carl's hat from the lab, I'll find a way to exchange it."

She agreed to call Logan and explain that she had the hat of a potential suspect and wanted a DNA test on the hair. She promised not to disclose how she got the hat but said it belonged to a person of interest and that she wanted to have it delivered directly to the lab to avoid any issues with the chain of custody.

Maggie called Robert later and told him Logan had exerted intense pressure to get more details, but she had remained stubborn. With great hesitation, he authorized the DNA test, even though he didn't know the circumstances. They arranged to have the hat dropped off. Robert was to deliver it personally to Aaron Jenkins, the coroner in Salt Lake, and request a DNA test of any hair found in the inside sweatband to match it with the DNA from the baby bones. The results were to be reported directly to Logan. Maggie had promised to reveal the name of the hat's owner if the results were important.

CHAPTER 30

Robert

Robert had one more task before taking the hat to the coroner's office. He drove into Medford and parked at the Lazy Q Tavern. It was early afternoon, and only one car was in the parking lot.

Harvey came out from the back room and greeted him.

"Hey, buddy," Robert said. "Got any cold beer?" He took a seat on the same stool as before. "Had to come into town and thought I would stop by."

They shot the breeze for a few minutes before Harvey said, "I've been asking around about your question."

"Any thoughts?"

Harvey started drying the glassware. "Well, I don't have anything specific yet." He moved a few items to their places behind the bar. "The general feeling is that Audrey kept to herself. She wasn't a drinking girl."

Robert waited quietly, pushing his Michelob around a bit. Sometimes Harvey took a while to spit out what he wanted to say.

"Those cabins are a bit isolated. Those folks don't come into town much," Harvey said. "And you know as well as I do that certain men like to brag when there ain't an ounce of truth behind what they say."

"You've heard something, and you're not sure if it's true. Is that what you're saying?"

"Well, I've put together some loose talk, shall we say? I don't want to disparage anyone's reputation if it turns out it ain't true, ya know what I mean?"

"I gotcha. I'm not asking you to swear on a stack of Bibles."

"All the Stevenson boys have reputations just like their previous generation did."

Robert rubbed his chin and decided to prime the pump. "Well, we have ole man Stevenson, Carl, who led the pack. I've always heard he chased anything in a skirt but never followed through. His cowboys don't fall far from the tree, is that it?" He gave Harvey a wry smile. "All hat and no cattle?"

Harvey's face remained deadpan until a grin slowly formed in acknowledgment.

Robert offered another thought. "Supposedly, Eddy was staying with his parents around that time. Eddy is bad news for women, so I hear. If he was out there, or even visiting, cute little Miss Audrey would've been in trouble."

"Eddy's bad news for every woman, but he's a Stevenson, so he gets away with it." Harvey nodded as he spoke. "Then you have that Stevenson kid who lives out there."

"You mean Randy? Randy's not a kid anymore. He's been in the army and just got married. You think he could've been sowing some wild oats before he settled down?"

"The word is that one of those Stevensons was playing fast and loose with Miss Audrey, but no one knows which one it was."

Robert casually twirled his beer bottle between both palms a few times. He didn't want to show too much interest in the rumor, but it was significant. "Interesting. Keep up the good work." He took out a twenty-dollar bill and laid it on the counter as he got up. "Keep the change."

When he got in his Jeep, he reported to Maggie that his source suggested they should look at three specific suspects with the last name of Stevenson.

From there, he drove to the crime lab in Salt Lake and dropped off Carl's hat.

CHAPTER 31

Maggie

Friday, September 25, 2020

Maggie called Logan to arrange faxing over Ben's credit card statements. She was also becoming concerned that he was letting the case slide. She wanted to keep him energized because she needed his cooperation to find the actual killer.

"As expected, I got the call from the mayor pressuring me to arrest Ben," Logan said. "I had to tell him the details, but I swore him to secrecy about the pregnancy. I told him we have evidence that Audrey may have died in March 2017, but I don't have probable cause against Ben. Obviously, I'm still looking for more evidence."

Maggie had already pegged Logan as a good ole boy like the rest of them, but believed he wanted to do the right thing. "I don't have an issue with that. We're looking at it from a different angle, of course. We're looking for the boyfriend."

"Sure." He chuckled. "Just do me a favor. Don't find the wrong boyfriend."

"Can't make any promises." She understood his comment as a signal that he would bury the case if the names of her suspects came too close to being the wrong people. She wasn't ready to tell him who was on her list.

"Mrs. Williams has asked me to release Audrey's body so she can have a funeral."

"Has that happened?"

"Not yet, but I think the paperwork will be finished in a day or two. The funeral will probably be in a week."

"What if Ben wants to attend?"

"Bad idea, but he's entitled to go. He was the husband."

"I'll let you know what his decision is. You'll want to have some security there if he attends."

"Give me a couple of days' notice, please."

"Speaking of Mrs. Williams, did you ask her about Audrey's furniture?"

"Yep. Carl contacted her right after she filed the missing person report. He was very sympathetic. Told her he had the furniture and wanted her to take it. She didn't have any room for it and didn't want it, anyway. He said he would get rid of it for her."

"Interesting way to get some furniture. Keeping it allowed the cabin to be rented as a short-term furnished place." Maggie stifled her sarcasm. "We'd still like to review that missing person report. Do you have it handy?"

"No, but I'll get it for you." He sounded like he was appeasing her.

"It should be very easy to find." She would have to follow up again.

"I know. I just have to send someone down with the properly signed paperwork."

Maggie frowned. "Would you ask Mrs. Williams a couple more questions?"

"Sure, what you got?"

"It looks like Audrey may have moved in a hurry and didn't take her personal possessions. This doesn't match with what Mrs. Williams said about Audrey's planning for several months to move in with her, but let's go with the possibility that Audrey changed her mind and suddenly moved out of town in mid-March."

"She didn't take any of her money."

"Randy said there was a note about her leaving quickly. Let's assume someone wanted her gone. Whoever got her pregnant could've given her money and a new phone and forced her out quickly."

"Where are you going with this?"

"If she made a quick decision, she would've taken clothes, but that's all. What did Carl do with the personal stuff she left behind? We know the furniture stayed in the cabin. Some leftover inventory was given to Claire over at the gift shop, but we want to know what happened to her business records, her remaining clothes, her bedding, her kitchen things, all that kind of stuff. Did Carl deliver these things to Mrs. Williams when he cleaned out the place? Would you ask her about that?"

"Good question. I'm sure there's a reasonable answer."

"There's something else she may know about if she was given Audrey's personal possessions. There's a rumor Audrey kept a diary. Her mother may know about that."

"I'll ask about that too. Where did you hear that rumor? Anything else on your mind?"

"Right now, I have to keep the source quiet, but it's a reliable source. There is something else. It's minor, but I heard Audrey had a cat. Would you ask her if she knows what happened to the cat?"

"Sure. We can't forget about the cat."

Actually, I do have one more issue. You and Charles agreed to postpone questioning Ben until there was more evidence, but you and I talked about a couple of people we should interview. Where does that stand? Shouldn't we bring them in?"

"Remind me who they are."

Maggie was a little stunned that he had not jumped on these witnesses, but she kept her concern to herself. She needed his goodwill. "She had a girlfriend. The name was Stacey. She also talked to Randy Stevenson."

"I'll get on top of those and let you know the interview schedule."

"Can I make a suggestion?"

"Sure."

"Let's get DNA tests on every male we interview. The DNA test is the key right now. Tell them we're doing an elimination process to match a DNA sample from something connected to Audrey. Let them know we expect the results to be negative. If someone refuses to take the test, he becomes a suspect."

"But...Randy? Why would you want to test Randy?"

"We have to start the DNA testing somewhere. Randy was friendly with Audrey. He helped with her garden. A romantic interest wouldn't be out of the question. That would explain the phone calls. Who knows? He could've been angry after being rejected and gotten a little rough with her. If we eliminate Randy from suspicion, he may be more forthcoming. Besides, he lives out there and would've seen any boyfriends coming or going."

"You know who Randy is, don't you?"

"Yes, heir to the Stevenson legacy. We need his cooperation. That's why we need to get him off the suspect list." She wasn't going to expose her suspicions to Logan yet.

"Just keep that in mind, and don't make waves."

When Logan called later to confirm the Monday interviews, he said Randy had refused to take a DNA test, insisting he wasn't a suspect. His refusal cemented Maggie's suspicions.

Logan had also talked to Audrey's mom. Mrs. Williams said she had suggested that Audrey start a diary, but she never heard anything more about it, and she received none of her belongings. She always wondered what happened to them.

"And the cat?" Maggie asked.

"When she went over to the cabin looking for Audrey, she found the cat outside. She picked it up and took it home. Mrs. Williams saved the cat and still has it."

Logan also said that Hank asked for a short appointment on the same morning as the interviews. He was expecting to be confronted and wanted Maggie there as a witness.

CHAPTER 32

Maggie

Monday, September 28, 2020

"Hello Hank, good to see you again," Maggie said, entering Logan's conference room for the interviews. She was wearing a light-gray pantsuit, a purple blouse, and flats.

A table with six brown leather chairs filled the room. Several straight-back wooden chairs lined the walls. Logan had already brought in recording equipment for the later interviews, and Maggie had asked for a water pitcher. She hoped to obtain DNA samples from the saliva.

Hank did not respond. He was already seated, and his Stetson was on the table.

She tried again. "Mrs. Madison was quite helpful. Thank you for setting that up."

He finally nodded. "Good to see you as well." His cold eyes pierced her.

She was seeing his bad side again and wondered how ugly it would get. *Does Hank have the power to stop the investigation? Is he the reason Logan is dragging his feet?*

She gently squeezed Audrey's sachet for comfort.

Logan walked in and sat at the head of the table with Hank on one side and Maggie on the other, as if he was a referee. Maggie casually poured water for each of them. Logan was grateful, but Hank pushed his glass away.

Hank turned to Logan. "Can we talk privately?"

"She represents the defense. She's entitled to be here if there's any discussion about the Stillman case. What's on your mind?"

Hank gave Maggie a stern look. The rebuke did not please him, but he softened his face to a congenial expression, as if Maggie didn't really matter. "I just want to touch base. This case is having an effect on the town, and that concerns me."

"I think we're all concerned," Logan said. "We definitely have a challenge."

"As you already know, my concern is always the citizens and businesses of this community. We're noticing a downturn in retail, especially with out-of-town dollars. People are afraid to visit because no arrest has been made. Logan, we've got a murderer out there, and it's scaring people. If it's Ben Stillman, well, he's up here running around like nobody's business."

Maggie winced. He was lying. Ben hadn't been near the town except for the day he visited his parents to report Audrey's death.

"Anything else?" Logan asked. His tone suggested he also realized Hank was lying.

"There's also the fact that property values and rents out there at Stevenson's Row will go down if we don't get this thing put to bed right away. The folks who bought that cabin site are already asking for a partial refund. They think I should've known about that body and got a raw deal because the property will always have a bad reputation."

He clenched his fists. "The owners of the rental cabins are also up in arms. Their winter bookings are backing out. We need to protect our business interests. It's bad enough we found a body, but it's an issue that we haven't made an arrest."

"I hear you, but sometimes justice is slow." Logan's face was resolute.

"The mayor's telling me there are complications, but he won't give me details." He folded his arms across his chest and spoke with an artificial softness. "If you tell me about these complications, I might be able to help."

"Hank, let's be blunt here. You're like everyone else. You're pushing me to arrest Ben Stillman." The veins along the side of Logan's forehead bulged, showing how hard it was for him to stand up to Hank. "We've got phone and bank records, and the defense team just gave me Ben's credit card statements. We believe Audrey died in mid-March 2017. Ben moved to Salt Lake in August 2016. I can't link him to Audrey's death, and I can't arrest him without probable cause. You know that."

Hank's control over the town was threatened. It showed in his tense demeanor. "I keep telling you that Salt Lake is close enough that Ben could've driven up here in less than an hour. Those cabins are remote enough that he could've done it, buried her, gone home, and no one would've known any better. He's the only one who had a reason to kill her."

Logan's face flushed. Hank had probably just confessed to unlawful interference.

Hank turned to Maggie, venom in his eyes. "Little lady, I know you're doing your best, and I don't have anything against you or Ben personally, but we need to get this murderer off the streets. You know this investigation isn't over. Your defense of Ben will fall apart." He seemed to dismiss her as unimportant to the conversation.

She had not heard the insult "little lady" in years. Her opinion of Hank tanked even further. He was no longer the affable man about town who carried the keys. She became suspicious of his motives, which seemed to be preventing acceptance of social changes and thwarting justice for his own profit.

Logan slapped the table and stood. "Damn it, Hank, I need evidence! No judge in this entire state would sign an arrest warrant on the speculation that you and everyone else are spouting. I would need to impanel a grand jury to get an indictment, and I don't have any evidence. They would laugh me out of the courtroom."

"You want me to talk to the judge privately? See what I can do to get a warrant signed?"

Logan tried hard to maintain control as he finally sat down, but his tone became hardened. "I appreciate the offer, but you know as well as I do that's called obstruction. There may be times when you get away with it in a civil case, but this is a criminal case, and you can't pull that kind of shit. If I were to even ask for an arrest warrant now, you and I would both be in trouble, and there are higher powers than just Madison County who would see to it. You may not have an issue, but I have a law license at stake."

Hank's voice changed. He was going for the jugular. "Logan, don't lose control, old man, but let's drop the BS, okay? You've got too much baggage to keep up this farce. How are we going to get this situation under control? Everyone out there believes Ben Stillman did it."

"Which means we have a tainted jury pool." Logan gestured toward Maggie. "Don't give the defense any ideas about changing the venue. The first thing we need is incriminating evidence. We have something, but we can't talk about it yet. You gotta let me do my job."

"Look at it this way. You're up for reelection in two years. This town is going to remember how you treated this case. You may have to think about retiring. You think that's what your wife and those college kids of yours will want to hear?"

"I've qualified for my full pension, and I'm vested. If I have to retire, then that's the way it is. At least I've kept my oath of office."

Hank leaned back. "Oh, come on, Logan. This case isn't worth your career, is it?"

Logan pushed his chair back and stood again. "Hank, we've been friends for a long time. Let me handle this. This 'little lady,' has been a fine investigator. Best I've ever seen."

Hank rose slowly and faced Maggie. His nose twitched, and his cheeks flushed bright red. "If you're such a good investigator, why haven't you found any evidence against your client? What are you hiding?"

He showed no interest in an answer, snatched up his hat with his boots thudding on the floor. At the door, he turned. "Logan, if that's the way you want it, we'll talk later, privately."

After the door closed, Logan seemed frozen.

While he decompressed, she took a drink of water. "Are you okay?" She closed her hand around the sachet. *Audrey, what just happened? You need to help me with this.*

Maggie glanced at the table where Hank had been sitting. A few hairs had fallen off his hat when he picked it up. Normally, she would have brushed them away, but she hesitated.

Logan stared vacantly into the room and shuffled some papers. His face was pained. "Hank isn't like his father. Carl got things done, but he stayed on the right side of the law. Sometimes he skirted the edges, but he would've never pushed me like that."

She stared at the pieces of hair and wondered if Logan had really seen the light. *Can he be trusted now?* "Logan, we need to test all the Stevensons for DNA, and they're not going to like it. Hank just left us some strands of hair. He's a long shot, but it's not out of the question. We have an opportunity here."

Logan stared at the hair, hesitating before he spoke. "You're right. I'll be right back."

He walked out of the room and returned a few minutes later with two sheets of paper. He folded one and used the other to sweep the strands of hair onto it. He folded it to look like an envelope and smiled. "I got this."

He paused at the door. "I apologize for asking you to be here. I knew it would be rough, and I needed a witness."

Hank had gone too far. She hoped Logan would be a changed man when he left the room.

CHAPTER 33

Maggie

"What's wrong, Logan? Why do you need to see me?" Randy fidgeted uncontrollably when he blew through the door fifteen minutes later. He wouldn't even glance at Maggie. "I'm missing school for this, so it better be important."

"Sit down." Logan, still angry with Hank, paced the floor and barked as if he was talking to a rebellious teenager. He leaned in, turned on the recorder, and put Randy under oath. Pulling out one of the straight-back chairs along the edge of the room, he leaned across the high back and gave a heavy sigh. "Look, you were friends with Audrey. We all know that."

"So what? I didn't kill her. Why aren't you arresting Ben?"

"I'm asking the questions here."

Randy eyed Logan as if he wasn't sure of him anymore. He squirmed. Sweat beaded on his forehead. He clenched his fists and scowled at the recorder. He wiped the sweat from his brow. He was a sheltered man who believed in his own invincibility. He was being accused by a man who had more perceived power than he did, and he didn't know how to react. His swagger usually got him out of difficulties, but it wasn't working.

Maggie poured everyone a glass of water as she watched each of them. With measured deliberate movements, she pulled Audrey's picture out of her case file and placed it on the table. "Randy, tell us a little more about Audrey."

He stared at the picture and turned away, frowning. "What do you want to know?"

She smiled and talked like the wise aunt who knew all the secrets of young men. "It's a small town. People talk. Audrey was pretty. Who did she hang out with after her divorce?" She cocked her head, keeping eye contact.

He avoided looking her in the eye and swiveled to Logan. "I don't know."

Calmed, Logan pushed the wooden chair aside and moved to one of the leather chairs. "Think about it. Is there a bar or a honky-tonk that she went to? You're someone who hears everything. Were there any guys who bragged about dating her? Getting her drunk, maybe? Anyone who bragged about having sex with her?"

Logan understood how to insult Audrey's reputation just enough to get Randy's goat. Maggie used her hand to covered her grin, then reached into her pocket and squeezed her sachet in apology.

Randy grimaced and shifted in his chair. He glared at both of them, but avoided the picture. Torment showed in his tightened muscles. Anger flashed in his eyes. "Is this about someone who had sex with her? You think he's the killer, don't you?" His face turned bright red. "You can't prove anything."

"We've got some DNA we're trying to match," Maggie said.

"She's been dead for almost four years. You ain't got anything." He pushed the glass of water away. "Audrey wasn't that kind of girl."

"What do you mean?"

"She didn't drink beer. She drank tea. She made tea from the plants she grew in her garden." His voice became petulant. "She read books. She stayed home, read, and drank tea."

"With you?"

"Yeah, sometimes." He looked at the wall. Moisture welled up in his eyes. He tried to regain his composure.

Maggie had gotten to him. "You were infatuated with her, but you were too young, weren't you?"

Randy didn't respond. He quietly wiped away a tear. He stared at the center of the table. His hands were clenched so tight his knuckles were white. He reminded Maggie of a cornered animal who still wants to please.

"You told me you helped her with the garden. What did you know about those plants? Did she ever tell you what they were?"

"No. It was just stuff to make tea. I don't know shit about plants, but like I already told you, I helped her clean out the garden in the fall. That's all. She was pretty and nice to be with."

"Did she ask you to help, or did you volunteer?"

"My grandpa asked me to help the first day, and I went back and finished the job."

"When was this, exactly?"

"I started the weekend before Thanksgiving. We finished up a couple of days into Thanksgiving week."

"Did she tell you about the plants? How they could be used in medicine or maybe that some of them were poisonous and you needed to be careful around them?"

He crossed his arms. "No, never. I wouldn't have gone near poisonous plants. I'm not stupid."

"You put a lot into helping her, didn't you? Most people would expect something in return. What did you expect?"

His eyes narrowed. "I didn't expect anything. We were neighbors. I helped out."

Logan jumped in. "Did she hang out with any of your relatives, maybe your older cousins, your uncles, or someone who came over to your grandparents' house?"

"Not that I knew about." His eyes glazed over, and he looked away.

She frowned. *Evasive. Who is he protecting?*

Logan let a long pause settle in before speaking. "Did you ever have sex with her?"

"No." A slow blush rose on Randy's face. He slumped in his chair and looked toward the door. "I was her friend. Don't try to pin this on me."

"Do you know anyone who bragged about having sex with her?" Maggie asked.

"No." Randy tensed. "And I didn't kill her."

"Don't jump to conclusions," Logan said. "We're not accusing you of murder."

Maggie drummed her fingers on the table. "Did you help Audrey move?"

"What do you mean?"

"You told me she left a note for Carl that she was moving. Did you help her move?"

"No."

"How did you know about the note?"

"My grandpa told me."

She sat forward. "Did he tell you this before or after she moved?"

"After, I guess. I don't know when she moved."

"Did your grandpa tell you where she moved to?"

214

"No."

"She left some things behind. Did your grandpa ask you to help move those things?"

He hesitated. "No."

She straightened. "You're sure about that? Your grandpa asked you to help with the garden, and later he told you about the note, but he didn't ask you to help clean out her cabin?"

Randy's face hardened. "That's right. What do you want from me, anyway?"

Maggie remained calm. "How about helping us make a list of the men in your family who might have had some contact with her?" She handed a yellow legal pad to Logan.

"Why just my family? Why do you have it in for us? Why not all the men around here? Isn't that who you're looking for?"

"We're starting with your family because the Stevensons live out there," she said.

Logan wrote Randy's name at the top as if he hadn't objected. "Okay, we know you had contact. Not sexual, just contact. You visited. You had phone conversations with her."

"What did you talk about on those phone calls?" Maggie asked.

"Not much." He stopped for a moment as if remembering. "Mostly, we just talked about me helping her with the garden."

Logan wrote the names Carl and Hank. "Your grandpa must have had some contact. He was the landlord. Hank must have also known her."

Randy said nothing. His stare suggested he knew something he didn't want to tell, but his back was up against the wall.

Logan looked up. "Who are your male cousins, your age or older? Your first cousins and second cousins who live around here."

Randy ignored him. "That DNA you have. You know it's a guy?"

"Yes," Logan said.

"You know anything else about it?"

"Let me ask the questions, okay?"

Randy huffed. "There's George and Kevin on my dad's side. And Barry, Manny, and Louis on my mom's side, but they're too young."

Logan wrote the names down. "Do they all live in Madison County?"

"Yes."

"Next generation up. Who are your uncles?"

"Jimmy and Eddy. None on my mom's side."

Logan studied the list. "Who on this list would've come around your place out there in the woods in 2016 and 2017?"

Randy shrugged. "Probably my dad's brothers, Jimmy and Eddy. Jimmy would come over to talk about the ranch." He lowered his gaze. "Eddy, well, Eddy just has a hard time with a lot of things. I think he might have been staying out there around the time Ben left, maybe a little later. He knew Audrey."

"Say that again. Eddy was staying with your grandparents when Audrey was living there alone?" Logan shook his head.

"Yes."

"Did he hang out with Audrey?"

"No. I never heard that. Never saw anything. I said he knew who she was."

Logan stood. "Randy, this is a good list. It gives us something to start with. Thank you for being cooperative.

We need to check out these names, but we'll most likely clear these guys. We'd probably clear you too if you did the DNA test."

"It would be in your best interest to clear your name," Maggie said.

"I didn't kill her. I'm not a suspect, and I don't need to clear my name."

Logan leaned forward. "This is important, son. Can we count on you to stay quiet about everything we've talked about?"

"Sure." Randy rose and grabbed his hat from a chair. "That's all you need from me?" He moved quickly to the door. "You're the boss. I won't talk to anyone."

After the door closed, Logan sighed. "What do you think?"

Maggie sipped her water. "He acted exactly like the son of the most powerful man in town. He wasn't going to tell us anything until you insulted Audrey's reputation. Then he came around and defended her. He's too nervous. He knows more than he's letting on. We don't know if there was more contact than the gardening incident, but I suspect there was. He obviously had feelings for her. He tensed up when you asked about having sex with her, but doesn't want to admit it or get caught. He got emotional when we suggested the DNA might be someone else."

She swirled her remaining water. "He could've made the tea and accidentally used the wrong herbs, or it could've been deliberate." She set her glass down. "Final thing. I think he lied about helping his grandpa move Audrey's things. It was written all over his face and his demeanor changed. He knows what happened to her stuff. However, it looks like she stopped talking to him in December, and we think she died in March. If they kept talking or if she told him she was pregnant, it was face to face. We can't make a connection with her death unless we can prove ongoing contact. Living in the neighborhood isn't good enough."

"Good points. There's no sense in ruining his reputation when he has a wife and a big future in this town."

"What do you know about Eddy?"

"Eddy should be settled down by now, but he's always been a drifter. He was out at the ranch and got into a brawl with Jimmy, so he stayed with his parents for a while. That's what Randy was talking about. Then Carl finally forced them to work out their differences. That hasn't worked out well, and Hank's trying to figure out what to do now."

"Eddy seems to have a bad reputation with women. We need to talk to him and get his DNA. Any chance we could get him in for an interview?"

"You really think it was one of the Stevensons?" Logan's voice betrayed his fear.

"It's beginning to look like that. Maybe not the killer, but possibly the father."

"Eddy's not easy to get along with. I'll ask, and if that doesn't work, I'll subpoena him. If we clear Randy and Eddy, we have to go after the cousins, which doesn't excite me at all."

"How many male cousins would be the right age?"

"Carl's nephew died in a horse accident a few years back. He had two sons, George and Kevin, who would be the right age. They both live out near the ranch."

"What do they look like? How likely is it they would've been around Audrey?"

"George is pretty hefty. His wife's a good cook. Kevin, the younger one, is tall and thin. Dark hair. Not married. Both would've gone over to Carl's place occasionally."

"Does Kevin usually wear a white hat and does he have a bad leg?"

"Yep."

"Robert told me about him. He was one of the cowboys who stopped me on the sidewalk."

"I wouldn't put it past him. He's a little rowdy. Got himself shot once. Hangs out with Eddy. I'm not sure what's going on with him. I'll find out." Logan rubbed his face. Finally, he pulled Ben's credit card statement out of a folder. He had circled the charge for gas that Ben had purchased in Ogden. "Do you have an explanation for this?"

"I saw that when Ben brought his statements in. He doesn't recall why he was in Ogden, but he's researching his records. I'll touch base with him and see what he has and get back to you. However, he's certain he didn't go to Madison County that day."

"You know I can easily argue that he had the time to drive over and kill Audrey. I think this makes my case."

"Let's see what his explanation is before we jump to conclusions. May I use your office to call him?"

"Certainly." Logan escorted her to his office and unlocked the door.

CHAPTER 34

Maggie

Ben answered Maggie's call right away. "I've worked it out. Just getting the documents together for you. At my brokerage firm, we have a client who was in town and needed to go to Ogden. I was his transportation. It was an all-day trip."

"Tell me the whole story."

"Our client is from Utah, and we've handled his investments for many years. He lives in California now. He's a doctor and was invited as a panelist for a workshop at Weber State University on March 18. As a courtesy, my boss offered his Mercedes, and I was the driver. He needed to be there by ten o'clock. I picked him up from his hotel at nine and drove him up. The meeting was in the student union building, and I hung out while the workshop was in progress. It ended around four o'clock, and I drove him directly to the airport. I had to get gas before leaving Ogden."

"What documentation do you have?"

"I found my old calendar and some emails. I also have an expense reimbursement for the gas money."

"The doctor will need to be a witness on your behalf if we go to trial."

"That can be arranged. I've asked him if he has any old records showing that he attended the conference. He's still looking for it."

"Good. What did you and the doctor do for lunch?"

"Dr. McKenzie invited me to their luncheon. As I recall, it started at 12:30."

"You know the DA will do everything in his power to disprove your story. It's the only evidence he has against you."

"I know."

"I need to see your documentation and go over the details with you. Would you be able to come to my condo on Saturday? You should plan to stay for a couple of hours."

She provided him with her address, and they set a time to meet before she connected with Logan to give him Ben's explanation.

CHAPTER 35

Audrey

Friday, September 2, 2016

Dear diary, I can't even trust my best friend for advice because she's never had this happen, so I'm talking to you.

I went down to pay the rent today and was almost at the bend in the road when Carl climbed up from the river. Carl's the landlord. He's always been friendly, and he recently offered to help me with local deliveries when he goes into town.

I gave him the check and started walking back, but he could see I wasn't in a good mood. Anyway, he started walking with me and asked how I was doing. Well, I had to tell him the truth. I couldn't hide it. I told him Ben left me and I was upset. He was very understanding, I must say, and I just kept talking. You know me!

I told him I was trying to figure out what to do. Like I've told you, I think I should move in with my mom to save on the rent. After all, she's by herself and would like the company. I would have to rebuild the garden, which would be a pain, and

*I can't move the plants right now. There is room in her base-
ment for a small shop too, but I can't face doing it right now.*

*I kept walking and talking with Carl, and pretty soon we
were at my place, and I invited him in for a cup of tea. I've had
Grammy for tea many times, but I've never had Carl, so it
seemed a little strange.*

*We must have talked for an hour, and I ended up telling
him why Ben left. I was so incredibly embarrassed, but he
took it in stride. I told him I'm worried about what people
will think. It was so good to have someone to talk to, and
he seems like he really cares. I've had such a shock that I'm
barely able to endure it, and I haven't yet told Grammy the
reason because she's so old-fashioned and might think less
of me.*

*Before he left, Carl gave me a hug, and I broke down and
cried on his shoulder. He told me he understood how things
were and I shouldn't worry about the rent for a few months.
Can you believe that? No rent! I couldn't thank him enough
and cried again out of happiness. I can stay here over the
winter and move my plants in the spring.*

*No one has come to my place since Ben left, and now I've
actually had a visitor. I hope I'm doing the right thing by
talking to him. It feels so good to have a friend.*

CHAPTER 36

Audrey

Wednesday, October 5, 2016

Dear diary, Carl has stopped by several times in the past month just to see how I'm doing. The first time, he brought some logs for my woodpile. He said he had more than enough for the winter. The second time, he wanted to see what needed to be fixed. He didn't try any funny business with me. I think he just wants to be friends.

I was in my garden yesterday, and his truck pulled up again. He brought several bags of fertilizer and mulch. He always stays for tea. He's started telling me stories about his life and the places he's been. He's gone to Wyoming many times, and he's even been to Montana!

It took a while before he told me how much he appreciated my hugs. I wonder if I should be hugging him, but I also need hugs. I've been very lonely without Ben.

It took even longer for him to tell me how lonely he's been. Can you imagine? Carl, who is popular with everyone, said he was lonely? He loves his wife, but she became withdrawn after she had a mastectomy twenty years ago and hasn't allowed him to touch her for more than ten years. He says he longs for physical affection so badly he can hardly stand it. I had no idea what was going on between them. I'm so willing to hug him, and his hugs are getting to be more frequent and more intense. He's actually kissed me on the forehead!

He's just a lonely man because he hasn't tried anything else besides friendly hugs and forehead kisses, so I feel safe. Besides, he's too old, and he's married. I guess I just appreciate his company because I'm lonely, too.

I'm feeling a little guilty because I haven't been to see Grammy recently. I'm not sure what I should tell her about these visits because I know too much about them, but I'm so looking forward to having Carl come for tea. He makes me feel good about myself again.

CHAPTER 37

Audrey

Wednesday, November 2, 2016

Dear diary, last Saturday, the weather was still warm, so we had our weekly gathering at the patio as a Halloween party. It was all the regular people and a couple of the summer families, so it was quite a group for this late in the season. Anyway, Carl and Grammy were both there, but so was their son, Eddy, who's been staying with them.

I don't like saying bad things about people, but Eddy creeps me out! I was sitting next to Grammy. Last week, I finally told her everything about when Ben left, and she was concerned about me, but then Eddy interrupted.

Eddy is tall like his dad, but his hair is black. His eyes are a piercing black, and his skin is tanned from being outside so much. He's also very muscular, but that's because he usually works at the ranch. He scares me. I don't know why Eddy has been around for the past few months, but it's like having a shadow.

"Well, you're by yourself now, ain't you?" he said.

Diary, that's not what you say to someone who is alone in the woods and doesn't like living by herself. What did he expect me to say?

I tried to be polite, but he just kept pushing it. He finally asked me if I would like to go into town and get a beer. I told him, "No, thank you," and left. I was really annoyed because Grammy's my good friend.

Eddy came to the door the next day, and it was bad. I guess that's why I'm writing now. I still need to get my wits together. He had a six-pack with him and wanted to come in. I said no, but he pushed his way in, sat at the table, and acted like it was okay. He drank a beer and stood up, and I knew he was coming for me.

I was able to get out the door. I ran to the sheriff's house and banged on the door. No one was home, so I stayed on the porch. I would have screamed if he came near. He finally left my place and got into his truck. As he passed, he lowered the window and shouted at me.

I don't know what he said. After he was far enough away, I ran home and locked all the doors and windows. I'm really afraid of that monster!

On Monday, I told Carl about Eddy. He apologized and said it wouldn't happen again. I'm still not over it, but I trust Carl to keep him away.

CHAPTER 38

Audrey

Friday, November 25, 2016

Dear diary, Randy came over with Carl last Saturday. Carl asked him to help clean out my garden. A lot of plants need to be cut back. I've been working on them, but Carl wanted me to have help. I tossed Randy some gloves, and we went to work.

I've seen him around since he was a kid and even talked to him once in a while. He's always been pretty decent. Anyway, Randy and I worked out a plan and got a good start.

On Monday, Randy came by himself because he didn't have classes during Thanksgiving week. We got the work done, but it was cold, so we went inside for tea. I watched him grow up, so when he flirted with me, it felt weird. He got back from the army a few months ago, so I think he's around twenty-five or twenty-six and still trying to figure out how to grow up.

On Tuesday, Randy came again, and we finished the work. This time, he brought some beer. The beer was nice enough, but I guess it made him aggressive, and I'm just not used to it. I let my defenses down because I was a little drunk and a lot tired of being alone. He tried to talk me into just lying on the bed because we were exhausted. When I said no, he picked me up and carried me in. I protested, but that didn't help, and he was too strong to fight. One thing led to another. I wanted to sleep, but he had other ideas. It didn't feel right, and I tried to get away, but it just made him more determined. I can't write it here, as it was too disgusting, but I will tell you that he pinned me down until he finished.

When he was standing next to the bed afterward, I told him to get out of my house and not to come back. I was really ashamed and humiliated. I shouldn't have drunk that beer.

I don't think I should tell Carl about this. He'll think I did it on purpose.

CHAPTER 39

Maggie

Monday, September 28, 2020

Logan escorted Stacey Lighthouse to the conference room thirty minutes after Randy left and introduced her to Maggie. She was fortyish, medium height, trim, and dressed in a faded denim jacket, pink turtleneck, and Levi's. Her blond ponytail bobbed from a pink baseball cap. She brought her own large coffee. Her hands clenched the cup, suggesting she was fearful.

Maggie intentionally took a seat across from her and adjusted Audrey's picture so Stacey could see it clearly.

Logan turned on the tape recorder and went through the usual routine. "Stacey, I've known you a long time. I'm sorry to tell you that the body out there by the river was Audrey Stillman."

"I saw in the paper that she was ID'd. She'd been my best friend since high school." Her voice quivered a little, and her eyes watered. She barely held back tears.

"I know." He rustled papers. "I called you in because I thought you might be able to help with information about her." He glanced up. "We believe she died in March 2017. We're looking at the last nine months of her life. That's when her life changed quite a bit. When did you last see or talk to Audrey?"

"A week or so before she disappeared, she told me she was getting ready to move to her mom's place."

"Did she ever talk to you about her marriage falling apart?"

Stacey kept her eyes down, avoiding the picture. She wiped away a tear and looked up. "We talked about once a week. She was angry when Ben left. She cried for about a month."

"Stacey," Maggie said softly, "Audrey's death isn't just a statistic. She still had many years ahead of her to keep being your friend. She was also her mother's only child. We know you were left with many unanswered questions because no one knew what happened. We're trying to find those answers. We need to sort out who she was spending time with those last few months. Do you know anyone who became close to her?" Maggie planned to lead the conversation to Randy.

Stacey put her elbows on the table; her chin rested on her left palm. "I don't remember anyone in particular. She just started getting on with her life. She started socializing."

"Did she begin dating?"

Stacey slowly shook her head. "Not that I can remember. I think she started hanging with the people out there at the cabins. You know, going down to the river for the group dinner and stuff. I remember she went to the Christmas party." She took a long drink of coffee. Her hand shook, and her bracelets jangled. "She came over to my place a couple of times after Ben left. My husband babysat, and we went out to eat, just us girls."

"Was she hanging out with Randy Stevenson?"

She brought her coffee cup to her lips before speaking. "Him? I think they were friendly, but, you know, he was too young for her." She glanced at Audrey's picture.

"Did she have a boyfriend?"

"Before Ben left? Nope, she wasn't that type. Afterward, not anyone I knew."

Maggie noticed how carefully she spoke, how nervous she was, and how little information she gave. She had not answered the question about Randy, and she evaded the question about other boyfriends.

"You know, Stacey." Maggie sat forward in her chair. She placed her elbows on the table, her chin in her palm, and waited for eye contact. "Sometimes you can tell when your girlfriend has a secret she isn't ready to tell yet. Have you ever noticed that?"

Stacey tensed. "What d'you mean?" She looked down, cupped both hands around her coffee, and stole a glance at Audrey's picture.

"I'm not implying anything specific, but when you're close friends with someone, you know things from the way the person acts. For instance, when Audrey disappeared, everyone said she had moved out of town. Did you believe that?"

Stacey stared at an easel at the back of the room. Her hand covered her mouth.

"I get the impression you didn't believe it."

Stacey shook her head.

"You think someone was lying about that, don't you?"

"Yes."

"We're like that too. We think someone's lying about who killed her. You could be the key to identifying that killer." Maggie picked up the photo of Audrey. "This is the Audrey you knew, isn't it?" She put it directly in front of Stacey. "What happened after Ben left?"

Stacey flinched. She glowered at Logan.

Logan looked away and seemed to ignore her.

Stacey turned her gaze to Maggie. She bit her lip. She stared at the photo, quickly looked away, and came back with a nervous stutter. "After a while...there was something different about her. I couldn't put my finger on it."

"What did it seem like? When did this change happen?"

"She said her life was going to improve a lot, but she wouldn't tell me anything more. It was a month or so before she disappeared." Stacey's hands loosened on the coffee cup.

"Could you guess? Did it have to do with moving? Did she have a boyfriend she was going to move in with?"

Stacey leaned forward on the table. She frowned. "Look, I'm not going to tell tales about someone who's dead, especially someone who was my best friend. I don't know the facts. Anything else is just speculation, and I'm not going to speculate."

Maggie mimicked Stacey's posture and sat forward with crossed arms. "Okay, not a problem. How about this? Let me toss out a couple of ideas, and you tell me what you think."

Stacey's stare was blank. Her hand trembled as she drained her cup.

Maggie looked up at a corner of the room and spoke as if she was pulling an idea out of thin air. Her plan was to reel Stacey in. "She had a boyfriend, and she was going to move in with him and get married?"

Stacey's expression didn't change.

"Let's try this one. She had a boyfriend. She knew something about him he didn't want to be known, and he was going to pay her a lot of money to keep quiet?"

Stacey frowned.

"Here's another one. She had a boyfriend. She was pregnant, and the boyfriend was going to leave his wife and marry her?"

Stacey's face flushed bright red. She sat back in her chair.

Bingo. She knew. Maggie was quick to catch her off guard. "How many children do you have?"

Stacey glared at the table, defeated, and clasped her empty cup with both hands. "Five."

"You know when your friends are pregnant, don't you?" Maggie picked up the photo. "They don't have to tell you."

Stacey didn't respond.

"Do you know who the father was?"

Stacey glanced up, paused, and finally shook her head.

"Can you guess?"

Stacey shook her head more slowly. Her eyes focused on the center of the table.

Maggie watched her intently. She had her answer. Stacey either knew who the father was or had a very strong suspicion. It was time to stop pushing. The next time they talked would clinch it. "If the father wasn't happy about it, he's the most likely suspect in Audrey's death. Would you continue to think about it and come back if you remember anything else that could be important?"

"Yes." Stacey exhaled; her body relaxed. She raised an eyebrow at Logan. "Can I go now?"

Logan nodded. She quietly stood, tossed her empty cup in the trash, and left.

After the door closed, Logan turned to Maggie. "When I asked her to come in, she was scared, and I promised her it would be easy. You were pretty rough. How did you know she knew about the pregnancy?"

"It's a thing with women. There's a signal out there in the universe. If you've ever been pregnant, you know when your best friend is pregnant." Standing, Maggie recognized the lack of understanding in his expression and put Audrey's picture back in her case file.

"Logan, I'd like to have another chat with Stacey, but I'd like to make it off the record, and I'll go easy on her. You know, just girl talk. She knows who the father was, and I may be able to get her to say the name off the record."

"I have no problem with you talking to her again, but if she gives up the name, let me know immediately, even if she wants it kept quiet." She agreed, and he gave her Stacey's phone number.

"Would you email these transcripts as soon as you have them?" She put her sunglasses on her head and texted Robert. With a smile at Logan, she walked toward the door. "I'm meeting Robert for lunch."

CHAPTER 40

Maggie

Within five minutes, Robert pulled up. Maggie asked him to take her to the gift shop.

He grinned, his eyes twinkling. "Forgot to tell you this morning, but you sure do look good all dressed up. It's okay if I admire you, isn't it?"

She laughed. "Of course it is! Thank you." She appreciated his compliment and had been looking forward to the warmth of his smile. Before getting out, she gave him a quick kiss. "Don't go far. I'll miss you."

Maggie opened the shop's door and gave a small wave. "Hello, Claire!" She browsed while Claire finished with a customer.

Claire came over quickly. "On the phone, you said you needed some important records from me. What are you looking for?"

Maggie gently touched her on the arm. "First, some news. We have the coroner's report. Audrey died from drinking a poisonous herbal tea. We don't know how or why, but we know the herb."

"I'm so sorry to hear that." She wiped a sudden tear.

"I'm trying to find out if she ever purchased the plant." Maggie waited for Claire to absorb the news and spoke gently. "You told me you and Audrey shared orders from your herb catalog. Would you tell me more?"

"They required us to place a minimum order. I didn't need that much, and neither did Audrey, so we would combine our orders, and she would pay me when the order came in."

"How far back do your records go?"

"I'm a small business. Keeping the records isn't a problem. I pulled out the information you asked for." She brought up a banker's box of records from under the counter. "This box is 2016. The boxes for 2015, 2014, and 2013 are in the back."

"Do you remember if Audrey ever ordered a belladonna plant? She might have used it to make a skin salve."

"I didn't pay much attention to her orders, but I can look for it." She thumbed through the catalog invoices from the 2016 box. Not finding anything, she went to her back room.

Claire emerged quickly, holding two files. She showed Maggie how Audrey's orders were identified on the invoices with a large A. "Look at this. In September 2014, she ordered a book on making herbal remedies and salves." Claire picked up the second file. "In March 2015, she ordered live root plants for arnica, Saint-John's-wort, lavender, belladonna, and foxglove."

"Good work!" Maggie examined the invoices. "She had the plant. It's still a puzzle, though. We know she was poisoned, but we don't know who gave her the tea or why." She glanced up. "Thank you, Claire. You've been extremely helpful." She asked for copies, and Claire made them quickly. "I'll stay in touch and let you know if anything develops."

Maggie waved a friendly goodbye and found where Robert was waiting.

CHAPTER 41

Maggie

Maggie settled into the Jeep. "I usually don't eat beef, but I'll try some of your western food. Where's the best hamburger in town?"

"The local places get their meat from Hank's ranch. They're all good. Best grass-fed steer in the state. Special wholesale prices for being a local."

He drove several blocks and parked at an old diner on the frontage road. They went inside and found a table.

After making sure no one was too close, Maggie said, "I know he's your old friend, but Hank did some serious backroom politicking this morning. He threatened Logan."

Robert frowned. "Any idea why?"

"Nope. He was a bit difficult when I first met him, but I thought we got past it. Looks like being a bully is the way he operates around here when things don't go his way." She stopped while the waitress came, took their order, and left.

"He didn't use to be that way. Any idea what Logan might do?"

"Not sure, but I hope he steps up the pace on the case. I have my own ideas about who the suspects are, but I can't get Logan's full attention."

"What do you mean?" He handed her a bunch of paper napkins as the food arrived. "We don't see city clothes up here all that often. Don't spill the ketchup."

"You're a sweetheart!" Taking the napkins, she smiled. "It was illegal pressure to arrest Ben. I'm not going to repeat what he said, but he's worried about something. Logan surprised me and stood up to him. I can now understand why Logan has been dragging his feet and why he wanted me as a witness."

Robert rubbed the back of his neck. "What did you find out about the plant?"

"Audrey bought a belladonna plant in early 2015. I've got copies of the invoices." She reached for the Heinz bottle, doused her fries, and sprinkled them with salt and pepper.

He looked at her plate. "What happened to all the healthy eating?"

"Oh, Lordy. After the morning I had, I need good comfort food. I forgot how draining it is to question witnesses." She feigned guilt as she picked up a fry soaked in ketchup and leaned over to eat without dripping.

"What do you make of the interviews?" He took his first bite of an overstuffed hamburger. A piece of lettuce fell on the table. He picked it up and put it on his plate.

"Hank is worried about something, and maybe it's just because we're interviewing Randy and Hank's protecting him. Randy knows something, but he isn't willing to tell. And I think Stacey knows who the father is, and she isn't telling. I was a little hard on her, but I'm going to change the scenery and talk to her again to see what happens."

She ate a few more fries. "We've established that Audrey had the plant. Now we need to know who knew about it. Was it an accidental poisoning? Did she drink the tea intentionally, or did someone else give it to her? Did someone poison her because she was pregnant? And last but not least, who buried her?" She licked the ketchup off her fingers.

He smiled. "That's quite a mouthful of questions. You'll do it, though. You're Nancy Drew who finds all the answers."

"How do you know about Nancy Drew?" Maggie asked between bites. "Those books were for girls."

"I have two daughters, remember? For many years, I read to them every night. Also, Sherlock Holmes. I still have some of those books at the cabin."

"You're amazing! You read to your kids?"

"By the light from the fireplace. Just like Abraham Lincoln." His wide grin and sparkling eyes teased her.

She stopped eating for a moment as she hid her feelings. Her father never read to his children. He had been an angry, aloof man who demanded obedience. She became estranged from both of her parents at an early age and retreated into the quiet world of books. A local librarian had encouraged her. In Maggie's effort to escape her reality, Nancy Drew became her hero.

"You hesitated to take on this case." He brought her back. "How are you feeling now?"

She looked inward for a moment. "It feels good to be back in the game, as long as we don't have any extra deaths. Being on the defense side instead of the prosecution side has its advantages because we don't have to prove the case, just defend against whatever the DA has."

"Another question. You were bothered because of a mysterious cry coming from Audrey's grave. Does that still bother you?"

Maggie sighed. "I still hear her, but in a different way."

A puzzled look crossed his face.

She spoke carefully. "This isn't something I usually tell people, but I can trust you. I always tried to feel the inner spirit of my rape and abuse victims. Sometimes I was able to get a small object that belonged to them, and I would hold it as I prepared a case. I took it to trial with me. I needed to feel the connection. I always thought it helped. That was just my quirk."

She gauged his nonverbal response. He didn't look astonished, so she continued. "The first time I went to Claire's gift shop, she had the last remaining item that Audrey made, and I bought it." She reached into her purse. "I have it with me every day." She showed him the sachet. "Sometimes I have it in my pocket, sometimes in my purse."

She put the sachet back. "You probably thought I was just a tough ole broad with a vendetta against men who abuse women. I'm really a know-it-all mystic." She smiled apologetically at her flippant tone and turned to the window. "After we visited Audrey's grave, I realized what the cry was. Audrey's spirit was asking me to take the case, begging me. I talk to her sometimes when I'm alone and puzzled about something. It's like having a special friend. I'm not sure she hears me, but it helps me understand her case."

He smiled. "I think it's your intuition you're talking to. It's telling you the truth and hoping you hear. You listen for everything. That's what makes you good at what you do."

"Two weeks ago, when I stayed at your cabin, I thought I saw Audrey's ghost. She was in a long cape the way Randy described her at the picnic. She pointed to a plant. That was a clue. The following week, Logan told me she was poisoned by a belladonna plant. It may have been my intuition, but it turned out to be very real."

He became thoughtful. "I believe you. I believe there could be spirits out there, but a lot of people will think you're nuts if you talk about it."

"I know." She sighed. "Sometimes when I stop and listen carefully, I find answers I hadn't thought about. I think Audrey's spirit is trying to tell me things I need to know."

She picked up her hamburger. She had said enough. He probably thought she was crazy.

"Can I make a suggestion?" he asked.

"Sure."

"Getting hints from Audrey is a good thing, but we don't want your credibility to go out the window. May I suggest you use the word *intuition* to describe what you hear? I'll understand what you're saying, and Logan Harris won't think you're nuts."

She chuckled. "Our secret?"

"Agreed. Do you think you'll hear from her again?"

"If I listen closely enough."

CHAPTER 42

Maggie

Wednesday, September 30, 2020

Maggie's appointment with Stacey was in Medford, and Robert had received a phone call from his secret contact and wanted to follow up in person. Before he dropped her off, they stopped at a coffee shop and loaded up with two large coffees and chocolate croissants for Maggie to take to Stacey's. They found Stacey's home easily, an older one-story brick rancher that had assorted bicycles, tricycles, and toys in the fenced yard. When Maggie rang the bell, a dog barked.

Stacey answered the door and invited her into a kitchen that showed signs of a hurried breakfast. Maggie dressed in torn jeans and a T-shirt, hoping she was portraying herself in a way that Stacey would find more trustworthy.

"Very sorry," Stacey said. "Do you mind if I finish cleaning up?"

"Not at all." Maggie smiled, remembering those days with her two children.

Stacey rushed to put away cereal boxes and load the dishwasher. Maggie asked about her husband and children, who ranged in age from six to fifteen. Her husband worked for the county as a fireman, and the kids were all in school.

Maggie coaxed the dog over and petted him.

Finally, Stacey sat at the kitchen table.

"Stacey," Maggie said gently, "I apologize for being hard on you the other day. I don't work for the DA. I work for the lawyer who represents Ben Stillman. We believe Ben isn't the one who killed Audrey, and we're trying to find the real reason she died. You knew Audrey was pregnant, and it wasn't Ben's child. We believe the father of her child probably isn't the murderer, but will know who the killer is."

Stacey nervously sipped her coffee until it was gone. "All of this is really hard on me. Couldn't Ben have killed her when he found out someone else was the father? Did you think about that?" She hesitated, as if she knew it wasn't a good argument.

"Ben moved out in August. He lived in Salt Lake. The divorce was finalized in November. She died the following March. If they were divorced, why would he care if she got pregnant?"

Stacey was silent.

"We have other suspects."

Stacey poured another cup from her coffeepot. "Who?"

"I can't reveal that right now. I'm hoping you'll give us a little more assistance so we don't target the wrong man. Please be assured that anything that comes up today will be confidential and completely off the record."

Stacey returned to the table. She pulled her croissant apart and nibbled on it.

"Tell me a little more about how Audrey's marriage crumbled."

Stacey was more relaxed than in the interview. "It was good in the beginning, but they disconnected, I guess you would say. It was a slow change. No one really noticed. She was faithful to Ben until he left. When she found out he was gay, we went to a bar to talk about it. She didn't want anything to do with men for a while."

"How did she handle the divorce?"

She gave Maggie a quick, angry glance. "How would you handle it? She was in love with him. She committed her life to their marriage. It wasn't like he had someone else and just didn't want to be with her." Her voice hardened. "What he really said was their marriage had been a fraud for fifteen years."

Maggie took a long sip of coffee. She wondered whether she should share one of her most private experiences. She decided to risk it. "I understand the anger you're talking about. I fell in love with a gay man when I lived in San Francisco. He knew he was gay, and he wanted to maintain our friendship without being dishonest, but that didn't stop my feelings."

"Well, at least you knew." Stacey stared. "How can you be in love with a gay man?"

"Love doesn't have borderlines. He was a fantastic person. We worked together and became friends in the late 1970s when people first started being open about it, probably the way it is now in Medford. It was awkward sometimes."

Maggie had a moment of melancholy. "He became like an uncle to my kids. I wanted him to be their stepfather, but he wasn't interested. It was hard to give him up." She closed her eyes.

"Did you finally break it off?"

"He died of AIDS."

"I'm sorry." Stacey's tension relaxed with her compassion.

"You can't get to be as old as I am and not have experienced loss. Grief comes alongside the birthday cakes."

Stacey drank her coffee. "I knew Ben in high school. He didn't seem gay then or when they were married. After Ben told her, Audrey was afraid. She went to Salt Lake and got tested for AIDS. I drove her."

"How did she handle the divorce?" Maggie asked again.

"You really want to know? She believed they would be together forever, have kids, and live in a three-bedroom house with bicycles in the driveway. Suddenly, she was thirty-six and didn't have a husband. She didn't have kids. She didn't even have nieces and nephews. She couldn't support herself on her business income."

Stacey became lost in her thoughts. Maggie waited patiently.

"There was a point where she couldn't go on." Stacey choked back her emotions. "She wanted to die." She reached for a napkin and wiped her eyes.

"Did she consider suicide?"

"I don't think so, but she didn't know what to do. I was calling her almost every day. I think she started a diary and wrote a lot about it."

"What made her feel better?"

Stacey hesitated. "She met someone. He gave her hope. He was someone special, but she wouldn't tell me who it was. She said it would cause a scandal."

Did Audrey withhold the name, or is Stacey the one keeping it a secret?

"How did she change?"

"Well, she was always into poetry and dressing old-fashioned. She was even into Shakespeare for a while.

When she met this new guy, she started talking like a princess who was being rescued, stuff like that, a little wacky. She said he was her Prince Charming."

"When did she start seeing him?"

"I'm trying to remember. Ben left in the summer. Audrey was pretty messed up for a couple of months. She started seeing this new guy before the divorce was final. You said she was three months pregnant in March?"

"Yes."

"That would be about right. I remember when she told me they finally had sex. I think it was during the holidays. She was crazy about him."

"Why did she keep his name a secret?"

Stacey stared for a moment. When she turned to Maggie, her gaze was guarded. "He was married."

"Did she expect him to leave his wife?"

"I think so. I kept telling her it really didn't work that way in real life, but she thought it would happen for her."

"Do you know who it was?"

"I think so." Her voice quivered.

"Would you give me a hint? If I gave you names, would you confirm or deny?"

Stacey had relaxed while remembering Audrey, but she became nervous. "I can't. I can't bring Audrey back by telling, and you haven't proved that he killed her. I'm having a hard time believing that."

Her breathing became rapid. "All I can say is a lot of lives would be destroyed if his name became public, including my own. My family would be punished. My husband would probably lose his job. My kids would be shunned. I can't bring that down on us." Her eyes pleaded. "You have to understand that. My husband and I were born and raised here. It's not like we would have any place to go."

Maggie couldn't push any more, or she would lose Stacey's cooperation. "I imagine it's hard to live knowing that this happened to your best friend."

"Yes, but I don't think he killed her. I can't tell you why, but in my gut, I just don't believe it. Someone else did it."

"It's not illegal to get someone pregnant. It would've been inconvenient and probably embarrassing if he was married, but that's not a crime. I'll trust you with what you think happened. If you feel certain, then I'm all right with it. If you can help us more, we would appreciate it. There are ways of keeping information confidential."

She cleared her throat. "Logan Harris and I believe that if we can identify the father of Audrey's baby, we'll be able to link that information to the actual killer." *I want that name more than anything else, but I have to play along with Stacey.*

Stacey didn't respond.

"I appreciate the time you've spent with me today." Maggie stood. "I have a better understanding of your situation." Maggie sent a text to Robert.

Stacey escorted her to the door. "Thank you for not pushing any harder. I'm having a hard time with Audrey's death right now. If you come up with something that won't ruin my family, call me, and I'll tell you more."

As they reached the door, Stacey said, "I got word the other day that Audrey will be buried soon."

"I expect Ben to be there as well. He'll have law enforcement escorts."

Robert's Jeep rounded the corner, and Maggie said a warm goodbye.

Stacey had confirmed much of what Maggie already knew. The father of Audrey's child was someone important in the community, but she still didn't have a name.

She squeezed Audrey's sachet. She needed help.

CHAPTER 43

Robert

Once Maggie was in the Jeep, Robert said, "I had a good conversation with my source. Let's grab an early lunch and talk someplace private. Where would you like to eat?"

"Subway. There's one over by that hamburger place."

"You're on."

"I'm all yours for two hours before the interview with Eddy."

He grinned. *I wish you were all mine, period.*

After they got sandwiches, he drove to a small, old cemetery and found a secluded spot in the parking lot. "These people won't eavesdrop, will they?" He grinned as he stopped the engine and turned sideways. "Today, I'm Sherlock Holmes at his best. I picked up something of interest, and I have a present for you."

"Well, don't leave me hanging!"

"I'm still not naming sources, and I don't have details, but it's worth following up on." Robert unwrapped his sandwich. "We all know how the Stevensons like to brag.

It's part of being rich and powerful, I guess." He shook his head. "Hank's youngest brother, Eddy, brags a lot when he's drunk. There's a bartender who's been listening to him for years."

He took a couple of bites. "This is background, so stay with me. Eddy has always been a problem. Basically, when he was born, Grammy wasn't doing all that well physically, so his sisters raised him, and he became a bully to show he was tough. He got into a lot of trouble in high school. Later, Jimmy kicked him off the ranch, and he stayed with his parents. Then something happened. No one knows what it was, but Eddy was suddenly back at the ranch, and he was a full managing partner. Carl made that happen, and no one knows why. He's been a major pain in the ass since then. Now that Carl's gone, Hank wants to fire him from the ranch, but Eddy seems to be holding Hank hostage over something."

"How do you know this?"

"Hank told me about Eddy a while back. He didn't outright say Eddy was holding him hostage, but it was easy to guess."

"What does that have to do with Audrey?"

"Eddy went back to the ranch around the time Audrey disappeared. Now that Audrey has been found, Eddy is talking too much when he's drunk. The bartender believes Eddy knows what happened to her and thinks someone in the Stevenson family is involved. He thinks Eddy knows who it is, and he blackmailed Carl into putting him back at the ranch."

"Eddy blackmailed his own father?"

"He's that kind of guy. Never been worth shit. You don't want to turn your back on him. The bartender says Eddy and Randy were in a few days ago, and Eddy was bragging about being the only one left who knows what really happened."

"Randy and Eddy hang out together? Interesting. Did Randy seem surprised?"

"Don't think so. My source says Randy didn't ask for an explanation."

"That could mean he knows what Eddy was talking about. I'll meet Eddy this afternoon. How do we get him to talk?"

"We don't. We don't want to get near him."

"It's too late for that. Logan subpoenaed him. He's also refused to take a DNA test, so we need to get a saliva or hair sample."

"I'm way ahead of you." Robert pulled a brown paper bag from under his seat and took out two beer bottles sealed in plastic bags. He turned the first one so she could see the name written with a marker: "Eddy." The second name was "Randy."

"Oh, my God!" Maggie's eyes widened. She kissed him smack on the lips. "Sherlock, you're the best!"

"I'm better than Sherlock. He never got kissed for his efforts."

Her brow wrinkled. "I have to know the chain of custody on these before I approach Logan again. Did you actually see Eddy or Randy drinking from these bottles?"

"No. My trusted contact is the bartender. He served them and kept the bottles for me. He said he took the bottles to the back room and put them in plastic within minutes of getting them. He would testify."

Maggie looked away and shook her head. "If I was prosecuting this case, I would try to get DNA off these bottles, but any defense lawyer in his right mind would object and would likely win. You probably don't have a trusted chain of custody."

He frowned. "You mean these are worthless to us?"

"We could send them to a private lab. If there's anything incriminating, we might be able to get a court-ordered DNA test through the crime lab."

"It's worth a try, isn't it?"

"I'll talk to Charles Cameron and see what he thinks. He may know a good private lab that could handle it."

She called Charles and told him what they had.

Hanging up, she turned to Robert. "Charles will wait for us before leaving his office this evening, and he'll get them tested. For comparison purposes, I'll send him the DNA report on Carl's hat when it comes in and the report on Audrey's baby."

She called Peter and Gwen and canceled the team meeting for that evening because they couldn't get back in time. She still had to attend Eddy's interview, and they needed to drop the beer bottles off on the way home.

While Robert finished his sandwich, she became quiet and distracted by the surroundings. "Robert, something bothers me. It's gnawing at my gut. I'm not sure what it is. I don't know why, but Carl's name is ringing in my ear. Consider this...he was married. He had money. He was the landlord. He was prominent in the community. Logan called him a womanizer. Somehow, he's involved in this. I'm glad you got that hat. Something tells me we're going to get a hit on it."

His heart pounded. "Do you think Carl was the father of Audrey's baby?"

"I don't know. I would be very disappointed in him if he was."

"So would I." He didn't understand it, but he believed in her intuition.

Had he misjudged Carl over the years?

CHAPTER 44

Maggie

Robert dropped Maggie off at the county office complex for Eddy's interview.

While walking toward the conference room, Logan also told Maggie that Eddy had gotten into trouble and was sent to a ranch for troubled teens. He ran away the first week and has been difficult ever since. For this interview, Logan didn't trust Eddy to come on his own, so a deputy was sent to pick him up.

"From his reputation, I suspect you've mistaken him for a human," Maggie said sarcastically. She was about to confront a difficult witness, but felt empowered by the bartender's report. "Does Eddy have any good or endearing qualities?"

"Depends on who you ask," Logan whispered as they approached two men sitting on a bench outside the conference room door.

Eddy was over six feet tall, with a build similar to Hank's and a darker skin tone than the rest of his family. Dressed in black, he was unshaven, haggard, and had shoulder-length, unkempt hair. He stared at her. His dark, hawklike eyes exuded meanness and anger.

Maggie was close enough to cringe at the barnyard smell remaining on Eddy's boots.

The deputy pushed slightly to get Eddy to enter the conference room and sat next to him. Eddy didn't bother taking his cowboy hat off. The deputy nodded to Maggie, but Eddy remained aloof and sullen.

Logan thanked the deputy, who rose to leave. He turned suddenly and removed Eddy's hat and tossed it on the table. For a moment, Maggie was afraid Eddy would jump up and confront him.

Logan nervously turned on the recorder and put his witness under oath. "Okay, everyone, let's get this show started."

Maggie poured water for everyone. Eddy ignored his glass.

His voice artificially gentle, Logan took the lead and used simple opening questions to calm Eddy. Logan asked where he had lived as a child, which schools he had attended, which sports he had played, and when he had graduated from high school. Eddy had been a football tackle in school and worked on the ranch for most of his teenage and adult life. Finally, Logan asked if Eddy had been in the military.

Eddy winced. His eyes froze. He lowered his gaze to the table.

"Where did you serve?"

He looked toward the end of the room. "Afghanistan."

Logan nodded, as if he understood. "I was a sergeant in the Gulf War, 1991."

The two men stared at each other as if a brief bond had been established.

"Honorable discharge?"

"You want to know my service history? You get the records."

Logan allowed a moment to pass. "Eddy, we're talking to everyone who was living out at Stevenson's Row at the time Audrey lived there. You stayed with your parents around that time, didn't you?"

"Yeah."

"Do you recall when you moved in with them?"

"Don't know exactly." Eddy's gaze was full of contempt. He leaned back in his chair, his hands clenching the table's edge.

"Would it have been sometime in the summer or fall of 2016?"

"Could have been." Eddy eyed Maggie.

"Why did you move from the ranch to your parents' house?"

"Personal reasons." His glare dared Logan to ask more.

"Was one of the personal reasons because you had a run-in with your brother, Jimmy?"

"Ain't none of your business." The protruding Adam's apple on his throat bobbed as if he started to say something and stopped.

"And when did you move back to the ranch?" Logan was reading from a list of prepared questions and making notes.

"Sometime in the winter. Maybe the late winter, early spring."

Logan glanced at Maggie with a plea to take over.

Maggie tried to remember everything she had heard about Eddy. *His father always had trouble with him. Where did the family go wrong with this child? How can we get through the hostility?*

She followed Logan's lead. "When you played football in high school, did your parents come to your games?"

His eyes momentarily flashed with pain. "What business is it of yours?"

"Were you injured in Afghanistan?"

His face hardened. "Yeah, but it healed."

"When you were living at Stevenson's Row, did you attend the 2016 Christmas party the sheriff always has?"

"Yeah." He looked away. His hand twisted the hair brushing his cheek.

"When you were at the Christmas party, did you see Audrey Stillman?"

"I saw everyone who was at the party."

"Did you speak with Audrey?"

He glowered at her, then scratched behind his neck. "I don't recall."

"Who did you leave the Christmas party with?"

"I don't recall." He sounded bored.

"Did you and Randy Stevenson leave the party together?"

"Guess so. If he says we did."

"Eddy." Logan created a pause before asking his question. "Did you ever have sex with Audrey Stillman?"

Eddy flinched. He leaned away, and his jaw tightened. He rubbed the back of his neck. Finally, he growled. "None of your fucking business."

Maggie eyed Logan to sense his reaction. He stared at Eddy and shrugged.

"Did Audrey die while you were living out there at Stevenson's Row?" she said.

"I don't know when she died."

"Eddy." Maggie was also tired of his noncooperation. She went for it. She sat forward and altered her tone so she sounded like she had the upper hand. "You're aware that both Carl and Audrey are now deceased, isn't that true?"

He hesitated. A puzzled look crossed his face. "Yeah. Everyone knows that. So what?"

"There's an investigation going on as to how Audrey died, isn't that true?"

"That's what I hear. That's why you're stirring up trouble. Doesn't concern me."

"If Audrey died while you were living at the cabins, you'd be a suspect, wouldn't you?"

Eddy scowled. "I moved back to the ranch before she died. You ain't got nothin' on me."

He just admitted that he knows when she died. Maggie smiled and glanced away before returning his stare. *I have something, but you don't know it.*

"Don't be so sure," she said, barely loud enough for him to hear.

She cleared her throat. "Actually, we've got a witness who overheard you make an interesting statement. You said that since Carl and Audrey are both dead, you're the only one who knows what really happened. Did you make that statement?"

Eddy's eyes flickered. His neck muscles twitched. He tried not to show that he recognized his own words being thrown back at him. He remained quiet.

"Isn't that a statement you made?" she repeated.

"I don't know what you're talking about." He brought his clenched fists to the table.

"So, Eddy, what is it you know about Audrey's death that no one else knows?"

His eyes pierced into her, but he said nothing. The muscles in his temples contracted.

"What if I told you we have a DNA sample from you? And we have a sample from Audrey that will help us identify her killer. Is that something you should be worried about?"

The smirk left his face. His eyes narrowed. Pure evil tainted his face. "You're bluffing. You have nothing on me."

Maggie had accomplished her objective. He was nervous. Eddy now knew he was a suspect. She wanted him to make a wrong move or do something that showed guilt.

"I have no further questions."

Logan went to the door and asked the deputy to return Eddy to the ranch.

After they were gone, Logan said, "Clue me in. What just happened?"

"Eddy's been bragging around town that he's the only one who knows what really happened. I just let him know that we're onto him. He got the message. You need to put a tail on him and see if he does anything that speaks of a guilty conscience."

"What was the DNA comment about?"

"We just got DNA samples from Randy and Eddy." She smiled. "Did you notice how he tensed up? There are some questions about the chain of custody, so we're processing the samples at a private lab. I'll let you know if anything interesting turns up. We can always go into court later and ask for a court-ordered DNA test."

Logan's eyes widened, a hint of concern in them.

She texted Robert.

She still needed to see the missing person report filed by Audrey's mother. She had already asked for it twice. "One more question, Logan. You told me about an investigation when Audrey first disappeared. Would you get that file so we can review it together? It may have some information about what happened to Audrey's belongings."

Logan reddened. "Sure, I'll get it. I guess we'll have to look at that."

CHAPTER 45

Maggie

Saturday, October 3, 2020

Ben arrived at Maggie's condo at two o'clock. She offered him a cup of coffee before they started working.

"First, I'd like to reconstruct the timeline for that day in March 2017." She invited him into her dining area, where she already had an easel set up.

He handed her the evidence he had collected. Spreading it out on the table, she examined each piece in detail.

She wrote the date at the top of the paper on the easel and listed the hours from 9:00 a.m. through 4:00 p.m. "These are the relevant times," she said as she started identifying them.

"9:00 a.m., you picked Dr. McKenzie up from his hotel.

"10:00 a.m., Dr. McKenzie began his workshop.

"10:00 a.m. to 12:30 p.m., you read a book.

"12:30 p.m., you had lunch with Dr. McKenzie as part of the workshop.

"After lunch, until 4:00 p.m., you read a book.

"4:00 p.m., you and Dr. McKenzie left Weber State University and drove to the airport. On the way, you stopped at a gas station in Ogden and filled the tank. Do these times seem correct?"

"Yes, except for one point I remembered after we talked."

"What's that?"

"I remember going for a walk on the campus. It was after I left Dr. McKenzie in the morning. I think I was gone thirty to sixty minutes. Also, there was a speaker at the luncheon, so lunch was probably ninety minutes."

She made the corrections. "Have you done anything to refresh your memory except going through all of this evidence? By any chance, did you go back to the campus after we talked, or have you reviewed an online map of the campus?"

"No."

"Good. We shouldn't be over-prepared because a jury might think we constructed the whole thing. I'm going to play the role of the DA, and I'm going to ask you detailed questions about your time on campus. If you can remember the answer, tell me. If you don't remember, say 'I don't recall.' My goal is to trip you up, so think carefully before answering. Is that clear?"

"Yes."

They pushed the table to the side of the room and pulled his chair out to the center. She asked him to consider himself in the witness box and sworn to tell the truth.

Maggie leaned against the doorframe and adopted the attitude of a prosecutor who was cross-examining Ben. "Now, Mr. Stillman, what was the name of the hotel where you picked up Dr. McKenzie?"

"It's the hotel on Main Street in Salt Lake, about Fifth South. I think it's the Little America Hotel."

"Which road did you take to get to Ogden?"

"Highway 89 that branches off from the interstate at Farmington."

"About what time did you get to the Weber State University campus?"

"My estimate is we got there around nine forty-five. We had enough time to walk in and find the location of the conference before ten o'clock."

"Where did you park?"

"We had a guest pass to park in a lot nearby. We entered the lower level of the student center on the west side."

"On which floor was the conference held, and approximately how many people attended?"

"I don't recall which floor, but we went up a couple of flights of stairs. My recollection is that it was a midsize room, but they had tables set up. I left as soon as Dr. McKenzie got to the right location, so I don't know how many people were there."

"Don't offer more than what I ask for. What did you do next?"

"I went for a walk on the campus. I had never been there before."

"Where exactly did you go, and what did you see? Do you remember the names of the buildings?"

"I recall walking out an east door because I remember how close we were to the mountains." He thought for a moment. "I think I turned left and found an outdoor map of the campus. I remember seeing a bell tower and hearing it ring at ten o'clock. I remember passing a large pond when we parked, so I headed in that direction. I passed several buildings, but I don't remember any of the names."

"Was there a fountain in the large pond?"

"Not that I can recall."

"After viewing the pond, what did you do?"

"I went back to the student center, found a comfortable place to sit, and read a book on my Kindle."

"Did you see anyone you know, or did anyone talk to you?"

"No."

"Did you talk to anyone on the phone?"

"I don't recall. You'll need to check my phone records."

Maggie sat. "Logan Harris will probably say that you could get to Audrey's place in thirty minutes, and two hours in the morning was enough time for you to make sure she drank the tea, bury her, and get back. How would you respond to that?"

"I recall I wore slacks and a sports jacket that day. I would expect my clothes to be dirty if I dug a grave, wouldn't you?"

"Yes, good point. Who would have noticed?"

"Dr. McKenzie. Also, I had my boss's black Mercedes. It would've gotten very dusty if I'd taken it down that dirt road. You could ask him about my clothes and the condition of the car."

"We will need to write this up as an affidavit for you to sign and submit. I'll keep both points in mind when I talk to Logan Harris about March 18. Quite frankly, your alibi for that day has at least one big hole in it. He isn't going to give up easily, so keep thinking about other reasons why you didn't leave Weber State University and go over to Audrey's place."

CHAPTER 46

Audrey

Sunday, December 11, 2016

Dear diary, I had such a fabulous time at the Christmas party last night! I'm starting to feel like a woman again, but I'm not sure I did the right thing. You know what I mean? I can't tell a soul about this, so it's between you and me.

I wanted to look perfect, so I made a new skirt for the occasion. It looks like a kilt and goes to the floor. He probably won't notice, but it's his ancestral clan's plaid. I also wore my black velvet vest over my peasant blouse. I don't usually wear makeup, but last night was special, and, if I do say so myself, I really looked nice!

I wore my woolen cloak because of the snowstorm. I also wanted to show Carl how amazing the Gaelic cloak pin looked with it. He gave it to me only a few days ago. It was his family heirloom, and for me, it's a symbol of how much I mean to him. I also wonder if he eventually wants me to be included in his family.

It was a short walk to the sheriff's place. He and Marion always host the Christmas party. This is the first time I've gone alone, but that's okay. I knew Carl would be there without Grammy.

When I arrived, he wasn't there yet. Randy found a place to put my cloak and got a glass of wine for me. He acted like nothing was wrong. I told you he had sex with me when he helped with the garden, and it was against my will. I haven't told anyone. He really repulses me now, but I don't know what to do because he's Carl's grandson. I guess what happened was really my fault.

When Carl came in, my heart skipped a beat. I was sitting on a stool and raised my glass to him ever so slightly. He nodded. As always, he was the center of attention, and I was happy just to watch him and notice how he glanced at me now and then.

Carl finally came over to talk to me. "Well, Audrey."

But then Bobby Parsons walked by, slung an arm around Carl's shoulders, and pulled him aside. Someone else guided Carl over to the food table and handed him a plate.

Oh, and Randy tried to be friendly again and was really revolting. "Looks like we got that garden cleaned up just in time, doesn't it?" He spoke a little loud and moved too close for comfort. He acted like he owned me.

"Yes," I said, "and thank you again for your help. It was kind of you."

He glanced at my bosom. I was disgusted.

"I think I'll check out the food," I said and pulled away.

I filled a plate and looked for Carl. He was at the table. The man next to him got up, so I slid into the empty chair.

"Greetings," I said casually, with a smile.

His eyes started at the top of my head and magically caressed my hair. I wore it down instead of in a ponytail, and it was wavy and shiny. His eyes locked with mine.

Finally, he smiled and said, "Merry Christmas."

Oh, diary, it was so sexy! I was in heaven!

He nodded toward my plate. "Food's good." As he turned, his gaze lingered momentarily on my cleavage.

I felt warm all over.

I picked up a forkful of turkey dressing and ate it slowly, keeping my eyes trained on the crowded room. "Um, yes. Delicious."

We ate in silence, not looking at each other. It was like something out of a medieval tale, and you know how much I love those stories! But then Eddy came over and sat across from Carl. He was dressed all in black, and he was evil.

"You know my son, Eddy, don't you?" Carl said.

"Yes, of course. You look just like your father." That really wasn't true, but what else was I supposed to say?

Eddy nodded. He stared as if he was undressing me in front of the entire room. He glanced at his dad and rose to leave. "I'll let you two finish your conversation."

Eddy's look shattered my sense of romance. I felt unclean. I ate in silence while I recovered my dignity.

After I finished eating, I whispered in his ear, "I would like to be with you tonight."

He thought for a moment. "I have my truck outside. May I give you a ride back to your place later?"

"Yes." I stood. "I'm going to check out the desserts. I'll see you later."

The party broke up around eleven because of the snow and wind. Several people had trucks. The people from the cabin next to mine were summer people, and they didn't like the idea of walking a few hundred yards in the blizzard.

"Climb in my truck. I've got crew seats, enough room for everyone," Carl said to them. "I'm dropping Audrey off. She'll never make it if I don't."

He hustled us into the cab, and they jumped out at their place. I'm not sure I liked having someone see him taking me home.

Before we got out, he wrapped his arms around me. "I want to be with you very much and hold you like this all night. It's not fair to you, but I can't stay the whole night. Can you understand that?"

I touched his cheek. "I cherish even brief moments with you."

Inside, he rekindled the fire, washed his hands, and turned to me. I can't tell you how wonderful it felt to have him bury his face in my hair for the first time.

"I've been dreaming of this moment," he whispered.

Ever so slowly, he unbuttoned my vest. I haven't been touched and held like that in years!

We moved toward the bedroom. For nearly two hours, we were together. You must know how good it felt! When I fell asleep, he left. I know he'll be back, so I've already started scenting my bedroom with the same lavender sachet I make for others. I feel like I'm falling in love already!

CHAPTER 47

Audrey

Tuesday, December 27, 2016

Dear diary, Carl has found me, the woman he needs, and he visited several times this month. It's like we have our own secret world deep in the forest.

He always brings a gift. The first time, it was a dozen roses, which I loved and displayed on my kitchen table. I have pressed one as a keepsake.

His second gift was a long red negligee for Christmas! I've never had anything like it. He asked me to dance in it! I put my cloak on over the negligee, untied my hair, and danced like I've never danced before. I felt like an exotic belly dancer! I dipped, twirled, and teased him. It ended with my cloak on the floor and me on his lap.

I've never felt so sexy! I finished the dance by kissing him on the back of his neck. Of course, it was late when he went back to his place. I've danced for him several times now.

CHAPTER 48

Audrey

Tuesday, January 3, 2017

Dear diary, what a horrible time it's been these last few days. If I can only get the words out, I might start feeling better.

What I didn't know was that Eddy knew about Carl's visits. Our secret hideaway has been violated. On New Year's Eve, when Carl was at a party, Eddy showed up, and he was already drunk.

I wanted Carl to come see me, and when there was a knock, I thought he had changed his plans. I already had the red negligee and cloak on and gladly opened the door. When I realized it was Eddy, I tried to push it shut, but he forced his way in.

I screamed and backed away. The sound bounced against the cabin walls, and probably filtered through the trees, but no one heard me.

Eddy's long hair and stubble made him look wild. His eyes burned with anger. He growled. "You're giving it to my dad.

I want some too. It's free for the taking, right?" He smelled of beer.

I was barefoot, but I wanted to run into the night. I inched toward the door, carefully circling him.

He didn't move. "You ain't goin' nowhere, bitch."

He grabbed me by the hair and pulled me closer. His gross hands wouldn't stop touching me. He held my head and tried to kiss me. I bit his lip.

"Dance for me." He snarled as he shoved me toward the fireplace. "I've been watching through the windows. I've seen you do it for him."

I couldn't move.

"Dance, bitch." He whacked me hard, knocking me against the wall.

I wasn't strong enough to push him away. He yanked my cloak off and threw it on the floor. His powerful arms encircled me below the elbows. He picked me up and carried me into the bedroom.

"Shut the fuck up, girl. There ain't no one to hear you. You either calm down on your own, or I'll beat the shit out of you to make you stop."

He slapped me hard across the face. I went limp.

I can't even write any more. I was too stunned to respond. I went to another place where I was dancing in a garden in my magical cloak.

After he left, I pulled the bedcovers up and slept through the night. When the sunlight came through the window, I stayed in bed.

Hours later, I made tea and sat at the kitchen table, alone with my pain. My cat, Muppet, was my only comfort. I snuggled in my cloak. With great effort, I went to the bathroom mirror. I was covered in bruises.

CHAPTER 49

Audrey

Thursday, January 5, 2017

Dear diary, for two days, I took care of myself, ashamed to call anyone for help. A warm shower soothed me. I dressed in woolens and sat by the fireplace, watching embers fall off the logs. I brushed my hair. I drank tea but barely ate.

On the third day, Carl startled me with a knock at my door. I looked out the window to make sure it was his truck, opened the door a crack, and stared at him.

"Is something wrong, sweetheart?" He gently pushed the door open.

His hand rose to caress my cheek. I brushed it aside but allowed him to come in.

He put his hands on my shoulders and looked at me. My bathrobe fell open. He took in the full extent of my bruises.

He almost cried when he asked me, "Who did this to you?"

He wrapped his arms around me and then made tea for both of us. He didn't push for more than I was willing to tell, but over two hours, he learned what happened.

When I finally gave a name to the man who had beaten me, Carl recoiled. "Eddy? My son Eddy?"

"Yes." I finally told him the horrifying details.

"I'll get the sheriff right now. We can handle this. Eddy belongs in jail."

"No." I clung to him. "Then everyone will know about us. Grammy will know. My mother will know. Everyone in town will shame both of us. I'll lose customers."

"Let the chips fall where they may. You didn't deserve this. I'll take care of you. I've always handled his problems within the family, but this is way too much. He raped you. What he did was wrong, and he needs to pay for it. If I didn't need to be here with you, I would be down there at my place, beating the crap out of him."

"Oh, Carl, please, for my sake, don't tell anyone! I'll heal. I'll get over it. I'm sure it was my fault."

"I can't allow him to treat you like this."

I fell to my knees. "Carl, my dearest friend and lover. Please don't make me go through the public agony. Please, I beg you. I would be humiliated forever and wouldn't even be able to walk on the streets."

He gently pulled me up and held me. "I'm so sorry for what my son did to you. This is also my fault."

A few days later, he told me he privately confronted Eddy, who showed no remorse. Carl told him he was no longer welcome to stay in his home. Eddy threatened to expose our affair and some of Carl's business dealings. He would expose how much Carl had hurt his wife and the community, and I would be shunned. Eddy offered to keep everything quiet if Carl would let him go back to the ranch in a full partnership *with Jimmy. Carl had no choice and forced Jimmy to accept. By the middle of January, Eddy was gone.*

Carl came to see me every day, brought me food and supplies, and sat with me. He shoveled the snow and kept the fire going. He kissed me gently on the forehead, but never expected anything.

I healed physically, and Carl's love and attention helped me heal emotionally. Every smile, every kiss, every moment caressed me. It was a hard way to learn, but I'm so sure of his love now.

CHAPTER 50

Maggie

Monday, October 5, 2020

Logan called Maggie early. "I have the missing person report. I have to be in court this morning, but I have time this afternoon around two. Do you want to see it then?"

"I'll be there."

She called Robert, but he had a commitment. It was important enough that she decided to go on her own. Her car was known, so she arranged a rental. She parked in the rear, and Logan met her at the back entrance. They went through the corridors to avoid being seen in any public areas. When they got to his evidence room, he closed the door and laid the file on the table in front of her.

"There it is. The investigation." His voice betrayed his feeling that the investigation was inadequate.

Has he been intentionally withholding this file? She opened it and reviewed the sheriff's summary report and confirmed that the witness statements were signed under penalty of perjury.

The second document was a statement by Mrs. Williams. She had a close relationship with Audrey and normally talked to her daughter every week. She last saw Audrey on March 8, 2017, for her birthday celebration. Audrey was planning to move in at the end of the month, and on Saturday, March 11, they talked in detail about planting a new garden. During the weekdays of March 13 to 17, while her mother was at work, Audrey cleared out the new garden spot and began preparing the soil. Mrs. Williams expected to see her on March 18, but she never came over or called. Mrs. Williams became concerned and started calling her. She tried numerous times and left messages. Finally, Mrs. Williams drove over to Audrey's cabin on Wednesday evening, March 22. Audrey's car was gone. Audrey regularly left the door unlocked when she was around, but Mrs. Williams found it locked. She also found Audrey's cat outside the cabin, and put it in her car to take home.

She walked over to the sheriff's cabin, but Marion had not seen Audrey for several days. Mrs. Williams called Carl. He said he had found a note saying she was leaving town. The note did not make sense to her, and she knew Audrey would never abandon her cat, so she filed the missing person report on March 23 with the sheriff's office.

The third document was a statement from Carl Stevenson, Audrey's landlord, who was interviewed on March 23. He had been helping Audrey during the winter because she was alone and stopped by every couple of weeks. Carl said he went to Audrey's cabin on Sunday, March 19, to ask about repairs or yard work that needed to be done. Her car was gone. He found a note taped to the door that said she had decided to start a new life and had left town. He tossed the note after reading it. He had a key and went inside and found some inventory, the furniture, and her personal possessions. Carl got his grandson, Randy, to help him clean out the cabin on March 20 and 21 so he could list it as a rental. He asked Mrs. Williams if she wanted the furniture, and she said no, so he kept it. They put the rest of Audrey's possessions in a dumpster.

A fourth document showed they filed a statewide missing person alert. There were no follow-up reports.

Maggie turned to Logan. "That's all that was done?"

He rubbed the back of his neck. "There were no indications of foul play."

"Was anything done to confirm any of this information?"

"Carl had cleaned out the cabin before it was reported. He didn't realize he should've kept the note. No one saw anything suspicious happening."

"It wasn't suspicious that Audrey suddenly disappeared? What about a statement from Randy? Did anyone talk to him? Did the sheriff or his wife provide a statement?"

"Doesn't look like it. Audrey's note to Carl was that she decided to start a new life. People do that. We had no way of disproving it."

Maggie eyed him suspiciously. "A young woman was born and raised in this county. She had a business in this county. Her father was a county official at one time, and she was planning to move in with her mother, but she vanishes. No one searches for her? Was there an alert placed at her bank? Were any relatives contacted?"

"We didn't have any clues, and we didn't have the manpower to handle a needle-in-a-haystack investigation."

"It looks to me like no one cared." Maggie felt angry because they didn't consider Audrey important enough for a more thorough search. *No wonder he didn't want me to see the file.*

"Logan, I'm having a hard time with this." Maggie was too angry to sit. She threw up her hands and paced. "We should have obtained this file as soon as you opened the case against Ben. How many times have I asked for it? We definitely should have had it before we interviewed Randy. This information says he's implicated. It looks to me like you've been intentionally withholding evidence."

"Maggie, there are many factors at play here." He winced. "We don't know who killed Audrey, and maybe we should just let this case go cold and let everyone move on."

"It looks to me like you're protecting Carl's reputation. He's implicated in this scheme. You're definitely protecting Randy."

"I'm not protecting anyone. It's a cold case. We did what we could. We need to let go of this and let the town get back to normal."

"Not as long as I'm still on the case. It's no longer a cold case because my client is being accused with no evidence. He can't even walk on the sidewalks in this town. He can't go visit his parents. Is that what you mean by letting the town get back to normal?"

"Ben has a life in the big city. He's moved on. You're here stirring up everyone with evidence on an old cold case that can't be solved. Give it a little time, and they'll welcome Ben back, I'm sure."

"Does this mean you're dropping the case against Ben?"

"Ben's purchase of gas in Ogden still makes him a suspect. I still need your sworn explanation and evidence for the gas charge on March 18. If he can't explain it to my satisfaction, we'll have enough to charge him."

"I've got that affidavit almost ready. I'll get it to you."

There was nothing more to say. She thanked Logan for getting the file, took her copies, and went to her car. She was furious about the injustices to Audrey and Ben and had to calm down before she could drive. She had experienced the same rage when law enforcement had ignored the disappearance of her victims in DC. *Maybe I'm overreacting, but I don't think so.*

On the drive home, she realized there was one important clue in that file she would not forget. Randy had helped Carl clean out the cabin. In his interview, Randy said he had nothing to do with it. He had lied. Logan didn't want me to see that. *Randy knows more about what happened to Audrey than he's told us.*

CHAPTER 51

Maggie

Tuesday, October 6, 2020

Maggie did not sleep well on Monday night. She intended to fight hard to resolve Audrey's murder rather than let it go cold.

On Tuesday morning, she called Robert. "I think the case got blown wide open yesterday, but I'm not sure where it's going. We need to talk. Do you have time today?" Carl was one of her prime suspects, and she wanted to respect Robert's close relationship with him by discussing it privately.

"Absolutely," he said.

They arranged to meet at her place in an hour.

When he arrived with coffee and croissants, she directed him to her dining area where she had taped three large, easel-size sheets of paper to the wall. "For this, I have to talk with a marker in my hand."

Nervously, she pried the lid off her coffee, took a sip, and smiled as she noticed he had remembered how she liked her coffee. Robert found a dish for the croissants and sat with her at the table.

"What's up, boss?" He took a croissant.

She met his eyes. "I think Carl is more involved in Audrey's death than we realize. I don't know the extent, but he was your close friend and mentor. We need to talk about this."

Robert looked down, frowning. "That's hard to hear."

"I know."

"I've also seen a connection, but I kept hoping we would find someone else." He broke off a piece of croissant and ate it slowly. "What happened to break open the case?"

"I finally saw the missing person report. Carl told the sheriff that he went to Audrey's cabin on March 19 and she was gone. Within a few days, he and Randy cleaned out the place. Mrs. Williams filed the report on March 23. Carl had destroyed any and all evidence by that point. Randy lied at his interview and said he didn't help. Logan wants to forget everything now and send the case back to the freezer. I think we've got a cover-up."

"Wow. That's all I can say. A cover-up? What a can of worms." He was pensive for a moment. "Want to tell me how it all fits together?"

"I can show you how this affects the facts we have, but we're still waiting for the DNA reports, so we don't have any confirmations yet."

She picked up a marker. "I need to start with our basic facts and a few assumptions. Remember the three words: *why*, *how*, and *who*?" She added the words to the top of the three sheets of easel paper.

"What do we know so far as to *why* someone killed her? We suspect it's because she was pregnant, but we don't know who got her pregnant, and that's the key to solving this case."

She turned to the papers and referred to her notes while giving each fact a bullet point as she wrote it down:

- When she died, Audrey was divorced and three to four months pregnant. The time of conception was late November or early December. It wasn't Ben's kid.

- In October 2016, she started getting free rent from Carl.

- Eddy lived with his parents from the summer of 2016 to the winter of 2017.

- On November 17, 2016, when they signed the divorce papers, Audrey told Ben she had a rich boyfriend. Stacey told us this boyfriend was married and important in town.

- Randy helped Audrey with the garden just before Thanksgiving in 2016.

- Audrey attended the Christmas party in early December.

- On March 8, 2017, Audrey visited her mother and started a new garden.

- Her mother last spoke to her on March 11, 2017.

- March 16, 2017, was Audrey's last phone call.

- On March 18, 2017, Ben was in Ogden, thirty minutes from Audrey's place.

"There are two long time periods when Ben's actions can't be verified."

- On March 19, 2017, Carl allegedly went to the cabin and found Audrey gone. Carl claimed there was a note saying she moved out of town. No one saw this note, nor can anyone prove it existed.

- On March 21 and 22, Randy and Carl cleaned out Audrey's cabin. Everything went into a dumpster. If there was any evidence associated with her death, it was destroyed.

- On March 23, 2017, Audrey's mother filed a missing person report.

Maggie moved to the second sheet of paper and made notes as she talked. "Audrey died of poisoning from a belladonna plant. That answers our *how* question. What do we know about that? We know Audrey purchased a belladonna plant in 2015. Who knew about the poisonous plant? We don't know yet." She waited for Robert's response.

Robert's face drained of color. "Tell me why you suspect Carl, Eddy, Randy, and even Ben. How do you tie them to this evidence?"

She moved to the third sheet of paper and wrote the names: *Ben, Carl, Randy,* and *Eddy.* "We get to the most important question—*who*? Our next questions are *means*, *motive*, and *opportunity*." She put her marker down and turned as if she was facing and connecting with one person in a jury box.

"We know from DNA that Ben isn't the father. His only motive would've been revenge, but they were far enough away from the divorce that a motive seems unlikely. He claims he didn't know about the poisonous plant. He was physically close enough and his alibi has two time periods when he might have gone to Audrey's place, so he had the opportunity, but it seems unlikely. He was driving a Mercedes, and he was dressed up on that day. The only way his alibi would fall apart is if someone saw the car or saw dirt on his clothes." Next to Ben's name, she wrote *Least Likely*.

"Let's take Eddy second. He's bragging about being the only person who knows what really happened. I take him at his word. We don't know what his motive might have been, but the bragging makes him a suspect even though he doesn't fit the profile. He had the means and opportunity. He's violent and angry. The only clue comes from his interview. Logan asked if he had sex with her, which he seemed to deny, but his body language said he was lying. I would be surprised if he knew about the belladonna, but if he got her pregnant through violence, she may have been despondent enough to make the tea, and then he could have buried her." She wrote *Not Likely*.

"Didn't Eddy move back to the ranch before her death?" Robert asked.

"Yes, but he was there when she got pregnant, and the move could've been because she told him she was pregnant. No one would have found it unusual for him to be in the neighborhood. He could've come back to kill her."

Maggie pulled her croissant apart and took some bites before continuing.

"Then there's Randy. At first, I thought Randy was just a kid with a crush who had been rejected. He was probably told to wear gloves in the garden because there was a poisonous plant. He denies this, but we know he lies. He had the means and opportunity because he lived there, but I'm not sure what his motive would've been except perhaps jealousy."

She sighed. "Randy was also asked if he had sex with Audrey, and he denied it, but his body language said he was lying. He isn't violent, and I can't see him exerting force. Could there have been a romance? Randy had an emotional attachment to Audrey, but he doesn't fit the profile either. I think he's mixed up in this, but I don't know how."

She tapped the paper. "Randy's credibility on everything has gone down the toilet because he lied about cleaning out Audrey's cabin. Why? We don't know. What else happened that he's lying about?" Next to his name, she wrote *Mysterious Involvement*.

Maggie sat at the table across from Robert. It was the first time she had to confront an issue with him, and she was notoriously bad with difficult situations in romantic relationships.

"We have to turn to Carl. It makes the most sense if he was the boyfriend. He had money, he was married, and he was powerful in the community, which fit the profile. He gave Audrey free rent for six months, and he had a reputation as a womanizer. He could've had a motive to kill her because he was married. He claimed he knew nothing about plants, but he took care of the gardening for the new tenant. I suspect it was because he knew about the poisonous plant. He admitted to being at the cabin, and he was responsible for destroying the evidence. Why was he so sure he could throw everything away?"

She waited.

Robert stared at the names. "We really need those DNA reports. I've known Carl all my life. Yes, he had a reputation, but he also stayed with Grammy. He had too much at stake to get involved with Grammy's best friend. I wish he was here to defend himself. There has to be a different answer."

She stifled a groan. She had made no progress in convincing him. "I also think Logan knew what was in that missing person report and he didn't want me to see it. Now he wants to drop everything. I still need his cooperation, but I can't trust him anymore. Either his life fighting crime has clouded his judgment or he has succumbed to the local political influences."

"I thought he had it out with Hank and he was on your side."

"So did I. But he's still afraid I'll accuse the wrong person. He doesn't dare bring charges against any of the Stevensons, so he's going to overlook anything they've done."

"If Ben is innocent, how bad would it be if Logan let the case go cold?"

"That's Logan's intent. There's no way he'll arrest anyone except Ben. The politics in Medford won't allow it. He was visibly shaken when I told him about the DNA tests we're doing. Now he can't close the case until the DNA comes in."

Robert didn't meet her eyes. His lightheartedness was gone. He seemed deeply disturbed by the time he decided to leave. He hugged her as he was leaving, but his kiss and the sparkle weren't there.

Later in the afternoon, Maggie sent an email postponing the next team meeting. Nothing would make any sense until they got the DNA results. She also let the team know that Audrey's funeral would be on Saturday, October 10.

Not the least of her worries, she wondered if her belief in Carl's guilt and her passion for justice would be the end of her budding romance with Robert. Sitting at the dining room table soon after Robert left, she cried.

CHAPTER 52

Audrey

Wednesday, February 1, 2017

Dear diary, as Valentine's Day approaches, I'm worried about something else, something I didn't think could happen. I'm not sure, and I can't ask anyone, even my best friend, and I can't tell Carl yet.

I've kept our affair a secret because Grammy is old and sick. I thought the future would allow me to step forward a respectful amount of time after her funeral. All I had to do was be patient, but that's changed. I've been thinking about my encounters with Randy and Eddy, but decided Randy was too early and Eddy was too late. I know in my heart that it's Carl's child because it's a love child.

I've been pretending that my cloak was long and white and that I was a bride again. I pretend there's a preacher in front of the fireplace. I've even imagined climbing a mythical old stone bell tower and proclaiming to the world that I'm the new Mrs. Carl Stevenson.

I went through so many tests, and no one could understand why I didn't get pregnant. I assumed I was sterile, but there it is. Or maybe there it isn't. My period didn't come again.

CHAPTER 53

Audrey

Tuesday, February 7, 2017

Dear diary, I waited almost a week before I thought about it again. I had cramps and thought it was coming. It didn't. I needed to find out without letting anyone know.

I looked up pregnancy tests online. I didn't dare walk into a local drugstore because I know all the clerks. They would all talk about it. So I drove down the canyon and found a Walmart in Ogden. It was a chilly day, so I hid behind a knit hat and layers of clothes. I picked the test kit off the shelf, checked the expiration date, and bought it.

I read the instructions carefully. I have waited for this day for more years than I can remember. I was frightened, but also excited. I read the instructions a second time. It would be a test for a hormone called HCG. If it was present, I was pregnant. I used the small vial to collect a sample. I waited for the required two minutes. The test strip indicated a positive!

I was stunned.

I wanted to share this moment with Carl, but he's in Wyoming on a trip to buy cattle. He didn't know I was concerned. I've been imagining how I would tell him and how excited he would be. A baby for me at last. A baby for us!

I'm practicing holding an infant. I'm learning lullabies and singing them as I work. I'm dreaming of the tiny clothes I'll make and wondering about names. At night, I caress my child in the womb.

Valentine's Day. Yes, it will be Valentine's Day when I tell him. The perfect day to celebrate our love for each other!

CHAPTER 54

Audrey

Tuesday, February 14, 2017

Dear diary, I invited Carl to come for a late lunch and spend the afternoon with me today.

Early in the morning, I made a trip to town and bought a single red rose and a valentine with a bouquet on the front cover. When I got home, I crossed out one word of the inside message and added another.

Carl got here at one o'clock and presented me with a beautiful bouquet of red and white long-stemmed roses. I was so excited!

I had put my best white dishes on the table with the single red rose as the centerpiece. I quickly took two chicken breasts out of my skillet and made a hot cream sauce. I pinched a few chives on top of the sauce, got the asparagus and rolls from the oven, and served my first proper meal to him, with a kiss planted on his cheek. I barely ate anything, as I imagined serving many more meals.

"I have a special valentine for you." I gave him the red envelope and a kiss.

He paused at the front of the card. "Beautiful flowers, my sweet Audrey." He flipped it open and read aloud, "We love you." He seemed puzzled. "Why did you change the 'I' to a 'we'?"

"Please guess."

He stared at me. A slow, hesitant realization emerged on his face.

"I'm pregnant! I'm so, so extraordinarily happy! You've become the most wonderful and important person in my life." I sat on his lap and flung my arms around him.

Automatically, his arms encircled me. "My sweet Audrey, what have we done?" He buried his face in my hair and gently caressed me.

CHAPTER 55

Audrey

Friday, February 17, 2017

Dear diary, Carl came today. I was thrilled to see him, but he seemed distant. He asked me to sit down and took my hands. Oh, diary, I shivered because this was exactly what Ben did!

"Audrey, my dearest friend, you have meant so much to me these past few months. We need to talk about this new development. I'm sorry I didn't ask. I assumed you had arranged for birth control or that it wasn't necessary. I'm not blaming you. I'm blaming myself for not thinking."

"What are you saying? Aren't you overjoyed? Aren't you happy for me?"

"Yes, I'm happy for you because this is what you want. The joy on your face makes you even more beautiful."

"Then what's wrong? Are you accusing me? Carl, I thought I wasn't able to get pregnant. I didn't do this on purpose."

"Oh, no, my sweet Audrey, I'm not accusing you. We have a problem that neither of us expected. We must come to grips with reality. For me, as old as I am, it creates many issues. I already have six grown children. You know that. Having another child is a big responsibility. I'm too old to do this."

"But you're still healthy. You'll live long enough to be a father while he's growing up, and I hope it's a boy!"

"Sweet, darling Audrey, you've been through so much." He kissed my hands. *"I can't leave my wife. As hard as these past few years have been, I can't. She stood by me and forgave me for so much. I need to forgive her for any faults she may have. I need to stay with her."*

"Oh Carl, you deserve to be loved. She stopped loving you. I love you with my whole heart, soul, and body. You're my hero." I leaned back and stopped pleading. *"Carl, my dearest lover, your wife has been ill for a long time. What if she dies soon? Can I wait for you?"*

"Don't go there, please. Don't wish her dead. Don't ask me for a promise."

I withdrew my hands, stood, and backed away from him. In my tiny kitchen, I paced nervously. I moved into the living room and stood in front of the crackling fire. Finally, I returned to the table. I felt an emotional strength I had never known before.

"Carl, I'm pregnant with our child." My feelings rose to the level of panic, but I spoke with the clarity of sudden awareness. *"Did you see me as simply a very needy woman who was available to you?"*

"No, no. We both had strong needs. We're in this together! I've come here to talk to you about a solution. We've been important to each other."

"I want to have this child and raise it. I will not give the child away. I will not have an abortion, if that's what you want to talk about."

"I'm not asking for that. I'm asking for something that would work for you and for me."

"What works for me is for you to be a father to the child you created."

"I can be a father by making sure I provide for you and the child."

"Are you saying that you want me to have your child and raise it alone, without a father? We live in a small town. Maybe I'm old-fashioned, but it matters to me what people think about me. You want them to look at me with scorn and talk about me behind my back? Is that it?"

"I think the best solution would be for you to move somewhere. Maybe Salt Lake where there are a lot of people. I'll give you plenty of money to get set up, and I'll give you a good amount every month. You'll never worry about money. I'll be close enough to come down and see both of you every once in a while."

"Money buys everything, doesn't it? You want to hide us away somewhere, is that it? Will I continue to be your sexual toy also?"

"Please think about it. I have the money. I can bring it tomorrow if you want. We could start making plans. I can continue to be close to you and help you in so many ways. It really is the best answer. Please see it that way."

"No, no. I will not be dismissed again! Ben tossed me aside because I became inconvenient. I will not hide because I'm inconvenient for you. My whole life has been here in Madison County. My mother wants to be a grandmother. I'm sorry this is a problem for you. Please leave. I must deal with this myself."

"What are you going to do? You need some help, and I can help you. Your mother will be close enough. We can make it work."

"Please, Carl, I need to be alone for now."

"How much money do you want?" His voice sounded cold.
I refused to respond and pushed him to the door. I began
to think about innocent ways of bringing about the death of
his wife, and I was horrified at my thoughts.

CHAPTER 56

Audrey

Wednesday, March 8, 2017

Dear diary, I've just come from my mother's house where we celebrated her birthday. I still haven't told her about my pregnancy. I want so much to keep the baby. She will be so happy, but I don't know what to say about the father, and I may have to keep it a secret. It'll end up embarrassing her if everyone finds out it's Carl's. I haven't even told her I was seeing someone.

We agreed that I'll move in with her. I have no other choice. I haven't seen Carl since I asked him to leave, and I'm sure he'll want me to pay rent on the cabin soon. I need to prepare a garden over at Mom's house and quickly move my plants.

I'm still afraid of being in the cabin alone, so it'll be good to be with my mother. Men just haven't been good for me. I also think I've written too much here. I worry about someone like

Randy finding this and reading my most private thoughts. He's such a squirrely person. I can't trust anyone right now.

Thinking about it, I have an idea where to hide you. I'll sign off for now and pack you away. It'll be a great place and will be very safe. I'll start up again after I've moved.

CHAPTER 57

Maggie

Saturday, October 10, 2020

The Thursday before Audrey's funeral, the local newspaper published a front-page story that laid out the status of the investigation as they understood it. The picture of Audrey in her dirt grave accompanied it.

By the end of the day, most county residents knew Audrey had died from the poison of her own plant. They also knew Ben could not be arrested because he could not be placed near her cabin, or in the county, around the time of her death. The story, attributed to the mayor, speculated about the possibilities of depression and suicide.

Her obituary was also an invitation to the funeral on Saturday, and most of the town was expected to attend.

Maggie told Ben, and he insisted on going. He wasn't afraid. She, Charles, and Robert decided to go with him for safety reasons, and a sheriff's escort was arranged.

Audrey was being buried at the South Medford Cemetery. Robert and Maggie picked Ben up, then Charles, and
arrived in Robert's Jeep. To avoid attention, they elected
not to go to the church service and parked near the cemetery, waiting for the hearse. Maggie wore a large-brimmed
black hat, a somber skirt suit, and low heels. The men were
in dark suits. As the crowd gathered, their group walked
up the slight incline to the site without getting any attention and selected folding chairs near the back of the seating area.

It was a beautiful autumn day. Mrs. Williams became
the center of attention when she arrived a few minutes
later. Hank met her car and escorted her to a seat in the
front row. She was thin and used a cane to steady herself.
She didn't wear a hat, and when the breeze caught her
short gray hairdo, she reached up and smoothed it. Several
women came over to hug her.

Hank joined his family, including Randy and Karen, in
the second row behind Mrs. Williams.

A tall man with the same auburn hair and husky build as
Hank and Randy helped Grammy alight from a car. She held
his arm as she walked toward the chairs and was quickly
surrounded by a blond woman with two elementary-aged
children. Once Grammy was seated next to Mrs. Williams,
the man sat on her other side and was joined by the woman and children.

"Who's the man with Grammy?" Maggie whispered to
Robert.

"That's Jimmy and his family."

In the large crowd, Maggie spotted Stacey and her family, Logan Harris and his wife, Sheriff O'Brian and his wife,
and Claire Pascal from the gift shop. Ben had mentioned
that his parents would be there. Handkerchiefs were si-

lently raised by those who were honoring someone who never had much attention when she was alive.

Maggie saw Kevin Stevenson with his distinctive white Stetson. She nudged Robert and nodded toward him as he walked behind the chairs and had an animated conversation with Eddy. Eddy finally broke away and took an empty seat in the third row.

Four uniformed deputies had been present from the beginning, and had taken their places at each corner of the canopy. The crowd became agitated as they noticed Ben. The deputy nearest Ben came over and stepped in front of him. The sheriff and the other deputies calmed the crowd.

Heads bowed as the preacher made his comments. Everyone stood for the final blessing and lowering of the casket. Maggie noticed Ben observing Mrs. Williams when she raised her head and glanced around. He caught her eye and nodded. She looked away.

After the final prayer, the deputy with Ben motioned for him to leave and escorted them to the dirt road where Robert had parked. The officer got into his vehicle and provided an escort until they reached the entrance to the freeway, then broke away.

As the Jeep escalated, Maggie turned to Ben, who sat behind Robert. "While I have everyone here, let me mention one small matter that needs attention."

"What's that?" Ben asked.

"When Audrey died, she left some money in the bank, and I recall you mentioned a safe deposit box. Those need to be closed. Your name is still on the accounts, so you're entitled to claim that money."

"I don't want any of Audrey's money. Give it to her mother to help pay for the funeral."

"You'll need to sign some documents."

"That means I'll have to go to the bank in Medford. Would you go with me?"

"Sure."

Robert merged into the main lanes. He glanced at Maggie. "I want you to stay turned around and watch our rear. I think we're being followed. Get 911 on your phone."

On the freeway a few miles from town, two pickups accelerated. One managed to get ahead of Robert, and the other stayed on Robert's left, preventing him from changing lanes. The front pickup slowed down, forcing him to do the same, and the second one veered toward him. The front pickup suddenly stopped. Robert hit his brakes and swerved onto the shoulder. The second pickup parked in a way that trapped Robert.

Maggie told the 911 operator that they had been forced off the road and asked for help.

Kevin climbed out of the pickup on Robert's left. He tapped on Robert's window and motioned for it to be lowered. Robert did nothing.

"Lower the goddamn window, or I'll shoot it out!" Kevin pulled a small gun from inside his shirt.

Robert lowered the window a few inches. Kevin put both hands on top of the vehicle and leaned down with his face close to Robert's. Four other men stood near Kevin.

"A gun is aimed at us, and we're surrounded. Please hurry," Maggie whispered to 911 and hung up. Hiding behind her hat, she crouched in the well of the seat.

"Bobby Parsons," Kevin said. "You know better than to be associatin' with scum like this." He glared into the back seat. "We don't tolerate dirty fags." He pulled back and eyed Robert. "If you know what's good for you and that property of yours, you won't show up again with him."

"I'll find you if there's any damage to my property," Robert said. "And you'll start having trouble with your other leg."

"Unlock the back door."

"You've got to be kidding." Robert quickly turned and whispered, "Get down."

Kevin took a step back and pointed his gun at Robert. "Do what you're told, or I'll blow your head off. I've been wanting to do that for a long time."

Robert slowly unlocked the doors while Charles and Ben ducked below the top of the front seat.

Kevin jerked opened the back door, pulled Ben out, and pushed him up against the Jeep.

Robert glanced at Maggie and whispered. "Stay down. I'm going to rush him." He grabbed the door handle and waited for Kevin to look away.

Kevin motioned with his gun. "Get over here, Joey."

A heavyset, muscular man covered with tattoos moved toward Ben.

Kevin kept his aim on Robert. "Bobby Parsons, you're going to be sorry you were ever born. If law enforcement will not do anything, we are."

Joey landed a sucker punch in Ben's ribs. He groaned and doubled over. The other cowboys were ready to join in.

Kevin turned to watch Joey execute a karate chop across the back of Ben's shoulders and knee him in the groin. Robert forcefully shoved his door open, throwing Kevin off balance.

Robert tackled him. A bullet grazed the top of the Jeep as the gun was knocked from Kevin's hand.

Joey pulled a knife from his belt and lunged. The knife caught Ben in the stomach. A siren got closer. Except for Kevin, the cowboys ran for their pickups.

Kevin scrambled for his gun. Robert kicked it under the Jeep.

Kevin ran to the passenger door of the nearest pickup and jumped in. Both vehicles sped off.

Robert grabbed Ben and helped him into the Jeep. Charles squeezed into a corner of the back seat, pulled Ben in, and tried to stop the bleeding. Robert found an old blanket in the back of the Jeep to cover Ben. Maggie took off her jacket and handed it to Charles, who pressed it against the wound.

Robert got in. "We're taking Ben to the hospital in Ogden." He started the engine.

A sheriff's patrol car pulled up. Both deputies ran to them.

Robert quickly told them what happened and that the gun was under his Jeep. He said they needed to get to the hospital. The deputies agreed to follow and stepped aside to retrieve the gun as soon as the Jeep moved.

Robert drove rapidly toward the canyon. Charles did his best to comfort Ben.

The deputies moved ahead of the Jeep and gave them a siren escort to the McKay-Dee Hospital complex. While Ben was being treated, Robert, Charles, and Maggie gave a statement.

After the deputies left, Maggie asked Robert, "Kevin Stevenson looks to be in his forties. Maybe we should put him on the list of suspects in Audrey's death?"

"Yep. Probably for several other things too."

Because his ribs had been broken and the knife had punctured his stomach, Ben remained in the hospital in a serious, but stable condition.

CHAPTER 58

Maggie

Sunday, October 11, 2020

Logan called early on Sunday morning. "Maggie, I heard what happened. Is Ben okay?"

"Yes, he'll be fine. They're keeping him for a couple of days."

"How are you? I heard you were also in the vehicle."

"I'm okay." She and Robert had recovered together when they returned to Salt Lake after dropping Charles off, but she wasn't going to disclose that to Logan. Robert had driven directly to his home, and they poured a glass of wine to unwind. Their differences on the case seemed to be behind them, but he was still melancholy.

Detaching from an ugly day needed to be done slowly and in increments. She didn't want to be alone and needed Robert's hugs, even if they weren't as warm. She had asked to stay in his guest room. She had seen too many people in law enforcement who used alcohol, drugs, and sex to blot out what they had seen during the day, only to create additional problems. She avoided these but needed to take it slow.

"Good," Logan said. "Can we talk a few minutes about a new development?"

"Sure."

"Several people are claiming they saw Ben Stillman in town around the time Audrey died. It's because of that story in the paper. Most of them don't have anything, but I have one person who can place Ben at Audrey's cabin during the winter and early spring of 2017."

"Can this witness be corroborated?" She was enjoying a cup of coffee with Robert on his deck and was cuddled in one of his bathrobes that was much too large for her. She didn't want to sound fatigued, but she needed a day of rest away from everything.

"A jury would find her testimony credible," he continued. "It's the sheriff's wife, Marion. She's very careful with the truth. She lives just down the road. She says she saw Ben at the cabin long after he moved out."

"Do you have anything besides her statement? Does she confirm he was there on March 18?" She glanced up at Robert. His eyes conveyed curiosity.

"It's beginning to look like he had motive, means, and opportunity. His credit card records have a gas purchase in Ogden on that date. He only needed a couple of hours. Audrey was saying ugly things about him, so we can presume he was angry. You have to admit, he's the most likely one to know about the poisonous plant. If we can prove he was spotted at the cabin on or about March 18, we've got probable cause."

"I guess the belladonna is the key, isn't it?" She was annoyed at his flimsy case. The car Ben was driving was the real key, and she had not yet mentioned it. *Logan isn't dreaming up this stuff. He's still clinging to Hank's version of what happened. Maybe the mayor is pushing it too.* "Logan, I believe you when you say people are coming forward. We both need to know what they're saying. Would you set up interviews?"

"Sure."

"One other thing." Maggie walked to the edge of Robert's deck. His house was in the foothills, and she could watch the immense Salt Lake valley coming to life in the early morning. "You remember that note on the cabin door when I was there? My guess is Kevin Stevenson did that. He's the one who threatened me on the sidewalk. Now we have this assault on Ben. He talked about taking the law into his own hands. You've got a vigilante issue up there in Medford. Someone is afraid of what I'll find out, and my life is in danger as well as Ben's."

She frowned. "Something is going on. We saw Kevin talking to Eddy at the funeral, and Eddy might be tied to Audrey's death. Eddy and Kevin pal around, and they're up to no good. Ben will probably file charges against Kevin, his pal Joey, and Eddy as well, if we can connect them to a conspiracy."

"We picked Kevin and his buddies up last night for the highway assault. We have the gun and also found the bullet and the casing. Kevin's refusing to make a statement without a lawyer. You think Eddy also had something to do with it?"

"Glad to hear you got them. Right now, we both know Eddy's got a lousy reputation, and he's uncooperative. From his body language at his interview, I suspect he could have assaulted Audrey."

"I've already alerted the sheriff to watch him closely. For your own safety, you need to stay out of town. You'll be okay with Bobby Parsons driving, but if we need to meet, be careful. Don't bring Ben up here under any circumstances."

"I need to take him up to close the joint bank accounts he had with Audrey. Could we get an escort for that?"

"Yeah, let me know when. Drive a vehicle no one will recognize. By the way, when will I get the affidavit about Ben's gas purchase in Ogden?"

"We've got it ready. Just need Ben's signature." *The affidavit mentions Ben drove his boss's car. I wonder if he will notice that.*

After hanging up, Maggie shook her head at Robert. "It's Sunday morning. Logan says hello."

CHAPTER 59

Maggie

Monday, October 12, 2020

Why am I doing this? Maggie thought as she drove to her condo from Robert's place. *Our client still appears to be innocent. That business with the gas purchase seems minor, and the Mercedes is our ace in the hole. I just put my life in danger because he wants to clear his name.* By the time she unlocked her front door, she was certain someone was trying to frame Ben and that person would not stop. The next murder could be him.

Maggie called Ben. "Trouble is brewing." He was being released from the hospital that afternoon and would be back at work in a week. "Someone thinks she saw your truck at Audrey's cabin during the winter and spring before Audrey died. She may testify that she saw it there in mid-March. I haven't mentioned the Mercedes you drove to Ogden on March 18 because you haven't signed the affidavit yet. If they're operating on faulty information right now, we aren't going to correct them until we get your signature under oath."

"I'll have no problem signing it. I never went back to the cabin after I moved in August 2016."

"I believe you, but we need to play along with them until you actually sign the document. Tell me about your truck. What's the brand? What color?" She was taking notes at her dining room table.

"It's a red 2015 Ford F-150 pickup."

"Anything to distinguish it? Decals? Any special equipment? A gun rack? Any damage that never got repaired?"

"No. It's just a regular truck. It has one set of seats. I didn't get the crew cab option. Nothing to distinguish it. No damage."

"When did you buy it?"

"Late 2015. It was a demo vehicle at the dealership. I bought it when the new models came out."

"I need to get pictures. Is it at your place? Can I photograph it?"

"Yeah, it's there. You've got the address. It's in the parking lot behind the building."

"I'll stop by today."

Ben became agitated. "Do you have any idea how many red Ford trucks get sold in Madison County? I probably sold ten trucks a month. At least two of them were red. Aren't they supposed to prove it's me? Why do I have to prove it isn't me?"

"I know. I know. You're up against prejudice. The town's grasping at straws. It sounds like Logan only has one witness who has anything credible to say. If we have enough ammunition, we can cut this off at the pass."

An hour later, Ben called her back. "I just remembered something."

"Tell me."

"I sold a lot of red trucks, and one of them went to Carl. It was in August 2016, just before I moved. He lived in the neighborhood. It may have been his truck and not mine."

"Describe it."

"Same as mine, but it was a 2016. He bought it when we were clearing out the 2016 models. The only difference was his truck had a crew cab, the extra seating for passengers."

"Good. We could get those records if we need them. I'll print out pictures from the internet as a comparison. We'll see what the witness can identify."

She researched pictures of trucks identical to Carl's, then drove to Ben's apartment about thirty minutes away and took pictures of his truck.

After returning home, she called Gwen and Peter to let them know about the highway assault and Ben's injury. Peter left the conference call after being assured that neither Maggie nor Robert was injured, but Gwen needed more assurances.

"Maggie," Gwen asked, "that must have been very jarring. Would you like to spend some time talking about it?"

"Robert and I talked quite a bit afterwards, and I stayed over at his house so I wouldn't be alone the first night afterwards."

"Oh?"

"Don't get your hopes up. I was in his guest room. There are some complications because of the case. I don't think you can expect any romance to develop. Sorry."

"What do you mean?"

"The evidence is starting to point to Carl Stevenson as being Audrey's boyfriend, and possibly her killer. That's becoming very hard on Robert. Carl was Robert's closest friend and his mentor when he was growing up. I'm not sure he will stay on our team."

"Oh dear. That's difficult. On top of that, the highway assault must have been hard on both of you. I'll call and check on him, too."

"That's a good idea."

CHAPTER 60

Maggie

Tuesday, October 13, 2020

Robert drove Maggie to Medford and dropped her at the back door of the county office complex for the interview with the sheriff's wife.

Mrs. O'Brian was already seated when Logan and Maggie walked into the room.

"Good morning, Marion," Logan said. "Nice to see you again. I don't believe you've met Maggie Anderson, the investigator representing Ben Stillman."

Marion was a short, slightly overweight woman in her early sixties. She was dressed in a black-and-white print dress with a black blazer and carried a boxy black handbag.

"Nice to meet you. I recently met your husband." Maggie extended a hand, but Marion looked away. Maggie ignored the slight but intentionally sat next to her.

"Marion, what you have to say is important. Don't let it bother you, but we need to record this session." Logan turned on the tape recorder. "Please state your full name and where you live."

"My name is Marion O'Brian. I live with my husband, Jeffery, who's the sheriff. We live at Stevenson's Row off Highway 84, the fifth cabin in. My husband grew up there, and it's been our home since we got married forty-three years ago."

"Do you work outside the home?"

"No. I'm involved with church activities and various charities, but I'm home most of the day." Her hands were firmly clasped in a small ball on the table.

Logan nodded. "Did you know Ben Stillman or Audrey Stillman?"

"Yes. They were our neighbors for about fifteen years."

"How far away from your place was their cabin?"

Her forehead wrinkled. "Maybe a few hundred yards, or maybe more. I'm not sure. It would need to be measured."

"From your front door, can you see the cabin Ben and Audrey Stillman rented?"

"Yes." Marion looked toward Maggie.

"Can you see the place where they parked?"

"Yes. The road ended at their place. They parked in front, where you turn around."

"Are you familiar with the vehicles Ben and Audrey drove?"

"Yes. Audrey had an old car, a station wagon. Ben got new vehicles every couple of years. He had a pickup."

"Do you recall what kind of pickup Ben had just before he moved out?"

She glanced at Maggie, telegraphing that she had important information. "It was a red Ford pickup."

"Why do you remember it so clearly?"

"All his other ones were dark. When the new red one showed up, we talked about it."

"Do you remember seeing anyone get in or out of Ben's red Ford pickup?"

"Well, of course. When Ben lived there, I saw him driving his truck." She relaxed as Logan got to the important part. "Sometimes Audrey rode with him."

"When you heard Ben had moved, did you notice that the red Ford pickup was gone?"

"Yes. I didn't see the truck for a while after he left. Audrey was there alone. I remember she came to the Christmas party alone."

"Do you recall whether the red Ford pickup started showing up again at Audrey's cabin?" Logan spoke slowly and emphasized every word.

"Yes, it was in the winter. I remember snow on the ground. I would see the red Ford pickup at Audrey's house, usually in the afternoon and early evening."

"Do you recall seeing the truck there overnight?"

She frowned. "It would've been too dark for me to see that far."

"How often did you see the red Ford pickup at Audrey's house during the day?"

"It was at least once a week, sometimes more than that. It could've been during the week or on the weekends. I don't remember any pattern."

"Did you see the person who was driving the red Ford pickup?"

"I recall seeing a man who looked like Ben. It was too far for me to be certain."

"Why did he look like Ben?"

"Well, he was tall like Ben. He had on a heavy coat when it was cold, so I couldn't see how thin he was, and he always had on a cowboy hat that was a light color like Ben's."

"Were you able to identify him as Ben?"

"I couldn't say absolutely—again, I was too far away—but he looked like Ben, and I assumed it was Ben who was visiting. Who else would it be?"

"When was the last time you saw the red Ford pickup at Audrey's place?"

"I remember seeing it when I hung a St. Patrick's Day wreath on our door. That was the last time I noticed it."

"Did you see the same man on that day?"

"Yes. I remember seeing him walk from the garden. He went to the truck, put some tools inside, and got in it."

"Was it Ben?"

"I couldn't tell for sure, but he had the same hat that Ben wore and that same heavy jacket. It could've been. It was Ben's truck. Who else would be driving it?"

"Thank you, Marion." Logan turned to Maggie. "Do you have any questions?"

"Yes." Maggie removed the pictures of the Ford trucks from her case file but left them turned over. "Is it okay if I call you Marion?"

She stiffened. "Yes."

"First, Marion, I don't doubt that you saw a red Ford pickup at Audrey's cabin, and I don't doubt that you saw a man who got in and out of this pickup. I would like for you to tell us why you haven't come forward before now?"

She relaxed a little. "Oh, no one asked me. It was natural to see Ben's truck there for so long. I didn't think anything of it. I thought maybe Ben and Audrey had remained friends. It was only when the story came out in the paper that I realized Ben was up here around the time Audrey disappeared. I saw him, and I thought it was my duty to come forward."

"Do you recall seeing other men around Audrey's cabin?"

Marion furrowed her brow. "Well, there was Randy. For a while, he spent a lot of time in her garden. Brought his truck over and hauled out a lot of dead plants. Audrey told me that, and I saw him. But his truck is white."

"Did you see any other men at Audrey's cabin?"

"No, she was very private. Not many people came over, and Audrey wasn't the type to entertain men."

"What about Carl?"

"Well, of course he was there. He was the landlord. He would come over and fix things."

"What kind of truck did Carl have?"

She hesitated. "I don't remember. He had a black one for a long time, and then he got his new red truck, but I'm not sure when that was."

"So, there was another red truck in the neighborhood?"

"Yes, but I think that came later. You would have to check with someone else on that."

"Do you recall seeing any other vehicles at Audrey's place around the time she disappeared?"

"No."

"Were you friendly with Audrey?"

"Oh yes! I went over for a cup of tea now and again. When she walked up the road, she would stop and chat if I was on the porch."

"After Audrey and Ben separated, did you chat with her or go over for tea?"

"Well, let me think. I walked over and told her the details about the Christmas party. We always hold it two weeks after Thanksgiving weekend. After that, I didn't go when there was snow, but I remember going over because I had a birthday card for her mother and I wanted Audrey to deliver it for me. That was in early March."

"When you chatted with Audrey, did she ever mention anyone she was dating?"

"Oh no, I would never ask those kinds of questions."

"Did Audrey seem depressed or anxious about anything?"

"No. Audrey was always cheerful and pleasant."

"Was she feeling well? Did she have any medical conditions that you knew about?"

"No, none that I was aware of."

"Okay, going back to the truck, would you be able to recognize the red Ford pickup if you saw it again?"

"Well, I think so, but trucks sometimes look a lot alike."

"Do you remember anything special about the truck you saw? Did it have any decals on it, or maybe a gun rack inside?"

She was silent for a moment. "No, not that I recall."

"What about damage? Do you recall seeing anything like a dented fender?"

"No."

"You said the man put some tools inside. Let's explore that. The man walked from the garden, carrying some tools. Is that correct?"

"Yes."

"Do you remember what kind of tools?"

She closed her eyes. "It was a shovel and a rake. I think he also had a bucket."

"Did he open the door on the driver's side or the passenger's side, or did he put the tools in the bed of the truck?"

Marion kept her eyes closed. She used her hands as if following the man in her vision as he walked to the truck and put the tools in. "Normally, I only see the end of the vehicle. But he had backed it up to the garden. That's why I saw the doors. He opened the door behind the driver's side and put the tools inside." She opened her eyes and looked at Maggie with satisfaction.

Maggie turned over the pictures and laid them on the table. "I'm going to show you three red Ford pickups. I've labeled them A, B, and C. Do any of these trucks look like the pickup you remember seeing?"

Marion picked the pictures up one at a time and took her time. "They're all similar, but I think C is the one I saw. It has two doors on the driver's side. The man opened the door behind the driver's door. I remember that."

"Thank you. One more question. When you put up decorations for a holiday, do you put them up early, or do you usually wait until the day of the holiday?"

She exhaled. "Oh, I put decorations up early and leave them for a few days after to get the full benefit. I do things like that on Sunday afternoon after we return from church because sometimes I need my husband's help."

"If St. Patrick's Day was on a Thursday or Friday, would you have put the decorations up the Sunday before that?"

"Yes. That's my way of doing things."

"When would you have taken them down?"

"The next Sunday after St. Patrick's Day."

"If St. Patrick's Day was on a Friday in 2017, you would've taken them down on Sunday, March 19. Does that sound right?"

"Yes."

"Between Thursday, which was March 16, and Sunday, which was March 19, did you see any vehicles at Audrey's place other than her car? Either a red pickup or any other vehicle?"

She tapped her chin after a moment of thought. "Yes, I think the red pickup was there, but I don't remember which day."

"Marion, you've been helpful. Thank you. I have no further questions."

After Marion left, Logan said, "What was that all about?" His voice betrayed that it had not been a productive interview.

"She saw someone who resembled Ben. She wants to provide information about Ben, but she can't positively identify the man she saw. He was tall and maybe he was thin, and he wore a light-colored cowboy hat and a heavy coat. That's all. Her husband is the sheriff. She's been coached on making identifications, and she knows better than to identify someone falsely."

She picked up picture A and handed it to him. "This is a photo of Ben's truck that was taken yesterday. It's a red 2015 Ford F-150 pickup that Ben bought in late 2015. He still owns it. Please notice it doesn't have the crew cab feature."

She handed him photos B and C. "Both of these came from the internet. These are 2016 models. Notice that B doesn't have the second door for the crew cab and C has the extra door. Marion selected C. She saw a red Ford pickup with the crew cab."

She put the pictures down. "We're looking for someone who's tall and has a red Ford pickup with extra seating. The extra seating option has become very popular. There are probably a number of them in the county. In fact, we know Carl purchased one. You may want to get the records from the dealership. It might have been the landlord she saw."

"Damn." Logan shook his head slowly. "We'll confirm when Ben bought his vehicle, but we can't prove he was there when we think Audrey died."

Maggie found the calendar on her phone and scrolled back to March 2017. "One other small point. Marion says she put the St. Patrick's decorations out on Sunday, March 12. That's when she saw the man with the gardening tools.

We have phone and bank records showing Audrey was alive until March 16. Marion hasn't proved anything."

The disappointment on Logan's face was palpable. "You're right. We got nothing."

"No, we got something. We think we know what kind of truck her boyfriend had, but Carl also had a red pickup. Maybe all Marion saw was the landlord." She shrugged. "Maybe the boyfriend was Carl." She put the pictures back in the case file. "Who's up next?"

"Carol Stevenson, Hank's wife. She wants to know what's going on, and I can't tell her."

"How much time do we have before her appointment?"

He looked at his watch. "An hour and a half."

"I'm getting some lunch." Maggie texted Robert. "I also have a question. Have you gotten the DNA report on Hank's hair strands? Did anything interesting show up?"

"I got it yesterday. I don't know much about interpreting those reports, but he's not the father. He's related to the baby, so it goes along with our suspicion that it was one of the Stevensons, but we have hundreds of Stevensons in this county."

"Can I get a copy? Hank isn't the most likely killer because he didn't live out there, but there may be a connection we don't know about yet. I have someone who is a DNA expert. We're going to meet soon to review all the DNA reports."

"Good luck with that. I'll send it. Let me know the results as soon as you can." His voice was apprehensive and measured.

"I'll absolutely let you know if we see anything interesting."

CHAPTER 61

Maggie

Robert and Maggie found a café a couple of blocks away. They stepped outside after a quick sandwich.

Maggie glanced around and spoke pensively. "Marion suggested that Audrey's boyfriend was tall, wore a light-colored Stetson, and had a red pickup with a crew cab. It could've been Carl because he bought a truck like that in 2016. The red truck was at Audrey's place a lot. Do you think there could be two men who look like that and drive the same truck model?"

She knew she could create reasonable doubt for the defense by asking the dealership to provide a list of all red Ford trucks with a crew cab that were sold during a certain time frame. For Robert's sake, she hoped the truck had not been Carl's and they could find someone else who fit the description who visited Audrey.

Slowly, Robert looked up and down the street. "Yep. There are a lot of them. I'm tall. Not as thin as Ben, but I wear a light-tan hat. Could even have been me if I had a truck like that."

Maggie checked the time. "It's a small town. Let's explore a little." It felt like a wild goose chase, but Marion had suggested the possibility, and Maggie wanted Robert to know that she wasn't targeting Carl without reason.

They circled several blocks and went through multiple parking lots, looking for red pickups. Two-thirds of the vehicles were pickups, and several of them were red. If the red truck had a crew cab, she took a picture of the license plate. In thirty minutes, they found three trucks that matched the description.

Robert had several places he wanted to check out and promised to keep looking after he dropped her off. It seemed important for him to still cling to the hope that it wasn't Carl.

CHAPTER 62

Maggie

Carol was chatting with Logan when Maggie returned. Seeing her up close, Maggie recognized her as tall, attractive, physically fit, and mid-fifties. Her shoulder-length blond hair, loosely tied with a scarf, set off her good looks. She was smartly dressed in fashionable jeans, a dark-brown turtleneck, and a turquoise necklace. She also wore a fringed leather jacket that matched a soft leather hand-bag. She was friendly, but had the air of someone who had authority and used it.

"Sorry, I'm late!" Sitting, Maggie nodded toward Carol, took out her phone, and wrote the tag numbers of the three red pickups on a piece of paper.

"No issue. We just started," Logan said. "Carol would like to talk off the record. Is that okay with you?"

"Sure." Maggie handed Logan the slip of paper. "Would you have these tag numbers run at the DMV?"

"Carol, go ahead and state your concerns again." Logan faced Maggie. "I haven't had a chance to respond to her yet. Why don't you take the lead?" He turned to a phone on a side table and asked his assistant to come get the tag numbers.

"Ms. Anderson, it's nice to meet you finally. I understand you're the one who's behind this investigation." Carol's voice started calmly, but slowly began to quiver. "I don't know if you know this, but my husband is the most prominent businessman in this county, and he comes from one of the founding families."

"I've met Hank." Maggie kept an even tone, although she was incensed by how Carol had started the conversation. "He provided some valuable rental information."

"I'm aware of that. My point is that you're targeting our family as suspects. The whole town knows, and people are asking questions. It isn't pleasant, to say the least. None of my family members had anything to do with Audrey's death." She stopped to catch her breath. "You can't possibly be suspecting any of the Stevensons. Why are you asking us for DNA? Ben's the one you should go after."

"May I call you Carol?"

"Yes."

"Carol, thank you for expressing your concerns, and I understand your frustration. I think we all want this case to be resolved." That was the limit of the syrupy response she could pour on Carol's fire. "You're aware, of course, that I work for the lawyer who represents Ben. When we got lab reports showing some foreign DNA on the skeleton, Ben was the first person who was tested. His results didn't match. Despite that, Logan has asked for every possible piece of evidence that could place Ben in Madison County around the time of Audrey's death. He's checked everything. Ben moved to Salt Lake in August 2016. They divorced in November 2016. Audrey died in March 2017. Ben was nowhere near Stevenson's Row in March." She was tired of being the villain. "There simply isn't any compelling evidence against Ben."

Carol's lips tightened. "Well then, since you've cleared your client, aren't you finished? Can't you just leave it to Logan to wrap up?"

"I agreed to keep working in order to solve the case. I think everyone would like to have an answer, including Ben. Audrey was his wife for fifteen years."

"Randy tells me you're laying the blame squarely on one of the Stevensons."

Maggie should not have been surprised that Randy betrayed his promise to Logan. He had discussed his interview with his mother and had made it sound like their family was under siege when, in fact, he had refused to give DNA to clear himself. Maggie looked at Logan to make sure Carol's angst had registered with him.

Logan frowned.

"Actually, it's the opposite of what you're thinking." Maggie squelched her rising anger and intentionally adopted a low-keyed voice as if she was updating a subordinate team member. "We want to use the DNA tests to eliminate your family from suspicion. Even if we find the match we're looking for, it doesn't prove who killed Audrey. All it does is give us someone who was close to Audrey, who might fill in some missing blanks."

"But why are you harassing us?"

Maggie crossed her arms and leaned forward. "Because someone with Stevenson DNA had something to do with burying Audrey."

Carol copied Maggie's posture. "Do you know how many people in this county are related to the Stevensons? Are you seriously going to test all of them? You're grasping at straws." She straightened and turned to Logan. "She's employed by the suspect. Is it proper for her to be involved in your investigation?"

"It's normal for the defense attorney to have their own investigator," Logan said. "They have every right to know all the evidence and interview all the witnesses."

"Have you arrested Ben?"

"No. There's insufficient evidence."

"Has the evidence cleared him like she said?"

"Pretty much. Unless something new comes up, we can't charge him."

"What you're saying is this case can't be solved. I'm also presuming that Ben doesn't need a defense attorney or an investigator since you can't charge him, isn't that right?"

Logan stared at her. "We haven't made a final determination yet."

Carol stood and picked up her handbag. "It sounds to me like I should talk with the mayor. I can't imagine why this county is spending our hard-earned tax dollars chasing after a dead-end case. Audrey is deceased and properly buried. We all know who did it, but we can't prove it in court." She moved toward the door. "Logan, you need to think hard about this one."

She closed the door firmly.

Maggie waited for Logan to speak. He had a frustrated look.

"Where do we go from here?" she asked.

Logan's research assistant opened the door and handed him some papers.

He studied the information, muttered under his breath, and looked up. "One of those red Ford pickups belongs to Hank Stevenson. The other two belong to ranchers in the eastern part of the county. I would hardly think of them as suspects."

"Any chance Carol would be driving that truck today?"

"Yep. That's the vehicle she usually drives."

"Does the printout show a history of the vehicle?"

He looked over the report. "Yep. It was originally owned by Carl."

"And after he died, it went to Hank, and Carol drives it." Maggie decided it was time to up the ante on Carl. "Could it have been Carl who was frequently seen at Audrey's cabin?"

"Well, he owned the cabin. He was the landlord."

"Was he tall and thin?"

"He was tall, about like Ben, but I wouldn't say he was thin. He was a bit husky like Hank is now." He shook his head. "Come to think of it, Carl lost some weight after he retired and stopped going to all those events that had too much food around. He was getting a little thinner, if you ask me, but not like Ben."

Maggie stared at him. "Marion said the man in the red truck showed up in the winter and was there several times a week up to March 12. That seems to be too much for a landlord who made occasional repairs."

Logan grimaced. "Carl gave Audrey free rent starting in October. Maybe there's a reason we don't understand yet."

She had made her point. "The evidence is beginning to look like Carl was also the boyfriend. He's the only one who fits Stacey's profile."

Logan crossed his arms, his voice petulant. "There are a lot of red pickups in this county. The fact that the truck she observed looked like his vehicle doesn't mean anything to us."

CHAPTER 63

Maggie

Wednesday, October 14, 2020

Logan called Maggie on Wednesday morning. "We just got DNA results on that mysterious hat you brought in. I'll email it to you. You need to tell me what it means."

"And?" She braced herself for Logan's results.

"There may be something there. Depends on where you got the hat and how reliable the sample was. They found enough hairs with root follicles to do the DNA test. The hair belongs to one of the Stevensons."

"Is he the biological father?" She moved from behind her home office desk to her kitchen. She needed a cup of coffee in hand for this discussion.

"No, but there's a blood relationship with the baby. The owner of the hat is related to the father, just like Hank, but not as close."

"I promised I would clue you in." She coughed. She felt relieved for Robert's sake but annoyed that her theory had a big hole in it. "Hold on a minute." She sat at her dining room table. "The hat came from Carl Stevenson's cabin. It's been on his hatrack since his death. What we've confirmed with Hank's DNA, and now Carl's DNA, is that someone in the Stevenson clan was the father of Audrey's baby. It wasn't Hank or Carl, but someone they are both related to, correct?"

Logan's frustration was audible. "I'm glad it's not Carl, but the fact that it's one of the Stevensons is the last thing I want to hear. Absolutely the last thing. You know that. Tell me how you got it and why you think the findings are valid."

She gave him a detailed account of how Robert had obtained it. "Grammy is like a lot of older people. Things are left lying around for a while after someone dies. I suspect that hat hasn't been on anyone's head since Carl passed. Charles and I have been suspicious that one of the Stevensons was the father of Audrey's baby, but we didn't know who. We now have evidence pointing in that direction."

"There're a lot of Stevensons in this town. Who do you think it is?"

"We haven't pinpointed it yet. Maybe my DNA expert will see something we don't."

"I hope you won't ask me to do DNA tests on all of their clan. You know what kind of ruckus that would cause? They could probably get a court order to stop massive DNA testing." Logan stopped. "Maybe Hank already knew it was someone in his extended family. Maybe that's why he has tried to head me off."

"I might ask you to test Kevin Stevenson." She cleared her throat. "I think Hank knows something he isn't telling us. Three of them lived out there, and they are all good suspects. We've just cleared Carl from being the father. If it's not him, he didn't have a strong motive to kill her. Randy and Eddy both refused to do DNA tests. Randy's unlikely because he was too young for Audrey, so that leaves Eddy or one of the cousins, and Kevin is now a potential suspect. Eddy's reputation might include murdering someone, but I can't see him relying on poison. Like I said, we'll know more when we review our private lab report."

CHAPTER 64

Maggie

Thursday, October 15, 2020

Charles called on Monday saying the DNA reports on the two beer bottles were back, but he didn't fully understand them. Maggie asked him to email the reports to her DNA expert, Peter. She had already emailed Carl's and Hank's reports.

On Thursday afternoon at four, Peter and Maggie arrived at Charles's office. Copies of the DNA reports were passed around.

"Peter," Charles said, "I hear you're an expert. Hope you can help."

"I'll do my best. My understanding is that Robert obtained two beer bottles that had saliva from Randy Stevenson and Eddy Stevenson, correct?"

"Yes."

"And the lab was furnished with a copy of the report on Audrey's baby for comparison?"

Maggie nodded. "We already have DNA reports on Carl and Hank that link Audrey's baby to the Stevenson family. Neither of them is the father. Right now, Randy and Eddy are the most likely suspects, but we will expand to more family members if they are cleared."

Peter picked up the reports on Randy and Eddy. "How much do you want to know about DNA results? I've testified in court before as an expert witness."

"Right now, only the high-level results," Charles said. "If it becomes important for court testimony, we'll dig into the details later."

"Okay. What we're looking for is a familial or a genetic relationship, and in this case, we're looking at the Y chromosomes, which give us the paternal inheritance. Sometimes they have to do a lot of work to extract perfect DNA specimens from a sample, but it looks like these samples were fairly clean, which is good. They can't certify a comparison with the DNA from Audrey's baby because they didn't perform the baby's test, but they've given us their preliminary analysis."

Peter flipped the pages of one report and looked up. "I'm looking at Eddy's DNA first. He's been matched to Carl, who is his father, but he's not the father of Audrey's baby."

Peter leafed through the pages as if he was stalling, but he also sounded like he was about to say something important. "This is a very thorough analysis. It says that Eddy's mother is primarily from the Iberian Peninsula, which is Spain and Portugal. It also says that Eddy has a mutation called MTHFR, which is pivotal in mental health issues like bipolar disorder and schizophrenia. It doesn't mean he has these disorders, just that he carries the hereditary marker."

"That's odd," Maggie said. "Grammy told me her pioneer ancestors were from Scotland. I wonder when a Spanish ancestor slipped in."

Peter set Eddy's report down and picked up the one on Randy. After a long sip of coffee while he reviewed it again, he glanced around. "Randy is the father of Audrey's baby."

"Randy?" Maggie stared at him. She had suspected Randy of lying about having sex with Audrey, but had dismissed him as the boyfriend because he was much younger.

"Yes, it's a perfect match. His report matches Randy to Carl as his grandson, to Hank as his father, and to Audrey's baby as the father."

Maggie checked her copy of the report. "This whole time, Randy has acted like an innocent bystander. No wonder he didn't want to be tested. Everything has pointed to Carl except the DNA." She looked up. "Could it be that Carl knew this and was protecting Randy?"

"Randy may be the father of the child, but it doesn't mean he killed Audrey," Charles said. "This murder occurred three and a half years ago. What we need to know is what his motive would've been to kill her." He waited. "I think you can use this report to confront Randy, but you don't have enough to charge him with murder."

Maggie nodded. "Stacey told us that Randy showed an interest in Audrey, but Audrey thought he was too young, and Randy doesn't fit Stacey's profile. Audrey said her boyfriend had a lot of money. Stacey said the boyfriend was married and had influence in the community. Only Carl and Hank fit that profile. Could one of them be protecting Randy?"

The reports distracted Peter. "I think there's another puzzle here."

"What do you mean?" Maggie shifted in her chair and frowned, still not ready to accept how Randy fit into the story.

Peter carefully laid out the DNA reports on the conference room table. At the top, he placed Carl's report. "I'm going to show you something." He tore a blank sheet of paper from Charles's yellow legal pad. "May I borrow this for a minute?"

He placed the yellow paper next to Carl's report and rested his hand on the paper. "This represents Grammy. Here we have the grandfather and the grandmother."

Hank's and Eddy's reports were placed just below. "Think of this as a family tree. Here are two of their sons. There's a third son, isn't there?"

"Yes," Maggie said. "Hank is the oldest, Jimmy is the second and runs the ranch, and Eddy is the youngest. There are three girls in the middle."

Peter set Randy's report below Hank's and the baby's below that. "This is the genealogy. Carl and Grammy had a son named Hank. Hank had a son named Randy. Randy's report makes sense. He inherited his father's genes, and his mother's genes are consistent with what we know about her. She's Caucasian, Anglo-Saxon with a small amount of Germanic. The baby had those same genes."

Peter picked up Eddy's report. "Eddy inherited his father's genes, but the markers for his mother are completely different. None of these markers show up in Hank's report, and none of them carry down to Randy's report. As you said, it's surprising to suggest that Grammy had ancestral roots in Spain." He put the report next to Hank's and gave Charles and Maggie a firm, penetrating stare. "I would stake my professional reputation on the fact that Eddy had a different mother. Hank and Eddy are half-brothers."

Charles and Maggie looked at each other in disbelief before turning back to Peter.

"How does that affect the case?" Maggie asked.

"Who knew about it?" Charles asked.

"Here's another thought," Peter said. "We know Eddy has a genetic marker for mental health issues. Could that have shown itself in some manner that led to killing Audrey?"

"We think someone gave Audrey a cup of poisoned tea," Maggie said. "That's not something Eddy would've done. He's capable of murder, in my opinion, but he's the type who would've used physical force."

Charles turned to her. "Maggie, you've uncovered the father of the baby. Good work. Now you need to identify who gave Audrey the poisoned tea. I'm not sure how this new information about Eddy fits in, but I'm sure you'll figure it out."

Maggie gathered up her copies. "Right now, I have no clues. I'll meet with the DA and see what he knows about the family history."

She asked Peter and Charles to keep the DNA results a secret until she could meet with Logan. She was also concerned because Robert had been close to the family and Carl. How would he react to the fact that Eddy had a different mother? Did he know about it, or would this be another unwelcomed surprise?

CHAPTER 65

Maggie

Friday, October 16, 2020

Robert drove Maggie to Medford. On the way, he asked about the DNA meeting, but she said there were some surprises and she needed to confer with Logan before disclosing any information.

"Did you know Eddy had a different mother?" Maggie said to Logan in his evidence room. She had already passed along to him copies of the DNA reports on Eddy and Randy and identified Randy as the biological father of Audrey's baby. She watched carefully for his reaction. She was now certain he couldn't close down the case because her DNA results would keep it alive.

"Nope," Logan said. "Surprises me as well. There must be a reasonable explanation for that, but don't ask me what it is." He sounded frustrated.

"I'm going out on a limb here." Maggie stood and paced. "Tell me if I'm completely off base." She picked up the report on Eddy and looked for his age. "I'm guessing Carl was a little too friendly with some woman about forty years ago and she got pregnant. For whatever reason, Carl took the baby and asked Grammy to raise it as her own." She put the report down. "How does that land on you?"

Logan listened intently and spoke hesitantly. "It could be. Carl was a very friendly, outgoing man. Eddy came along after all the other kids."

Maggie nodded. "Grammy came from a polygamous family. She grew up with men who had multiple wives. The women were subservient, and they raised their children together. Forty years ago, when she was told to raise someone else's child, I bet she did exactly what she was told to do."

"I can't speculate on that, but it could be true. Hank must know. I wonder if Carol knows."

"I think she does, but she'll never tell. She's been in the family for over thirty years. Grammy would've confided in her at some point, but Carol protects the family secrets."

"It's beginning to make sense." Logan's eyes were fearful.

"I'm also speculating that Carl was doing it again four years ago. Only there's a hitch. Audrey was also involved with Randy, and she kept her second boyfriend a secret. Carl probably thought the baby was his kid."

"We also have the possibility that Carl was never the boyfriend, and they knew all along it was Randy's baby," Logan said. "That secret would also be protected."

"Randy knew about the poisoned plant, but he doesn't fit Stacey's profile. If it's him, why would Audrey imply Carl was the boyfriend?"

Logan's eyes narrowed. "What are you suggesting?"

"I'm not sure yet. We heard a rumor that there could be some type of blackmail in the family. I think we've uncovered the blackmailer's secret. I'm not saying it's true. I'm just putting that possibility on the table."

Logan raised his eyebrows. "Tell me what you heard."

"Robert has a source that believes Eddy was blackmailing Carl. There's no evidence, just someone who knows Eddy pretty well. Robert thinks it's a reliable source."

Logan stared at her. "I don't rely on rumors, but I also have reason to believe that could be true. I won't name names, but someone in the Stevenson family told me before Carl died he was being blackmailed. I never saw any hard evidence, but Carl seemed to be under a lot of pressure in his last year. What do you think the possibilities are?"

"I think we have three." She counted with her fingers. "Carl could've been the boyfriend, and Randy was Audrey's secret. She told Carl she was pregnant, and he thought the baby was his. Or Carl was just the friendly landlord, and Randy was the boyfriend. Randy panicked when she got pregnant and went to his grandpa for help. Third possibility, Randy was the boyfriend, and Carl had nothing to do with it. In any of these possibilities, Eddy found out and blackmailed Carl because Carl had the money and power."

She drummed her fingers on the table. "Carl knew how to handle problems diplomatically. You knew him well. If you were Carl and you thought a young woman got pregnant either by you or by your grandson, what would you do?"

The air was still. Maggie kept her gaze on Logan.

Logan frowned as he doodled on a piece of paper for several seconds before looking up. "If I was Carl, I'd have walked across the street to the bank and taken out enough cash to convince Audrey to leave town. Then I would quietly pay child support for the kid. He had the money to do it."

He became quiet. "And I would never tell my wife or Randy's mother."

"Would you have killed Audrey if she refused the money and went public?"

"No, I would never risk a murder conviction, and neither would Carl. Everyone has a price. I would pay whatever it took. It would've been in her best interest to start fresh somewhere else and not embarrass her mother. Kids born out of wedlock are still frowned upon in this county."

"Do you think Audrey would've refused the money no matter what was offered and one of them poisoned her?"

Logan's mouth opened and closed. He shook his head slowly. "I can't answer that."

"Do we have enough to subpoena Carl's bank records?"

"Probably not."

"I have an idea. I think I can get evidence to support this, if there is any. Give me a day or so."

Logan's assistant knocked and opened the door a crack. "Logan, the mayor wants to see you ASAP."

Logan rose and walked toward the door. "I'm an elected official. The mayor can't fire me. Do what you need to do. If Carl is the one who poisoned her, he's already dead, and the case can be closed."

Maggie called Mrs. Madison at Hank's office to say she needed to ask about a financial issue and wondered if she could come over right away. She didn't want to give Mrs. Madison time to talk to Hank.

CHAPTER 66

Maggie

Maggie's first impulse was to walk over to Hank's office, but she thought about what happened the last time she ventured out alone. She called Robert. He was curious about what she was after, but she would only say she was following a hunch. He took her to Hank's office building.

"What can I do for you?" Mrs. Madison said politely as Maggie entered her office.

"I'm following up on a piece of information that needs to be checked out. It probably has a reasonable explanation, but, you know, investigative work is often a process of just getting these explanations. I'm sorry to bother you with this."

Mrs. Madison frowned.

Maggie assumed Mrs. Madison was well connected to the gossip circuit, so she acted gossipy. "For instance, we have an odd DNA sample that was on the corpse, and we're trying to get DNA tests to prove certain individuals had no connection with Audrey's murder. We've been able to eliminate several people already."

Maggie wanted this information on the grapevine. She watched Mrs. Madison's face carefully. Little twitches on her otherwise stoic face confirmed she already knew what Maggie was talking about.

"Not a problem. If I can help clear anyone, I'm glad to do it. What do you need?"

"We've run across some information related to a large sum of money. Large enough that I think it could only have come from Carl, and it's probably totally normal for him. Did he ever take large cash amounts out of the bank?"

Mrs. Madison was quiet for a minute. "Well, if they were purchasing a new property, there would be the down payment, but it has been several years since they purchased property. You also have the annual trips where Carl bought new cattle for the ranch. That's all I can think of right now. He was pretty much retired before he died."

"Tell me about the cattle trips."

"Well, he usually went to Wyoming or Montana to make a deal for spring calves. We would pick the animals up after they were born and take them down to the ranch to fatten up for the slaughterhouses. There's a slaughterhouse near Ogden that we use, and it's much cheaper to transport calves than grown animals."

"When did he make these trips?"

"It usually depended on the weather. It would've been between January and April when the breeders knew what they had to offer."

"Would you check your records for January and February 2017 and see if he took a trip then? That might be the explanation I'm looking for."

"Certainly." Mrs. Madison turned and concentrated on her computer. "It looks like there was a buying trip in early February 2017." Her voice sounded wary. "What are you looking for?"

"We have information about a large chunk of money, probably in January or February, maybe as late as March. It was probably just a normal transaction for Carl. I can't disclose more than that right now. Do you see anything like that?"

"Well, let's see." She scrolled through the records. "He went on a trip, and I paid his expense report for February 2017. He went to Wyoming. Let me look at the bank account transactions and see if there was anything else. He usually left a check with the breeder on those trips, and then we paid in full when the calves were delivered."

"I'd appreciate getting those details. Sounds perfectly normal and would explain a lot."

Mrs. Madison squinted. "In early February 2017, he wrote a check to a breeder in Wyoming for $125,000 as a deposit. The balance was paid in May. He wrote another check for $100,000 later in February. That was a loan to Carl." She kept searching. "Here, in late March, the loan is paid back. That's a little unusual, but he paid it back, so I didn't need any paperwork."

"Ah, that must be it. Maybe that's why we found a reference to $100,000. It was a loan. Nothing wrong with that. Thank you. You've been very helpful." She intentionally softened her voice. "Could I get copies of the bank statements for the files so we can clear up this confusion?"

"Of course." She sounded more assured, found the documents in the old records, and made the copies.

Maggie thanked her again and left quickly, walking out with proof that $100,000 had been withdrawn on February 17 and redeposited on March 21 in 2017. It was useless as court evidence because she couldn't prove Carl's intent, but it might be useful in smoking out a confession.

Maggie wondered how long it would be before Hank learned she had been back to his office. Hank simply didn't realize what the records contained.

CHAPTER 67

Maggie

"Did you get what you needed?" Robert asked as Maggie climbed into the Jeep.

"Yes." She didn't know what to say. She had just implicated Robert's mentor in a bribery effort that might have led to murder. "Logan has a theory we're trying to confirm. I think I got what we need, but I must go over it with him to see what it means. It's not something I can talk about right now."

She mused about her new evidence as they drove home. Carl most likely attempted to persuade Audrey to move out of town. One logical conclusion was that Audrey refused the money, and as a result, she was poisoned and buried. Carl could have forged the note he claimed Audrey wrote.

She had not kept anything from Robert before and had poured out her innermost suspicions about Carl. It was now becoming too difficult. Marion's confirmation that the red truck had frequently been at Audrey's cabin confirmed Carl's involvement. The bank withdrawal suggested he had attempted a payoff. The only other complication to resolve was Randy's involvement. The facts were coming in fast, and she needed to talk them over with her team.

They were mostly silent on the way back to Salt Lake. She understood his loyalty to the man who had mentored him and stayed his friend for life. She feared bursting his balloon.

She also wondered whether her budding romance with Robert would survive if she identified Carl as the person who poisoned Audrey. Would Robert forgive her?

When Robert pulled into the parking lot at Maggie's condo complex, she had a heavy heart. She reached for the door handle.

Robert put his hand on her arm. "Let's talk for a minute. Something seems to be bothering you, and it probably has something to do with me."

Her heartbeat was loud. She could barely talk. "The case is getting sticky. I've probably broken some ethics rules by bringing you into the investigation."

"Please don't talk in legalese. Would you tell me what's on your mind?"

She stared out the front window of the Jeep, too conflicted to respond. She had never learned to successfully communicate difficult issues with a romantic partner and usually walked away when things got tough.

"Can I guess?" Robert said. "You've stopped talking about the case. It has something to do with Carl, doesn't it?"

"Yes."

"You've proved your theory. Some of the new evidence isn't looking good for him?"

She barely nodded. "That's about right."

He gently turned her face toward him. "Look. I wasn't going to say this yet, but I want you to be my girl. We're not there yet, and you may change your mind, but I hope you don't. I'm not going to change my mind, no matter how the case goes. You're all about truth and justice, and I hope you always stay that way. I don't want you to think I'm not on your side. I don't ever want you to think you have to be afraid of telling me the truth because I won't like it."

"Carl was like a father to you." Her voice quivered.

"Yes, and I'll always love that memory. Nothing will ever take that away. But I know he wasn't an angel. Let's just let things fall where they will. When you told me about the red truck, I suspected it was his, and he's probably the one Audrey was having an affair with. You may even have some DNA results you don't want to tell me about. I don't need to know all of it right now, but whatever the evidence is—good, bad, or sideways—I'll be okay with it. Let's just get that out there and move on."

She hugged him to hide the tears of relief in her eyes.

"Are we good?" he said.

"Yes. I'll tell you the details next time we're together." She leaned forward and gave him a quick goodnight kiss.

CHAPTER 68

Maggie

Monday, October 19, 2020

Maggie called Logan first thing on Monday and arranged to meet in the early afternoon when he returned from a court appearance.

Robert needed to go back to the cabin early because he was working on a broken window. He picked up the materials in Salt Lake, and he and Maggie were there by ten thirty. On the way up, she told him about the DNA results and her new theory about Carl's involvement. He wasn't happy, but understood where she was going with it.

It was the third Monday in October, and the cabins seemed deserted. The weather was crisp, the sun was shining, the leaves were quietly falling, and the forest was still except for the rushing river. Since her time was free until the afternoon, she walked to Audrey's cabin.

She had grown accustomed to holding Audrey's sachet while it was in her pocket and talking to her as a way of clearing her own thoughts. She was never sure if these imagined talks were a way to sort out her intuition, or a way of getting messages from Audrey, but it always worked. *Give me more guidance, please. Help me find the truth. If Carl was involved in poisoning you, it's going to devastate Robert.*

Gwen's car was parked at Grammy's cabin and she wondered how Grammy was doing now that Gwen was involved. Maggie knew she couldn't stop for a visit because Carol would hear about it and would cause trouble. Passing Randy's cabin, she wondered if Karen would become interested in caring for Grammy.

When she reached the sheriff's home, Maggie stopped and looked toward where Audrey's old cabin had been. The yellow police tape had been removed. The remains of the garden were still there, but the faltering fence and the old cabin were gone. She understood more completely what Marion had seen when she glanced out and saw vehicles and people.

Maggie went closer, climbed partway up the small hill, and tried to find the spot where the body had been buried. She was close, but the foundation for the new cabin had been poured, and the hole was no longer visible. As she turned to leave, a truck carrying a fresh supply of lumber turned the corner.

Standing near where the grave had been, Maggie saw the sheriff's house directly behind the truck and realized that nothing obscured the line of sight. If Marion had looked out the window at the right time, she would have seen someone digging. *Is there a chance she saw it happen? Would she have understood what the person was doing? Is she withholding this information because no one has asked her?*

She also recalled that Grammy had talked about visiting Audrey's place occasionally. *Did Marion remember seeing her come up?*

Energized, Maggie scrambled down the bluff. She waved to the truck driver, made her way to the sheriff's cabin, and knocked.

Marion opened the door and stared. "Yes, what can I do for you?"

"I'm sorry to bother you. I walked over to where Audrey's cabin was and realized I had a couple more questions for you, just a few details, actually. Would you have a minute to talk?"

"Yes, come in." Marion was businesslike. "I know there's so much protocol." She hesitated before offering a seat in her cozy living room full of chintz, trinkets, and old-fashioned furniture. "I worked at the sheriff's office when I was young. That's how I met my husband. Should I be talking to you alone? Shouldn't Logan Harris be here also?"

"You're right. I can turn on the recorder on my phone. I'm meeting with Logan this afternoon, and I can play it for him." She placed her phone on the coffee table.

"That should be enough," Marion said.

"Marion, I have just a few questions, if I may—"

"Shouldn't you do the oath first? I want this to be proper. My husband always insists on following the rules."

"Of course." Maggie administered the oath.

"Now," Maggie said, "I was just over at Audrey's cabin and realized I still had a few questions. Did Audrey's cabin have a back door?" She needed an opening question that was easy and would not cause Marion to become defensive.

Marion was quiet for a moment. "No, I don't think it did. The cabins all started out as one-room log structures with one door. Some things were added on, like actual bedrooms, a bathroom, and a shed for the firewood. Audrey's place had four rooms. Two bedrooms and a bath were added on to the original. The firewood was kept outside in the front under the eaves."

"So if you were sitting on your front porch, you could see everyone who went into her cabin?"

"Well, yes, I could have, but I wasn't any sort of busybody. I didn't sit on the porch and watch her place, if that's what you mean."

Maggie shook her head. "No, I didn't mean that at all. I was simply wondering if someone could go in and out without being seen. I also remember that I only asked you about men who might have visited Audrey. Do you recall seeing any women going to Audrey's cabin?"

"Well, let me think. I sit outside and shell peas and beans once in a while. She didn't have many visitors. Her mom came out, but that's been quite a while. Sometimes I would wave. Audrey also had a friend who came to visit—that girl, Stacey. I'm sure there were others, but I don't recall right now."

"What about Grammy?"

"Yes, Grammy came down occasionally. She would stop here sometimes. She used to be quite the walker, and they were friendly. It was nice to see since Carl was always busy. Grammy was interested in the plants and the ointments. She told me about that."

"Do you recall the last time you saw Grammy visit Audrey?"

"I can't tell you exactly when it was." She cleared her throat. "It was after the snow had melted, sometime in the early spring. I remember because she hardly ever came out, and she was walking with a cane."

"Do you think it was in the early spring of 2017?"

Marion closed her eyes. "I visited Audrey just before her mother's birthday that last year, just like always. The road was muddy. It was after that when I saw Grammy come this way. I thought about going out and helping her, but the road was dry, and she was doing okay. It was a week, maybe ten days, after I had gone over to deliver the birthday card. She was probably going down for a cup of tea like she usually did. I didn't like seeing Audrey in that cabin all alone. I worried about her, you know. I was always glad to see a vehicle there or someone going to see her."

"Did you see Carl at the cabin?"

"Well, of course, he was the landlord. I think he did repairs and some of the yard work. In fact, he had his new red truck at the Christmas party that year. I remember we had a bad snowstorm, and he gave Audrey and some other folks a ride back to their cabins."

Maggie tensed slightly. Marion had just confirmed that Audrey had left the party with Carl. She tried not to show a reaction. "By any chance, did you see anyone digging on the hill next to the cabin? It would've been in the daylight, and it could've been on the weekend, maybe Sunday. It would be very useful if you could remember seeing someone up there, even if you couldn't identify him."

Marion glanced down as if she was trying hard to remember. She finally looked up apologetically. "No, I want to be useful, but I don't think I did."

"One last question, if you don't mind. I believe you said that you usually go to church on Sunday morning. Is that correct?"

"Yes. Every week."

"Does your husband go with you?"

"Yes."

"What time do you leave?"

"Usually around nine thirty. It only takes a few minutes. We should be there by ten, and we like to get there a little before services start."

"What time do you usually get home?"

"We always have lunch with a group of friends. We don't get home until around two or three in the afternoon."

Maggie thanked Marion for her willingness to answer more questions and turned off the recorder. Before leaving, she assured her that Logan would hear her new testimony.

Walking back, she mulled over what she had learned. None of the locals would have dug that grave if the O'Brians were home, but on Sunday mornings, they were always gone.

CHAPTER 69

Maggie

Maggie walked into Logan's office. "We don't have everything, but we're getting closer. By the way, what did the mayor have to say the other day?"

"He's still putting pressure on me to arrest Ben, but I haven't found anyone who saw him around the time she was killed. I also told the mayor we've got new DNA evidence, and I would get back to him with the results." Logan frowned and shook his head. "If Carl poisoned Audrey, it's a good thing he's already dead. If he was still alive, this town wouldn't be able to handle it."

"Let's go over everything and see how it fits in." She opened the door to the evidence room. "I saw something today that will interest you."

Maggie took out a yellow pad and sat next to him. "First, let's review the days in 2017 that we care about." She drew eleven small boxes horizontally and labeled them from Sunday, March 12, through Wednesday, March 22.

She tapped each date as she identified what had happened. "Marion O'Brian saw the red pickup and the tall, thin man on Sunday, March 12. He could've been Audrey's boyfriend, or he could've been Carl. We know that Audrey's last banking transaction was on March 15. Her last phone call was on March 16." She made Xs on each of those days.

She pulled out the new bank statements from her case file. "I talked to Carl's bookkeeper. I didn't tell her what we suspected, but I got what we needed. Carl cashed a check for $100,000 on February 17, 2017. He probably learned she was pregnant around that time. I have no doubt he offered the money to her. We can't prove it, but it's circumstantial and suspicious. She probably turned him down."

"Why was the bookkeeper so willing to give you that information?" Logan asked.

"When I met with her the first time, Hank told her to be cooperative and give me anything I wanted. Mrs. Madison was still following his initial instructions."

Logan grinned and shook his head.

She kept filling in the dates. "We suspect Audrey died on March 18. I think she was buried on Sunday morning, March 19. On March 21, the $100,000 was returned to the bank."

Logan studied the chart. "Why do you think she was buried on Sunday?"

"Let me show you." She tore off a sheet of paper and drew a map. Along the left edge, she wrote the word *highway*, and along the right side, she wrote the word *river*. Between the two, she drew horizontal lines to represent the dirt road that curved to the right before it reached the river. She put ten small squares beside the road. Five were along the top of the road, two more were on the river side, and two were on the right after the curve. The last one was at the end.

Starting on the left, she identified the houses. "This is cabin #1, summer residence." She put a large *X* on it.

"Cabin #2 is Robert's place." She made another *X*.

"Cabins #3 and #4 are Carl Stevenson's and Randy Stevenson's." Two more *X*s.

"At the point where the road curves, the O'Brians live in #5." It was labeled with an *O*.

Cabins #6, #7, #8, and #9 all received an *X* because they were summer residences.

She got to the last house. "This is where Audrey lived." She labeled cabin #10 with an *A*.

Using a finger, she traced her route. "This morning, I walked down the road and saw the view that Marion O'Brian sees every time she looks out her front window. It's a direct line to Audrey's cabin and the hill where her corpse was found." She stopped at the O'Brian's home. "If that grave was dug during the daytime, Marion or Sheriff O'Brian could've seen someone digging. It's too dark out there to dig at night."

She drew a straight line from the sheriff's cabin to Audrey's place. "Anyone who lived in Stevenson Row knew that Audrey's cabin was always visible to the O'Brians. Marion is home most of the time. They attend church on Sunday mornings. They leave at nine-thirty and get home around two o'clock. The time for someone to dig unnoticed was on Sunday morning. I'm suggesting the person who buried her knew the O'Brians would be at church on Sunday morning."

She let her theory sink in. "Robert told me he wasn't there much during 2017. I suspect none of the summer folks were there in March, so only four cabins were occupied the day Audrey was buried: Carl's, Randy's, the O'Brian's, and Audrey's. Carl and Randy were the only men who would've been available on Sunday morning to dig a grave."

Logan examined the map, frowning. "It's a good theory, but it's all circumstantial and speculative. Right now, we still don't have enough to prove anything in court."

"We'll get there. One more question—Do you think Grammy knew anything?"

"Three and a half years ago? Maybe. She was quite the matriarch at one time, a lot like Carol is now. She's become reclusive since her health deteriorated."

Maggie eased back in her chair. "The day I met her, she was adamant that Ben Stillman should be arrested. Maybe something weighs heavily on her mind."

Logan eyed her thoughtfully. "If she knows something, she'll never tell. The Stevensons keep their problems to themselves. Carl used to be the one who handled the family troubles. Now it's Hank."

"Let's mesh all of this with our theories." Maggie paced like a prosecutor speaking to an investigative team. "Audrey told Stacey her boyfriend was married and powerful. Carl fits that description." She leaned against the whiteboard. "Maybe Carl thought he was the father. He withdrew $100,000, and Audrey turned it down. He was accustomed to getting his way and didn't like what Audrey intended to do, so he did something about it. He visited her and made sure she drank the tea. He dug the grave on Sunday morning. Then he covered it up with a story about a fake note and cleaned out the cabin before anyone could look for evidence." She crossed her arms, anticipating Logan's response.

Logan's face betrayed he could believe Maggie's assertions, but didn't want to. He planted his right elbow on the table and buried his chin in his palm. "The alternative is that Randy got Audrey pregnant, told his grandpa, and Carl covered for him." He paused. "Carl wasn't a rash person. Randy could've made the tea. I can't see Carl poisoning her, even if she wouldn't accept the money."

Maggie offered another idea. "Randy didn't have his act together. He might have thought he could get away with poisoning her because it would look accidental, then he freaked out and went to Grandpa."

"I don't think it's quite that simple. Listen to this." Logan rose and paced. "Carl was having the affair. I can buy that." He whipped around. "Audrey told him she was pregnant. He panicked because she wouldn't take his money. He said something to Randy, not realizing that Randy was also involved with her."

Logan gripped the back of a chair. "Even better, let's say Audrey told Randy she was pregnant. He's a rash kid. He knew about the poisonous plant and decided to solve the problem. He went up the road, picked a few leaves when the plant was just starting its spring growth, and had tea with her. Or maybe he knew she had some leaves leftover from the previous year. When she died, he confessed everything to Carl. Together, they buried her. Carl wasn't going to turn his grandson in. Then Eddy figured it out and blackmailed Carl to get his job back up at the ranch."

"So now Carl is dead, and Eddy is blackmailing Hank because Randy is Hank's son," Maggie said. "It all worked until I came along and started asking questions. That's why Eddy sent his goons to run me out of town."

Logan sat in his chair. "We've got pieces of the story, but we can't prove anything. She could have drunk the poison herself, and they found her body and buried her. The point is, they kept it a secret, which tells me something was up and someone broke the law."

He gave her the serious scowl of a DA. "I can't move on this any further until I get either hard evidence or a confession."

Maggie agreed. She had finally convinced Logan of something, but wasn't sure what it was. She had more work to do.

* * *

"Any progress on the case?" Robert asked as they drove home.

"Yes, and no. We're speculating about a couple of possibilities, and we think we have pieces of the puzzle, but we don't have the full picture and don't know how to put it together. Either Carl or Randy was having an affair with Audrey. Either Carl or Randy poisoned her. It's a hornet's nest right now."

Robert frowned.

"There's something else I'm puzzling over," Maggie said. "Grammy was seen going up to the cabin around the time Audrey disappeared. We don't know the exact date, and it could've been totally innocent. She could've just gone for a cup of tea, but it's another wrinkle."

"Who told you that?"

"Marion, the sheriff's wife. It looked totally innocent to her."

Maggie squeezed Audrey's sachet as they drove, hoping Audrey's spirit heard her. *Audrey, who poisoned you? Did you commit suicide? Am I completely wrong about this? Are Carl and Randy both innocent? Did they just find your body and give you a decent burial?*

CHAPTER 70

Maggie

Tuesday, October 20, 2020

Maggie left a message when she couldn't reach Ben. "Ben, we still need to get up to Medford and close those bank accounts. I'd like to drive up early and be there when the bank opens so that very few people will see you."

He called back later in the day, and they planned a trip for the following morning.

Maggie picked Ben up at eight in the morning in a rented car. They arrived before nine and parked in front of the bank until the doors opened. Maggie had arranged for a deputy to meet them at the door. Although the employees recognized Ben, they were polite. The bank manager closed the old joint accounts and arranged for a cashier's check to go to Mrs. Williams. Finally, the manager asked him if he also wanted to close the safe deposit box.

"Yes. I don't think there's much in there, but we should close everything."

The manager grabbed some keys. "Would you like to check it before it's closed?"

Ben agreed. He and the manager went to the safe deposit boxes. A few minutes later, he returned with a small cardboard box with a couple of papers and a dark-blue spiral-bound notebook.

"It looks like she started keeping a diary. It starts about the time we split up. I'm not sure why she put it in the safe deposit box." Ben handed the diary to Maggie. "I'm uncomfortable reading it right now."

"Do you want me to look at it?" She did her best to subdue her excitement.

"Yes, please. When we get home."

She gave it back without looking inside.

Maggie smiled as she thanked the bank manager for his assistance. Ben gathered everything from the safe deposit box, put it in a small briefcase, and they left.

She drove toward Salt Lake in silence, allowing Ben to have his private thoughts and memories. About halfway, she suggested getting something to eat. They pulled into the same Wendy's where she and Robert had stopped.

"We heard there was a diary, and we were worried that it had gone missing. I'm glad we found it," she said as they settled into a booth.

"I don't want to know what she was doing. That was her business."

She patted his hand. "I respect your reason for not looking at the diary, but we may find some clues about what happened to Audrey. Would it be okay if I open it and silently look for anything relevant?"

Ben slowly nodded. He removed the notebook from his briefcase and handed it to her. She opened it to the first entry on July 4, 2016, and read. On an almost daily basis, Audrey had written about her activities, along with her fears and anxiety. Maggie read until she reached the day when Ben revealed his secret. She looked up but didn't say anything.

Ben watched Maggie's face as he sipped coffee. She took a couple of bites of her sandwich.

Maggie, with her years of experience in failed relationships, understood Ben, and now she empathized with Audrey. Her heart went out to the confused young woman, who no longer knew what to do with her life. Maggie had been there.

She breathed a little harder when she read about how Eddy attempted to make friends.

When Maggie got to November, she glanced up again. "Audrey was very lonely. Carl befriended her and helped her around the cabin. She also talks about the day you both signed the divorce papers." She stopped for a sip of coffee. "How are you doing?"

"It's like she's speaking from the grave. I don't think I'm quite ready to hear it."

Maggie continued reading silently. She twitched when Randy got Audrey drunk and had sex with her. "Do you want me to tell you about some of the tough parts?"

"Not now. I want you to read it because you're doing the investigation. I'll read it later."

Maggie read on. She experienced Audrey's joy at finding a new lover at the Christmas party. Tears came to her eyes a few pages later when Eddy raped her on New Year's Eve. Under her breath, she mumbled, "He's such a reptile."

She appreciated how Carl took care of her afterward, but despised him after Valentine's Day and when he proposed his solution. She felt the irony of the fact that Carl wasn't really the father. She cringed at his reaction. Carl had used Audrey for his momentary pleasures. His cold intention, when their affair became inconvenient, was to force her out of town.

She finally closed the notebook. The look in Ben's eyes suggested he wanted her to say something.

"The story ends right after her mother's birthday in early March. Audrey sensed that trouble was brewing, so she hid her diary. She was getting ready to move in with her mother. She put the diary in the safe deposit box."

"Does she give any hints who might have killed her?"

"No, but we're getting closer." Maggie had not yet told Ben about Randy's DNA test. "We know who the father was, and this confirms it. When you want to hear about it, I'll tell you our theory."

CHAPTER 71

Maggie

Wednesday, October 21, 2020

On Wednesday morning, Maggie called Charles. "We found Audrey's diary. It confirms that she was seeing Carl and believed he was the father. As you know, we have information that suggests he was a seasoned player. Logan has suggested that Carl believed he was the father and told Randy about the pregnancy; Randy took matters into his own hands; and Carl covered for him. I'm guessing the murderer could be either one."

"Why do you suspect Carl?" Charles asked.

"Carl had a motive. The diary tells us Audrey didn't realize Randy was the father." She told him about Logan's theory about how Carl would have behaved when he learned about the pregnancy. "There's evidence suggesting that he offered Audrey a large sum of money and she rejected it. She was planning to move in with her mother and probably anticipated keeping the baby, and Carl would've eventually been exposed. Also, he probably knew about the poisonous plant because he hung around her place."

"Why is Randy a suspect?" Charles asked.

"Randy had a romantic interest in Audrey, and the diary confirms they had sex once. He denied they had sex, so we've caught him lying. He also denied knowing about the belladonna, but that doesn't make sense because he helped her with the gardening. I think he knows more than he's telling. I have no clue what it is or how to get it out of him."

She cleared her throat. "Logan thinks Carl said something to Randy about Audrey's pregnancy, and Randy took matters into his own hands. Logan thinks Carl was protecting Randy, and Randy gave her the tea."

Charles was thoughtful. "What else do you have?"

"Eddy has surfaced as a possible suspect and a blackmailer. He recently bragged about being the only person still alive who knows what really happened. However, we can't prove anything. The diary tells us Eddy bullied Audrey, beat her up, and raped her. Eddy's motive for killing her was that she could've sent him to prison on the rape."

She sighed. "We also believe Eddy and his nephew Kevin are the ones who have been trying to chase me out of town."

Finally, she ended with her theory that the burial occurred on Sunday morning. The diary said Eddy was gone by the time Audrey was killed, so it was probably Carl and Randy who dug the grave.

Once they had gone over everything, Maggie said, "Charles, there are still a couple of things that bother me."

"What are they?"

"I'm still puzzled about why someone buried Audrey with an old wooden cross in her hands. There's no indication that either Carl or Randy was religious or owned anything like that. The cross feels important, but I can't find the answer."

She bit her lip. "And second, when I first met Randy, he talked about an ancient Gaelic cloak pin Grammy had given to Audrey." She told him about the brief conversation at the picnic. "It always seemed odd that Grammy would give away a valuable family heirloom, and the diary says Carl gave it to Audrey, not Grammy. Randy's wife, Karen, said she had seen it, but Randy didn't even know Karen when Audrey was alive. So how could she have seen it unless Randy took it from Audrey after he killed her? I think there's a missing link involving that pin."

She grimaced. "We have a witness who saw Grammy going to the cabin the same week Audrey disappeared. I haven't asked Grammy about it, and we aren't sure which day it was. It could've been an innocent cup of tea, or she may be tangled up in it, too."

Charles blew out a breath. "Your evidence against both Carl and Randy is still circumstantial and speculative. Randy and Eddy are the only ones still alive, and Eddy won't be of any help. Randy is your best source for additional information, but you're going to have to get him to talk."

"I know."

"I would put pressure on Randy and see what happens. Keep in mind that a mistake is always made. If he was involved, he made a mistake somewhere. Find it. See if you can nail him on it. That may force him to talk."

CHAPTER 72

Maggie

Thursday, October 22, 2020

Maggie reached Logan the next day. "Charles suggested I confront Randy. We know he hasn't been telling the whole truth. I'd like to meet with him at his cabin, off the record, and push him fairly hard. What do you think?"

Logan hesitated and was slow to respond. "You could probably get away with it, but he has to talk to you voluntarily. I can't be there because I would have to follow all the official procedures, and this needs a unique strategy. Would Robert go with you?"

"I haven't asked him yet, but I think so. If Randy slams the door in my face, I'll let you know, but I think I can intimidate him into talking to me."

"Let me know when. I'll call the sheriff and have him on standby in case anything goes wrong." He coughed and sounded worried. "Keep in mind that Randy may have already murdered someone." He told her to keep the sheriff in the loop before providing her with Randy's number.

He paused. "Touch base with me before you go in. I'll have deputies nearby."

CHAPTER 73

Maggie

Maggie called Robert in the early evening. "I need your help again."

"What's up?"

"I went over everything with Charles. Logan and Charles both say we won't solve this case without a confession. Besides Eddy, Randy is the only one left who was around then and might know something. Charles suggested I confront him to see if we can break it open. Logan will provide backup, but he won't be present."

"That's another thing I like about you. You never, ever, ever give up, do you?" Robert laughed. "What do you need from me?"

"That's my job. I don't give up. It's too late for today, but I'd like to make it happen tomorrow evening. Would you go with me and be there just in case it gets difficult?"

"Of course I will. Do I ever miss a chance to be with you?"

Maggie paused. "Carl's name may come up. We don't know what to expect."

"I know. I'll handle it. Do you want to stay at the cabin, or should we plan to come back to Salt Lake?"

"I'm not sure what time I can set this up. We should be prepared to do either."

Her last call was to Randy. She told him she and Logan had a few additional details they needed to confirm and asked for a meeting. Randy was nervous as usual, especially when she asked to have Karen there, but her tone was insistent, and he didn't dare say no. She set it up on Friday evening at seven.

After the plans were made, Maggie realized that she and Robert would stay at his cabin and wondered what his expectations were. Had she given him the wrong signal? As much as she enjoyed his company and was drawn to him, she wasn't ready for the sexual level of a relationship.

She faced two confrontations. For the first one with Randy, she didn't know what the answers would be, but she knew how to handle it. The second would be the real challenge. All of her previous romantic relationships had been more about sex than love. She wanted to fall in love with Robert first.

She had mishandled romance so many times she didn't know the right way to act.

CHAPTER 74

Maggie

Friday, October 23, 2020

As Charles had said, a mistake is always made, and she needed to find it. On Friday morning, Maggie reviewed her small spiral notebook and the evidence in her case file one more time. She planned to take a walk and let the evidence filter into her subconscious, where she always came up with answers. She knew the mistake was there, but she couldn't see it yet.

Since moving to Salt Lake, she had found two places that were good for long walks and thoughtful musings. One was the zoo. The other was an aviary in Liberty Park. Both were already closed for winter. She decided on a new place, Sugarhouse Park, where a road meandered on gentle hills in a large grassy park that had several outdoor pavilions.

She placed the photo of Audrey on her passenger seat and talked to her like a friend as she drove. "Audrey," she said aloud, "I know you were hurting when your marriage fell apart. I've been there too. For me, it was anger, frustration, and hurt all rolled into one. I wasn't strong. Like you, I had to find someone who would let me cry, and I made mistakes." She reflected on her own periods of grief and how she had survived them. "I've learned so much about you, especially from your diary. I wish you could tell me what happened at the end."

When she arrived at the park, she sat in her car for a few minutes, closed her eyes, and imagined sitting with Audrey over a cup of tea. *I've tried to understand what happened to you. I still need one last piece of the puzzle. How did you die?* She breathed slowly and deeply to clear the chatter in her head and sharpen her intuitive powers. When she finally opened the car door, she felt an inner calm, as if she had connected with Audrey without words.

It was late October and early on Friday morning. At the park, a few people were walking, jogging, and riding bikes. A slight breeze tossed a few leaves around. Maggie started walking, enjoying the softness of the wind and the easy flow of nature.

How would she confront Randy? While walking along the road, she felt panic at first. But she swallowed it and tested aloud her various approaches and anticipated his responses. She tried many styles, and the wind absorbed her efforts. Before she knew it, she had covered the main circular road and was returning to her vehicle.

It was time for her to trust herself again and to trust the process. She sat on a bench and breathed heavily to quiet her remaining anxiety and let her subconscious take over. As she concentrated on her breathing, her mind cleared. She knew Audrey would be with her.

Late in the afternoon, Robert and Maggie drove to Madison County. Before heading down the dirt road, they stopped at the diner for dinner. This time, they chose the red booth at the end, and she faced away from the door so she would not be seen. The place was full and busy, but no one noticed her, and Robert distracted the waitress with his joking.

After their entrees were served, Robert put his fork down gently. "There's one thing we haven't talked about yet."

Maggie stopped eating.

"There are some things I tend to be slower about than most men." He waited. "We're going to be at the cabin alone tonight. You're a very desirable woman, but I don't think it's time yet to sleep together. I don't want you to feel any pressure in that regard. If we get to that point, I'd like for you to make the decision."

She wasn't sure she heard him right. No man had ever spoken to her like that, but she felt relieved. Had he recognized her nervousness? "Thank you. It's been a long time since I've been romantically involved with someone. I think I have some issues to deal with first."

"Well, I have an issue as well." He pretended to be embarrassed, but his face lit up with a grin. "I snore."

"Oh, no!" The tension was relieved. She leaned into him, feeling sarcastic. "I have my own confession." She gave him a dramatic look. "I wear socks to bed."

"Oh God, no! I can't sleep with a woman who wears socks to bed." Robert shaded his eyes and faked a look of horror.

Thirty minutes later, they were at the cabin, and without fanfare, they put their things in separate bedrooms.

CHAPTER 75

Maggie

A few minutes before seven, Maggie called Logan as promised, and they arranged a signal if something went wrong: she would autodial his number and hang up so it would ring once.

She and Robert walked over to Randy's cabin. Maggie knocked and heard someone turn off the TV.

Randy was testy when he opened the door and saw Robert. "What's he doing here? I thought Logan was coming with you. I thought it was something official."

"Oh, Logan couldn't make it, so Robert came instead." Maggie had not planned to mislead him, but it worked.

They entered without an invitation. "It's all right, isn't it? You're old friends."

Maggie greeted Karen, who was apprehensive, and looked at Randy furtively. The dim lighting in the room was foreboding, and a fire crackled in the fireplace.

Randy didn't have a choice. He wasn't cocky enough to ask Robert to leave. Robert's unexpected appearance caused him to be off his game and unsettled, and it gave Maggie a little more advantage. He nervously took a seat at one end of the couch.

Maggie intentionally sat at the other end. She turned toward Randy and placed her case file on the center cushion. Karen offered each of them a glass of water and sat in a nearby rocking chair.

Robert stayed close to the door. He sat on a leather stool pushed against the wall. His hands were on his knees. Maggie had arranged for him to gauge whether he thought Randy was telling the truth. If Robert suspected a lie, he would fold his arms across his chest.

Maggie took out her small spiral notebook and flipped through it in her best offhanded manner. For effect, she studied the notes carefully before making eye contact with Randy.

"Randy, officially, you're a suspect in Audrey's death because there are some inconsistencies. I'm trying to clear them up. It would be in everyone's best interests if we could get these questions answered." It was hard for her to hold her tongue and feign being casual.

"I told you I didn't kill her."

"I'm going to tell you a little more about that."

He squirmed.

She spoke calmly and slowly for emphasis. "Audrey was about three to four months pregnant when she died, which means she got pregnant around the beginning of December."

"What?" Randy stiffened and practically jumped off the couch. He immediately turned to Karen. "I had nothing to do with that!"

"You refused to take a DNA test, remember?"

"Yeah, I didn't need to. I never had sex with her." He was flippant.

Karen stopped rocking and stared at him. The look on her face suggested she didn't believe him.

"That was the same time that you both were exchanging phone calls and you were helping in her garden." She allowed her statement to sink in. "You'll remember I said we had DNA evidence. We've been testing to match the DNA of the baby."

Maggie braced for her next surprise. "The thing about saliva is that it can be taken off a lot of things. We got a saliva sample from you without you knowing. The DNA test says you were the father of Audrey's baby."

Randy's jaw dropped. He froze. His voice rose and shook. "You're lying. You haven't been around me to get any sample. Whatever you have is fake. You're framing me. My dad's lawyer will fight you in court."

"He'll certainly have the right to do that, but we plan to ask for a court-ordered DNA test to confirm what we found. If it's fake, you're in the clear, but we have something else that confirms you had sex with Audrey."

Randy stared at her with fear in his eyes. His face flushed a bright red. He was unable to look at Karen for support. Her eyes demanded the truth.

"Audrey kept a diary. We found it."

"And you think everything written in a diary is true?"

"She described how you got her drunk on beer and carried her into the bedroom and had sex with her. That could fall into the category of date rape."

"That was her fantasy. I never did a thing to her."

"Let me repeat what I said earlier. There's a reasonable possibility we can get a court-ordered test to confirm the DNA findings."

"So what? What would that prove? It doesn't mean I killed her. You're barking up the wrong tree."

"You're right. But you lied under oath when you told Logan Harris that you never had sex with Audrey." She tapped her notebook. "There's something else you lied about that creates additional suspicion."

"What?"

"Do you recall that I asked you, under oath, whether you helped your grandfather remove things from Audrey's cabin?"

Randy glared at her. His voice was cockiness mixed with fear. "My grandfather is dead. All you have is my word on that."

"There was an investigation into Audrey's disappearance in 2017. Carl signed a statement under oath. It was in the sheriff's records. In his statement, Carl said you helped him remove her stuff and take it to the dumpster."

"So what? That doesn't prove anything."

"It proves you lied again."

"I forgot. I helped him a lot."

"It means you knew more about her disappearance than what you have admitted, and you knew what happened to her stuff. Randy, what else have you lied about?"

He sat upright on the couch and turned to his wife. Karen's eyes were wide with fear and flitted from Maggie to Robert to Randy.

"I didn't kill Audrey." Randy's gaze implored Maggie to believe him. He was shaking.

Maggie sat back a little. "The fact is that Audrey was romantically involved with someone else while you were flirting with her and cleaning out her garden. She might have been just using you to get her yard work done."

Randy looked down, clearly embarrassed at being accused of playing the fool. His face reddened. Maggie gave him time to absorb her comment. He planted his forearms on his knees and hung his head.

"Do you know who the other man was?" Maggie asked. "She may have gotten pregnant the one time you had sex with her. The other guy may have thought the baby was his and killed her because of it."

Randy slowly shook his head. Sweat beaded on his brow.

Maggie glanced over at Robert. He folded his arms across his chest.

She watched Randy for several minutes. "Do you suspect who the other man was?"

Randy looked up. He had composed himself and stared directly at her. "No." He reminded her of a defiant child. "Doesn't her diary say who it was?"

Robert's arms remained folded.

"Okay." Maggie eyed him with disbelief. "Let's talk about something else. Did Audrey ever make tea for you with leaves from her herb garden?"

His eyes narrowed. "Yes."

Robert's hands went back to his knees.

"When you worked in the garden, did you help her pick some of the leaves for her teas and ointments?"

"Yes."

"Did she tell you to wear gloves when you were handling the plants?"

"Yes."

"Why was that?"

He looked at her hard and clasped his hands together, but said nothing.

"Was it because some plants had poisonous berries?"

It took longer than normal for him to respond. "Yes." His face showed he had been caught in another lie.

"You knew there were poisonous plants?"

He closed his eyes. "Yes. She talked about them. She used tiny amounts in her ointments. We had to be careful."

He looked at Maggie like a young child being forced to admit the truth.

"Did anyone else know about the poisonous plants?"

"I don't know of anyone else." He squirmed and glanced toward the ceiling.

She waited.

"Maybe my grandpa did. He worked in her yard a lot. She must've told him. Maybe my grandma did. She went over to visit Audrey. But I don't know for sure. I'm just guessing."

"Randy, you know Audrey was poisoned with tea from that plant because it's been in the paper. At the time she died, you knew about the poisonous plant, so you're a suspect." She made sure her voice was firm and intimidating.

"I didn't kill her. I didn't bury her." He looked her straight in the eye with regained composure.

"Do you know who did?"

He hesitated, gazing at the floor. "No."

Robert folded his arms across his chest.

Maggie imitated Randy's posture, her forearms resting on her knees. She stared at him as if her eyes could penetrate him.

He's lying. Who is he protecting? He needs to admit the truth. She picked up her spiral notebook and flipped through it until she landed at one of her unanswered questions. "Randy, do you remember telling me about the Gaelic cloak pin?"

Randy flinched. "Yes."

"Didn't you tell me that your grandma gave it to Audrey?"

"Yeah. After I saw it, I asked my grandpa. That's what he told me."

Maggie raised an eyebrow. "When did you see it?"

"At the Christmas party. When Audrey came in. I helped her with her cloak."

"That was in 2016, wasn't it? Were you surprised your grandma gave it away?"

"Yeah."

"Why?"

"That was one of her most prized possessions. It was a family heirloom that came across the ocean with our ancestors and then across the plains in a covered wagon. She treasured it."

She narrowed her eyes. "Did you ask your grandmother about it?"

"No. Grandpa told me not to. He said she might change her mind, which wouldn't be fair to Audrey."

She faced Karen. "Karen, you mentioned that you saw the Gaelic cloak pin. When did you see it?"

Caught by surprise, Karen spoke as if she was afraid of how her answer would affect her husband's situation. "A few months ago, maybe last spring. Randy and I were visiting Grammy after we got engaged. She was welcoming me into the family. She told me some of her family history and showed me her treasured heirlooms. The pin was in her jewelry box."

Randy's mistake was to brag about the pin to strangers at a picnic. The Gaelic cloak pin had been returned to Grammy's possession. Randy must know how this happened. If he knows this, he also knows more about what happened to Audrey.

She sat still for a minute. She had found another of Randy's lies, but she didn't know its impact. She glanced at Robert, then over to Randy and Karen. Randy rubbed the back of his neck and shifted in his seat. Something bothered him.

Maggie leaned forward again and slowly leafed through the pages of her notebook. She raised her gaze to him. It was time.

Even though she disliked him, her motherly instinct took over, and she spoke with rehearsed compassion. "Randy, there are several times when you haven't told us the truth or you haven't kept your promise. I'm going to ask you to be truthful with me. Your credibility with your wife, right here and now, depends on it. This isn't about Logan Harris or me, or even Robert. It's about whether your wife can trust you to speak the truth. Trust is more important than love." She spoke from her own broken heart. "It's the foundation of all relationships."

The room was quiet except for the sound of logs crackling in the fireplace.

Randy's eyes were uncertain. Beads of sweat rolled down the side of his face. He looked long and hard at his wife, pleading. Karen stared back at him. She got up and went to the kitchen. Maggie could see her at a counter. She was dabbing her eyes with a tissue.

"Did you know your grandpa was romantically involved with Audrey?" Maggie inhaled deeply. "Think about your answer, Randy. Carl is already dead. Nothing's going to happen to him if you tell the truth. We can probably put this case to bed quietly if we know what really happened."

Karen returned and sat quietly.

Randy hung his head. He waited a long time before answering. "Yes." His swagger was gone. His position in the family was forever changed. He had been forced to choose between protecting his family and being truthful in front of his wife.

"When did you know?"

He swallowed hard. "I saw them together at the Christmas party. It was only for a minute or two, but it was obvious. He took her home because of the snowstorm. I couldn't sleep. I watched for his truck to show up at his place. He didn't come home for two hours."

"Were there other times that you suspected him?"

"Yes." He sighed deeply. His entire demeanor had changed. He was letting go of the tension.

"And?"

"His truck was often at her place when I came home. I looked for it, and if it wasn't at his place, I drove to the bend in the road and saw it. I turned around in the sheriff's driveway."

"Did you tell anyone?" Maggie asked.

"No. I was ashamed. He was married. He wasn't supposed to do those things."

"As far as you know, did anyone else know?"

He hesitated. "Yeah. My uncle Eddy knew. He also saw them at the Christmas party."

"Do you believe Carl poisoned Audrey?"

"I don't know."

"I didn't ask you what you know. I asked what you believe deep down inside your heart. What does your gut tell you? You knew Carl was involved with her. She thought he was the father of her child. What do you think he did about it?"

"I don't know. I couldn't tell him what I knew. I couldn't ask him what happened to Audrey when she disappeared."

Randy began to cry. Without shame, he wiped the tears away as they trickled down his cheeks. He lowered his head. His shoulders shook. Everything became still as his muffled sobs filled the room.

Karen looked at Maggie. Her eyes silently asked if she could comfort him.

Maggie shook her head. He needed to do this alone. Randy had finally told the truth. His pain was coming to the surface. He was afraid his grandpa had killed Audrey. He didn't need to cover it up anymore.

Randy wiped his eyes. "Her car disappeared, so I hoped he was right when he said she decided to move. I helped him clean out her place."

"What happened to her stuff?" Maggie asked.

"It went in the dumpster."

"Including her cloak?"

"He didn't know it, but I saw him take the cloak pin off and put it in his pocket before he threw her cloak away."

"Did you think it was strange that she didn't take her cloak with her?"

"Yes."

"What did you think when you heard Audrey's body had been found?"

Honesty was in his eyes. His voice trembled. "I figured he did it."

Maggie let his admission sink in. Randy had been protecting Carl's reputation.

"You believed your grandpa killed Audrey, but you were leading the outcry in the town against Ben. You were going to let Ben take the blame?"

He closed his eyes. "He was my grandpa. He was dead. I couldn't tell on him."

"Maybe you owe Ben an apology," Maggie said softly.

Randy stared at the floor. His elbows were still on his knees, and his hands were together as if in prayer. "Yeah, I guess so."

"Do you think Carl buried her?" Maggie asked.

"Yeah, he must have."

"Did you help him dig the grave?"

"No."

Maggie had not expected his answer. *Randy's letting go of the burden he's carried for three and a half years.* "There's also the possibility that Audrey was upset about being pregnant and drank the poisoned tea herself. Maybe your grandpa just found the body and buried her."

Randy looked up. His eyes questioned the possibility. She let it hang in the air.

"Carl must have given the Gaelic pin back to Grammy or maybe put it back in her jewelry box. Do you think he would've told Grammy what happened?"

"Yeah. You can't keep anything from her. She doesn't know that I know about it, but she hasn't been the same since Audrey died. Whatever she knows, it's eating her up."

Maggie leaned back on the couch. *Grammy has also been burdened by a secret.*

"Would you and Karen go over with us tomorrow to talk to her? It might ease her mind if she knows it's out in the open. All we have to do is confirm what happened, and we can close the case. We can keep this quiet."

Randy glanced at Karen. She nodded slowly.

Randy and Karen agreed to meet at Robert's cabin in the morning before going to Grammy's place.

CHAPTER 76

Robert

It was after eight when Robert and Maggie left Randy's place. The sun had set, and the forest was darkening.

"Thank you for being my lie detector," Maggie said. "Your signals gave me the direction I needed."

Robert walked in silence. When they reached his porch, he turned to her with a heavy heart. "This is my hometown. These are the people I've always trusted to do right. Carl was the one person who could do no wrong. I could deal with him having an affair, but I'm having a hard time with the thought that he killed Audrey. I always looked up to him. I'm feeling wounded. That's about all I can say."

She took his hand and hugged it close to her chest. She could feel his pain. They had finally resolved Audrey's death, but it was painful for his memories.

They entered the cabin and hung their jackets on the pegs. The room was still warm.

Maggie called the sheriff and told him they had some answers but were going to meet with Grammy in the morning to clear up the last question. He said he and Marion would stay at home in case their assistance was required. Feeling exhausted, Maggie asked him to notify Logan.

Robert went to the small table where he kept the liquor and poured whiskey into a tumbler. He sat on a bench, staring into the embers and downing his drink. He put another log on the fire. Maggie hung back, allowing him time to be alone. After a few minutes, she came over and softly massaged his shoulders. He pulled her around and onto the bench and wrapped his arm around her shoulders. No words were spoken as they watched the fire burn.

The log finally crumbled.

Robert sighed and stared into the fire. "I don't talk about my own feelings. I'm just a tough ole cowboy, even an asshole sometimes. I can get angry in a split second, but I can't talk about when I'm feeling hurt. Right now, I've got a huge pain in my gut."

"I'm here to listen when you're ready."

"You'll probably hate me when all of this is over." He wrung his hands. "My dad didn't do much with his life. Carl was my hero. I looked to him for advice. I went to college because he found scholarship money for me. When my wife died, he was the one who kept me going."

"He was a good man, but like everyone, he had faults," she said.

"He succeeded at everything and was the glue that held this county together and made it grow. He knew what to say, when to say it, and how to get people to work together." He turned to her. "But he killed Audrey. How can that be? How could he have done that?"

"We haven't confirmed that yet. Maybe Audrey just couldn't take losing her husband and then losing Carl because she got pregnant. Maybe she poisoned herself."

"He should've known better. He should've had enough character to avoid getting involved. I can't tell you how many times he talked to me about my behavior as a kid and how character counts. A married man with good character doesn't have an affair."

"What are you feeling now?"

"Randy felt betrayed." He winced. "I feel betrayed." He resumed looking into the fire.

After a time, he squeezed her shoulders. "Sit with me on the couch. It's more comfortable."

They pulled the couch closer to the fireplace. Robert took a blanket off a nearby chair and wrapped it around them. He pulled her close so her head rested on his shoulder. They stared at the fire. She kicked off her shoes, left her socks on, and tucked her feet under her. He closed his eyes and drifted off.

CHAPTER 77

Maggie

Saturday, October 24, 2020

Maggie was the first to wake up. She discovered it was five thirty and went to her room to begin her morning routine.

At six o'clock, she put on a pot of coffee and was frying sausage links when she heard Robert stir.

He walked into the kitchen, stretching. "There's nothing I like better than the smell of fresh coffee and the sizzle of sausage. That's cowboy food."

He sat at the counter while Maggie poured two cups of coffee.

"I don't know how you take your coffee."

Robert reached for the sugar bowl. "Sugar, two scoops."

She handed him a spoon. "Is that what makes you so sweet?"

With a grin, he cradled his cup with both hands. "Thank you for being my friend last night. I needed that. I rarely let emotions get to me."

"It was my pleasure." She considered his sensitivity. "You know, you don't have to go with me this morning."

"It won't be easy. I'll be there with you. I need to hear the story from Grammy."

Maggie cracked two eggs into the frying pan and popped whole wheat bread into the toaster. Moments later, she scooped the eggs out, added a couple of sausages and the toast, and set it in front of him. After preparing her plate, she took a seat on a stool next to him, and they ate breakfast like a couple of old friends.

Randy and Karen arrived at nine o'clock. They shed their coats, quietly accepted fresh coffee, and sat on the couch. Randy seemed contrite, and Karen had an air of assertiveness. From their demeanor, Maggie guessed they had a serious talk long into the night.

Maggie joined them and turned to Randy. "I'm concerned about how Grammy will handle this. It looks like we've uncovered a secret that she's been holding on to for over three years. I can't imagine knowing your husband killed someone." *Now I understand why Grammy wouldn't talk about Audrey. I wonder if she'll be as relieved as Randy is when the truth is out.*

Randy stared at Maggie over the top of his coffee cup.

"How do you think I should handle her?" she asked.

"I don't have any idea. Can you keep me out of it? She doesn't need to know how much I know."

"I can try, but I can't promise anything."

Maggie glanced at Karen. "I believe the Gaelic cloak pin is essential for getting Grammy to open up, but I'm not sure how we can bring it up. I was wondering if you had any ideas."

Randy and Karen looked at each other. They shook their heads.

"I have a thought. Tell me if this would work for you. We're close to Halloween. What if you tell her you were invited to a costume party and you want to borrow the pin for a costume you're putting together?"

"I could do that," Karen said.

"Okay." Maggie thought for a minute. "Let's do it this way. The two of you go visit for about ten minutes, then ask about the cloak pin. Offer to go upstairs and look for it. Robert and I will come over around that time. After we get there, wait a few minutes before coming down. If we assume she knew about Audrey, talking about the cloak pin will help us cut through some of the pretense, and we'll get to the truth faster. I'll take the lead, and we'll see what happens."

CHAPTER 78

Maggie

Robert knocked on Grammy's door fifteen minutes later. Grammy opened it, exclaiming that she was lucky to have so many visitors in one day. Karen had already made a pot of coffee. Robert tossed his hat on the antlers next to Randy's and gave Grammy a long, heartfelt hug. He sat on the couch near her recliner. Randy was opposite her on a chair in front of the window.

Maggie pulled a kitchen chair over next to Grammy. "How are you? Gwen tells me you're doing well."

"I'm surviving. It's nice to have visitors." She turned to Maggie. "I heard you're the one investigating that Stillman death. Have they arrested the husband yet?"

"No. We're still working on it."

"It's taking too long!"

Karen came downstairs. "Grammy, I found it. May I borrow this for my costume?"

She held the tarnished old iron ring with a linchpin through the middle. It took up most of her outstretched hand. Where the ends of the disconnected circle came to-gether, carved gold eagle heads provided the hooked beaks where the linchpin rested tightly and held the fabric of the cloak in place.

While the Gaelic pin distracted the others, Maggie se-cretly turned on the recording function of her cell phone and put it in her pocket.

"That medieval cloak pin belonged to my grandmother, who got it from her grandmother, who came here from Scotland," Grammy said proudly.

"I remember when you showed it to me last spring. That's why I wanted to borrow it." Karen showed the pin to Robert.

"What kind of costume are you making?" asked Grammy.

"Oh, it's going to be a queen costume. I'm going to have a cape over it." Karen twirled around as if she already had the cape on. She was perfect.

Maggie sensed the time was right for her to switch from being a friendly visitor to being the investigator. *I have to let Grammy know we've already uncovered the story.*

Maggie patiently waited for everyone to finish admir-ing the pin before she faced Grammy. "How did Audrey get the Gaelic cloak pin?"

Grammy's head whipped around. Her eyes were fierce. Her body jerked, and her thin hands tightened on the arms of her chair. The crocheted throw on her lap fell to the floor. Just as quickly, she looked away. "How did you...?" Her voice slipped away.

The room became quiet. Grammy remained silent for several seconds. She glanced at Randy as if looking for help. He didn't speak and turned toward the window, hanging his head. She stared at her small bookcase of family pho-tos and said nothing.

After a long, tense moment where no one moved or said anything, Maggie looked at Randy. "We know Audrey had the Gaelic cloak pin that belonged to you."

Grammy stared at Randy, her gaze wounded. "Carl gave it to her." She sighed heavily, and her chest sank into a concave.

"It's your treasure. Why would he have done that?"

"We went through a rough time." She shifted her gaze to her lap. Her hands shook.

Maggie leaned in. "How did you get it back?"

"When she died, he found it in her things and gave it back to me."

The air was thick. No one moved.

Maggie took a deep breath. "Grammy, I need to ask you a question, and I know it'll be painful, but I have to ask it as part of the investigation."

"Go ahead." Her body tensed.

"Did Carl give it to Audrey because he was having an affair with her?"

Her face darkened. Her eyes closed. "Yes."

Maggie's heart ached for her. "Did Carl tell you that Audrey was pregnant?"

Her chin hardened, and her lips pursed. She barely breathed. "Yes."

"This happened once before, didn't it?"

She coughed suddenly, then glared at Maggie, startled. "How did you know?"

Grammy lifted her head toward Karen and asked her to put the kettle on the stove to make more tea. Slowly, she took a small blue tin of loose tea leaves from the knitting bag at her side and pinched some leaves into the teapot on the small table next to her. Maggie waited. It seemed fair to let her have a cup of tea. Moments passed.

Everyone in the room was silent.

A clock ticked in the background.

Grammy motioned for Karen to pour the hot water into her teapot.

"Grammy, Carl can't be hurt anymore, but we need to know what happened. Did Carl give poisoned tea to Audrey?"

She closed her eyes and braced her body. "No."

Maggie blinked. She had expected Grammy to admit that Carl had poisoned Audrey. "Do you know how Audrey died?"

"Yes."

"Did she prepare the tea herself?"

Grammy poured from the teapot. She picked up the cup and saucer with both hands and brought the cup to her lips. Her hands were shaking.

"No. I made the tea she drank." She sipped until it was gone. Her eyes focused straight ahead, as if not seeing anything.

Something's wrong. Grammy didn't put sugar in her tea. Maggie gently took the tin from Grammy's lap. The old woman didn't resist. Her eyes closed. Maggie smelled the tea. It didn't smell like any teas she knew. She examined it carefully—crushed leaves and small dried berries. She put it on the table next to Grammy's chair.

Maggie's heart lurched. The belladonna. She took the cup and saucer and mouthed to Robert, "Call 911."

He reached for his phone and moved toward the front hallway.

Grammy's eyes opened, and she turned to Maggie. "Once was enough. I wasn't going to go through that again." Her voice was hoarse. "After Carl told me Audrey was pregnant, I went up to have tea with her. I brought the tea. I picked it from Audrey's plant in the fall when I first suspected he was courting her." Her face begged for sympathy. "Carl buried her the next morning. He took his old tarp, and we went together." Her shaking hand seemed out of control.

After several more seconds, she slumped in her recliner. Her eyes remained open and fixed on Maggie as if she was asking to be forgiven.

Her body twitched. Seconds passed before she went limp.

Maggie froze momentarily, then reached for Grammy's hand. "Grammy?" She felt for a pulse. It was weak. "Grammy...?"

Karen ran to Grammy. "No! No!" She rubbed her arms, trying to revive her.

Randy stood, nervously wanting to help but not knowing what to do. He came closer.

Robert rushed to Grammy's side. He moved the teapot and cup to the kitchen table. "They're on their way." He felt for her pulse. Her head slumped forward. Tears glistened in his eyes. "I need to be alone for a few minutes." He backed away and stepped outside.

"She's my grandma." Randy stood over Grammy and held her hand, tears streaming down his cheeks.

Karen put her arm around her husband's waist. They hugged each other silently with their grief.

"I'm so sorry, Randy," Maggie caught his eye. "I believed it was Carl. I thought she would reveal he'd done it. I never thought..." She couldn't find the words.

Karen covered Grammy's face with her gray shawl. She knelt and laid her head on the old woman's lap.

"She had so much pain." Randy bowed his head. "She's with grandpa now." He choked back tears. "Their secret destroyed both of them. They have forever to forgive each other." He sat on the edge of the couch beside Karen.

The paramedics arrived, but it was too late. They assessed it had not been a lot of poison, but she was too frail to withstand it. They moved her to the ambulance.

Randy went back to his chair and cradled his head in both hands.

When he finally looked up, Maggie said, "Would you go down the road and ask the sheriff to come here?"

She gathered the coffee cups.

Randy comforted Karen for another moment before taking the blue tin from the small table and putting it in his pocket. Maggie didn't have the heart to confront him for tampering with evidence. He hadn't changed. She would tell someone later.

Randy left to fetch the sheriff and his wife.

Karen stared out the window.

Maggie washed the coffee cups. Robert came back in. He gently pulled her into a silent and heartfelt hug.

After a long moment, Maggie drew back. "You've lost someone who was special to you. I'm so sorry. I made another mistake. I didn't accurately judge what would happen."

"It's not your fault. She had the poisoned tea with her and has probably kept it in her knitting bag since Audrey died. She knew this day would come." He wiped tears from his eyes. "She's at peace."

CHAPTER 79

Maggie

Maggie stepped outside, called Logan, and told him what had happened.

Randy and Sheriff O'Brian returned. Marion was a few steps behind them. They went inside the cabin and came out a few minutes later. Randy's arm was around Karen's shoulder. They joined Robert on the front porch.

Logan had been nearby and arrived almost immediately. He parked close to Randy's cabin and spoke privately with the sheriff before they pulled Maggie aside. "Give me the specifics."

"The confrontation worked. Randy was evasive at first, but he came around and told me he believed Carl had been responsible for Audrey's death."

"Did he know for sure?"

"No, he assumed, and it ate him up thinking his grandpa had done it. We agreed to ask Grammy to confirm. That's why we came over here this morning."

"What did she say?"

"I recorded it, but essentially, she said Carl confessed that Audrey was pregnant. Eddy's history still bothered her, and she wasn't going to let it happen again."

"Are you telling me that Grammy poisoned Audrey?"

"Yes. She admitted it. Afterward, she reached for the belladonna she had with her and prepared a cup of tea. On Saturday, March 18, she went to see Audrey. She made the tea and watched Audrey die. Carl buried her on Sunday morning."

"Damn. All of this because he couldn't keep his britches zipped up." Logan frowned. He turned away and wiped his eyes.

Sheriff O'Brian wrapped the cabin in yellow tape and stood guard. When he finished, Logan and Maggie explained to him how the DNA had uncovered Eddy's story. Maggie played Grammy's comments. The sheriff and Logan decided to record her death as an accidental poisoning in the county files, although they had to report it as a suicide to the state. The file would be kept under a court seal for as long as possible.

Logan and Maggie walked over to where Robert, Randy, and Karen were sitting and explained the underlying meaning of Grammy's final comments. Robert had already been briefed, but Randy was unaware of Eddy's background.

Hank and Carol arrived within minutes. Logan and Sheriff O'Brian took them aside and filled them in. After Logan played the recording, Hank asked everyone for a short meeting.

"The family will not ask for nor will we permit an autopsy," Hank said to the small group. "The Sheriff and Logan Harris have agreed with me that the press and the general public will be told that she died of natural causes. Our family will remain secluded and in mourning for a while. No good will come from the community knowing the details, and I don't want my mother's memory desecrated. I'm asking everyone present to respect our family's wishes."

Maggie felt sympathy for the family, but couldn't help noticing how Randy had learned his deceitful behavior.

As Logan handed Maggie's phone back, he said he would bring Audrey's mother up to speed and quietly close Audrey's case. A press release would be issued, and Ben would be exonerated.

The sheriff asked if anyone knew where the small tin with the remaining tea was. No one offered an answer. Maggie pulled him aside a few minutes later and told him she had seen Randy take it. He thanked her and said he would handle it.

Carol called Grammy's other children. The shock had worn off, and tears flowed as she talked to each of them. She invited Karen to help choose a dress to give to the mortuary. The sheriff let them go upstairs together. Randy left the group and went to his cabin.

A few minutes later, Carol brought down a garment bag holding a long white dress. "We found the dress she wore when she and Carl were sealed together for eternity in the Salt Lake Temple. This will be her burial garment."

Robert and Maggie walked to his cabin, and sat on the front steps. She quietly reached over, took his hand, and leaned against his shoulder. "It started out so easy. We had a body and a cold-case murder. How did it get this complicated? I'm not condoning anyone, but how did this happen?"

"There are so many ways this could've played out. Where does the blame start?" He surveyed the people standing around. "Ben found himself in a no-win situation, and no one paid much attention to Audrey after the divorce."

"Except for Carl. His family had just as many problems."

"And no one knew. We saw this family as being too important to have issues. I'll always have good memories of what Carl and Grammy did for me, but Carl got away with hurting his wife. He was involved in Audrey's death, and I suspect the stress finally killed him. It also killed Grammy. Times have changed. Carol would never let Hank get away with what Carl did. It'll take a while, but they'll recover."

"I barely knew her, but I can guess that Grammy's life was shattered a long time ago. She pretended that Carl's behavior didn't hurt, but it ate her up from the inside and shattered her self-esteem. I've been there, too. Every day, you have to pick up the pieces, knowing you have no one to talk to about it, but you'll never be the same."

A few minutes later, Maggie held a conference call with Charles and Ben. Charles was thankful the truth had been uncovered. He sent his condolences to the family. Charles said he and Logan would work out the formal details of closing the case.

Ben took the news with more emotion. His voice cracked as he asked questions. Maggie told him the details of Audrey's death and asked him to keep it as confidential as possible.

Maggie called Gwen and Peter and made arrangements for a team meeting that evening.

Carol approached Robert and Maggie on the steps. "Robert, could I speak to Maggie alone for a minute?"

With a nod, he went inside.

Carol took his place on the steps and dried her eyes. "I want to apologize for the way I talked to you. I know you were just doing your job. I was out of bounds."

"Thank you. It's been a stressful time for you." Maggie hesitated. *It would be easy to dislike Carol, but at times people say ugly things. She's really a decent person.* "Randy helped break the case last night. I hope the family won't hold that against him."

"No. It won't be like that. I think this will solve another issue we're having with Eddy."

"Let me guess." Maggie glanced at her. "We picked up a rumor that Eddy had something he was holding over Carl to get what he wanted. We guessed that after Carl's death, Eddy switched to blackmailing Hank."

"Yes. He didn't know everything, but he knew enough. He made it sound like Randy was the one responsible. Hank and I didn't know all the facts. Randy said he didn't do it, but we weren't sure. We were afraid you would unravel the mess and the whole town would know our family business. Hank can now fire Eddy from the ranch."

"Another little crime put to bed." Maggie shook her head.

"Grammy told me a lot about her life, but she never told me about Carl and Audrey. I thought something bothered her, but I didn't know what it was."

"I visited Grammy about a month ago. She seemed lonely, even depressed."

Carol sighed. "She didn't know what to do with herself when her kids were grown. No one noticed except Audrey. I didn't understand why Grammy turned against her, and she wouldn't say."

"Did you know about Eddy's background?"

"No. He never fit in. It was obvious Grammy didn't like him. He was the youngest, and we thought she was just tired of raising kids."

"For forty years, she's been angry about Eddy's circumstances." Maggie frowned. "When it started to happen again, she couldn't handle it. I don't blame her for that."

Carol shifted on the stairs. "How did you solve the case?"

Maggie stayed silent for a moment. "We learned Randy had some involvement, but I'm going to spare you the details. I spoke with him last night, and he told me he thought Carl killed Audrey, but he wasn't sure. Carl was his beloved grandfather, and he's been living with that pain for a while. When we went over this morning, the purpose was to confirm that it was Carl, not to accuse Grammy."

"Why won't you tell me? I'm his mother. I need to know these things."

"I'm going to leave some details up to Randy to talk about. He still has some growing up to do. I'll let him take responsibility when he's ready."

Carol crossed her arms. "I don't understand, but there's not much I can do about it."

Maggie's hand closed around the sachet. She leaned back, as if she expected to reconnect with Audrey. A mist formed a few yards away on the dirt road. Maggie saw Audrey in her long woolen cape emerge and slowing walk toward her. In her outstretched hand, she held the wooden cross.

Maggie turned to Carol. "There's still one mystery. Audrey was buried with a small wooden cross. Do you know where that came from?"

"Her wooden cross? I looked for it in the house a few minutes ago and couldn't find it. She made it from a tree in her mother's yard when she left home. It was all she had from her childhood, and it meant the world to her. Do you know where it is? It should be buried with her."

"Yes, I know."

Maggie got up and walked over to Logan. "Do you remember that wooden cross that was found with Audrey?"

"Yes."

"It was treated as evidence, wasn't it?"

"The coroner's office had it, but they sent it back when they released the body."

"That cross belonged to Grammy. She must have placed it in Audrey's hands when they buried her. Since Audrey's case will be closed, do you think it could be released?"

"I suppose so. Who wants it?"

"Grammy."

CHAPTER 80

Maggie

Just before noon, Maggie and Robert left his cabin and drove back to Salt Lake. Robert dropped her off and planned to return for the team meeting.

It was a somber group that met in the evening. Maggie wore black in recognition that another person had died. Gwen made arrangements for all the food and brought an array of Chinese takeout.

"Thank you for getting shrimp egg foo yung," Maggie said. "I remember telling you once it was my favorite." She poured green tea for everyone as they gathered around her coffee table.

"It's difficult to know where to start," Maggie said. "When I met Grammy a few weeks ago, I was drawn to her because she was courageous and strong-willed. I was also bothered because she seemed haunted by something. I had no idea the depths of her pain."

She turned to Gwen. "You made her last few weeks more pleasant. You were also able to provide us with the first clue that Hank and the whole family were involved."

Gwen put her plate down. "I'll miss her. She was just starting to be comfortable with me. I still don't understand everything that happened."

Maggie sipped her tea. "Carl was a good man in many ways, but he was a womanizer, and Grammy tolerated it. Forty years ago, one of his girlfriends got pregnant. For whatever reason, Carl brought the baby home and asked Grammy to raise the child. That child was Eddy. She detested every moment spent with him. When she heard about Audrey's pregnancy, she vowed to never be humiliated like that again."

"That's horrible," Gwen said. "He asked too much of her."

"She was raised to be subservient and do what she was told to do. Her feelings weren't important to anyone."

"But how did Eddy play into the actual murder?" Peter asked.

"I'm only guessing. Robert may understand it better." Maggie looked at Robert.

"I was in college when he was born, so I don't know much about it. All I know is Carl always had trouble with him."

"But what was his role in the murder?" Peter repeated.

"I'm going to make some guesses," Maggie said. "Eddy was pretty aggressive. We know he was at the Christmas party with Randy and he detected Carl's affair. Audrey's diary told us that Eddy brutally raped her, but she was too ashamed to tell anyone. He had an axe to grind with his family and used that to blackmail Carl to get his job back at the ranch. Once he saw that the blackmail worked, he used it on Hank."

"I imagine Eddy will be even harder to deal with now that the circumstances of his birth have been uncovered," Gwen said. "He seems to be someone who moves through life by causing tragedy and disaster."

"I have a hard time feeling sorry for him, but from what I have heard, he was the rejected child in the Stevenson family." Maggie sighed. She carefully lifted a large bite of egg foo yung.

Maggie nodded to Peter. "Your help with deciphering the DNA was critical."

"It was Robert who set it up so we could get the beer bottles." Peter raised his cup of tea to salute Robert.

"Who was your secret contact who got the beer bottles?" asked Gwen.

Robert grinned slyly. "A bartender. I had to be discreet so no one would know what I was doing. In fact, I owe him one more visit to thank him." He cleared his throat. "We all did a great job. We should name our team and do this again."

"Again?" Maggie frowned. "Grammy was a good woman who should've been treated better. She died because I was too insensitive. I keep making mistakes. I should've understood her better."

Robert patted her hand. "Grammy wanted to die. She was just waiting for the day when someone uncovered her secret. She was trying to deceive us into believing that Ben was the murderer. That wasn't your fault."

"I know." She sighed. "Carl did not deserve Grammy's loyalty. If I had been her in those circumstances, I might have thought about doing what she did. Gwen, what would you have done?"

Gwen took a long pause. "I would not be able to kill anyone. I'm not sure what I would have done. She should have left him."

"She had five kids. She didn't have the means to leave him." Maggie sat back and let out a long breath. Her eyes twinkled. "How did I ever get through all those years as a prosecutor? It's a tough job. I'm glad I'm retired. I'm going to sit at home and knit."

Robert's eyes twinkled. "Somehow I doubt that."

THE END

I hope you enjoyed reading Buried Bones.

Please consider leaving a review on Amazon.

If you are curious about Maggie Anderson's next investigation,
please go to my website and sign up for our mailing list:
BonnieMooreBooks.com

QUESTIONS FOR READERS

For those readers wishing to understand the story in more depth, and for members of book discussion groups, I offer the following questions for evaluation and discussion:

1. Why was Maggie drawn to this investigation? What did she get out of it?

2. Was Justice served? Maggie was able to uncover the truth about the death of Audrey Stillman, and Ben Stillman was no longer accused. What other elements of 'justice' played out in this story? How will the townspeople be affected?

3. Underneath the investigating a wrongful accusation, this story is about the lives of three women: Maggie Anderson, Grammy Stevenson, and Audrey Stillman. Each woman addressed her challenges in a unique way, and the outcomes were very different. What does this story tell you about how women must address their challenges. Could any of these women have acted in a different manner?

Consider how each woman faced her challenges. Which events in her background motivated her? Was she treated fairly by those around her? Was she put in her place by a controlling bully or someone who was very insensitive? Did she let a fear of failure overcome her? What did she do, or not do, that affected the outcome?

4. Two hidden secrets are exposed in this story. Grammy had carried the secret about Eddy's parentage for forty years. It bothered her every day and caused her reaction to Carl's affair with Audrey. Why was Grammy unable to address the issues that gave rise to both of these secrets?

5. Was Logan Harris ever up to the task of solving the murder of Audrey Stillman, or did he go along to get along? What was going on behind the scenes? Why did it become important to him that the case be sent back to the cold case files? Why was it important to Maggie Anderson that the truth be uncovered?

6. Discuss how Maggie's attitude toward Grammy changed during the story. Why do you think she became sympathetic toward her?

7. How do you feel about the Stevenson family?

8. There is an indication that the sheriff, the DA, and the Stevenson family will continue to cover over the truth when it is inconvenient. How common do you think this is in the administration of justice. How do you feel about this?

ACKNOWLEDGEMENTS

This story started as a class project in a non-credit writing class at the University of Utah in October 2020. The seven-week class was called *A Study in Mystery* and was taught by Johnny Worthen, a popular writer and instructor in Utah.

Each student was required to work on a mystery story idea. I had no 'idea' in mind, but I remembered that someone at a party had told me about an old pioneer cabin in the mountains that his family had inherited. I had a location! I started on the story. I recently went back and reread the initial idea that I submitted. All I can say is that it's come a long way, baby!

Perseverance helped. My story became my COVID project. Long days and sleepless nights. Rewrites. Editing. Books and workshops on developing writing skills. I remember critiquing a fellow student's first chapter. I had to stop in the middle of a sentence because I realized I needed to follow my own advice. More Rewrites.

When I thought I was finished, I sent the first draft to friends and cousins. I quickly heard back that it was awful. Some readers couldn't even get to the end. There was one strongly implied suggestion: Get an editor.

So, I hired a professional editor, Miranda Miller, a very patient woman, who saw me through four editing/coaching sessions over a three-year period. Every time I thought it was good, she made it better. The woman is also a genius with punctuation and paragraphs.

As I progressed through the rewrites, I joined a support group for writers led by David Duhr who leads a group called WritebyNight. David suggested I have one of his team members, Thomas Andes, critique it. Little did I know Tom would take a cleaver to some of my favorite passages. Oh well. My pride survived.

I reached the stage where I examined every word and rewrote most sentences. I finally let two friends read the manuscript again. They said it was now a page-turner, but again, they were friends.

Finally, I started submitting to contests for unpublished manuscripts. I was a finalist in one major contest. I thought I had it made and publishers would come running!

Nope. David Duhr took on the task of doing submissions. One publisher asked for the full manuscript. After months, I got a rejection letter. It had too much dialogue. Too Much? What were they talking about? The dialogue defines the characters and moves the story along!

I kept editing. I kept rewriting. I fine-tuned the plot. This never ends for an obsessive author.

Also, I can't forget my law school professors who taught me the basics of criminal law. Hope I got it right.
On New Year's Eve, 2023, I made a commitment to two friends that I would get it published by the end of 2024. So here I am, and the plan was that it will be launched in late September, 2024. Well, we finally got the launch date set for April 8, 2025.

I thank everyone who was involved, even in the smallest way, in keeping this project going. Without your willing-ness to tell me that my writing could be improved, I would not have pushed for something better.

I've now become good friends with "Maggie Anderson" and I'm taking notes of her newest escapade. She just never quits! Hope you will join us in the next story.

If you've ever wanted to write a story, I simply encour-age you. There is nothing more satisfying than typing the words, THE END.

Here's to burning the midnight oil!
Bonnie Moore

www.ingramcontent.com/pod-product-compliance
Lightning Source LLC
LaVergne TN
LVHW040812240425
809439LV00001B/1